AMERICAN TIGER

AMERICAN TIGER

ADAM SKOLNICK

COPYRIGHT © 2025 ADAM SKOLNICK
All rights reserved.

AMERICAN TIGER

FIRST EDITION

ISBN   978-1-5445-4986-6   *Paperback*
            978-1-5445-4985-9   *Ebook*

Cover Design by Rachael Brandenburg
Original cover art and cartography by Aidan Yetman-Michaelson

For A & Z

BASED ON A TRUE STORY

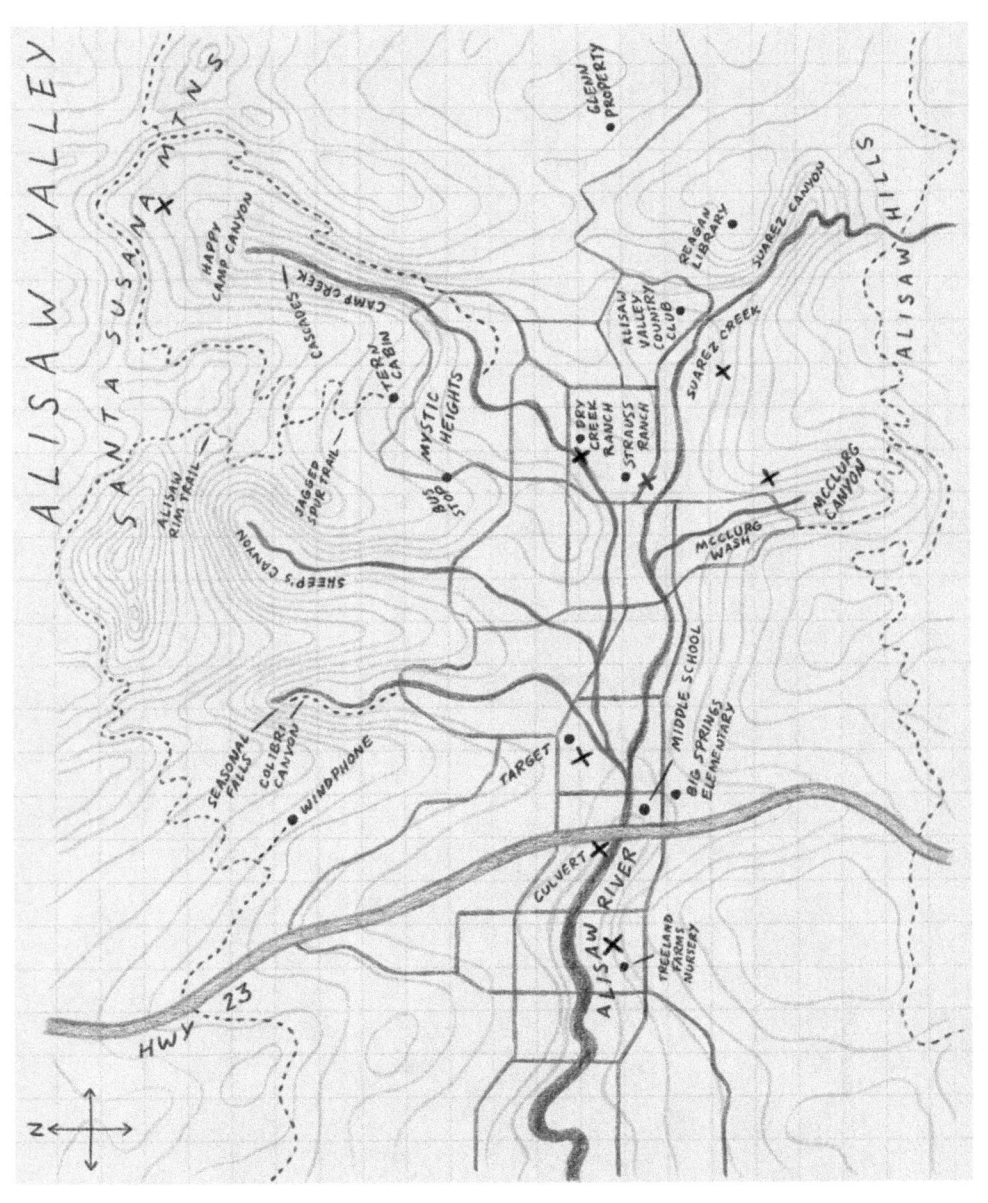

Part I

1

JANUARY 17, 2005

BELL TERN WAS THE FIRST PERSON IN ALISAW VALLEY TO SEE THE tiger, and nobody believed her. Not even Jay Tern, who, as a local game warden for the California Department of Fish and Wildlife, should have been genuinely interested. Of course, he knew better than anyone that his daughter had an "imagination problem."

Just five months earlier, the day after her ninth birthday, Bell woke Jay before dawn, insisting she'd heard a troop of baboons on their rooftop. She swore that she'd rushed outside to find them clambering through the oak trees that spread around and above the six-hundred-square-foot, one-bedroom, wooden cabin they shared. That she'd watched them pick ticks from one another's fur and raid the avocado grove. Bell said one of the babies climbed to the edge of the new tin roof Jay had installed the previous summer and reached out a small hand, creamy with guacamole, until the mother pulled them back and flashed her fangs.

As usual, Bell had the illustrations to prove it. She was obsessed with Jay's collection of tattered, old field guides, and she'd use the early twentieth-century drawings as inspiration to animate wildlife in intricate, swirling detail. Jay knew they were to be treated as evidence, not art. Proof that whatever she'd "seen" was, in fact, real.

"Ticks, huh?" Jay asked as he leafed through her evidence file. He took off his baseball cap, caught his reflection in the kitchen window, and ran his fingers through his salt-and-pepper hair, which he couldn't help but notice used to be thicker and darker. "I do respect ticks."

Bell arched her left eyebrow. No physical trait had been passed from Tern to Tern quite as directly as their improbably charismatic left eyebrows. Ever since wrangling control of the muscle as a toddler, Bell had used it to induce laughter or signify suspicion, surprise, frustration, or deeper interest by bending, sharpening, or buckling it. She deployed it here, making it stand on its tiptoes like a cat stretching after a nap. "Why do you respect ticks?" she asked.

"Because they can live for eighteen years without eating a thing and then, when they're really hungry, they find some unsuspecting mammal and suck its hot blood until they can't possibly drink another drop."

"Then what do they do?"

"Then they lay their eggs...and die!"

Bell's smile spread slowly, then she let loose that undulating giggle of hers that hit all the high notes on the scale. Jay loved that laugh, and he loved her imagination, neither of which came from the Tern side of things. Her elaborate illusions were generally harmless, he thought, and she usually retracted them within a few days. Often over breakfast.

"You know, I don't actually think it was baboons on the roof that night," Bell said four days after her ninth birthday. "I don't know why my brain works like this." She shrugged as she tucked into a steaming bowl of oatmeal with almond butter, cinnamon, nutmeg, peaches, and strawberries.

Jay responded with his own inquisitive left eyebrow. "Doesn't everyone want to believe they've seen something as sensational as a troop of renegade baboons migrating through Alisaw Valley?"

he asked, sipping his latte. "Or giraffes marching through Chavez Ravine?"

The giraffes were a reference to an earlier episode that had been brought to his attention as they watched their beloved Dodgers play in early May. Four times a season, they made the ninety-minute, traffic-choked pilgrimage to Dodger Stadium. During the seventh-inning stretch of this particular game, she'd pulled a rolled-up evidence file from the inside pocket of her secondhand Dodgers Starter jacket and smoothed out a carefully conceived illustration on her lap. The illustration proved that exactly sixteen years earlier, during the Dodgers' mythic 1988 championship season, a tower of giraffes had marched down Stadium Way before the game, causing even worse gridlock than usual. When describing the scene, she'd said it just like that, "a tower of giraffes," because everyone knows that is the proper term for a group of giraffes. She claimed to have read all about the episode on microfilm in the library. Jay had pretended to believe her and had locked her illustrated evidence in the green, metal filing cabinet in his home office. That was where all evidence wound up, real and imaginary.

There were times Jay worried about Bell's willingness to let her towering imagination trample her reality. He knew she bent the truth in other ways, too, but it never seemed to serve a dark purpose. She didn't steal candy at the shop or palm money from his wallet. Whenever she broke rules that some grown-up laid down, it was for the sake of adventure or curiosity rather than selfishness or outright rebellion. Wasn't that instinct natural for kids her age?

The morning Bell changed her tune about the baboons, Jay watched his daughter devour her breakfast, cheeks stuffed with oats and puffed out like a ground squirrel's, and thought back to the time she ditched school. He was scheduled to work the graveyard shift that night and had made plans for her to sleep over at her friend Miles's place. Then he went and told her that Ben's mare, a buckskin beauty of a quarter horse named Luna, would most likely give birth to her first foal that evening.

When Jay called Miles's house to check in around dinner time, Miles's mother sounded surprised to hear from him. Miles had told her that Bell went home sick at lunch and that the sleepover was off.

Jay overheard the subsequent interrogation. Apparently, Miles stood watch at lunch time while Bell scaled the old oak tree on the back corner of the school's athletic field. Its branches extended over the fence, offering an easy escape route. Jay was more annoyed than worried because he knew exactly where to find her.

He stepped into the horse barn on Dry Creek Ranch just as contractions rocked Luna onto her side, where she lay, trembling. Bell watched in amazement from the hayloft, her clothes and boots streaked with dirt, courtesy of the four-mile march from school. Armed with her colored pencils and drawing pad, she attempted to capture the scene in real time.

The mare quaked and swung her backside twice. The foal's long legs appeared at odd angles. When the next contraction hit, Ben, still plenty spry at over six feet tall and eighty-one years old, ducked into Luna's stall and tugged on those spindly legs. Luna stood up tall, and the foal fell onto the hay below her, where it was doused in warm, pink afterbirth. Luna turned to Ben, glared, and huffed, and the old man made a hasty retreat. Her privacy restored, Luna licked and nuzzled her baby and then devoured the placenta.

"Evening, Ben."

Ben and Bell seemed to notice Jay at the same time. Jay was in uniform, dressed for the night patrol, and as he stepped toward the action, it was difficult to tell who was more surprised by his presence.

"We didn't mean to startle you." Jay said and gestured toward Bell, implying he and his daughter had come together. Ben glanced up at the hayloft, where Bell kept her eyes glued to her sketchpad.

Fresh and fragile, the foal already had her mother's regal bearing. Her stockings were speckled black and white. So were her flank and backside. Confirmation that Luna had mated with a neighbor's Appaloosa.

"Well, since you're here," Ben said, peeling off gloves soaked with afterbirth. "Bell may as well name her." Ben winked up at Bell, who stared down at the foal.

"She looks like a Billie to me," Bell said.

Ben nudged Jay, who was still caught somewhere between concern, irritation, and pride. "Billie it is," he said.

On the drive home, Jay debated punishing Bell, but he knew she'd learned more in Ben's barn than she would have in her classroom. Hadn't he pulled her out of school before to explore the high desert in bloom and count migrating gray whales from the craggy bluffs? He understood most parents would come down hard, but hadn't Bell been through enough? She didn't need a lecture on how life can reach up out of nowhere and stab you in the soft place. She knew that already.

Yes, if you asked Bell, she would gladly tell you that she saw a tiger licking its front paws in the sun, but there was a flaw in her story: she insisted she'd seen it behind the dumpsters at Target. When was the last time a large, exotic cat turned up behind a suburban superstore? How could anyone ever believe such a thing? Especially Jay, who was on a first-name basis with the alpaca herders and the atheist rattlesnake breeder who shipped vipers to sweaty Pentecostal preachers in Missouri. He knew the older couple with the cartoon-sized Burmese pythons and flamboyant monitor lizards and the hippie lady with two crazy-eyed, half-breed wolves. One odd, older fellow owned a rather dignified moose who starred in television commercials. Jay held all their permits and visited each of them every six months. He knew for a fact there were exactly zero tigers in Ventura County, and that included a certain patch of asphalt behind a certain Target. But there definitely could be one running loose through the imagination of a certain nine-year-old.

Bell, on the other hand, considered her sighting a quirk of fate. Normally, she found a window seat on the right side of the bus on her way home from school because she preferred mountain vistas to parking lots, but on the day in question, she'd been held after school. Instead of paying attention during math, Bell had been caught drawing herself into a trance. Again. This time, her illicit illustration depicted her teacher at the blackboard surrounded by a snickering gaze of raccoons. Four scrambled around her desk. Three hung from her extended arms, and one bit her on the behind. Ms. Levine seemed especially irked that Bell was confused by her reaction.

Bell insisted it was all a giant misunderstanding. Her father used cameras to record evidence, and he'd told her that law enforcement agencies had relied on sketch artists before the age of photography. Newspapers too. That was what Bell considered herself to be: a sketch artist who had captured her teacher's harrowing ordeal in real time. Unfortunately, Bell's attempt to explain illustration's investigative history only made things worse. The terms "fib" and "liar" were bandied about. As in, "You cannot continue to *fib* your way through my class, young lady," and "You know the other kids think of you as a *liar*, don't you?" Eventually, Bell was sent home with another exasperated note for her father penned in an elegant, looping cursive Bell couldn't help but admire. Jay would have to sign it, or Bell would not be welcomed back to class.

Deflated, Bell was the last to board the bus. The only window seat still available was on the left side, and she claimed it. Seven minutes later, the bus chugged up the overpass spanning Highway 23, skirted the backside of the new mega-shopping center, and stopped at the most infuriating traffic light in town. The one that took forever to change.

The school bus was filled with the tedious chatter of happier children. Bell peered out the window toward the sagebrush, beyond Target's sparkling, supersized loading bays and dumpsters. And that was where she saw the tiger, halfway in and halfway out of the brush, its front paws on the asphalt, one directly in front of the other. It was staring right back at her. Stunned, Bell tore open her pack; sifted through such essentials as pruning shears, a compass, a collapsible butterfly net, and a space blanket; and dug out her field glasses.

She raised them up and focused in. She was no longer on a rattly old bus packed with the Smelly, the Irritating, and the Stupid—the three scientific classifications she used to categorize her fellow students. She was in her own bubble, suspended in time and space. That was how absorbing it was to watch a tiger—an actual tiger!—on the loose in the real world. Or was it? She had her doubts. She pinched her ears and clenched her eyes shut, but when she opened and released them, the tiger was still there, less than sixty feet away.

Bell watched it lick its front paw. She noted its liquid-amber eyes, and was that a mane bunched up around its shoulders like a ruffled collar? Did tigers have manes? She'd have to research that. Its coat was the deepest ochre and a creamy ivory brushed with jet-black stripes. Its nose was two-toned, half baby pink and half black as beach tar. With each inhalation, its nostrils pinched closed, then opened wide. Through her lenses, she felt as though she could reach out and touch it.

The tiger snarled and flashed its pearly canines. A flatbed truck stacked with pallets of recycled cardboard came squealing around the corner, pulled up to the dumpsters, and obscured Bell's view. As the clueless driver got out of the cab, Bell saw a banded tail float to the edge of the fresh blacktop and recede into the brush.

Bell dropped her field glasses. The traffic light turned green. Mrs. Parker eased her foot off the brake. The bus sighed dramatically and pulled away while Bell cursed herself. She should have ditched the bus and tracked the animal. That was what any decent investigator would have done. Tail the suspect, no matter how menacing. Don't let any witnesses slip away. Roll out of a moving vehicle if you must! But bailing out the side door of a school bus demanded training she did not have. Instead, she went public.

"There's a tiger behind Target," Bell said. Then came one and a half seconds of silence before laughter rolled toward her like a flood. It bounced off the steel walls, poured into her ears, and threatened to wash out the pixelated image still coming together in her mind's eye. Fingers pointed in her direction; stale accusations hurled like hand grenades.

"Remember when she said she survived a plane crash?" one boy asked.

"Um, no. She said she was born on a plane," said another.

"She told me she was born at Everest Base Camp," said a familiar voice. It belonged to Ashley, from Bell's pod in Ms. Levine's class. Ashley only rode the bus a few times a year for street cred, and her timing and memory were as perfect as the rest of her. A few rows up, one of the fifth-grade boys Ashley was sitting with leaned into the aisle and sneered back at Bell.

"Wild tigers don't live in Southern California, retard," he said. Once again, the bus erupted in laughter.

"That's enough!" Mrs. Parker's sympathetic eyes flashed in the oversized rearview mirror. "I will not have hateful language on my bus! Next child to talk like that is getting reported to Principal Ono, and I know none of you want that!" Mrs. Parker nodded at Bell in the rearview. "You don't know what she saw." For a moment, Bell thought she had an ally, until she noticed the bus driver shaking her head and chuckling to herself.

"Maybe it was a bobcat," Miles said, leaning over the seat behind her. He was all tousled brown hair, wet lips, and glasses.

"I know what bobcats look like, Miles. One had kittens in our garden last spring. And I've seen a wild tiger before too." Bell glared at Ashley. "In India!"

"Oh, right. You've been to India," Ashley said. "That's why you live in an outhouse and ride around in that *embarrassing* truck." The boys sitting with Ashley laughed and high-fived her, and Bell slumped down to make herself invisible. For the rest of the ride, she scribbled notes on the inside of her forearm so she wouldn't forget.

"Had to be the smell," she said later that evening over a dinner of spaghetti with chopped, pan roasted garlic and pistachios. "It was probably hungry and trying to raid the dumpsters, like bears do."

"Possibly," Jay said. "Or maybe it was confused or afraid and hiding out."

"Yeah. The suburbs are not exactly tiger habitat."

"Far from it," he said while spooning himself a second helping of wilted spinach.

Bell didn't much like his tone. A dangerous cat was out there somewhere, and he was obviously humoring her. Then again, if he had done his job and interviewed her properly, she wouldn't have had much valuable information to share. She hadn't seen where the tiger disappeared to. She couldn't tell him its length or weight. She'd utterly failed as a witness.

After dinner, Bell retreated to the three-dollar flea market drafting table in her room. The top edge was lined with spent jam jars stuffed with a palette of Faber-Castell colored pencils bought for half price at a moving sale for Alisaw's failed art-supply shop. She gathered ten shades of yellow and six shades of orange and spread them out in an arc. She flipped through the vintage field guides from India and Russia that Jay had bought at flea markets for pennies and traced the photos and sketches of Bengal and Siberian tigers with her fingertips until she'd had enough inspiration. Then she shut her eyes and zeroed in on the image etched in her own brain.

Two barn owls called out to one another as she sketched an intense and inquisitive feline face poking out between candy-appled-red dumpsters stamped with a familiar logo. The tiger's pupils floated like inky, obsidian islands in vibrant amber lakes. Its subtle mane—she'd confirmed that tigers did, indeed, have manes—stood on end. She blended four shades of orange to get the right tint of ochre. Then, she crafted the stripes. Some were thick and curved like elegant tree trunks, others wispy like clouds. They arced and slashed like the blaze of a falling star. One stripe under the cat's left eye folded at an angle, like a bolt of lightning.

That was it. That was what she had seen. No matter how many kids laughed at her or what her father thought he knew. There was a tiger all right. On the loose in boring old Alisaw Valley. She was 96 percent sure of it.

2

JANUARY 31, 2005

BELL WOKE BEFORE FIRST LIGHT. THREE PORTRAITS OF THE TIGER were strewn across her quilt. She'd been drawing the same animal, the same scene, for two weeks, hoping to perfect it. She turned on her bedside lamp, raised one of the sketches, and scanned the animal's elongated whiskers and lip curled to reveal its upper-left canine. Then, the screen door slammed, and a gust of wind blew through her cracked bedroom window, snatching the sketch from her fingers. The snarling tiger settled on the floor at the foot of her bed among a burial ground of crumpled false starts and a fan of previous days' sketches from a file folder labeled: *EVIDENCE: Tiger behind Target, supplemental drawings.*

It was another cool, dry morning, and Bell heard her father cough and blow into his bare, cupped hands outside her window. That was his version of a wake-up call. This was supposed to be an El Niño year. Experts claimed Pacific Ocean temperatures had spiked, which typically encouraged monsoon-like weather patterns on the California coast, but so far, those had failed to materialize. Cold desert winds still blew in from the east, as they had for weeks, and the hills were crisp as kindling. This morning's trail run would double as an inspection. Her father planned to see just how imminent the fire danger was.

Bell slipped out of bed and peered between the gaps in her shutters. Jay was dressed in his usual decades-old running shorts—she could practically smell them through the window—and a similarly antiquated long-sleeve thermal with a frayed crewneck and moth-nibbled cuffs. He shivered and sunk his thumb into the soil of their vegetable garden, where broccoli and cabbage, radish and leeks were coming in nicely. His morning routine was as predictable as ever. She rolled her eyes and pulled on secondhand running tights that were too short, a baggy hand-me-down thermal top, and an oversized beanie large enough to corral her unkempt hair.

She stepped outside and gave her dad a curt nod. He nodded back and grabbed hold of the pull-up bar he'd anchored to the eaves of the back porch. Any time he went in or out the back door, he knocked out a set of five and dimes: five pull-ups followed by ten push-ups. When he was finished, Jay picked Bell up so she could grab the bar. She managed three pull-ups of her own before Jay slipped on a small backpack, and they started up the Jagged Spur Trail, a narrow, single track that dangled like a stray thread from the county trail system into their avocado grove.

They loped up the switchbacks Jay had hacked into the mountain, enduring the silent suffering that comes from forcing a cold body up a steady grade at a pace that pushes the breath out ahead of the heart. Jay was a mountain goat. Lean and long at six feet two inches tall, he was blessed with the natural ability to chew up steep terrain. He'd placed in his age group at a handful of trail races, but they had to be at least thirty miles long for him to have a chance. His gift wasn't speed; it was endurance. He could force himself to do almost anything for as long as it took to find the other end of the pain. Bell tried to keep up, but she had always been a slow starter. Both wore top-of-the-line trail runners, footwear being the one consumer item Jay refused to scrimp on. He had wide feet and favored Salomons. Bell had the small feet of a sprinter. She wore Nikes.

Their trail split a landscape of chaparral that included aromatic native plants—black sage, white sage, and artemisia—and beautiful yet invasive exotics, including thick stands of wild fennel and fields of mustard. Each year, before fire season, Jay and Bell took to it all with pruners and a McLeod rake. They clipped and cleared dead brush to create a fire-resistant buffer of safety between the wild mountainous saddle above their cabin and the subdivision of stucco McMansions, called Mystic Heights, below them. That buffer usually held long enough for the rains to come, but there hadn't been a drop of autumn rain, and the parched hills looked desperate for the smallest spark to set them ablaze. Fire season was supposed to be summer trouble, not a winter problem.

The Tern cabin was originally built as a foothill outpost of the Jagged Spur Ranch, before Alisaw Valley was named and incorporated in 1932. It would take another forty years for cops, teachers, firemen, nurses, contractors, grips, and gaffers to leak over from Los Angeles, put down roots, and raise kids here, transforming this once agrarian valley into a suburb. Back when valley life was still oriented around ranching and farming, the nearest structure to the Tern cabin—the main Jagged Spur ranch house—had been miles away. Yet despite the growth of Alisaw Valley's population and construction footprint—and the never-ending expansion of the Mystic Heights Neighborhood Association, which now included the Tern cabin, to Jay's perpetual chagrin—Jay and Bell still lived on the margin, where the suburbs ended and nature reigned. The way Jay saw it, that interface between the planned contours of human civilization and the wilderness was his responsibility.

By the time Bell reached the T-junction above the switchbacks, her father was already busy examining last season's fire buffer and identifying areas that needed immediate attention. A sheen of sweat glistened on his forehead and in his beard. Most mornings, they ran the two miles up eight hundred feet in elevation to the junction, then jogged home. This was not most mornings.

Jay ran on ahead and waved for her to follow. Bell groaned. There was no telling how long she'd have to run now. None of this was mandatory. Her father didn't believe in that sort of rulemaking. But she did need to qualify for the two-week backpacking trips she loved in the Sierra Nevada and the daylong cross-country rambles into the nearby Sespe Wilderness. Plus, she was small for her age and determined to be as strong as her father one day.

From the junction, they had the entire Ventura County trail system at their disposal, a spool of more than one hundred miles of single track and fire roads. Since Jay had veered left, Bell knew the next stopping point was Hawk's Nest Overlook, another mile and a half up a gentle grade on a single-track trail that hugged the ridge. With the incline more manageable, Bell stayed on Jay's tail. Within fifteen minutes, they were standing at the overlook, enjoying a pink dawn over Alisaw Valley.

She could see it all: Ben's ranch, her school—with its still-naked thirty-foot flagpole out front—the community college, the Ronald Reagan Presidential Library, the shopping centers and parks, the mountains cradling the valley, and Highway 23, a north–south throughway that carved a gentle arc through town. The buildings and cars looked like toys in the rosy light, but Bell's attention didn't linger on the valley floor. She was more interested in a cathedral valley oak in a sloped meadow directly below them. The bare tree had to be over a hundred years old, and at its top was a red-tailed hawk. The fearsome bird's breathy call was surprisingly gentle but had enough length to latch onto the Santa Ana gusts. Soon, a second red-tail, who had been spiraling in the thermals, feathered down beside it.

Bell watched her father fish a pair of high-powered field glasses from his pack and focus on the hawks. He handed the glasses to her, and she peered through the lenses. The raptor couple looked to be scanning the valley and plotting their next move. As Bell observed them, the sun rose above the eastern rim of the valley. The first blades of sunlight stung her eyes and spoiled her view, so she panned to the northwestern ridge, where the light glanced off an artful steel frame.

Bell adjusted the focus, and the image sharpened. She counted six gently curved posts connected to a crosshatch of overhead beams and spied the silhouette of a small, slender figure in a wide-brimmed hat balancing on top.

"Huh. Someone is…building something," Bell said. She handed Jay the binoculars.

"Always," he said without bothering to look. "Someone is always building something around here." With the glasses secured, he zipped his pack. "Race you home?"

"Sure," Bell said. "Loser makes breakfast."

Jay took off hot, but Bell was built for the downhill charge. She caught him after the junction, when the steep switchbacks and rocky trail slowed his long stride. Bell giggled as she hopped from rock to rock with ease, attempting to find a way around her lumbering father. He blocked the trail by splaying his legs out wide, so she slid between them and darted downhill. He couldn't help but stop and laugh as he watched her sprint all the way home.

Breathless, Bell arrived in the avocado grove and kept sprinting toward the back door, where a coiled rattlesnake was warming itself on a paving stone in a patch of morning sun. Bell skidded to a stop, inches short, and fell backward. The snake wasn't full-grown; she could tell that much. It had dark-green and gray scales, and its head was shaped like a squashed diamond. Frozen in fascination, Bell watched the rattler lift its chin off its slick haunches and unfurl a flickering, forked tongue. It did not appear ready to relinquish its post at the sight of a mere human.

Bell backpedaled to the tool shed, pulled on a pair of heavy gloves, plucked an oversized pickle jar from the shelf, and grabbed the long stick with a forked tip. Jay kept it among his gardening tools for one purpose: capturing rattlesnakes. The trick was to slot the head into the V. That gave you control. Do it right, and there would be no danger of a counterattack. Jay never missed. Bell had never even attempted it.

"Gently," she said, channeling her father, her eyes locked on the suspicious viper, "but quickly!" With one well-timed scoop, Bell lodged its head in the fork. She twisted the stick, and the snake coiled around it instinctively. With great care, she inserted her bundle into the jar and shook the stick hard until her captive dropped to the bottom. Then, she sealed its exit with an aluminum lid punched through with air holes. The snake was young and thin, and she watched it rattle and coil through the glass.

"You know I don't want you handling rattlesnakes," Jay said.

Bell glanced up, surprised. She'd been so absorbed in her task she hadn't heard him coming. He peeled off his sweaty shirt, grabbed the pull-up bar, and rocked another set. "Especially baby rattlers. They don't know how to control their venom. When adults latch, they release enough to stun and inflict pain so they can escape with enough—"

"—venom to defend themselves or feed again," Bell said. "You told me."

"Babies release it all and kill whatever they sink their fangs into." He dropped to the deck and started in on his push-ups. "Ponies, dogs...little girls."

"I'm *nine*, Dad."

Jay stood and did that thing where he nodded and shook his head at the same time. Then, he palmed the jar, kicked off his shoes, and stepped inside.

The cabin hadn't changed much since the days before Bell was born, aside from the new roof. One living room wall was taken up by a bookcase Jay had built from reclaimed pallets. He'd stuffed the shelves with his vintage field guide collection, a small selection of Beat literature and poetry, pulpy murder mysteries, and nonfiction from naturalists he loved, like Rachel Carson, Archie Carr, and Aldo Leopold. There was a shelf of oddities—rare succulents he'd harvested from canyons and islands in Baja, an old mason jar filled with sea glass, frames of colorful dead butterflies and moths, tree frogs and lizards shellacked and suspended by dental floss. There was a decent young adult section that featured two copies of their all-time favorite novel: Scott O'Dell's classic *Island of the Blue Dolphins*. One was Jay's childhood copy. Its pages were frayed and falling out. The other was Bell's, also well-used but still in decent shape. Jay read it to her once a year—a tradition that began when she was four years old. She would be ten this summer. On their last lap, he'd wondered how many more times she'd be willing to sit through it.

The living room's two cedar walls were mostly bare, though a trio of framed photos of Bell and Jay, taken when Bell was five, hung side by side. The first one was deadpan. In the second, they appeared to be screaming. In the last, they smiled wide, as if enjoying a more spectacular view than the tired wood coffee table and sad eleven-year-old futon where Jay slept.

While Jay fixed breakfast, Bell knelt on the threadbare rug and folded his bedsheets. He heard her click the futon from the inadequate bed position into the inadequate sofa position and turned to her as she grabbed flint from the mantle above the fireplace, preparing to spark a pile of kindling.

"Did it flick its tongue?" Jay asked. She lit the fire and glanced over. "Your friend here." He gestured to the jar with his elbow. "When you approached it, did it flick its tongue at you?"

"Yes," she said, watching her flames grow. "Three times."

"And why do you suppose it did that?"

Bell added a log to the fire, then stood and crossed to the slab bar. She climbed aboard one of their three barstools. Jay slid her a bowl of granola and Greek yogurt topped with sliced dates and pears. She pulled a spoon from a jar of clean utensils at the end of the bar, scooped, and crunched.

"It was trying to scare me."

Across the bar, Jay ate while leaning against the tiled counter of the galley-style kitchen. Pots and pans were stored in low cupboards behind him. The upper cabinets were stocked with dishes. The sink, range, and wheezing refrigerator he refused to replace were to his right. Above the sink was a sliding window large enough for Bell to climb through when they locked themselves out. He leaned forward and slid the jarred snake between them. The snake swirled along the bottom, rattled, and flicked its tongue toward the lid.

"Nope."

"Why then?"

"It was trying to smell you."

"You're saying rattlesnakes smell with their tongues?"

"No. I'm saying all snakes smell with their tongues." He scooped a heaping spoonful. "They flick that tongue out, collect whatever is floating around in the atmosphere, and rub it onto a receptor on the roof of their mouth."

"Wow," Bell said, eyes fixed on the snake. "Nature is so…weird." Jay arched his acrobatic eyebrow. "It's also weird that you know that," she added.

"I think it makes me cool," he said while using the edge of his spoon to scrape the sides of the bowl.

"Duh." Bell's bowl was still half full. She was the slower eater, even when she wasn't hypnotized by a snake. "We should build her a terrarium."

Jay chuckled and turned his attention to kitchen patrol. Ever since he could remember, Bell had been trying to turn pests into pets. There was the tarantula she discovered in the vegetable garden when she was six. He found her giggling uncontrollably as it crept up her arm from her open palm. When she met a mouse under the sink in the kitchen when she was seven, she turned a cardboard box into a painfully cute mouse house, complete with a cotton ball bed. It pained him to have to drive her mouse down the hill and set it free while she was at school. She refused to speak to him for two days after that. It was his own fault. They didn't have a fenced-in yard, so a dog was out of the question, and cats didn't live long in coyote country.

"Rattlesnakes aren't pets," he said as he scraped fruit scraps destined for the compost pile into a small pail he kept under the sink. He recalled a Joan Didion essay he'd read the summer after he'd dropped out of law school. She'd argued it was the obligation of every Californian to kill a rattler whenever they saw one. He'd agreed with her at the time, but that wasn't his style anymore.

"You know people who raise them as pets."

"They raise them as a commodity. They don't consider them pets. Neither does the state. That's why we require a special permit. I'll let it go in a safe place. End of discussion."

Bell's drawings dominated the kitchen. Recent renditions graced the old refrigerator, and Jay had framed a self-portrait from last year and hung it on the wall beside the back door. She'd copied a photograph he'd taken with his vintage Leica, bought on the cheap. She was laying on her back in a field of poppies after a long hike in the Sespe. Her outstretched arms and legs were brown from the late-spring sun. The beauty mark below her left eye was the brightest star in a galaxy of freckles dusting her nose and cheeks. Although he'd meant to, he hadn't gotten around to showing her the prints from that roll. She'd found them in his locked desk drawer, which meant she'd picked the lock—a crime he'd only discovered after she'd pinned the evidence to the fridge with a magnet to surprise him on his fortieth birthday. When he'd found her illustration hanging there, he'd stared at it in silence for nearly fifteen minutes.

She'd broken the cabin's most sacred rule that day. His desk, filing cabinets, and nearby closet, where he kept his dresser and gun locker, were off limits to her, and he required her permission to enter her quarters. But she had a way of seeing through him like he was made of her tracing paper, and she knew her reproduction would stop him from citing her for her crimes. His eyes found that self-portrait for the thousandth time while he guzzled fresh-squeezed orange juice straight from the bottle.

"I might want some, too, you know," Bell said. Startled, he set the bottle down on the bar. "We have clean glasses. Plus, that's just... gross."

"You're right." Jay wiped his mouth with the back of his hand and poured her a glass she regarded with suspicion. "Sorry."

"Humans!" Bell slammed her spoon down and stormed off. Jay drained the glass.

Ten minutes later, Bell stood before a vintage standing mirror from the 1950s, still dripping from the shower. She wore a thrift shop rainbow bathrobe with a coarse, navy-blue towel swaddled around her head. She leafed through her closet, paused on her patched denim overalls, and slid them off their hanger. The legs no longer reached the tops of her ankles. None of her pants did, and most of her shirt sleeves were either too short or too long and baggy. The solution was the same either way: she rolled them up.

She needed new clothes and would have to say so. But aside from shoes, her dad didn't buy her anything brand new. New clothes, like vehicles and furniture, came with a loathsome environmental footprint. By buying secondhand, they could reduce their impact. Translation: Bell was destined to be eternally dressed in someone else's discards. She compensated for the high-water pant legs with long, colorful secondhand socks.

Dressed for school, Bell pulled the towel from her hair and uncovered a thick, dark-brown entanglement. Hidden somewhere within it were three wood chips, a long-lost hair tie, and a binder clip, which she'd once used as a makeshift barrette. Jay was clueless to this catastrophe because she'd hidden it from him. Whether inside or out, she wore a hat, usually a beanie, though she'd also deployed scarves and hoods. It had started as a protest—that Jay either ignored or failed to notice—and had since mutated into a full-on hair hive. She knew what it symbolized but didn't have the time or energy to deal with it. Not now. Not today.

When Bell returned to the living room, Jay had his nose in his hand-drawn topographic map of Alisaw Valley. The original was ten pages taped together, and he'd been sketching and correcting, recopying and editing it for all of Bell's life. She had her illustrations; he had his maps. Somewhere in his files was a hand-drawn map of Ventura County and another of the Los Padres National Forest, which stretched up to Big Sur. She sat down on the futon beside him, her backpack slung over one shoulder, her hive stuffed into a cloudy-gray winter cap that was impossibly soft despite, or perhaps due to, its long chain of ownership.

"Humans oppress scary animals," Bell said. The jar with the distressed reptile rested on the coffee table in front of them. "We're, like, genetically influenced to be prejudiced toward the venomous, so we persecute them."

"Persecute?" Jay gazed at the snake coiled in confinement, checked his watch, patted his pockets, and came up empty. "Like I said, I'll let it go in a safe place, but I am impressed with the vocab this morning."

"They're on your desk," Bell said, nodding to the sheet metal throwback in the corner of the living room. He walked to his desk and palmed his car keys.

"Rattlesnakes live more than twenty years in the wild," he said. "Less than five in captivity."

"You *would* know that." There were times his encyclopedic knowledge of the natural world was seriously annoying. "Have you heard anything about the tiger?"

"Not just yet."

"Because you're not looking."

"That's not true." He tossed his keys in the air and backhanded them. "We have a three-man team rotating in shifts down at the Target."

"Ha ha ha. There are only two game wardens in Ventura County. You and your *boss*."

"Oh, right. And it's almost my shift. We'd better move out."

"You're not taking me seriously."

"Fine. We have a few minutes. Let's go over the evidence again." He unlocked his filing cabinet and pulled out a thick file folder tagged: EVIDENCE: Tiger behind Target, 01.17.05.

Bell's initial drawings of the incident were all sketched on sheets of sketch vellum—her preferred gridded tracing paper—and transferred to thicker stock by scrubbing the backside of the vellum with a soft black pencil. Once the image was transferred, she added color and detail with her Faber-Castells. Bell only showed Jay the finished pieces. She shuffled over and stood beside him so they could leaf through the drawings together.

She often hated the early versions of her illustrations, but sometimes, she managed to bottle something real, and the one at the bottom of the pile did exactly that. Thick stripes arced and rippled along the cat's muscular front shoulders, and its dark-yellow eyes burned with life. Jay traced the stripe beneath the tiger's left eye—the one shaped like lightning—with his thumb. "You really are talented," he said. "What made you add a lightning bolt of all things?"

"I knew you didn't believe me," she said, gutted.

Their warm breath became fog on the windshield as Jay turned the key in his 1981 Chevy Silverado a second time. Still, no joy. He loved almost everything about that truck, especially the original burgundy-and-cream paint job and almost flawless tan interior, but he'd have loved it even more if the driver's side door wasn't a chipped sky blue, that saucer-sized patch of rust on the tailgate wasn't spreading, and if it were a touch more reliable.

"Am I seriously gonna miss the bus again?" Bell stared out the window at his work truck: a brand-new, forest-green Ford F250. "Can't we just take the patrol truck, like, everywhere?"

"Against regulations." He tried again. The starter whirred but wouldn't spark. "And I like my job. You should too. It's all we've got."

"Everything we own is old," Bell said. "Like, ancient."

"Never seemed to bother you before."

"Maybe I've changed."

Jay took a sip of coffee from the travel mug slotted between his legs, checked his watch, and tried again. This time, the spark caught, and the V8 roared to life. He leaned on the throttle, revving it before letting it settle into a deep, chortling hum.

"Ah, yeah," he said, pleased with himself. "Listen to that tiger purr."

Bell glared at him. "Tigers don't purr."

The five-minute descent down Milpas Road snaked beneath a canopy of gnarled oaks—the last green gasp of a woodland that once covered the entire slope before ground broke on Mystic Heights, beginning with the garish gateway where the yellow bus stopped each weekday morning of the school year at 7:53 a.m. They arrived a few minutes early and leaned against the warm hood of Jay's classic hunk of junk while they waited. Bell faced away from Jay, toward the mountains. She had a way of freezing him out when she was angry that felt familiar. She could wall the entire world away if she wanted. He didn't like it much, but it was a byproduct of her willfulness and toughness, and he had to accept it, even when it hurt.

The bus arrived and folded open its accordion doors. A knot of kids ranging in age from six to eleven lingered with their parents, who doled out goodbye hugs and high fives and performed last-second spot checks.

"Be good today," Jay said. If Bell heard him, he couldn't tell. She was the first kid on the bus that morning, and he watched as she selected her preferred seat on the middle right, directly opposite where she had sat on the way home from school fourteen sunsets before. The seat that promised the best possible view of the Target parking lot.

As the bus rolled away, Jay's work phone vibrated and squirmed on his dashboard. He slid in behind the wheel and answered. "Warden Tern."

"Hi...yes. I live up Chelsea Road in Alisaw Valley, and...well...I don't know what kind of wild cats we have running around out here, but I thought I'd better call. Not that you'll believe me. The sheriff's department certainly wanted nothing to do with me. They gave me your number. And trust me, I know I sound ridiculous. I honestly can't believe my own eyes, but I swear, it's right there under my pepper tree."

Calls from anxious residents unfamiliar with the local wildlife were routine, and bobcats were frequently described in outsize proportions. This lady's voice had a tremor to it. Jay pegged her as an older woman caught somewhere between disturbed and fascinated.

"Bigger than a house cat?" Jay asked. The caller laughed dismissively. *Okay, a mountain lion then*, he thought. Drought occasionally lured big cats down into the valley in search of food and water.

"Warden Tern, allow me to describe this marvel for you so you get the picture. Yes, it is much bigger than a house cat or even a bobcat. Also, it has a tail, and it just so happens to be orange and white with—"

"Black stripes?" Jay clipped his seat belt in and turned the key. So much for routine.

"I told you," she said. "Ridiculous."

3

THE BUS RUMBLED TO A STOP IN FRONT OF THE FLAGPOLE AT BIG Springs Elementary, where it discharged its children with a great exhale. Bell trudged past the small army of fourth and fifth graders assigned to raise the American flag that was an orientation point for nearly everyone in town. Her inspection of the Target grounds from the bus window had been fruitless yet again, and she was beginning to accept that the cat had fled Alisaw. A tiger couldn't hide in the suburbs forever.

She watched two of the kids who'd mocked her on the bus that day pull the halyard line through its squeaky trucks until the enormous star-spangled banner rippled in the dry wind. She wondered if the tiger had used the flag as a landmark when it was still roaming the valley.

Students squawked and shrieked like a flock of seagulls as she made her way into the main building, a sprawling single story wrapped in freshly painted, cream-colored stucco with bright-blue trim. No, not a flock. A squabble. Bell had a soft spot for just about every member of the animal kingdom, but she never had liked seagulls much. She did her best to avoid them as she meandered through the hall and down a corridor that extended like a wing along the northwest end of the school, where Ms. Levine had propped her classroom door open. Bell stood with her back against the wall to the left of that open door until the bell rang.

Ms. Levine shut the door behind her as Bell shuffled inside and took her sweet time stuffing her backpack into its cubby at the rear of the room. She hung up her puffy jacket and made her way to her pod, where she had been assigned a desk in a back left corner by the windows. She had a view across the playground. She could even see Highway 23 twist like a black ribbon into the hills.

Ms. Levine marched to the front of the room, where *Plan for the Day* was written on the board. As the teacher went over it, Bell surreptitiously pulled a sheet of sketch vellum and a pencil from her desk drawer and began to sketch seagull children.

"Oh my god, Charlotte, look at her fingernails," Ashley said. Ashley sat kitty-corner to Bell in their six-student pod, an advanced learning group within Ms. Levine's class. Ashley was the head seagull—in life and in Bell's sketch. She was the tallest and the shiniest—she had golden hair and bright-blue eyes. She was also the loudest and wielded the most influence. She could carry a tune, dance, dress, and speak French, and she had penmanship almost as perfect as Ms. Levine's. The girl was popular, and like all well-coiffed seagulls, she was a bully. "She chews them but doesn't wash her hands. Isn't that an interesting/disgusting choice?"

"So interesting/disgusting," Charlotte said. Petite Charlotte sat next to Bell but worshipped at the altar of Ashley. Bell examined her ragged fingernails and found them as nibbled and filthy as charged. The tips were rimmed with black dirt. Two of her knuckles, freshly scraped from that morning's trail run, were gooey with partially dried blood. These were not the perfectly scrubbed hands of a well-brought-up nine-year-old. She thrust them into Ashley's face. Ashley leaned back theatrically, pretending to be horrified.

"Isabella Tern! That is quite enough." Ms. Levine was a severe redhead with straightened hair that curled gently toward the nape of her neck, and she never failed to use a child's full name to publicly admonish them. It seemed as if the entire class snickered as Bell retracted her paws. "And remember, we are implementing a new rule this week, people. No hats in the classroom." Dressed in one of her joyless pantsuits, Ms. Levine extended a manicured finger toward the top of Bell's head. Bell gave her a pleading look. Ms. Levine wasn't having it. "Outdoors only."

"It's called good etiquette," Ashley said.

"But...I...I can't take it off," Bell said, one hand on her gray winter hat. "The doctor said it would help with my headaches."

"So it's not just an inside hat then," Ms. Levine said. "It's also a magic hat." A larger ripple of laughter swirled. Ashley and Charlotte watched with anticipation. The unspecified Bell Tern hair problem was about to be revealed.

"I'm just telling you what the doctor said." Feigning confidence, Bell locked eyes with Ms. Levine. To survive the squabble, one had to be a seagull. "Insisted, actually. He mentioned something about keeping the scalp warm to increase blood flow. Although, he did admit the theory hasn't been proven one hundred percent. Not enough double-blind studies or something. But even if it is just a placebo effect, it can still help."

Ms. Levine stepped closer. Bell placed both elbows over her notebook to hide yet another unauthorized illustration as she strained to remember when she'd last seen a doctor. Was it eighteen months ago? Two years? All she knew was that it was before the headaches began, and the subject of preventative hat wearing had not come up. Ms. Levine did not appear to be buying any of it, which was no surprise. A hat that prevented migraines was a preposterous argument, but since everyone already considered her a liar, Bell didn't see the harm in pushing it.

"You have heard of the placebo effect, haven't you?"

"Honestly, Isabella. It's not even nine in the morning." Ms. Levine glared at Bell for a moment, then retreated to the front of the room. "Fine. Just please tell me this will not be another day of daydreaming and drawing and that you plan on joining us here on planet Earth for the rest of it."

Bell savored her victory and Ashley's and Charlotte's obvious disappointment.

"Everyone, please open your math books to page thirty-four." There was a delay as the students remained fixated on Bell. "Eyes front!"

The class snapped to. The percussion of math books landing on desks, the flutter of pages seemed to soothe Ms. Levine, and Bell followed along the best she could, but when it came to schoolwork, her attention was often unbridled. Within the hour, she'd followed it out through the cracked window to her left, where she was free to soar over the blacktop, the green field, and the golden hills beyond.

4

JAY RACED HOME TO HIS WALK-IN LIVING ROOM CLOSET, WHERE he buttoned up his green polyester uniform, pinned his badge and nameplate to his chest, and punched in the code to his gun safe. He holstered his Glock and two extra magazines packed with twelve forty-caliber rounds then grabbed his .308 assault rifle and Pneu-Dart tranquilizer rifle from the rack.

He seldom ran the lights on his state-issued Ford F250, but this call had him gunning his patrol truck and slaloming motorists. Partly out of concern for the homeowner and whatever was awaiting him on Chelsea Road, but also out of a gnawing curiosity tinged with wishful thinking. After dismissing it with half nods and forehead kisses, he was surprised to discover he wanted Bell's story to be true. Even if it meant he'd failed to track an escaped tiger who had been loose for weeks, an extreme dereliction of duty. That beat the alternatives—either his overimaginative daughter was completely losing touch with reality, or he was raising a pathological liar.

His lights flashing, he zoomed past the last of Alisaw's rangeland, three of the town's seven public parks, and at least a third of the housing blocks that had gobbled up much of the valley over the past sixty years. Housing developments were still spreading like an invasive species, sucking up groundwater, crowding out or killing wildlife, and trading in native savanna and chaparral for chemical-green lawns, wrought-iron fencing, swimming pools, and pavement. Jay kept up on the literature—sound science showed that biodiversity was crashing worldwide. This was what that looked like in Southern California.

Two new housing developments were currently under construction, both in the Alisaw Hills. A third, only a few miles from Mystic Heights and funded by those same developers, had been stopped after a certain game warden had discovered a half dozen nests belonging to the endangered southwestern willow flycatcher on the property. The developers were furious. They'd contracted a team of field biologists to survey the land, and according to the environmental impact statement they'd filed, there were no endangered species on the property at all, much less in the canopies of the trees slated for removal. Jay's report said otherwise, and his report carried more weight than their bought-and-paid-for version. Lawsuits were filed—including one that alleged a game warden had planted evidence of endangered species on the property. That one didn't get very far, and the developers and their lawyers had long since moved on. All that remained of the project were a few concrete foundations, an abandoned excavator, and an ostentatious gateway to nowhere. *At least I was able to stop that one*, Jay thought as he sped by.

He slowed down and killed his lights as he reached Alisaw Home Estates, one of the oldest developments in the valley. He pulled up to a tidy, single-story midcentury. Mrs. Hester waved from the doorway. She was a small woman, about seventy years old, with thin wrists, short gray hair, and bright eyes.

"Thank you so much for coming," she said, "but I'm afraid you've just missed him." The tremor in her voice was still there, but she seemed much more at ease. She said it so casually, as if the cat had headed to the store for a pint of milk. She pointed to a large California pepper tree on her lush lawn, with its fern-like foliage and red berries. "He was lying under that tree for half an hour."

Jay knelt beneath it to search for clues. He noted an impression in the sod where a cat might have been. There was a vague outline of folded front paws and extended back legs, but the bed wasn't as big as he'd expect for a tiger. Then, he inspected the tree trunk and plucked a snag of orange-and-white fur from the cracked bark. He bagged it, snapped photos of the shadow in the grass, and grabbed the rifles from his truck. He wore one on each shoulder and, with no tracks to follow, scanned the neighborhood for clues. A symphony of barking and howling dogs lured him southwest, deeper into the subdivision, where he picked up a trail of toppled trash cans. Bell had seen her cat among Target's dumpsters. *Must be the same cat.*

Jay stopped to arm his tranquilizer rifle. He slid a fresh CO_2 cartridge into the lower barrel, slipped a medicated dart into the chamber, and cocked the gun. He had the .308 strapped to his back and held the Pneu-Dart in his hands as he inspected mostly empty driveways and searched lawns, hedges, and tree canopies. The neighborhood was quiet. Most folks were at work or school. The few residents who were around—retirees, a mother with two toddlers—watched him through their front windows as he moved slowly and silently down the street. His heart rate was up, and his mouth was dry. Was this fear or adrenaline? Probably both. He wondered if he wasn't making a terrible mistake leading with his dart gun instead of the lethal .308. In all his years as a game warden, he'd never tracked a tiger.

He'd recently completed his twelfth year on the job. 2005 was lucky number thirteen. This career, this life he'd built all started at a CDFW booth he'd stumbled onto at an outdoor job fair thirteen months after dropping out of law school. He'd be a cop, the recruiter said. The type that patrols mountain ranges and golden valleys during deer, bear, elk, rabbit, and waterfowl seasons. It was a steady job with good benefits, and the fines he'd levy would pay for conservation. The crimes he'd solve would benefit Mother Nature. Upon graduating from the warden academy, he was assigned to the Central California backwaters east of Fresno. It took him two years and three attempts before he could transfer back home to Ventura County, where he was born and raised.

He became the deputy of a two-man, work-from-home precinct. A couple years later, while in the field, he stumbled upon a ramshackle one-bedroom in the Santa Susana foothills, a holdover from Alisaw's ranching heyday. The cabin was affordable, even on his modest salary, and still surrounded by open space. He and Ling hadn't been together long—about thirteen months, by his calculations—but he asked her to meet him there after he got off work. They made an offer that evening and moved in three months later with dreams of an addition or two. Soon after, Ling became pregnant.

"It's a girl," she'd said, standing barefoot in front of the open back door dressed in one of Jay's oversize black tees, a bead of fresh urine still clinging to the business end of a drug-store pregnancy test. "I know it." Jay had been sinking railroad ties into the earth to create a raised planting bed for their vegetable patch. Stunned, he pulled off his gloves. Ling stepped toward him, and he could see she wasn't trying to be cute. She was certain, and the twenty-week ultrasound proved her right.

Jay and Bell still lived in that cabin in the southeast corner of Ventura County, where Alisaw Valley sat in a three-sided bowl, cradled by the lower-lying Alisaw Hills to the south and wrapped by the crescent moon of the Santa Susana Mountains to the north and east of town. Some 150,000 people lived in Alisaw Valley in 2005, twenty-eight miles from the coast and roughly an hour from Los Angeles by rail or road. Most saw it as a suburb. Jay had always considered it an ecosystem.

In Alisaw Valley, fox and raccoon, rabbit and bobcat, deer, coyote, and mountain lion patrolled undulating fields of wild grasses and brushed against thick patches of sage and the serrated, dark-green foliage of the ubiquitous ceanothus bush. In February and March, vast clumps of dark-blue ceanothus blossoms infused the valley with the scent of honeysuckle. Alisaw was clustered with a handful of remnant live and valley oak woodlands as well as manzanita groves, and its streambeds and canyons were dominated by California sycamore, all of which lured in red-tailed hawks, golden eagles, and great-horned and barn owls.

This tapestry of animal and plant life rambled south to the Santa Monica Mountains and the Los Angeles County line in Malibu. The coastline was dotted with sea lion rookeries—the ocean depths a wealth of lobster, squid, white sea bass, California halibut, and yellowtail. The coastline meandered north from Malibu, past the naval base at Port Hueneme, the berry and lettuce fields of Oxnard, and the twin Ventura and Channel Island harbors and onto Ventura's golden beaches, where perfect waves rolled in.

Inland from Ventura, the hills piled up again and formed the Santa Ynez range that encircled the Ojai Valley and then rose ever higher as the county spread north and east into the Sespe Wilderness, up Alamo Mountain to Mount Pinos and Frazier Mountain, where rocky spires and steep slopes were frosted most winters. In those northern reaches, spruce and pine took root, black bears made their mark on conifers, and deer grew thick winter hides. The southern slopes of the Santa Ynez range cascaded toward the Santa Clara River Valley, best known for the farming towns of Santa Paula and Fillmore and its vast orange groves and avocado orchards.

To Jay, all that suburban sprawl, ag land, and open space was one web of life. An energy transfer system comprising soil, sunlight, and water. Plants and animals feeding on one another and evolving together under the nose of that one conspicuous ape at the tippy top of the pyramid. "Game wardens," he once told Bell, "are the police for those who can never call but are always under siege from planet Earth's apex predator: human beings."

It was an impossible job, of course. The entirety of Ventura County's two thousand square miles was the beat. Jay and his boss, Lieutenant Corey Krull, had only recently finished monitoring the overlapping hunting seasons, which required four months of intense six- and seven-day work weeks. He and Krull patrolled fire roads, trailheads, and private ranches to check hunting licenses and gear and ensure nobody exceeded the legal game limits. When someone was found with more than their share, any hunters involved were cited for poaching, and all the game was confiscated. They typically didn't take that too well. Jay let them vent, and once they'd calmed down, he attempted to explain how ecosystems worked and why they must be managed and respected. With each citation or arrest, Jay tried to educate and inform, even if his lessons fell on deaf ears.

In January and February, Jay and his lieutenant focused their patrols on the fishery. Meaning Jay was supposed to be in the harbor by now, not hunting a tiger in a subdivision. Forecasts called for a calm day in the channel and minimal swell on the open water, and it was lobster season. All the commercial crews would be out hauling up their traps. Plenty of sport fishermen too. Most of the regulars respected the rules, but Jay had learned to never be 100 percent certain about anyone on any given day until after he'd checked their coolers and cargo holds.

Roughly a mile and a half from the caller's pepper tree, Jay noticed two shrieking scrub jays on high alert. They took turns dive-bombing the object of their scorn, which was concealed from Jay's view by a one-story rambler at the end of the block. Jay slowed his approach even more as he drew closer, each step soft and deliberate, until he reached a parched lawn that edged a brick driveway. He found the cat sitting up on the front steps.

Jay laughed to himself. Yes, its face was orange and white with black stripes, but this was no tiger. The markings on its flanks were more like dashes and spots. The tips of its ears were crowned with long threads of jet-black fur. Plus, it was way too small, about the size of a juvenile mountain lion or large German Shepherd. He'd need to confirm the breed, but at first blush, it looked like a lynx. This cat wasn't native to California. It belonged to someone. He flipped through his mental files, searching for a permitted lynx in Ventura County, and found nothing.

The lynx tried to muster the energy to hiss at the birds, but it was clearly exhausted. Jay backpedaled to a secluded vantage point about seventeen yards away. He took aim, pulled his trigger, and watched his dart sink into the cat's rump. Confused, the cat leaped to the lawn and whined, then stumbled and collapsed in a heap against a rear fence. It would soon begin to snore. Jay lowered his rifle, checked his watch, and opened his notebook. He'd need to file an incident report and preferred to jot notes while the action was fresh.

11:11am. 31 Jan. Big cat, exotic. 75ish pounds. Probably a lynx. One dart, 50ccs of azaperone from a distance of approx. 52 feet. Bell's "tiger" is fast asleep.

5

AT LUNCHTIME RECESS, BELL AND MILES FOUND ONE ANOTHER by the back corner of the lumpy athletic field, beneath the infamous oak tree. Standing side by side, they monitored Principal Ono, who scanned the playground wearing her typical stern expression as she chatted with two teachers by the ball box. Their field research would be on hold until she left. Climbing the tree was against school rules, and every kid at Big Springs was deathly afraid of being called into the new principal's office. Better to stay off her radar entirely.

"What do you think the tiger is doing now?" Miles asked. Turned out, someone believed her after all.

"Hunting or sleeping, probably," Bell said, "and trying to stay out of sight. I mean, it's a fugitive."

"Yeah. A *fugitive*."

"It had to have escaped from somewhere, but it'll never be free. Not completely. It's too dangerous." Bell gazed at Principal Ono impatiently, willing her to wrap up her conversation and leave, then swiveled and stared into the canopy, searching for her target, which was difficult to see from the ground. "Anyway, it's been almost three weeks. Probably left the valley the day I saw it."

"Right," Miles said as they watched Principal Ono say her farewells and turn her back on the playground. "Or someone else would have seen it by now."

Once the principal had disappeared into the main building, Bell flung her backpack to the turf. The tree was so old and the canopy had spread so far that some branches nearly grazed the grass. Bell grabbed one that was only about four feet off the ground, hugged it tight, clasped her legs around it, and tossed her neck back, hovering above Miles like a sloth. They shared a giggle as she maneuvered her right leg a bit higher until the branch slotted into the crook of her knee, which gave her enough leverage to pull herself up into the tree.

"We've still got those two teachers on playground duty," Miles said. He was her lookout as usual, peeking over the top of a paperback. "Better be quick."

"Roger that," Bell said. She crab walked up the sloping branch and climbed into a higher tier of the canopy. For weeks, Bell and Miles had been staking out a hummingbird nest, and the only way to observe it properly was to climb above it and look down.

Two years earlier, there had been momentum to remove the tree, but native oaks had just been designated a protected species, and Jay Tern—not the sort of parent to involve himself in school issues—went to a board meeting and said so. His lecture on the importance of oak trees to the Alisaw Valley ecosystem was remembered as informative, moving, and sprinkled with veiled threats of criminal charges. That was enough to convince the board to sheath their chainsaws. Even the most accessible branches of the forbidden tree remained untouched. In fact, Bell used them a few weeks later to hop the fence and cut school. If anyone in the district noticed the irony, they never mentioned it to Jay. This was Bell's third time climbing that tree during school hours in the last month, and thanks to Miles, she hadn't been caught yet.

The mother hummingbird was nowhere in sight. Perhaps her egg had already hatched, and she was out foraging for her fledgling or watching over the nest from afar to avoid attracting predators. Bell had seen that behavior in the garden at home, and yet she had an uneasy feeling, which was confirmed once she'd crawled into position above the nest.

"Shears, please." Bell's wasn't the typical school bag. She hauled tools: a Pringles can stuffed with a reduced palette of colored pencils, a sketch pad, a headlamp, a portable water purifier, and flint for building a fire in case she got lost on the trails or caught up in a natural disaster. She also carried pruning shears. Miles retrieved them from the outside pocket, glanced across the playground, and noticed a huddle of kids around Ashley, who was pointing in their direction.

"We've been spotted," he said as he handed them up.

Bell took a moment to peer through the foliage at Ashley and her mob, who were sneering in her direction. She handed Miles a V-shaped live oak cutting supporting a flexible nest the size of his palm. Inside that was a dead hatchling, not much more than one inch long. It lay rigid among salt-and-pepper shards of eggshell. Its elongated beak was yellow, its body brown and black and covered with a thin coat of tiny feathers.

"It's so light," said Miles. He fixated on the lifeless baby bird as Bell swung down to the grass.

"Its bones are hollow," Bell said. "That's why they can fly so fast."

"How long do you think it lived?"

"Two days, maybe. Look close. The nest is insulated with moss and lint, and the twigs are bound with spider silk. Its mom was a good builder."

"I wonder what happened to her."

"Maybe nothing," Bell said. "Some mothers just leave." People didn't like to think about that, but it was true. She glanced over at Miles, who was still staring at the dead chick. "You can help me bury it if you want."

Bell knelt on the turf. Miles set the cutting down beside her, and retrieved a small trowel from a side pocket of Bell's pack. They took turns digging into the grass beneath the tree, keeping their backs to the playground to shield their handiwork from prying eyes.

"What a freak show. Of course you killed a baby bird."

Startled, Bell turned and accidentally knocked the chick out of the nest and onto the toe of Ashley's brand-new high top. Ashley's lips twisted with disgust. Five other kids, including Charlotte, formed an arc behind her.

"It was already dead," Miles said. Bell scooped up the bird and hid it behind her back.

"Um, no," Ashley said. "We saw her in the tree, hunting her latest victim. Guys, this is what serial killers do. They torture and kill defenseless animals when they're kids." She poked a finger into Miles's chest. "And you were helping her, which makes you guilty too. Murderer." Miles glanced at Bell, his cheeks pink with stress. "It's either that or you guys play with dead animals, which is also totally normal behavior."

"I'm gonna throw up. Like, for real," Charlotte said. "She literally has a dead bird in her bare hands right now. My mom would have a panic attack if she saw me holding a dead animal."

"My mom's head would explode," Ashley said.

"Mine encourages it," Bell said, standing. "She's not one of the boring soccer moms around here. She's an artist. In Milan. Studying taxidermy for an upcoming installation. Not that you even know what taxidermy is."

"Charlotte, make a note. Today she's an artist in Milan. I believe in third grade, she was a mountain climber from Nepal." The mob snickered. Charlotte was leaning against the tree, trying not to hurl.

"I never said she was *from* Nepal. She and my dad just happened to be at Everest Base Camp when I came five weeks early. So yeah, that's where I was born."

"Do you ever *not* lie?" Ashley asked. The lunch bell sounded. It was time to line up and head back to class, but Bell was too busy staring Ashley down to worry about protocol. Ashley didn't seem to hear it either.

With a shove and a quick swipe, Ashley grabbed Bell's beanie and tugged it free, revealing a different sort of bird's nest: a tangled mess of thick, dark-brown hair. "Charlotte, you're missing it!" Ashley held the hat over Bell's head with one hand and stiff-armed her with the other. The seagulls squawked with laughter. Bell lunged for her beanie. Ashley shoved her head down hard and sent her spinning to the turf. Bell popped up quick with her right fist clenched. Enraged, her face felt hot. Her lower lip trembled.

"Oh, look," Ashley said. "The future serial killer is gonna cry."

"I. Don't. Cry!" Bell charged and dug her uneven fingernails into Ashley's perfect neck, yanked at her perfect glossy blonde hair, and dropped the baby bird down her perfectly pressed blue denim dress. Ashley shrieked as she shoved Bell in the face with both hands then grabbed her by the shoulders and flung her down again.

"Charlotte! I can feel it on my skin! Get it off me! Get it off me!" The other kids backed away as Ashley tap danced and shimmied. Charlotte stepped up, held her breath, and helped Ashley shake out her dress until the bird dropped between her oversized feet, which she used to stomp the baby bird, twice. "You're a psycho!" Ashley said. She glared down at Bell, her eyes welling with tears.

"Come on, Ash." Charlotte tugged Ashley's arm, but she wouldn't budge. "Seriously. It's time to go." Charlotte tugged her arm again, and this time, Ashley retreated with her friends to the opposite end of the yard, where, beyond the fence, a blur of cars roared up and down Highway 23, the flow of traffic separated by a trim, grassy median.

"Are you okay?" Miles asked.

Still on her knees and clutching five strands of Ashley's hair, Bell shook her head. She knew what was coming.

It often started slow and dull like this, sprouting from the throbbing vein in her temple and mushrooming until pain narrowed her vision and occupied her entire body. All she could do now was breathe slow and deep like her father taught her and hope to stave it off. In the meantime, while all the obedient children formed up for their teachers, Bell went back to digging. Miles backed away, jogged across the playground, and joined the end of his line.

"I'm sorry I did that to you," Bell said as she placed the chick in a smooth, shallow grave, and buried it. She was still sitting beneath the oak tree when her migraine hit. She shut her eyes, took the pain, and watched a sphere of swirling color spin like a disco ball. She didn't budge until an errant pass sent a football tumbling toward her feet. Fifth grade P.E. had begun. A boy came over to retrieve his ball and watched, mystified, as Bell staggered to her feet and stepped awkwardly around him. Eyes open or closed, that searing ball of color was there, which made it difficult to navigate, but she made it into the building and found the calm of an empty bathroom.

Her soiled fingers smudged the white porcelain as she gripped the sink to remain upright. She stared into the mirror, her head pounding. Dirt streaked her flushed cheeks. There was a bloody scrape on her chin. Clumps of grass clung to her tangled hair. She looked like a cautionary tale. Like a punch line.

She wasn't one of them. Her father didn't have the money their parents did. She had zero interest in dolls or dancing or video games. She didn't watch the movies and shows they all watched. The Terns didn't even own a television. Bell's zip code was the same as everyone else's, but the Tern cabin may as well have been on a different planet.

Bell groaned. Her pulse raced. She gagged and vomited into the sink, then rested her forehead on its cool edge. The pain kept coming in waves—one was strong enough to take her knees out, and she crumpled to the chipped-tile floor. Her eyes stung. She shivered and moaned, but she did not cry. That bold claim she'd made in the heat of battle with Ashley was no lie. Bell Tern hadn't shed a tear since she was three years old.

6

WITHIN FIFTEEN MINUTES OF RECEIVING JAY'S CALL, MIRIAM LONG arrived in her retrofitted van, modified for animal transport. Sixty-three years old and all of five feet two inches, she wore high-waisted work pants cinched with a beige leather belt and a turquoise button-down she'd bunched and tucked into a style that elevated the otherwise baggy and pedestrian Alisaw Valley Animal Control uniform. She wore a knot of jangling keys on a ring strung through the belt loop on her right hip bone. Six of her ten tanned fingers wore sterling-silver rings. Her graying hair was cropped at the shoulders, and her face was sun kissed and lined with expressive grooves that made you want to believe whatever she had to say. Which was helpful because in Jay's experience, she was usually right. Miriam didn't just run Alisaw Valley Animal Control; she had a PhD in wildlife biology and was on the faculty at the community college.

She pulled on a pair of gloves lined with chain mail and hauled an epoxy shield over to Jay, who was standing beside the cat. Miriam knelt and peered over her shield to observe the mischievous stranger laid out before them. "Someone around here lost themselves a Siberian lynx," she said. Satisfied that the animal was in a deep sleep, she set her shield aside and rolled the cat toward her to expose its belly and other relevant bits. "A male Siberian lynx." She pried his lips back to inspect his teeth, which were white at the tips and yellow near the gums. "About five or six years old." She searched for a radio frequency with a handheld scanner. "Not chipped."

"I thought it was a lynx," Jay said, pleased with himself. The cat looked peaceful enough to pet, though Jay never would. Privately owned or not, Jay didn't consider this lynx, or any exotic animal, to be tame. Even if the lynx had been raised in a loving human environment from birth, which was an open question, his genetics were wild, and that made him impossible to predict and potentially dangerous. But it was most definitely something to see. "He sure is a beauty."

Miriam gestured to the empty kennel in the back of her van and offered Jay a pair of armored gloves. "We only have about an hour before he wakes up mad."

Jay grabbed the gloves and retrieved the kennel. Together, they slid the animal inside, and Jay hefted the entire nearly one hundred pounds into Miriam's van.

When they arrived at Animal Control, they were met by Joel, a wiry veterinary student holding a furniture dolly. Jay helped him steer the cat toward the labyrinth of fenced pens and outbuildings Miriam used as a wildlife way station. Typical animal control duties, centered on lost pets and stray dogs and cats, were handled in the main building. Distressed or orphaned wildlife were tended to in the way station until they were healthy enough to be released back into the wild. Miriam figured a lynx would be more at ease near the other wild things. His temporary home was a ten-by-ten-foot concrete-and-glass pen connected to a swatch of mulched outdoor space. Miriam slid her armored gloves back on and unlatched the kennel door. When the lynx woke up, he would have a clean, dry room with a sun porch all to himself. *There are worse fates*, Jay thought. But he still felt bad for the guy.

"I guess I'd better figure out what to feed this bugger," said Miriam.

"I'll call the *Star*," Jay said. "Hopefully, they'll send a photographer. Do you mind if I bring someone up here after school?"

"VIPs are always welcome. You know th—" Miriam was interrupted by the scraping sound of the kennel pivoting on the concrete slab. One paw stretched out of the kennel, then another, but that was all the poor lynx could muster. He moaned in protest, which faded into a whistling snore. Jay watched and listened, so fascinated he lost track of time, until his vibrating phone broke the spell.

7

BELL WAS ASLEEP ON A COT IN THE NURSE'S OFFICE WHEN JAY arrived, one of Miriam's armored gloves still dangling from his back pocket. A woman Jay had seen but never met joined him in the doorway, and he knelt beside his daughter. He inspected her grass-stained overalls and the gash on her chin and was stunned by the condition of her tangled locks. *When did that happen?* he wondered. *And how could I have missed it?*

Principal Ono watched from the doorway. She was in her early fifties and impeccably dressed in a black pencil skirt, fringed navy blouse, and designer eyeglasses. Her identification and a substantial keychain dangled from a lanyard around her neck.

"She gets these headaches," Jay said.

"We're aware. Nurse Silva has seen her quite a bit lately," Principal Ono said. "While she rests, I was hoping we could talk for a few minutes."

Jay followed the principal down the short hall and around the office reception bar. Her hair—black with a wide gray streak—bounced below her shoulders as her heels click-clacked on the waxed tile floors. Her minimalist office was decorated with abstract black-and-white photos. She gestured to a leather chair opposite her tidy, frosted-glass desk, which contained a single file folder in the center and a MacBook off at an angle. Jay sat and noticed the small but serious espresso machine behind her on the low-rise bookcase.

"She was found alone in a bathroom after lunch," Principal Ono said. "There was an altercation. It sounds like your daughter attacked another child. But to be fair, we don't have her side of the story because she hasn't felt well enough to speak to anyone."

"Well," Jay said, "I'm glad we're being fair."

"She was holding this." Principal Ono pointed to the oak cutting and empty nest, which were resting on the edge of her desk next to a weathered, slightly rusted binder clip. His mood brightened a fraction as he noticed the egg shards.

"Hummingbird. That's a nice find on a playground."

"She found it up the oak tree. I'm told you know the one."

Jay locked eyes with the principal and recognized for the first time that she hadn't been around for all that. He vaguely recalled reading a letter from the school last summer introducing her as an education innovator from Seattle. But Big Springs was often exalting itself in self-congratulatory and mostly irrelevant junk mail, and he hadn't gotten through her whole bio.

"Climbing it is against the rules," Principal Ono said, "which I suppose is why she recruited Miles to be her lookout." She reached for the binder clip. "Nurse Silva peeled this out of her hair. It doesn't appear she's brushed or combed it in quite some time."

Jay glanced at the clip, then out the window. Outside, the blue sky was going gray. There hadn't been any rain in the forecast, but his eyes itched like they tended to before a storm. The bell rang, and the saccharine soundtrack of hundreds of liberated children filled the halls. Principal Ono leaned in with a look of concern. Whether it was genuine or practiced was hard to say, but he was struck with the realization that he was being assessed for his parental fitness.

"She's not the only one who is hurting. It was an ugly fight today," she continued. "The other child has a nasty scratch down the length of her neck. Apparently, Bell put a dead bird down her dress. Which

I'd expect you'd agree is unsanitary and, frankly, unacceptable. I'm considering suspension."

Jay wanted to respond with something like, "That doesn't sound like my kid at all," or "Bell would never even think of doing something like that," but that was what the suspects he encountered or their relatives said when confronted with reality, so he kept quiet. Though he'd have bet a year's salary the other girl started it. Why would Bell climb a tree and take a specimen like this only to attack another girl with the bird inside it? It didn't compute. Bell revered hummingbirds, and if she used the dead nestling as some sort of payback, she probably felt terrible about it.

Principal Ono paged through the file. "Ms. Levine mentioned that you skipped the parent-teacher conference and that Bell has been difficult lately. She hasn't turned in a single homework assignment since Thanksgiving. But you know that, right? It was explained in three separate notes she sent home with Bell. You signed them."

"Right," he said, covering. "I signed them."

"Are you sure? I have them here if you'd like to read them again."

"That won't be necessary." Bell and her pen skills. Jay didn't need to see the evidence to know the forged signature would be a perfect match.

"Have you spoken to your daughter about it?"

"Not...specifically."

"Uh-huh. Well, Nurse Silva believes the headaches could be what's impacting Bell's concentration and is adamant she needs to see a doctor. And beyond that, Mr. Tern, I think it might help if she had someone to talk to. Someone besides her dad, I mean."

Jay picked up the nest and inspected it. This wasn't the first time someone had suggested therapy. Which was fine. He had a good idea what else was in that file folder and understood the two of them fit the patient profile, but he'd always shrugged it off. The natural world was their therapy. It was their escape and their renewal. He wasn't sure of a whole lot, but he knew Mother Nature had healed them once before and could be counted on to heal them again.

"The school can arrange free resources. You know, if money is tight."

Jay arched his acrobatic eyebrow.

"It's okay to feel overwhelmed, Mr. Tern. It's okay to ask for help."

"I know it is, ma'am." Jay glanced at his badge. "People call me for help all day long."

"Then you also know that needing help doesn't excuse someone from their responsibilities."

"No, ma'am. It doesn't." Jay stood, still holding the oak cutting. He didn't doubt this principal meant well, but he had heard more than enough for one afternoon. "We are sorry for all the trouble." He could feel the principal's gaze as he marched back to the nurse's office, scooped Bell into his arms, and carried her down the hall and out through the double doors.

Jay watched Bell take stock of his weapons and electronics when she woke up ten minutes later. He didn't allow her in the work truck very often. They were stopped at that long light alongside the Target parking lot, and Jay gestured to the nest he'd rested on the dashboard. "That," he said, "is pretty dang cool."

"I didn't trust that mama bird," Bell said wearily as she stared out the window toward the loading bays. "I should have checked on the baby every day. We could have brought it up to Miriam's."

Jay had questions about what had happened on the playground and what he'd heard from the principal, but he could see that Bell didn't have the strength to discuss it. *We'll get to it*, he thought, *eventually*.

The light changed. Jay accelerated toward the foothills, which cowered beneath a welcome invasion of storm clouds. Was this the famous El Niño at last? He hoped so. It felt like Southern California was in perpetual need of rain, but especially now, when the slightest spark could trigger devastation.

"Funny you should mention Miriam," he said. "I found something today too, and I think you're gonna like it."

8

MIRIAM'S KEYS JANGLED BRIGHTLY AS SHE ESCORTED THE TERNS down a long hallway lined with kennels holding dogs and cats. Bell counted them as they barked and cried. That was always the worst part of visiting Miriam's place. Not everyone would find homes, and it felt like the animals were pleading for help. Miriam didn't euthanize animals in her shelter, but it was still a relief to slip out the back door and into the way station.

Bell immediately glimpsed three spotted fawns in a hilly, fenced-off area beside a modest aviary. When she was four and a half, Bell and Jay had brought in a one-legged crow fledgling they'd found stranded beneath an oak tree. Miriam determined it to be a birth defect and decided that she had been orphaned, a rare occurrence among crows. Even at her meekest and most exhausted, the bird had a pecky, plucky spirit, and she grew strong in that aviary, thanks to Miriam's regular foraging tutorials. Bell and Jay watched a few of those lessons themselves, and they were there for her release six months to the day after they'd found her.

"How's our special guest?" Jay asked as they entered the last outbuilding in the compound, the one built for full-grown coyotes, black bears, and mountain lions. Jay's work camera—a digital Olympus—hung from around his neck.

"Still ticked off," said Miriam, "but he ate three pounds of ground beef in less than a minute. Poor thing must have been starving."

Bell's pulse quickened. Ever since she first saw the tiger tucked between the red dumpsters, she'd been wondering if she would ever get to see it again. She surveyed the large, empty kennels as she followed Miriam down the corridor. A few seemed big enough to hold a large tiger for a day or two. Miriam stopped in front of the last kennel in the block. Bell was too thrilled to speak, but when she arrived at the window, her anticipation curdled into disappointment.

She stepped closer to the zoo-grade glass and watched the lynx pace back and forth. Until he noticed her, bared his teeth, and snarled.

"When you kept pushing, I should have known something was out there," Jay said. He raised his camera and triggered the shutter in rapid-fire succession. The lynx was strutting in circles, probing for possible escape routes, while Bell searched for any evidence that would allow her to accept him as the animal she'd seen from the bus window. He was big all right. The biggest cat she'd ever seen this close. His eyes were a lighter shade of amber than she remembered but just as penetrating. His coat was orange and white, and his face was striped. That was where the similarities ended. This cat's body was marked with spots and dashes, and the lightning bolt she'd seen under the left eye wasn't there. Bell thought back to that day on the bus three weeks ago. How could she be so certain of what she'd seen? She'd seen so many odd things lately.

"I guess it does kind of look like a tiger," she said, finally.

"This species comes from the same place as the largest tigers in the world," Miriam said. "It's a Siberian lynx." Miriam stepped close enough for Bell to feel her warmth. "You have quite the eye for wildlife, kid."

Miriam waited until the cat moved into the mulch. Then, with the push of a button, she dropped a gate that divided the kennel. Bell retrieved his water bowl and refilled it, then helped Miriam dish up more ground beef. A cub reporter from the *Ventura County*

Star turned up, and Jay and Miriam went off to speak with him while Bell sat on the floor and watched the cat feast. After he'd devoured every scrap and licked the bowl clean, he lay on his side, facing away from Bell.

She watched his tail swish back and forth in a steady rhythm as the last light drained from the sky.

On their drive home, the first raindrops of the season splashed on the patrol truck's windshield, and Bell considered the version of reality in which Jay had found the cat she'd seen behind Target. Maybe she did have a runaway imagination. Maybe that was the source of all her discontent, especially her sense that she was out of step with the entire human race.

When she got home, Bell dropped her bag in her room and headed for the shower. The water was just shy of piping hot when she stepped into the stream face-first. She closed her eyes, washed away the remaining grime, turned around, and let the water saturate her hair, which she attempted to detangle until that proved both excruciating and impossible. She turned her attention to her forearms, noting her latest collection of scratches, bites, scabs, and bruises. *When you live close to nature,* her father had once told her, *it marks you from time to time.*

With Bell out of earshot, Jay slipped a tray of broccoli florets into the oven and tossed tofu in sesame oil, almond butter, and tamari. Then, he dialed a specialist in LA recommended by Miriam's sister, who was a pediatrician in Oregon. Dr. Ambrose sounded warm and upbeat, with none of the heaviness Jay had expected from a pediatric neurologist. Jay steered the conversation toward Bell's migraines.

"She had another one today. That's three in the past two weeks."

"I'm sensing that's an uptick," said the doctor. "How about hallucinations? Does she see things? Things that aren't there."

"I'm sorry?" Jay spilled the tofu into a hot skillet and set a timer for ten minutes.

"Some patients see shapes and colors that blur their field of vision. Or it could be an exaggerated version of events. Sort of a halfway point between fantasy and reality." Jay stared at the sizzling pan. The flame was too hot, and the sesame oil was burning, but he was too stunned to do anything about it. "Warden Tern? Are you still with me?"

"Yeah. I'm with you." Jay shut off the burner, opened the back door, fanned at the haze gathering near the ceiling, and stepped outside into a soft rain. With the phone to his ear, he watched his daughter enter her room through her bedroom window. Swaddled in her rainbow bathrobe with a towel wrapped around whatever had become of her hair, she paused at her drafting table and raised one of her lifelike illustrations of the tiger to the light. "What if she is...seeing things?"

"Well, Bell is at the age when more serious neurological issues can present in children."

"Meaning?"

"Meaning it would be a good idea to start ruling some things out."

9

FEBRUARY 1, 2005

IT WAS A TICK AFTER SEVEN IN THE MORNING WHEN JAY EXITED the 101 and continued east on Hollywood Boulevard. He noticed that the liquor stores, Armenian bakeries, and Thai sweet shops all seemed to roll up their metal security gates and blink their lights on at the same time. Bell picked at the cracked vinyl beneath her thigh.

"So this is a checkup," Bell said as Jay steered his Chevy into the Children's Hospital parking structure on Sunset Boulevard.

"In a way," Jay said. He considered the best way to phrase his explanation of what this appointment was all about as he rolled past the empty reserved spaces with easy access to the hospital until he reached the fourth level, where the lowly patients were permitted to park. He found a space with a view and pulled in. "These are very smart people who can help us figure out what's causing your pain and hopefully get you some relief."

Despite the early hour, the waiting room was full. A stone-faced receptionist handed Jay a clipboard stacked with new-patient paperwork and pointed to two available seats in a far corner. He knew from experience it was generally a good sign when medical staff didn't engage in casual chitchat. When doctors, nurses, and office staff gabbed too much, it often meant they were nervous the patient had floated toward the outer edge of their influence, beyond which lay an ethereal space between the practice of medicine and whatever forces determined the ultimate outcome of things. He wondered how friendly she would be after Bell's CT scan.

First, however, they had to wait. Bell pulled her vellum sketch pad out of her pack, shook a black pencil loose from her Pringles can, and began a new drawing while Jay filled out paperwork. Halfway down the first page, he hesitated at the heading he'd dreaded: *Family History*. Beneath it was a list of some two dozen diseases and disorders. He'd shared this information over the phone already. Now, here it was again, in print. He glanced over at Bell, who was busy sketching the lynx pacing in its stall. She added the lightning bolt he knew wasn't there and showed him her work in progress. Jay cranked up an eyebrow while raising his knee to shield his clipboard from view. Then he checked one box.

Dr. Ambrose met them in a treatment room. She was dressed in the standard crisp white coat and wore blue Coach eyeglasses. Her salt-and-pepper dreadlocks were wrapped into a ponytail that grazed her midback. She had a kind face, but the exam room felt sterile and cold.

The doctor traced Bell's spinal cord with two gloved fingers and instructed her to follow a pinprick of red light with her eyes. Then, she asked Bell how her headaches began, and they discussed gradients of pain and the disco ball of light Bell saw on the playground.

"Do you ever see stuff that others miss?" Dr. Ambrose asked. "I'm talking big, obvious things."

"Only sometimes," Bell said.

Repressed memories attempted to claw their way out of the burial ground in Jay's mind as he followed the doctor into an adjacent room where he was expected to watch his daughter have her brain scanned through a tinted window. The CT lab had an aluminum table on tracks, glossy floors, and severe overhead lighting. A tech in black scrubs boosted Bell onto the table and slipped her head and neck into the cradle. He placed an emergency buzzer in her right hand, oversize headphones on her ears, and a plastic coil over her face.

"Will we get the results today?" Jay asked.

"I'm afraid not," said Dr. Ambrose. "I'll need to examine the scans thoroughly, and I'll have other doctors on my team go over them as well. It's a process, but it won't take too long. Days rather than weeks."

Dr. Ambrose leaned in as the tech used a control panel to move the bed up and into the machine. Lasers crosshatched Bell's third eye. Jay shared her anxiety as he read her lips. "A parliament of owls. A prickle of porcupines. A gang of bison." It was the usual gambit to stave off panic. "A band of coyotes. A streak of tigers. A murder of crows…"

We're an atomic riddle, Jay thought. *All of us. We are not our dramas and desires, our successes and struggles, our identities and personalities. We are a mosh pit of colliding protons, neutrons, and electrons, mass and light.* It was what he believed to be true and what he taught Bell, but in that moment—with technicians and doctors attempting to decode whatever was going wrong inside his daughter's head—it did not soothe him.

Too wound up to watch, he slipped into the hallway, leaned against the wall, and slid to the floor. He sat with his knees pinned to his chest and listened to the lights buzz. Docs, nurses, and techs, color-coded in pressed coats and fresh scrubs, tossed awkward smiles and sideways glances toward the strange guy sinking into the quicksand of worst-case scenarios as they stepped around him. Jay knew he needed to focus on something, anything, else. If not for his sake, then for Bell's.

He retrieved his topographic map from his pack, zeroed in on Chelsea Road, and marked the location where he'd found the lynx. He'd been so certain he had solved Bell's mystery, yet he had noticed she was less than impressed. At the time, he'd chalked it up to disappointment and Bell's headstrong, overimaginative tendencies, but in that desperate moment in the hospital hallway, he allowed himself to consider a more generous possibility. The one that didn't involve Bell seeing things that weren't there. The one in which headaches might only be headaches. And he recalled her troubling question—the one she had asked as they breached the Mystic Heights gates on the drive home from Animal Control.

"Dad, do you think the owner of that lynx might own other big cats? Because I was thinking, since one animal escaped from someone you weren't even aware of, isn't it at least possible there is another one out there? Another lynx? Or something else? Something…bigger?"

Jay's instincts told him it was improbable. Doubtful even. Owning a lynx was one thing. Owning a full-grown tiger was a whole other magnitude of management. If someone in his jurisdiction had lost one of those, he'd have heard about it. Because nobody would dare lose track of a tiger in Southern California and keep it to themselves. But after he'd pulled into their carport, he took a moment to contemplate the human animal's capacity for self-delusion. Bell's eyes were on him when he turned to her and killed the engine.

"It's certainly not impossible," he said.

10

MIRIAM WAS STANDING BEHIND THE RECEPTION DESK WITH JOEL, cleaning out old files, when a middle-aged man she hadn't seen before strolled into Alisaw Valley Animal Control. "I believe you have my animal," he said.

"Terrific." Miriam sized him up. He was a big, handsome man in his mid-fifties, round in the belly but still barrel chested, with silver hair and bronzed skin. He wore pressed khakis, a pink polo with an open collar, a navy blazer, dark mirrored glasses, and cowboy boots. Clearly a dog person. "Joel here can help you with that."

"Which animal might that be, sir?" Joel asked.

"The Siberian lynx, son." He extended a manila envelope to Joel. "Sierra's paperwork." Joel turned to Miriam. She reached over and accepted the envelope.

"You know, Joel, I think it makes better sense for you to tend to these files in my office. I'll help Mr...?"

"Glenn." He popped a stubby stick of peppermint Trident into his mouth. "Aubrey Glenn." A symphony of howls, yips, and barks escaped as Joel did a double take in the doorway, then disappeared into the back with an armful of files.

"Okay, Mr. Glenn. You're missing a lynx. How on earth does something like that happen?"

"You'd have to meet the missus. She's the one who tells the tale about how we became lynx aficionados. We've owned several over the years. Wonderful kitties."

"That's not what I meant." Miriam opened the envelope and skimmed the permits inside. "You live in Temecula? That's down in Riverside County. He sure wandered an awfully long way."

"Used to. We just moved in across the valley."

"Got lost on the move, did he?"

Aubrey appeared to bristle at the question. "I'm sorry, ma'am. I didn't get your name."

"I'm Dr. Miriam Long," she said. "I run the place."

"Dr. Long, I should have thanked you right off. For looking after our Sierra, I mean. We were worried half to death, but if you wouldn't mind..." He removed his sunglasses and checked his watch. "I've got a big new property and a honey-do list as long as my arm."

Miriam assessed the husky gum chewer and couldn't decide if he was a total fraud or simply a quirky animal lover who hoped his folksy charm could grease her wheels. Not that it mattered. There were laws on the books when it came to exotic cats, and she would abide by them. "Unfortunately, we are not prepared to release the animal to you today."

"Why not? You're looking at the documentation. I have pictures too." He pulled a pack of one-hour prints from his inside jacket pocket and spread them out on the desk. There were snapshots of him and Sierra stretched out on a wide green lawn, a portrait of Sierra alone, and another of Sierra jumping through a hoop held by Aubrey in a horse corral. "Take a minute to compare the markings on his face. That's how you can tell..."

"I know how to identify individuals, Mr. Glenn, but your exotic cat was found by a game warden, which means the state is involved."

"Oh, I see. You gotta cross the t's and dot all them i's too." Aubrey sighed, gathered his photographs, and folded up his paperwork. "I don't mean to be pushy, it's just that Sierra is part of our family, and we're real eager to have him home."

Miriam had a similar opinion about exotic wildlife as Jay. They should never be considered pets, much less family members, but she also knew that moving could stress animals and that most runaways weren't mistreated. In all likelihood, the confused lynx had gotten himself lost and worried his owners terribly. As for Aubrey, Miriam had been around enough devoted animal lovers to know they could be different. Her quirky volunteer roster was evidence of that. Heck, she was one of them. Still, there was something about this man that raised the fuzz on her forearms.

"I know one of the local game wardens very well, Mr. Glenn," she said. "He'll perform a simple compliance review of your property, and if it all checks out, you can take Sierra home that same day. I'll see that he prioritizes it."

11

FEBRUARY 3, 2005

EVER SINCE THE FIRST DROPS FELL ON MONDAY AFTERNOON, THE rain hadn't stopped, but it was mostly light rain, and Bell refused to use it as an excuse to skip the morning trail run. She had hoped to see a genuine storm blow over the valley. What she had gotten instead was glorified drizzle. "We'll need a lot more rain than this to refill the reservoirs," Jay said from the lookout. "Hopefully, it picks up. We haven't had a decent wildflower season in three years."

Bell's school did not embrace the rain. Lunchtime recess was held inside the cafeteria. Her classmates played board games or watched old Disney movies while Bell sketched a tiger in the hills creeping closer to the silhouette of a girl with unkempt hair. Or that was what she was aiming for. She rarely achieved what she envisioned on the first go, which could be frustrating, but something about the scratch of the pencil on paper soothed her into an openness that encouraged improvisation. The rest of the world zeroed out, and time became elastic. When she was in her zone, hours evaporated like minutes.

"Is *that* what it looked like?" Ashley asked, popping Bell's bubble with her massive finger. She was pointing at the tiger but staring at the little girl. "Because we know that's what your hair looks like." Bell paused to consider the proper response.

When she'd returned to class the day after her CT scan, Bell had found her beanie on her desk, resting on a clean sheet of lined paper with the heading, *MAGIC HAT*. It looked and smelled like it had been freshly laundered in orange blossoms and honey. Meaning it smelled like Ashley. As much as Bell did not identify with that scent, an effort had been made, and she supposed that had to count for something. She'd nodded toward Ashley, who wore a scab as long as a tiger's stripe up the side of her neck. Ashley nodded back, and whatever elevated tension remained between them melted back to normal. Normal being a palpable, mutual dislike but not a blood feud. Bell preferred to keep it that way, which was why she opted against engaging and turned her attention back to her illustration.

"I'm saying you're a good artist," Ashley said as Bell assessed the tiger's expression for authenticity. "Um...that's a compliment, weirdo."

"Oh," Bell said. "Thanks for the compliment."

At the end of the day, Ms. Levine drew a straight-trunked tree with a billowing cloud for a canopy on the blackboard and turned to face the class. "Who can tell me what this is?"

Charlotte's hand shot up. As usual, she was way too eager to be called on, considering her record for getting things exactly wrong.

"It's a tree!" Charlotte shouted. Laughter rippled through the room.

"Yes, but what type of tree?"

Bell sharpened her focus. It looked like a ficus, the type of generic street tree that had a habit of buckling sidewalks and siphoning sprinkler lines, and it wasn't terrible for a quick sketch. However, Ms. Levine's point clearly wasn't the tree itself. It was in the horizontal lines she'd drawn within the canopy. Bell couldn't guess where this was going, and that made it at least semi-interesting.

"It's a family tree," Ashley said.

"I told you," one kid muttered.

"Very good," Ms. Levine said. "And what is a family tree?"

"It's like a map of your relatives," Ashley said.

"Precisely. Class, this assignment is about tracing your roots." Ms. Levine weaved between pods as she lectured. "Like trees, we all also have roots that lead us back through time to our parents and grandparents and their parents too. Creating your own family tree will enable you to learn about the lives of your ancestors and discover how you came to be right here, right now, and all the little miracles that aligned to make that happen."

She went on to explain where students' names belonged and how to organize the tree by generation. "Include as many generations as you like. Get creative. Use old photographs, handwritten letters, excerpts from diaries. Clippings work if you have newsmakers in your tree." She pointed to a due date circled on the blackboard: February 28. "This will be a longer-term project, but do not take that as an invitation to procrastinate. Research should begin immediately. Ask your parents about your extended family this weekend. Start digging. The point here is to discover who and where you came from because when we engage in that sort of work, we learn valuable lessons that will stay with us."

The class was rapt. All around her, children were thrilled at what would amount to a joyful march down memory lane, a family bonding exercise, an investigation into their own root systems. But Bell's roots were all dried up. They led nowhere. She hadn't even met her grandparents and knew she couldn't bother her father with this. The vein in her temple began to throb. She was in desperate need of fresh air. Another migraine was imminent.

"In nature, each tree is unique and beautiful in its own way," Ms. Levine said. "Just like each one of you."

Bell's stomach rumbled with nausea. While she conceded that was objectively true, each successive Hallmark-quality phrase increased the odds that she would puke publicly. To stave it off, she focused on the clock above the blackboard. There were two minutes left before the bell would ring at 2:55 p.m. Two more minutes, and she was free.

"Don't look so nervous," Ashley said. The clock ticked to 2:54 p.m. "Ask your mom to help. Maybe she can stuff something for you."

Ms. Levine placed her manicured hands on the back of Bell's chair. "I cannot wait to see what you come up with, Isabella."

Bell glanced up at her teacher and around the classroom. All eyes were on her, and the thought of revealing something, anything true about herself to any of these people made the taste of bile rise higher in her throat. The clock ticked over. The bell rang.

Bell bolted out the door, but the hall was choked with oversized seagulls. They brushed past her, squawking at one another. The pressure in her head made Bell squint as she slalomed them on her way to the main exit. Except all the shrieking birds destined for the bus were stopped short of the doorway, and she was herded to the wall along with them. They were meant to wait for the bus inside, to keep dry. Nauseous and claustrophobic, Bell dashed back down the hall toward three more preening gulls—Ms. Levine, Ashley, and Charlotte—marching side by side. She cut left to avoid them and ducked through the side door that was always unlocked.

Out on the blacktop, Bell tilted her head back and let raindrops splatter her cheeks. She took two deep, cooling breaths and opened her eyes to find Miles staring up at her. "I didn't want you to miss the bus," he said.

Bell wasn't much for conversation on the ride home. She kept her forehead glued to the sliding windowpane sprinkled with fresh rain as Miles chatted about the dozens of burrows built by the chipmunks around his condo complex. When they stopped at the light next to Target, she looked toward the loading bay and dumpsters but didn't have the angle. It was impossible to tell if anything was rummaging around. Not that the back end of a Target was a desirable place to curl up and wait out a storm. If you were a big cat in unfamiliar terrain, it seemed the kind of place you'd wind up by accident. But how could a tiger get there without anyone else seeing it?

Bell sat up, wiped away the condensation on her window with her sleeve, and stared at the shadowy gap between the strip of tarmac behind the superstore and the chaparral-draped slope behind it. That gap was one of several seasonal washes that threaded between the highways and subdivisions, shopping centers and avenues of Alisaw Valley.

"It's using the washes, Miles," she said. Miles looked puzzled. Bell tapped the window. "The tiger. It has to be." The light changed. The bus lurched and chugged onward, and Bell relaxed her head against the cool window. This whole time she'd been waiting. Waiting for her father to finally take her seriously, for the tiger to reveal itself again, for someone else to act. Why hadn't she ever considered lacing up her boots and searching for it herself? "It may not know where it is, but that doesn't mean it's lost. And neither was that lynx. Like my dad says, wild animals need to be wild."

Bell could see that Miles was barely listening as he stared up at the scarred ceiling, surveying its many dents, scratches, and missing rivets. Maybe she'd finally bored him with her tiger talk.

"What's it like to have a dad?" he asked.

Bell flexed her left eyebrow at him. "It's smelly," she said. Miles wasn't in a laughing mood. "I thought you saw your dad sometimes. You told me that you did."

"I guess I lied," he said with a shrug. "I was four last time. We have two pictures. Otherwise, I probably would have already forgotten what he looks like."

Bell leaned her head against his. "I was three the last time I saw my mom," she said. "The only thing I know about her is her name."

12

THANKSGIVING DAY, 2004

HOLIDAYS WEREN'T A PRIORITY IN THE TERN CABIN. WHILE MOST of Bell's classmates enjoyed traditional Thanksgiving meals with extended family, she and Jay usually stayed home and ate a quiet meal by themselves, as if it were any other Thursday. This Thanksgiving morning, however, instead of hitting the trails, Jay told Bell to grab her go bag and packed the Chevy with camping gear and his vintage metal cooler.

They drove northeast into the high desert and veered onto a dirt road that led them deep into the Mojave wilderness. They set up camp at the base of a rocky bluff overlooking a desert plain populated with Joshua trees, and after hours of hiking and scrambling up boulder columns, Jay hauled the old cooler to the ground and built a small cook fire. Bell popped the latch on the cooler to find a bag of Yukon golds with soil still clinging to the skin, vines of late-season cherry tomatoes, and meaty asparagus spears, all from their garden. Beneath the produce sat two fresh, thick-cut albacore steaks gifted to them by one of the more mindful fishermen on the docks. Jay had marinated them in olive oil, Meyer lemon, and fresh thyme and sealed them in a baggy.

Bell washed and chopped per his instructions, and he seared and roasted it all up in his prized cast-iron skillet, purchased at an army surplus store fifteen years earlier for under ten dollars. He told her that story for the hundredth time as he drizzled the asparagus with balsamic reduction then set the Albacore steaks down in that same pan. It was a fitting tale. Almost everything they owned shared the same traits: overlooked, inexpensive, indestructible.

After dinner, he brewed up hot chocolate, poured some bourbon into his, and sliced a halfway-decent store-bought pumpkin pie—because all pumpkin pie is halfway decent at its worst, which is better than good enough. When they were done pigging out, he tamped the flames to ash, and Bell dragged their sleeping pads out into the open. The stars were innumerable. You couldn't count them all in a year, a decade, a lifetime. There were clouds of galaxies, planets shining and fading, and commuting satellites. Meteors blazed the black dome sky. Jay cracked a ratty hardcover. It was thin and so well worn that the title had been rubbed off. He clicked on his headlamp and read aloud.

> *Do you imagine the universe is agitated?*
> *Go into the desert at night and look out at the stars.*
> *This practice should answer the question.*
> *The superior person settles her mind as the universe*
> *settles stars in the sky.*
> *By connecting her mind with nature, she calms it.*
> *Once calmed, it expands, and ultimately her mind*
> *Becomes as vast and immeasurable as the night sky.*

"What's that book?"

"It's an old translation of a classical Chinese text called the *Hua Hu Ching*," Jay said. He passed her the book and his headlamp. She read the verse again, then switched off his headlamp and handed them both back. He stashed the book. Bell waited for stars to repopulate her field of vision. "Guess where I found it."

"The Rose Bowl flea market, obviously."

"Obviously."

"I mean, duh, Daddy."

"Total duh."

"I don't think I get it all the way, but it sounds really nice."

"I'm not sure I completely get it either," Jay said, "but it makes me feel like there's more to us than we know. For instance, you, Bell Tern, are made of stars." Cocooned in her sleeping bag, Bell rolled onto her side to face him. He was chattier than usual, which tended to happen when he sipped from that flask. "That's why you have so many freckles." He pinched her nose.

She blinked and sneezed. "Gross!" She laughed as he wiped his hand on the desert sand.

"I'm not kidding, though. All life is made up of atoms, which are basically little pixels assembled like in a digital photograph. We have pixels of carbon and nitrogen, iron, oxygen, sulfur, and so many other elements. And scientists figured out that those atoms, those elements, are all byproducts of stars that burned so hot they exploded. Their dust rained down throughout the galaxy. Some landed on our little planet, and when these atoms bonded, they helped seed life on earth."

"We're stardust," Bell said.

"And so many people have forgotten that."

"Or never knew it in the first place."

"True. No wonder we all walk around wearing pants and shoes and ordering pizza. No one knows we're a herd of mysterious space creatures made of stardust."

"Pizza's good, though," Bell said, laughing.

"Pizza is the best," Jay said.

Their laughter faded to silence. "That means Momma's a dead star too," Bell said.

Jay's smile flickered when he turned to face her and laid his cheek down on the desert floor. A few minutes later, his eyes closed, and his glow was gone.

By the time she woke up the next morning, he was already packing the truck. On the drive home, she brought up her mother again. "I've been thinking it's weird that we never talk about her," Bell said. "Don't we have any pictures?"

"You know I don't."

"I know that's what you say." Bell stared out the window, trying to figure out a way to bust through the brick wall. "Which is sort of weird. Like why? You always have a camera with you. What did you do with them?" The question bounced off him as if he were dressed in that old flak jacket that hung in his precious closet with the tag still on it. "Can you at least tell me how you guys met?"

"We'll discuss it when you're older." She'd heard that before. "When you're mature enough to process everything." This time, even he didn't look like he believed it.

"I'll bet it was scandalous," Bell said. "Probably why we aren't in touch with her family. Because they hate you."

That prompted him to turn the radio up. After fifty miles of silence, he pulled into the cracked asphalt parking lot of the taqueria they liked in Santa Paula.

"You're mad at me," she said. They sat across from one another in a Formica booth, overlooking spent paper plates streaked with oil and scattered with chopped onions—the last remnants of some damn fine carne asada tacos. "For asking normal questions. And I don't understand why."

"I'm not mad," he said. "I just choose not to think about her, and neither should you. When she went away, I had to figure out how to rebuild a life, a future, for both of us, and that required some difficult choices."

Bell stared down at the greasy plates and her own uneven fingernails. She didn't like how he looked or sounded. Cold and distant, like some far-off moon.

"Now, your curiosity makes sense. You think these answers will help you. That's natural, but I promise they won't. That emptiness you have because she's not here, if you add shape and form to it with details, it will only feed the emptiness. It won't fill it up. That emptiness will grow so big that it defines you, and I've never wanted either of us to be defined by what should or could have been. Do you understand?"

She looked into his eyes—they were lighter than hers, like his skin. Similar in character, but in shape and symmetry, more different than the same. It was so obvious, but he refused the obligation of explaining why. Whenever she looked in the mirror, she saw a riddle to be solved, and he wouldn't offer any clues. He wasn't the moon. She was the one trapped in his orbit.

A quirk of geology had created the moon. He'd taught her that too. An ocean of fire and gas had churned on the surface of the Earth until it gathered into a tsunami that threw off a chunk of basalt rock so high and deep it flew into the earth's lonely orbit. Was that something all celestial bodies did—lose vital pieces of themselves?

"Aren't you afraid you'll forget her?" Bell asked. Tears gathered in the reservoir, prepared to flow, but she shut down the main.

"Afraid?" He stood and trashed their plates, peeled off a paper napkin, and wiped the table clean. "Forgetting is how wild animals recover from trauma. If they remembered the hell they'd survived, they wouldn't be able to keep going. It would be too much." He pinned a five-dollar bill beneath the stainless steel dispenser and threw the napkin away.

Before bed that night, Bell brushed her hair like her dad had taught her when she was five. Thirty times on the left, and thirty on the right. Then, she dropped her discount, wood-paddled, faux-boar-bristled hairbrush into the army surplus trash can beneath her drafting table.

She hadn't brushed her hair since.

13

FEBRUARY 3, 2005

JAY TURNED UP A GRAVEL DRIVE IN THE ALISAW HILLS THAT LED TO a property scattered with wild walnut trees and shaggy California peppers—which, despite the name, were indigenous to Brazil, not Southern California. They'd been planted over one hundred years ago by Luis Suarez, the head of Alisaw's original ranching family. Properties like this were designated "unimproved" by the county pencil pushers. Most were owned by absentee landlords anxiously waiting for the suburbs to reach them, with their promise of publicly funded water, sewage, and electrical lines. Jay preferred the land remain unimproved.

At the end of the driveway was a waist-high chain-link gate. Beyond that, a new solar-powered double-wide trailer was bolted to a concrete pad and fringed with a wooden skirt freshly painted aquamarine. A weathered barn stood behind the trailer and adjacent to a whitewashed horse corral, where a rusting horse trailer was set in a pasture gone to seed. Before Jay had a chance to cut his engine, Aubrey Glenn limped toward the front gate dressed in a purple polo tucked into black jeans. Jay pulled down the bill of his baseball cap, grabbed his moleskin notebook and Olympus E-1 from the passenger seat, and stepped out of the cab.

"I was wondering when one of you boys would turn up," Aubrey said as he rolled the gate open and flashed a cosmetic grin. They shook hands and introduced themselves, and Aubrey led Jay around the trailer toward the barn. On the way, Jay scanned the trees for claw marks and sniffed around for urine and feces. "You're starting to remind me of one of our cats, game warden."

Cats. Plural. Between Bell's headaches and CT scan and his regular patrol duties, Jay hadn't had time to dig into the Glenns, and as they approached the barn, a powerful scent tumbled their way. It grew stronger with each step.

"Relax, Warden Tern. Have a good sniff. We have nothing to hide. We're proud of the work we do." Aubrey rolled the barn door partially open to reveal three full-grown African lions behind a ten-foot-high chain-link fence. One male and two females in a single horse stall. The male had a gorgeous golden mane. Aubrey pierced a sliver of gray meat with a spiked metal pole and extended it to the male. He sauntered to the fence, licked it off the spike, and snorted his appreciation. The two females came over next, and Aubrey repeated the performance.

"What kind of work do you folks do, Mr. Glenn?" Jay wanted a reboot. He'd stumbled into what he had expected to be a simple inspection egregiously unprepared.

"We ran a popular exotic animal sanctuary down in Riverside County for a number of years. We've downsized considerably but still have some holdovers from Cat Heaven."

"Catchy name," Jay said.

"Not sure if we'll keep it. New beginnings and whatnot."

Jay pulled out his notebook and scribbled down the details. "You must know that the department expects professionals who move animals like these across county lines to give us a courtesy call."

"Yeah, but that law includes a thirty-day grace period before we're required to alert you. And frankly, we've been a bit busy getting this place set up."

When the male lion circled back to the fence, Aubrey knelt and rubbed his own whiskers on the wire. The cat returned the favor, nuzzling Aubrey's cheek with his nose. Jay raised his camera and started shooting.

"I'm guessing you've never seen anything quite like this before."

"No, Mr. Glenn," Jay said. "We do not have any other exotic cat owners in Ventura County."

"Not just that. I mean a person who has become more comfortable around big cats than he is around other people." Aubrey sounded wistful, and Jay lowered his camera. "Most folks in our community hate having to explain to outsiders what it feels like to lose the fear. It's too much work, and no matter what we say, they still consider us stupid or crazy and gaze at us with a patronizing gleam in their eye. Kind of how you're looking at me right now."

"It isn't personal," Jay said. "I look at just about everyone this way."

"I suppose I deserved that one." Aubrey laughed, grabbed the barn door with both hands, and slid it all the way open, revealing a second, larger stall occupied by two adult tigers. One was enjoying an afternoon nap, its head resting on its front paws. The other licked its left paw and then brushed its nose and head, bathing itself like a house cat.

Their presence felt confrontational, and Jay's attention was fractured. He thought of Bell. Could she have been telling the truth? Was there actually a tiger on the loose somewhere in the area? He'd have a better idea about that if he hadn't been so derelict in his duties as a game warden.

Then there were the tigers themselves. Even penned up in what Jay considered unreasonable, if not, by the letter of the law, inhumane, conditions, they projected a regal aura.

Jay raised his camera and became entranced. With his eye glued to the viewfinder and his shutter firing, he had no idea Aubrey had slipped into the cage on his hands and knees until the man crawled into the frame. Reclining on the ground beside the grooming tiger, Aubrey threw his arm over its striped flank and nuzzled his pet.

Jay was shocked, but he kept shooting. The second tiger woke up, moseyed over, and nuzzled the back of Aubrey's head with its powerful skull. Aubrey stood and ran his right hand up and down the back of the larger beast. The tigers did not seem put off by Aubrey's presence. In fact, they seemed to enjoy it.

Jay's head was clogged with questions as Aubrey made his way out of the barn. "What's the matter, Warden Tern?" he asked. "Cat got your tongue?" Aubrey laughed as he fetched scraps of cheap meat from a disposable Styrofoam cooler and tossed them into the enclosure. Not enough for a meal. More like a tiger's version of a treat.

"Are they littermates?"

"Common question. Until you learn to see tigers for who and what they are, the assumption is they all look alike. But you know what I love best about tigers, besides the fact that they are the most affectionate cats on the planet?"

"I couldn't possibly guess, Mr. Glenn."

"When you focus on the details, their differences become obvious. They all have roughly one hundred stripes, but the patterns vary to such a degree that they're like fingerprints: unique and individualized."

Bell had shared that same factoid with Jay recently, and hearing it again now compounded his guilt.

Aubrey whistled as he led Jay toward a gathering of patio furniture set up around a firepit. "Anyhoo, with the big kitties to look after, I suppose you can see how easy it would be to lose track of a little lynx."

"You say that like it's a common mistake," Jay said, "but your lynx is not indigenous to our ecosystem, and in this county, we take that seriously."

"Understood. We do apologize for the inconvenience, Warden Tern." He gestured to one of the sun-bleached patio chairs. "Coffee should be done by now," he said. "I'll bring out our permits so we can set your mind at ease."

Aubrey trotted up his back steps and disappeared inside the house while Jay sat down to consider how thoroughly he'd been played. He'd been wowed by the big animals for a reason. Aubrey wanted to control the inspection, and he had…so far. Annoyed, Jay scanned the property and homed in on the broken-down horse trailer in the pasture. He closed the distance quickly and heard a muffled rumble coming from within. He grabbed the door's rusted handle, but it didn't give easily. He yanked it three times, each tug stronger than the last, until he managed to open it wide enough to step inside. The air was fouled by the filthy sawdust lining an enclosure not much bigger than a travel kennel that housed a one-hundred-fifty-pound spotted white cat that was trying to bash its way out.

"Hello, pretty girl!" The cat recoiled, and Jay turned to find Aubrey holding a French press filled with black coffee in one hand and a thick file in the other. "I see you've met Lenora. Poor dear is having trouble adjusting."

"Lenora the snow leopard." Jay's favorite feline. Rare and reclusive, snow leopards were molded by evolution to range for hundreds of miles in the harshest, rockiest terrain from Mongolia to Kazakhstan, Afghanistan to Bhutan, from Nepal, India, and Pakistan to Russia. And this one was stuck in a cage on the floor of a raggedy horse trailer in Alisaw Valley. Or was it *Cat Heaven*? Jay's temper surged as he hammered the trigger on his Olympus.

"Good eye, Tern," Aubrey said. "The small enclosure is temporary. We're working on a nice habitat for her. We have big plans for this facility. Big plans for Alisaw. This beauty of a town needs a zoo, don't you think? Now, what do you say we have that coffee? It's good. I promise."

Jay followed Aubrey out of the trailer and settled into one of the outdoor chairs around the firepit. His camera in his lap, he sipped his mug of admittedly good coffee and sifted through the Glenns' paperwork while Aubrey watched his every move. "I'd like to take the file with me, if you don't mind," Jay said. "I find it's best not to rush this process."

"Fine by me, but those are originals, and the boss is in charge of all Cat Heaven paperwork." Aubrey gestured to a silhouette in the kitchen window. "Let me run it by Eden. If it means getting Sierra back home soon, I think she'll share copies with you."

Aubrey carried the French press, still sloshing with grounds, up the back steps to his mobile home. Jay waited for Aubrey to shut the door behind him, then looped around the side of the house, stepped up onto the wraparound porch, and peeked through a high window. All he could see were cardboard boxes stacked floor to ceiling, but he could hear a tense discussion between Aubrey and a woman he assumed was Eden.

"This was supposed to be a formality," she said. "He'd look at the paperwork and walk the property, and we'd get Sierra back. That's what you said."

"That's what I was told, dear."

"God knows how much weight he's lost. From now on, I'll handle these people like I handle everything else around here."

Jay nosed around to the front of the house, where he discovered the Glenns had made a critical error: the front door was slightly ajar. As an officer of the law, Jay could not open someone's door or enter their property without their permission or a warrant. If he did, any evidence he found inside would be thrown out of court for being obtained in an illegal search. But because this door was already open and he'd found it through the normal course of his duties, he had every right to look inside. The front door opened into the living room. Jay peeked through the slender crack. Six cat eyes stared right back.

They belonged to three full-grown lynx. One was curled up on the floor, while another sat up straight on the sofa, and a third lounged in a leather recliner. The one on the couch was a Siberian lynx that weighed upward of seventy pounds. The others were Canada lynx. Compared to the Siberian lynx, the dark spots of the Canada lynx were faint on their thick gray-and-white coats. They were smaller, too, weighing in at about twenty pounds each. Keeping exotic cats in a family home was a violation, and Jay had never seen anything like this. He'd met several exotic animal afficionados over the years, but none invited their beasts to lounge on the sofa like lap dogs. Jay raised his camera but only managed to take two pictures before Eden opened the front door, barefoot and oozing aggression.

"This is indecent!" she hollered as Aubrey hovered behind her. Her toenails were polished baby pink. She was dressed in torn blue jeans and a white tee. Her dark, wavy hair tumbled to her shoulders and was bleached at the tips. She was pretty and slightly overweight, and she used her extra to back Jay up a few steps. "You can't peep inside a private residence without permission!"

But the law was on Jay's side, and once he explained that the pictures he'd already taken would net him a warrant and enable him to perform a deeper and more invasive search of their home, she opened the door a bit wider and stepped aside.

"Fine," Eden said. "You have three minutes."

When his time was up, Aubrey and Eden joined him on the porch and shut the front door behind them. "Fun and games aside, we will do the right thing," Aubrey said. "We haven't had time to build the proper enclosures for everyone yet, but it's on the top of my list. That I can tell you."

"It had better be," Eden said. She wore three silver chains around her neck. One dangled a religious figure Jay recognized as Saint Blaise, the patron saint of wild animals. Before he was made a bishop in Armenia seventeen hundred years ago, Blaise of Sebaste was a physician with a reputation for miraculous healings of people and wild beasts alike. Eden also wore a strand of pearl-shaped stones on her scarred left wrist that gleamed with the colors of sunrise. Jay knew the stone. It was tiger's eye.

14

JAY'S FIRST SUPERVISOR IN THE DEPARTMENT HAD TAUGHT HIM never to trust his own memory. Memories were questionable at best, he'd said, no matter who they belonged to or how fresh they were. The camera, on the other hand, told the truth, and evidence was everywhere, attached to any complex case with tiny tendrils often hidden in plain sight.

While his images from the Glenn property downloaded, Jay sat at his six-dollar sheet-metal desk—a cast-off from a 1950s military base—opened his notebook, and read their names aloud. "Aubrey and Eden Glenn." He searched California and federal law enforcement databases for warrants and convictions. According to the system, the couple was clean. A web search for "Cat Heaven Temecula" revealed an expired site and a smattering of local news stories. The reporters had called it "a refuge," without explaining how the Glenns came to own big cats.

Once his photos were ready, Jay zoomed in on each frame, checking for signs of malnourishment. The lions and tigers looked reasonably healthy and well fed, and their pens were bordered by a ten-foot-high chain-link fence. The two-foot-wide gap between the top of that fence and the roof of the barn was a violation, and big cat enclosures were supposed to be wrapped with a second taller fence to prevent escape.

The snow leopard didn't look good at all. Her coat was patchy, which didn't surprise Jay. She was meant to roam at high altitudes in subfreezing temperatures. But was it only climactic stress? Jay had his doubts. Irritated, he checked his watch and sipped his green tea. In less than two hours, he was due at the bus stop to collect Bell.

The generous analysis was that the Glenns loved big cats too much and failed to see how dysfunctional their situation had become—for them, the cats, and the community. The less forgiving analysis was that a couple who claimed they were saving cats were jamming them into small enclosures or letting them run free in their living room. Jay had made sure to aim his weapon of choice into every cranny of that room.

In one photograph, the two Canada lynx were curled up on a couch beneath a framed poster of a vintage advertisement. Jay zoomed in. Bold-faced Thai script arced above a tiger sprinting in full stride. In Jay's own medicine cabinet, an updated version of that same tiger could be seen striding across the label on a half-spent jar of Tiger Balm.

He flashed to images of the Siberian lynx in Aubrey's easy chair. Behind it, a box tower leaned precariously into the kitchen. In one shot, Jay had managed to catch the side of the fridge, which was covered in cat magnets. There were housecats, jaguars, leopards, cheetahs, lions, and one solitary tiger with its tail in the air.

Eden had turned out to be as much of a showman as her husband. She'd wiggled between the two cats on the couch and rubbed the underside of the closest one's neck until it was pudding. Jay could still hear that purr as he marveled at those images. Jay had also captured the moment when Eden pried open its mouth, revealing two-inch canines that could slice a finger off in one chomp, and the next, when it hissed and bared its twenty-eight teeth at the lens.

Jay thumbed through the permits. Each had an animal's name, description, species, weight, and length from nose to tail, and he did his best to match them with the cats in his photographs. He counted eleven cats on the property, but the Glenns held permits for sixteen felines. Miriam had Sierra, which left two tigers, a cheetah, and a lion unaccounted for.

Were they all on the loose? Unlikely. The exotic animal trade was fluid. In most states, big cats could be legally sold and traded at any time, and when they were, sellers were not required to inform the government. That was what made tracking privately owned exotics so difficult. Conscientious owners kept the state wildlife department informed. Many, however, were like the Glenns—if they weren't outright hostile to regulation, they didn't feel the need to report their every move. When there was a grace period on the books, they took all the time afforded to them under the law and never did anything one minute sooner than they had to. Before he'd left their property that morning, Jay had asked the Glenns if there were other cats missing. Both reassured him only Sierra had run off.

He was holding the last permit in the file when an alarm sounded on his cell phone. Time to meet the school bus. He set the paperwork down, grabbed his keys, and pushed back from his desk. As he stood, he noticed that the permit was for a four-year-old male tiger named Bolt. He'd already matched the tigers he'd seen with other permits, which meant this one was unaccounted for. Jay felt a surge of adrenaline as he recalled what Aubrey had told him. *A tiger's markings are its fingerprints.* He slid open the bottom drawer of his filing cabinet and plucked one of Bell's illustrations from her evidence file. His eye went straight to the jagged stripe tattooed below the cat's left eye. He checked the permit. There was a space to note "distinguishing marks."

That field had been left blank.

15

FEBRUARY 4, 2005

SINCE BELL WAS DOING HER FATHER'S JOB FOR HIM, SHE FELT SHE deserved access to his maps. She used her pocketknife to pick the lock on his forbidden file cabinet, quickly found the maps she was looking for, and spread them out on the floor in front of the fireplace. Some were professionally printed by the US Geological Survey. Others were copies of the master he'd sketched himself. That was the one Bell was most interested in. USGS maps used generic greens, browns, and blues for managed or protected lands and waterways and left everything else colorless. The map her father had drawn wasn't a street map—only the major roads were represented—but it told the story of Alisaw Valley as she knew it. He'd traced their private trail and plotted their cabin. Her school had a plot point. So did her bus stop. His map was shaded in a range of colors, and the five canyons in the Alisaw watershed were rendered in more detail.

She sat on her hands and knees and inspected that map from edge to edge. There were two canyons in the Alisaw Hills, both named for ranchers among the original homesteaders. Suarez Canyon, named for a grazing magnate from Mexico, was a shallow cut in the gently sloped hills split by Suarez Creek. McClurg Canyon was a few miles west of Suarez Canyon and had a similar profile. Suarez Creek absorbed the smaller McClurg Wash on its journey west along the southern edge of the valley.

The Santa Susanas were younger than the Alisaw Hills and threaded with three seasonal streams that flowed one to two months a year. Happy Camp Canyon was the closest to the Tern cabin, and Camp Creek was steep enough in places to form ribbonlike falls that gave way to gentle, foaming cascades that dumped into the occasional swimming hole, though there was rarely enough water for any of that. Colibri Canyon was a box canyon on the opposite end of the range with a four-mile, out-and-back trail that could get packed on weekends, especially during wet winters, when runoff sheeted down the cliff to create Alisaw's only reliable seasonal waterfall. Seldom-explored Sheep's Canyon, its southern access walled off by subdivisions, had no trails at all. Its stream had eroded into a deep crack due to generations of grazing, and it only saw running water in rare years.

Below the housing blocks, Sheep's Creek fed Camp Creek, which ran through culverts and underpasses, alongside horse corrals and pastureland, skirting housing developments and shopping centers before absorbing Colibri Wash and colliding with Suarez Creek immediately east of the Highway 23 culvert. The water that flowed out the other side, west of the highway, was the Alisaw River.

Those predominantly dry corridors weren't just out of mind for most locals. They were mostly out of sight, though they could be glimpsed here and there from the edge of a road, the back of a parking lot, or over barriers built to keep livestock safe, housing developments organized, and wayward golfers rerouted to the clubhouse. Even Bell, who was raised to be dazzled by the natural world, rarely thought of the dry creeks she passed every day. She scoured the playground for evidence of wild things—feathers, prints, scat—but seldom bothered to consider how animals moved undetected throughout the valley.

Bell's fingertips tingled as she traced the Alisaw River from the edge of the valley back to Camp Creek and on to its origins in the mountains above the cabin. She noticed that after it rippled through Happy Camp Canyon, the creek banked west and ran below Mystic Heights, whose lawns and rain gutters drained into it via a rocky irrigation ditch. For the first time, Bell realized that ditch was an unmapped tributary to Camp Creek, which meant at that very moment, she was a quarter mile from the same network of hidden pathways available to a tiger.

She folded and sealed one of the three copies of Jay's hand-drawn map in a plastic bag, tucked it into her back pocket, and slid the file back into place. She locked the filing cabinet with her knife, zipped her house keys into the side pocket of her go bag, and hiked down the driveway dressed in her denim overalls, a long-sleeve thermal crewneck, an army-green rain shell, and a grey fleece beanie stuffed with her unruly hive.

Bell's first steps were nervous. After all, the tiger had flashed its fangs at her, or at least she'd thought so. She paused and asked herself if she'd swim at a beach where someone had just spotted a great white shark. The answer was a loud no, so why was this any different? If anything, a tiger in Alisaw Valley would be more dangerous. It was an apex predator in an unfamiliar land, and it was probably starving, which made Bell potential prey. She was about to turn back to the cabin when she spotted a chirping quail couple picking through the underbrush. She followed them, knowing their inherent skittishness would alert her to any danger. After a few minutes she heard a faint trickle, pushed through a thicket of sage, and found a shallow depression with a squiggle of water flowing southwest.

Bell followed the gentle flow along fences made of wrought iron and walls built from flagstone, brick, and rock. She liked the wrought-iron fences best because they offered a view of backyard pools, manicured lawns, hot tubs, fire pits, and barbeques. Fancy Mystic Heights had erupted from sandy soil and imposed its will on the land, yet it felt so empty because everyone was inside playing video games, watching television, and avoiding the rain. Or almost everyone. There was one girl alone in her backyard behind the biggest house of them all. She was tall and blond, spinning with a hula hoop in one hand, her chin tilted back as if sipping the mist. She wasn't in a raincoat. She wanted to get wet. Bell stood on a boulder and watched her twirl counterclockwise. After her second revolution, Bell realized it was Ashley. Surprised, Ashley stopped and offered a curious wave. Bell hesitated before waving back.

"Ashley! Come inside right now!" Ashley's frantic mother called out a back door. "I'm not going to ask again!" It was raining a bit harder now. Ashley rolled her eyes and made two more revolutions—chin tipped up and mouth wide open to catch raindrops.

Ashley's mom wore yoga pants and rage. Her shoulder-length hair, styled with auburn and golden highlights, bounced as she stormed out through oversize French doors toward her daughter. The fingers she used to snatch a fistful of Ashley's shiny blond locks were long and elegant, and her nails were lacquered a deep burgundy. "This morning! You got your hair done this morning, Ashley! Do you have any idea how much that cost?" Ashley shrieked and fought her way toward the fence where Bell stood, frozen in shock. But Ashley's mother didn't seem to care who saw her drag her daughter back inside the house by her perfect hair.

Bell turned and sprinted downstream, splashing down the middle of the ditch. Running made it impossible for her to think. If she were to dwell on the strange look in that woman's eyes, the anguish on Ashley's face, and her own conflicted feelings about it all, she might roll an ankle or stumble and fall on her face. Or worse, feel bad for her tormentor. It felt natural to block it out. Ignoring difficult or inexplicable things was a default Tern setting.

Bell ran the cut past the garish stone gates Jay loathed until it fed into Camp Creek, which she followed as it skirted three large horse ranches, including Ben's. When she reached a culvert built from ridged galvanized steel that tunneled beneath a two-lane country road, she did not pause to contemplate the darkness or the vicious beast that might be lurking inside. She dashed right through.

The rain was coming down hard by then, and Bell stopped under the far edge of the culvert to zip her shell, catch her breath, and watch it dump. She couldn't quite place why she so badly needed to see the tiger again. Was it the desire to be proven right? That did feel good, especially when you felt out of step so much of the time, but it went deeper than that. The lost beast was like something out of one of her visions. It was proof that animal magic existed outside her overactive mind. Even in the mean, smothering suburbs—even if nobody could see it but her. And if the tiger *was* real, it needed help.

When she neared the valley floor, Camp Creek arced around a mature oak that had shed its leaves for winter and stood like a lighthouse overlooking a golden-brown grassy sea. It grew next to a modest stack of boulders that Bell used as a ladder to scramble onto a thick limb about ten feet off the ground. She climbed a bit higher, then edged out onto a longer, thicker branch. She raised her field glasses and scanned the northwestern end of the valley, peering down upon Alisaw's empty streets.

There were no pedestrians at all, which was standard. Alisaw was built for cars. Shops and restaurants were couched in large developments linked by wide avenues with high speed limits set up on berms above those streambeds everyone ignored. Bell wondered how long it would have to rain until they overflowed. Until water swallowed everything up—the big-box stores, downtown thoroughfares and country roads, her school, Mystic Heights, and the highway, even the flagpole. She wondered what it would be like to tool around Alisaw by canoe.

There were also very few cars out. Nearly every living, breathing thing had hunkered down to wait out the overhyped El Niño. She hadn't seen or heard a single hawk or jay. No squirrels, snakes, or lizards either. Bunnies had headed for their holes to hide out. Foxes too. Even the quail she followed must have sought shelter by now. In fact, the town and the hills looked so empty, it was the perfect time for a fugitive tiger to roam. She'd been reading up on tigers and had learned they were plenty comfortable in wet weather and preferred to hunt in broad daylight. That surprised her because she'd assumed they were nocturnal. They averaged one kill every eight days and ate up to forty pounds of meat at a time. Bell weighed less than sixty.

When she turned to scan the nearby ridgeline, a flash of orange almost shocked her out of the tree. There was someone else out in the downpour after all, but it was not her tiger. It was another civilized primate dressed in an orange poncho. He was carrying a ladder on his shoulders toward a six-sided, metallic frame, the one she remembered seeing from Hawk's Nest Overlook. He'd made a lot of progress, and Bell watched him use a cordless drill to add to the structure for a few minutes before she climbed down and returned to Camp Creek.

The banks grew thick with ceanothus, artemisia, and white sage on the valley floor. Behind shopping centers, the underbrush was scattered with consumer castoffs—spent aluminum cans, plastic water bottles, packaging, and shopping bags. Most of those bags were from America's favorite superstore. Bell followed them to a tiger-sized hole in the chaparral and crawled through it.

She emerged onto the strip of asphalt that led to Target's loading bays. Rain clouds had darkened the sky. Overhead lights reflected off the slick tarmac and the hood of a familiar forest-green F250 with a CDFW decal on the door. Next to the truck, Bell saw her father, in uniform and on all fours, squirming between two red dumpsters.

"What could you possibly be looking for, game warden?" Jay flinched at the unexpected sound of his daughter's voice and banged his forehead against one of the dumpsters. Bell cringed. "Sorry, Dad."

"It's fine," he said, wincing. He checked for blood and found none. "I'm fine." Bell squatted beside him and peered between the dumpsters into the shadowy brush. Jay noticed her cheeks were flushed and her boots were caked in mud. "You ran here, but not on the street." Jay unfolded a copy of the same map she had in her back pocket. With his fingertip, he followed Camp Creek back into the hills, where it came within a quail's stroll of their humble cabin. "You're not looking for—"

"Has there been another sighting? Is that why you're finally here?"

"You know I can't discuss casework with you." He folded up his map.

"So it is a case," she said. "An actual case. You're here, like, officially."

Jay studied Bell as he would any witness. If she had made the whole thing up, would she really run for miles in the rain to make a point? He couldn't rule it out. It wasn't any more unreasonable of a possibility than a tiger roaming undetected in Alisaw Valley for three weeks. Of course, according to Dr. Ambrose, Bell might be convinced that what she saw was real even if it were pure fantasy or an embellished version of reality. Meaning it was more reasonable that Bell had seen the lynx between those dumpsters, and whatever may or may not be growing inside her brain had transformed it into a tiger.

Why, then, was he sitting between two stinking dumpsters instead of working the harbor? Because he believed her, despite all available evidence? Because the Glenns smelled dirty, and their permits allowed for the possibility that Bell was telling the truth? Or was it the most reasonable possibility of all: because he could not bring himself to accept that his daughter's beautiful brain wasn't functioning properly and she might be seriously ill?

"You must be hungry," he said finally. "I skipped lunch too. What say we grab a pizza from Delmonico's, and you tell me everything you remember about that tiger of yours?"

"Again," she said. "I'll tell you everything I remember. Again."

Part II

16

FEBRUARY 4, 2005

WHILE MOST RESIDENTS OF ALISAW VALLEY WERE FAST ASLEEP, BOLT woke from another bad dream. The sky was black. The rain hammered down, and the tiger was all alone. She sat up, alert. Every raindrop felt like a threat, each second she remained in the same place, a risk. Bolt felt compelled to move.

She roamed the rolling pasturelands and sniffed the soil, shrubs, and drip line of a valley oak, still hoping to locate Sierra's scent, but the rain had rinsed away all traces. Bolt rubbed her haunches against the crackling bark, leaving behind a lock of fur. Exactly the type of clue a game warden sought when tracking a suspicious animal, but enough water ran down the trunk to carry it off to a mud puddle, though one or two strands may have hitched a ride on the wind, spinning like liberated tendrils from a wish flower.

Led by her awakening instincts, propelled by fear and loneliness, Bolt followed McClurg Wash to Suarez Creek and the valley floor. Late-night traffic was always sparse in Alisaw Valley, and during a storm, it was nonexistent. Bolt dashed across a dark road and into an empty public park, where she stepped through a gap in the chain-link fence and traipsed across the Little League baseball diamond. Despite the weather, the sprinklers were on full blast. Her paws sunk into the manicured infield and the top of the pitcher's mound, but water was her magic eraser. The rain and the sprinklers made her tracks disappear as she pranced into the outfield.

She hopped the short back fence where decomposing baseballs went to seed, skirted the outdoor climbing wall, and dropped into the new skate park's smooth bowl. When the skate terrain was unveiled three years earlier, businesses and homeowners celebrated. No longer would their handrails, driveways, steps, and curbs be assaulted by punk acrobats in elbow- and kneepads. Kids of all ages packed the park at any given hour of almost every day. Late at night, when it was supposed to be closed, teenagers often took turns perfecting tricks until sheriff's deputies inevitably showed up and scattered them. That rainy night, however, it was deserted.

Bolt sprinted through the snake run, banked right on the quarter pipe, and dashed up the stair sets to the ledge, where she heard a loud metallic clang, and then another. Spooked, she swiveled and surveyed the empty lawns and colored-concrete pathways illuminated by solar lamps. The persistent clanging came from a distant playground. Two swings had been caught in a crosswind that rattled their chains against the pipe-metal frame. The stiff breeze also carried an animal scent, which triggered a twist of hunger in Bolt's gut.

Tucked into the shadows, she waited as the scent grew stronger. Soon, she could hear the shuffle of feet and caught the passing silhouette of a tall, full-figured, middle-aged man with an umbrella walking his half-blind golden retriever through the park. Until that moment, Bolt had never considered humans or canines to be food. People were always a food source, never the actual meal. But she was used to being fed twice daily and hadn't eaten in weeks. Her belly rumbled. Saliva dripped from her swollen tongue, which hung from her open jaw. She moved in silence, edging ever closer as she debated which would make the easier kill and tastier treat, the dog or its owner.

Thirty feet, then twenty, then fifteen. She followed the pair into a cluster of cookie-cutter homes near the park. She knew she could take either of them without much trouble, but she also sensed the reward would not be worth the risk. Bolt was hungry, not starving. Plus, she was still getting used to freedom and learning her territory. She chose to watch from a distance as the dog led its owner up their well-lit front steps and into the safety of their warm living room. Yet she had learned something valuable: it was possible to stalk humans undetected—even some dogs wouldn't notice—and it would be easy to take them if she had to.

Slipping from shadow to shadow, Bolt's haphazard route took her through one housing development after another, including one still under construction. She galloped past a sleeping excavator, hurdled a six-foot construction fence, and found the empty parking lots and walkways of shopping centers that served gourmet cheese, corporate caffeine, burgers and nutritionists, video games, firearms and personal injury attorneys, hair replacement and electrolysis.

She reached the ivy-covered fence of the Alisaw Valley Country Club and plunged into the sagebrush that skirted the back nine. She sniffed, detected the mineral musk of water rolling over stones, found the creek, and followed it to a large culvert that plunged beneath the highway. Unsure, she stepped through it gingerly. The thunder of passing traffic filled her with dread, but once she'd reached the other side, she continued west, moving slowly through ankle-deep water. She left the cover of the creek for a gathering of young trees, lapped pools of rainwater from a clean black tarp, and watched the fog roll in until the sky brightened enough to frighten her.

She leaped into the creek and turned back in a rush. She streaked beneath the highway and reached the place where the shallow river branched into tributaries. Desperate to outpace the dawn, she selected the middle route and followed it northeast into the Santa Susana foothills, where the corridor became a boulder-strewn crack studded with sycamore trees. Bolt bounded up a tumble of boulders, where pioneering threads of water began an ambitious migration to the sea.

At daybreak, she reached the top of the canyon, where she found a large, empty cave blessed with expansive views of Alisaw Valley. She crawled inside, exhausted. With one full revolution and another half turn, Bolt curled up into a tight ball and slipped into yet another nightmare. Her dreams weren't of capture. They were of the life she was attempting to outrun.

17

FEBRUARY 26, 2000–NOVEMBER 11, 2000

TIGER CUBS ARE BORN BLIND, SO BOLT NEVER SAW THE TONGS THAT yanked her from the hay bed where her hyperventilating mother lay exhausted and in pain. A pair of gloved hands deposited her in a cardboard box lined with newspaper and old bedsheets that sat beside a heating vent. The box had been filled with empty baby bottles when it arrived the day before addressed to a middle-aged former big-rig trucker named Cooper Stills. Now, it was home to two fledgling cubs who squawked like baby birds, desperate for their mother's milk. In the wild, tiger cubs stayed with their mothers for the first two and a half years of their lives, but Bolt never spent a single night with hers, and her mournful screeches echoed through the sparsely furnished two-bedroom house on a defunct horse farm on the outskirts of Indianapolis.

Cooper's Tigarium had been in business for nearly three years. He'd launched it after his wife left him with a note and a drained savings account. Dazed and depressed, he'd stumbled onto a peculiar pop-up at a mall in Minnesota, where he knelt among other paying customers hoping to pet a tiger cub for the first time. He didn't have to wait long. One charismatic rascal strutted straight up to him and nuzzled his fist before lying down on its back, begging for belly rubs. Others followed, and soon, every cub on the mat wanted to nuzzle his meaty fists.

Cooper didn't notice the tears streaming down his cheeks until he was in the parking lot, walking toward his rig. He felt alive with gratitude for the first time in over a decade. Within days, he'd sold his trucking business to buy three tiger cubs of his own. Within a year, he had a half dozen adults and a plan to produce three litters each year. Breeding enabled him to turn a nice profit. Tigers under three months old brought in tens of thousands of dollars at roadside petting junkets before aging out. He kept the cats he wanted to breed and sold the others for up to four thousand bucks each.

When Bolt was born, Cooper thought she wouldn't make it through the night. Her sister had been stillborn, and losing two cubs in a litter was not unheard of, but he loved her markings and fell for her sparkling eyes. Tigers had saved him when he was at rock bottom, and he vowed to save this runt. He bottle-fed her at the bottom of every hour and cuddled her at night, and she thrived. Once she found her feet, Bolt followed Cooper everywhere. She rode with him in the cabs of his pickup and box truck and walked his pastures alongside him, as if she were a farm dog. She remained a runt up through her first five months. That allowed her to stay in the petting rotation a bit longer, and she was good at her job. She was more curious about humans than the others. She knew how to elicit the oohs and aahs.

Everything changed in an afternoon, at the Town Centre in Kenwood, Ohio. Cooper had six cubs with him, and the line to see them stretched into the parking lot. He plopped Bolt and the others down on the rubber mats he'd set up. Twenty-four people at a time—six on each side of the mat—lay on their bellies and extended their hands. Cooper instructed his guests that his cats were not to be grabbed, tugged, kissed, or picked up under any circumstances, and Bolt worked the crowd, as usual. She rubbed up against the tips of outstretched fingers or playfully batted them. There was never any sign she might snap.

But she did. Toward the end of the fourth session of the day, Bolt ambled over to an attractive college-aged couple. The young man rubbed noses with her. It was an overstep, but Cooper let it go. The young woman cooed and clucked her tongue. Bolt ignored her and turned away. In response, her boyfriend tugged Bolt's tail, hard. Bolt lunged and swiped. The man ducked, and his girlfriend bore the brunt of Bolt's strike. Bolt's claws shredded her cheek. The force of her paw blackened and bloodied the young lady's eye.

Cooper grabbed Bolt by the scruff and stuffed her in a kennel while the girl shrieked and bled and her boyfriend hyperventilated accusations. The rest of the crowd bailed for the exits or demanded refunds. The line outside dissolved. Parents corralled terrified children. Paramedics arrived, and as they tended to the young woman, her boyfriend threatened to ruin Cooper.

After the couple left for the hospital, Cooper followed a deputy to the sheriff's station. He knew the liability waivers his guests signed weren't ironclad. Lawyers would poke holes, and his insurance was patchwork. Even if his business survived, the deputies assured him Bolt would be euthanized. Cooper wasn't surprised; he knew how these things went. Be it pit bull or tiger, when an animal scarred a person for life, certain dominoes tended to fall.

The fallout was swift. US Department of Agriculture inspectors showed up the next day. Everything Cooper owned was accounted for, and all his cats were inspected against the permits he held. The claws of every cub were examined too—the inspectors wanted to confirm the proper cub was in custody. Cooper had anticipated every bit of it. Which was why he'd swapped Bolt out for a chunky three-month-old female named Dervish before he'd left the mall. Dervish was almost as big as Bolt and tended to turn and snap when grabbed from behind. Cooper hid Bolt and swabbed Dervish's claws with the rag he'd used to wipe up the girl's blood.

Before the week was over, liquidation had begun. That was how quickly it all unraveled. Cooper needed to raise money for a lawyer, which meant he had to scale back his business, maybe even retire altogether with just a few cats for companionship. He desperately wanted to keep Bolt, but he knew the safest thing would be to find her a new home far away from him.

The Craigslist ad he placed through a pseudonym found Eden Glenn the day it posted. The two met for coffee, and as soon as he saw Eden, with her thick, shoulder-length hair and no-nonsense attitude, he felt reassured. "When I read your ad," Eden said, "I got this strange feeling that my life was about to change."

She explained that she was newly single and living in Temecula with two Siberian lynx and that she loved all exotic cats, especially tigers, but had never felt confident enough to handle them. Cooper had planned to keep his motives a secret. She didn't need to know that everything he'd built was melting away. He was there for one reason: to save Bolt. But after chatting for ten minutes, he knew he couldn't lie to her.

"Look, I don't mean to discourage you, but you should know something…"

"I already know about the accident in Ohio."

Cooper couldn't believe it. She knew who he was. He felt completely exposed.

"It's all over the chatrooms, for gosh sakes."

"Well, what you don't know is that I switched—"

"Shhh!" Eden checked for eavesdroppers and lowered her voice. "I suspected as much. The timing was curious." She reached out and took his hand. "You did good, Cooper. You did right. You did what you had to do to save a loved one's life."

"She's the best damn animal I ever knew."

"Cats are better people," she said.

"More interesting."

"More loving, and a hell of a lot smarter."

"Ain't that the truth." Right then, he decided to give Bolt to Eden as a gift. He didn't want her money, and all the paperwork and permit applications she would need were already in his briefcase. She accepted but asked him to ride back to California with them.

"I don't feel comfortable driving back with her on my own," she said.

They fell into each other's arms on the first night of their trip in a motel outside Kansas City while Bolt slept on the bathroom floor. They stopped in Las Vegas two nights later to catch a Siegfried and Roy show and hit a drive-through wedding chapel, where a trained ocelot on a leash acted as their ring bearer. They were married three minutes before midnight, and he took her name. She'd been calling him Cooper since they'd met, but that was just a nickname that had stuck. When he signed the marriage license, she learned his real name was Aubrey.

Not long after they arrived in California, Bolt's late growth spurt began. Within three months, she'd blossomed into a large female, a beast capable of tremendous damage. Aubrey was afraid of what might happen if that switch he saw in Kenwood flipped again. He and Eden spent entire nights debating what to do with her. Then, one day, after more than eight months of constant companionship and being treated like a member of the family, Aubrey led Bolt from the house. He'd just finished retrofitting an old barn to create kennels where horse stalls used to be. Bolt glanced up at him, confused, but when Aubrey clucked his tongue, she dutifully followed him into the cage. He had tears in his eyes as he locked her inside.

Months became years. Cat Heaven took off. The kennels multiplied. Animals came and went. Stripe patterns, scents, roars, and chuffs bled together, but Bolt showed no interest in bonding with anyone, human or feline, for years.

18

JANUARY 12–FEBRUARY 4, 2005

IT WAS SIERRA WHO FINALLY GOT TO HER. THE LYNX HAD THE RUN of the property, and for weeks, he'd been visiting the tiger cage to watch the inmates through the fence. Bolt shared her cage with two other full-grown tigers. Cyborg was a male and fancied himself the alpha, and though Bolt was smarter than him and every bit his size, she let him have the title. Ever since winning the allegiance of Chai, the other female, he had mostly left her alone. Bored and lonely, Bolt started looking forward to Sierra's daily visits. He'd usually turn up after lunch and stay for an hour or two.

They fell into something of a routine. Sierra would stare up at Bolt through thick-gauge chain link, and Bolt would respond with a chuff—a powerful exhalation that was a gesture of pleasure or joy. Then, Bolt would saunter to the fence until their noses touched. Their breath would commingle. The fur on Sierra's head would stand on end, betraying at least some trepidation, yet it was Bolt who always yielded first. She would step back and lower her nose to the earth, back straight and hind legs coiled, poised to pounce or play. Sierra would respond by strutting along the fence with his nose and tail in the air. Amused, Bolt would mirror the lynx and stroll from one end of the enclosure to the other, which was only about twelve feet wide. At either end, they would stop and stare into one another's eyes for minutes on end.

Then, one day, it was all abruptly interrupted by the hasty pack and dash to Alisaw. Sierra was supposed to be loaded into a kennel and then a van, but on the morning of the move, he burrowed into the sheetrock in the half bath to hide out. While Eden searched for Sierra, Aubrey loaded the lions and the other two tigers, Chai and Cyborg, into the largest of the two rented horse trailers. Chai and the lions boarded without incident. Cyborg seemed irritable at the prospects of upheaval, so Aubrey darted him and, with the help of six volunteers, muscled the unconscious tiger onto a pallet. He used a forklift to load Cyborg into the trailer, and when he was done, Aubrey was sweaty, spent, and on edge.

Eden had finished loading all the lynx except Sierra, who was still missing. Aubrey found him curled up in the wall behind the toilet, leashed him, and dragged him to a kennel, but Sierra refused to get inside. He hissed, bucked, and pushed the kennel away with his front paws. Eden attempted to calm him. Sierra bared his claws and teeth and lunged at her. She used both hands to shove his head down and away with every bit of force she could muster. Sierra used the momentum to tear out through the open front door. He ran around the house toward Bolt's enclosure, where he was cornered by Aubrey, who brandished the same pole dart gun he'd used to tranquilize Cyborg.

Sierra stood on his hind paws and pushed at the gate tucked beneath the barn's eaves, hoping his friend might help him slip inside. Bolt approached the fence as Aubrey backed Sierra into the corner with an epoxy shield. She swatted at the fence. Aubrey didn't seem to notice, so she backed up and charged, smashing into the chain link with all her weight. The posts buckled but held, and Aubrey tumbled to the hard earth. Bolt backed up, her eyes blazing with anger, and charged again.

The posts snapped at the base when she made contact, and the fence toppled over, pinning Aubrey. Bolt wheeled around and found him crawling out from under the fence on his belly and lunging for his pole dart gun, but it was out of reach. Bolt's mane flared, and she let loose a low growl as she stepped toward him.

"Eden!" Aubrey's voice cracked. "The shotgun!"

Eden came running. Slugs fell at her feet as she loaded her weapon on the move. Their volunteers watched from a distance as she stepped in front of her husband and cocked the shotgun. That was enough to halt Bolt's approach. When she growled again, Eden spread her stance and raised her weapon.

"Hush now, baby," she said. "You know momma loves you. Don't make me hurt you."

It never came to that. Sierra sashayed between Eden and Bolt. He wrapped around Eden's right leg then circled back to the tiger and nuzzled her, nose to nose, until she calmed right down.

"I told you about that one," Aubrey said, breathing heavy. "She's turned on me for good. She's dangerous!"

"She's family, Aubrey. We'll work through it at the new place. You'll build her a nice, big habitat, and the two of you will get back to how things used to be."

Aubrey pushed up to standing, dusted himself off, and glared at Bolt. Bolt peeled back her upper lip, flashed her canines, and moaned.

"Oh, knock it off, you!" Eden said. "Go on, Aubrey. Get cleaned up. I'll sort these two out. They'll be fine so long as they ride together."

And it was true. Docile as house cats, they allowed Eden to leash and walk them to the smaller of the two horse trailers. Of course, cats are shrewd by nature, honed by evolution to find angles to attack or flee. That suspicious independent streak, that apex predator point of view, can be found in all feline brains, no matter how well domesticated, even when perfumed, fluffed up, and marbled in belly fat or locked away in a barn stall long enough for their wild instincts to go dormant. However, they tend to be most daring when the risk–

reward ratio is high. Bolt had lived in Cat Heaven long enough to know it was surrounded by houses. There was no use running from there. It would be impossible to get lost.

The sixteen-foot horse trailer had been subdivided into sections for the lions and the other two tigers. Sierra and Bolt were left unrestrained in the nine-foot trailer. Aubrey towed both with his navy-blue Ford F250 while two Canada lynx roamed free in the cab of his truck. Eden led the way in her Dodge van, carrying a free-range Siberian lynx and a snow leopard stuffed in a kennel meant for a large dog. The drivers who swerved around them on their three-hour journey were oblivious to the type of cargo this quirky convoy was hauling.

The trip was going smoothly until Aubrey took a tight turn too quickly after exiting the highway and rolled over a troublesome curb blackened by the countless tires that hit it day after day. The jolt jostled the entire rig, throwing a bolt from a hinge on the door of the nine-foot trailer. It clattered to the asphalt.

Aubrey turned up the gravel driveway that led to their new ranch, and the rig rumbled slowly over uneven ground. Though the latch was locked, the compromised door offered flickering glimpses of a landscape thick with sagebrush, walnut and pepper trees, and no neighbors at all. Sierra stood on his hind legs and shoved one paw through the gap in the left side of the door. Bolt straddled her friend and gave the door a tap. It wobbled for a moment, and Sierra pulled his paw back a split second before the door settled flush against the frame with a thud. The rig rolled to a stop. Sierra placed one paw on the lightning bolt below the tiger's left eye. Bolt chuffed and nuzzled the top of her friend's head. Their trailer door looked closed from the outside.

The Glenns exited their vehicles and toured their new property, clueless that their equipment had failed. Inside the trailer, Bolt's ears swiveled like satellite dishes. She tuned in to the hammering of a downy woodpecker, the tittering of a white-breasted nuthatch, and the high-speed whir of a black-chinned hummingbird's wings. A distant howl from the closest neighbor's Australian shepherd hinted at the empty acreage around her.

Eden had rented a tractor to tow the trailers closer to the new big cat barn. Aubrey hitched it to the longer trailer first. As he towed the lions and other tigers away, the smaller trailer shuddered, and the door dangled from its one sound hinge. Offered a pie-slice view of a whole new Cat Heaven, Bolt could see Aubrey on the tractor receding into the distance followed by Eden, who marched behind the trailer armed with her shotgun.

Once the Glenns were out of sight, Sierra turned to Bolt and moaned. The tiger coiled her back legs and flew toward the door. It broke off like a toy. The exposed edge of the bad hinge gashed Bolt above her right ear, but she didn't even feel it for all the adrenaline coursing through her. She spun in the driveway, looking for Sierra, who had dashed toward a six-foot-high wooden fence topped with a strand of barbed wire behind a windbreak of pepper trees. Bolt caught up and hurdled the fence from a standstill. Sierra leaped into a tree, scurried along a branch that stretched over the property line, and dropped into the dry grass on the other side of the fence.

Sierra had enjoyed some autonomy as a house cat, but ever since she'd been caged at eight months old, Bolt had been a prisoner, so the smaller cat continued to lead the way, and by sunset, they'd found shelter in McClurg Canyon, a slender fissure in the Alisaw Hills thick with old live oaks. Night settled around them. Sierra tucked himself in between Bolt's left flank and front left leg. Flares of fur shot up from his ears and tickled Bolt's nostrils. Bolt pressed her itchy nose against the top of his head. Sierra purred like an idling race car while he slept, which inevitably lulled Bolt to sleep too.

For the next several days, they explored their ravine together. Each hike was a slow navigation, a mapping of their territory. There was a dry streambed running through the ravine with live oaks rooted on either side. Sierra had no trouble navigating the steep grade, sandy soil, and narrow footing. Bolt's paw pads were torn and bleeding from the long trek after their escape, and she had more weight to carry. She was content to watch from a distance as Sierra rampaged through the crispy underbrush, chasing rabbits and chipmunks.

Their dry streambed led to a larger one that snaked between subdivisions, across horse ranches, and eventually along the backsides of shopping centers. The wider sojourns were conducted under the cover of night. In the utter darkness of the bush, Bolt's eyes dilated to allow her to see. Her sensitive whiskers helped detect any shifts in the wind or movement nearby. When they traveled, Sierra walked upright and moved quickly. Bolt stalked slowly through the limp, drought-ravaged savanna, staying as low to the ground as possible. Night sounds felt sudden and foreboding—the suspicious squeak of a possum, the gravelly shuffle of a western fence lizard, the bark of a Labrador, the roar of an engine. Bolt responded to each by taking cover, pinning her white belly and banded tail flat to the sandy red soil. She'd wait like that for minutes, sometimes hours, and Sierra would wait alongside her. Once, they stayed out all day, and Bolt popped up, unnerved to find the back end of a parking lot, where she glimpsed a curious girl gazing at her from a school bus window.

Two weeks of living free changed them. Neither had eaten a thing, but tigers could last weeks between feeds in the wild, and the growing emptiness in Bolt's gut sharpened her senses, especially her hearing. When she absorbed the sounds that washed in from the distance—the squeal of a tire, the yelp of a dog, the layered caws of Alisaw Valley's crow mafia—she could estimate their distance and build a reliable auditory map of her territory. Her sense of smell became more penetrating and her sight more telescopic. She could zero in on lizards and sparrows from great distances. Her pads calloused; her stride became more confident. Bolt was rewilding.

Sierra experienced similar changes, but he was so much smaller that his hunger took a rapid and maddening toll. He wasn't good at stalking prey and was easily outmaneuvered. As his need to eat took over, he lit out into neighborhoods, where small dogs, cats, raccoons, and squirrels lived and roamed. Where trash cans were put out twice a week. Where there was food in abundance. Where there were humans. The first three nights Sierra prowled the subdivisions, he managed to make it back to the ravine before first light. Shivering and still starving, he curled up beside Bolt, who licked the top of his head and did her best to warm and soothe him. On the fourth night, Sierra did not return. Bolt waited in the ravine beneath a large, spreading oak tree all day, and when night fell, she set out on her own, hoping to find him.

The rain had washed away all traces of Sierra's scent, and Bolt found herself roaming the valley in ever expanding ovals, unsure of where to go and what to do. The pattern repeated itself. She searched for her friend with less to go on each passing night and then attempted to find a safe place to sleep before daybreak. Her hunger fed her anxiety. She had no home, no food, and no security at all, but she knew exactly where she was.

She was living free in a human world, and humans could not be trusted. Although some seemed warm and gentle, everything bad that had happened to her was their doing. They were dangerous. In many ways, they were her enemy, and though they certainly seemed to rule the world, they did not rule her anymore.

19

FEBRUARY 5, 2005

BEFORE DAWN, ASSISTANT MANAGER MARCO MACIAS UNLOCKED the gates to Treeland Farms—a wholesale nursery perched on the western edge of Alisaw Valley—as he had every workday morning for the past eleven years. Right away, he knew they'd had a visitor. Mulch and compost were strewn about. Rows of fruit trees in black fifteen-gallon buckets had been toppled. A dumpster was tipped onto its side. *This is not the work of vandals or the rain*, Marco thought. *This was animal.*

Raccoons, possums, and ground squirrels were the usual pests. They gnawed irrigation lines and ravaged seedlings, but this was a different scale. Marco flicked on his Maglite and searched for bear tracks as he walked up and down the line of fallen trees. He righted them, then searched around the dumpster. He did three laps of the steaming compost and mulch piles. Nothing.

The sun came up. Coworkers trickled in, and the first customers arrived while Marco circled the property hunting for clues. Fruit trees were not the only plants that had been ruffled. Nearly forty trees had been knocked over, including burlier specimens in twenty-four-inch boxes. He put his shoulder into them, set them upright, and inspected the pots, bark, and branches for fur and the soil around and between them for tracks, but he didn't find a thing. Although the mess was substantial, damage was minimal. Their dumpsters were padlocked for a reason, and he doubted whatever the bear found would inspire it to return. He resolved to search the rear of the property one last time, but when he reached the back gate, his radio chirped.

"Yo, if anyone's on the back forty, we need some mulch up front. Over."

"I got you," Marco said. He hooked his walkie-talkie onto his belt between his Leatherman and pruning shears and made for the open tool shed, where he grabbed a McLeod rake and a wheelbarrow. When he closed the shed, an impression in the soil caught his eye. Beneath the shallow eaves, where the dense clay soil had been protected from rain, was a cat track, the biggest one he'd ever seen. He grabbed his walkie-talkie, feeling compelled to warn his staff and customers, but after pressing the button to speak, he stopped himself. There was no reason to cause a panic. The cat—a mountain lion, he assumed—was almost certainly gone. Marco decided he'd better make sure.

He placed a fifteen-gallon pot over the track and shimmied behind the shed. He stepped through the barbed-wire fence and found a cougar-sized hole in the chaparral along the banks of the Alisaw River. Marco had always loved mountain lions as a kid, and he half hoped he'd see one in the wild one day, but he wasn't stupid. Torn between fear and fascination, he sang one of his go-to karaoke classics as he made his way through the cut. "Sometimes I feel like I don't have a partner." He projected his voice, but the early hour and his racing pulse made it impossible to stay in tune. "Sometimes I feel like my only friend is the—"

He stopped singing when he found two more eroding tracks. One paw pointed toward the nursery, and the other was heading east, back toward town. This confirmed his suspicion that their visitor had left. Marco had written the company protocol on dealing with nuisance animals, and the first move was to call Fish and Wildlife. He grabbed his cell phone from its holster and was about to dial when his radio chirped.

"We still need that mulch, Marco."

"Hey, boss? Do you know the status of the Ritz-Carlton order? I can't find anything in the system."

Marco returned to the yard and craned his neck toward the commercial gate, where a line of five flatbeds idled. There were orders to fill. His staff needed support, and business was business. He filled his wheelbarrow with mulch, hustled to the front lines, and kept the mountain lion to himself until lunchtime, when he revisited the eroding paw prints.

What a magnificent beast, he thought as he gazed upstream. *It doesn't make a whole lot of sense to call the game wardens now. What are they gonna do? Hassle a long-gone cat who already lives in a hostile world?* He removed the fifteen-gallon bucket protecting the track by the shed, snapped a picture with his point-and-shoot, and scrubbed the area with the soles of his boots until the paw print was erased. *So a mountain lion knocked over some trees? Big deal.*

Actually, it was a pretty big deal.

It was the coolest morning he had ever had on the job.

20

FEBRUARY 6, 2005

WHEN JAY RETURNED TO THE GLENNS' PROPERTY, HE FOUND THAT a new five-foot fence truncated the driveway two hundred feet from their mobile home. He was deciding whether to holler up toward the house or call them from his car when he saw a motion-sensor security camera mounted on one of the fence posts and waved into the lens.

"Business or pleasure?" Aubrey asked as he and Eden strolled down to greet him.

"Making some security improvements, I see," Jay said.

"As promised," Aubrey said.

"That's good, Mr. Glenn. Mrs. Glenn. I'm pleased to see this, but I imagine there is still a lot more work to do." Jay held up a file. Clipped to the front were eleven citations for the improper storage and care of exotic animals. Included in the bundle was a seventy-two-hour notice to bring the property up to state standards or find their animals new homes. He passed the file over the fence.

"Three days, Warden Tern?" Aubrey asked, leafing through it.

"He's taking our cats from us, Aubrey," said Eden. "You don't know the first thing about handling these animals. You'll murder them!"

"Is that what you're planning to do, Tern? Kill our business and our cats?" There was an edge to Aubrey's voice. Eden's too. They looked ready for a fight. Jay had been here before, and as usual, he downshifted into educator mode.

"Folks, I know this isn't easy," he said, "but these laws are meant to keep everybody safe. You, your neighbors, and your animals. Now, I'll be back here in three days for a full inspection. My hope is that if you don't have the time or money to tidy things up, you have friends who may be able to board your cats while all this gets straightened out. Because you're correct, Mrs. Glenn. I don't know how to handle your animals, but I'll find people who do, and we will keep them safe. I promise."

"Oh, a government promise ain't worth squat!" Eden snapped. "We cooperated. We were honest with you, showed you around, and how do you respond? Not by bringing our Sierra home from that filthy pound but with a hefty fine and another government promise."

Jay considered probing their anger. Sometimes, angry people let things slip. Useful things. "As long as we're on the subject of honesty," he said, "do you both stand by your statements that no other cats have run off? Because if there's something you're not telling me—if, say, you're missing a tiger and my community is in danger—now is definitely the time to come clean."

"Let's go, Aubrey," Eden said, gripping his hand. "We've got work to do."

LIEUTENANT COREY KRULL PULLED UP TO THE TERN CABIN AFTER ten that night. Jay stepped outside to meet him. The nocturnal version of Krull tended to be loud and longwinded, and Bell was asleep. Well, she was supposed to be anyway, though she was probably still reading *Tigers in the Field* by the light of her headlamp. She had been spending a lot of time with that hardcover lately.

"Tern, my boy," Krull said. "Read your report on the Glenns over dinner. Those photos. Yeesh! Nice of them to let us know they were bringing a gall dang cat zoo to the county." Krull was taller than Jay and still strong through the chest but had gained nearly twenty pounds of beer belly in the past five years. He was also a close talker, and even in the dark, Jay could detect dandruff flakes on the lieutenant's shoulders, see salsa splotches on his uniform, and smell at least two beers on his breath. "This world is filled with loons."

Krull stepped to his right, unzipped his fly, and relieved himself in the vegetable patch while Jay stewed. It wasn't that Jay was against peeing outside—it was one of his favorite pastimes—but he would never urinate on someone else's vegetables. Krull, though? He'd always been an overstepper.

They'd met during Jay's seventh year on the force, when Bell was four years old. Jay had been selected, along with five other wardens from three districts, to join a regional task force focused on a long-term poaching investigation in the San Bernardino Mountains. On Jay's drive into Big Bear to report for duty, dispatch had sent out a radio alert to all units. Enforcement officers from every government agency in the area were instructed to be on the lookout for an armed suspect in his early thirties. It wasn't one of the poachers. It was an ex-cop who'd shot and killed two uniformed police officers in San Bernardino that morning and stolen a bystander's Land Cruiser at gunpoint. He was last seen heading into the mountains.

The San Bernardino mountains were vast. Big Bear was one small town among many, and with three metro police forces and an entire sheriff's department chasing the suspect, Jay had not expected to get involved. Until he happened to see the suspect gassing up on Highway 38. He looked to be humming to himself, as if he were just another tourist out for a Sunday drive. Except for that pistol stuffed in his waistband. Jay was so startled he dropped his coffee cup between his feet. He could feel the suspect's eyes on him but managed not to swerve or accelerate as he drove past the gas station.

Once he'd traveled up the road and around a bend, Jay reversed into the trees and radioed for backup. He envisioned an incoming tidal wave of badges and guns, but two minutes later, he was still waiting for reinforcements when the suspect zoomed past him.

Terrified, Jay hesitated for fifteen seconds, maybe twenty. As usual, he wasn't wearing his flak jacket. Most wardens wore them all the time because they dealt with armed hunters, but Jay didn't like how the armor made him look or feel. He believed in de-escalation, not physical intimidation. But this situation had a different set of rules, and he'd been caught unequipped. He thought of Bell and what would happen to her if this thing went wrong, and he realized if he chose not to pursue this suspect, he would be dishonoring her and himself and may as well turn in his badge. So be it. He hit his lights and let his siren ring through the pines as he skidded onto the highway and floored it.

The suspect fired his pistol blindly behind him as Jay closed the distance. His accuracy was startling. His first shot sawed off Jay's side mirror. His third pierced the windshield, the smoldering shell lodging in the passenger seat. Jay had never been shot at before, and every instinct told him to slam the brakes, make a hasty U-turn, and smash the gas back down the winding hill. Instead, he grabbed his radio.

"I'm on the suspect, traveling northbound on Highway Thirty-Eight into Big Bear. Shots fired. I repeat, shots fired!" He knew the call was being recorded but couldn't stop his delivery from sounding an octave higher than normal. Jay ducked as the suspect kept firing until the mountain road switched back on itself like a python, and the shooter had to focus on cornering.

Backup arrived in the form of Warden Krull, another member of the task force, heading southbound on Highway 38. Krull spun around and fell in behind Jay as gunfire sprayed his tailgate. A third CDFW truck appeared ahead parked diagonally, blocking the road. The suspect fired two quick shots and veered into the trees, where he broadsided a ponderosa pine, shattering the driver's side window. He leaped out of the SUV holding a loaded assault rifle and bleeding from the forehead. He weaved between trees for cover and sprinted uphill toward a huddle of cabins. Jay charged up the slope after him and gained ground, but he ran out of real estate. He could only watch the suspect burst through a flimsy screen door and take shelter in one of the cabins. Jay heard a woman scream, ceramic or glass smash—perhaps a lamp or a wine bottle—and then a single gunshot. The screaming stopped.

Bullets raked the pines, and Jay dove beneath the back deck of the cabin. The cold air filled his burning lungs as he heard slugs penetrate bark, metal, and glass. The suspect was aiming downslope toward Krull and the other warden, who remained huddled behind the smashed SUV. Jay was on his own, but the suspect had no clue where Jay was.

The suspect's gun ran dry. He paused to reload, then stepped from the cabin out onto the deck above Jay and resumed blasting. Spent shell casings clattered on the redwood planks as he continued to pepper the trees and the stolen SUV. So far, nobody down there was sticking their neck out far enough to shoot back. That is, if they were still breathing. The back steps bent with the shooter's weight. Crouched in the darkness, Jay aimed his Glock. He had a clean shot at the suspect's leg and squeezed the trigger three times. The suspect crumpled, smacked his head on the edge of one of the steps, and rolled all the way to the ground.

"Drop your weapon! Drop it now!" The suspect moaned and attempted to lift his head. Jay heard heavy footsteps and watched an onrushing Krull discharge his pistol six times. For two long minutes, nobody moved as blood pooled.

Jay's legs shook as he crawled through the bloody soil out from under the deck and into the daylight. He pushed up to his feet, holstered his weapon, and scanned the scene. The suspect's body was splayed awkwardly, his arms and legs twisted and lifeless. His assault rifle was on the ground well away from him, and given the angle, it looked to Jay like he had lost his weapon after his knee and thigh had been hit.

"You were in harm's way," Krull said. "He had a bead on you."

Jay watched the blood coalesce and filter through the topsoil.

"Radio San Bernardino. Tell them I got their man."

Krull was identified as the hero of the gunfight in the mountains by the *LA Times*, CNN, and ninety-six other news organizations around the world. Jay read some of the press and was grateful to avoid the attention. His personal life was still in shambles, and he figured survival had been reward enough. But he hadn't considered the long-term consequences. A month after the incident, Corey Krull received a commendation from the state and was promoted to lieutenant. Eighteen months after that, he became Jay's commanding officer in Ventura County.

"Granted, the Glenns sound dirty," Krull said as he zipped his fly, "but do we have any physical evidence that there's another big cat loose?"

"We have an eyewitness."

"Right," Krull said. "The mysterious eyewitness. Why keep them anonymous?"

"It's a matter of discretion, Lieutenant. Reporters comb through our files. You know that." Jay could see Krull wasn't going to let the matter drop without a fuller explanation. "And there was a school bus incident."

"A school bus incident?" Krull sounded alarmed. "With a tiger? Where the heck was that in your report?"

"No. I mean our witness saw the tiger…from a school bus."

"Oh," Krull said. "So it's a kid."

"Yeah," Jay said. "A little girl."

"How old is she?"

"Nine." Jay said.

"Nine." Krull deadpanned. Then he unleashed his hee-haw laugh. "Well, what are you waiting for, Tern? If the kid says she saw a tiger, let's put out an APB. Rally a search party. Alert the media! I want an around-the-clock curfew until the devil cat is found!" Krull said, catching his breath. Jay glanced at the narrow gap in Bell's bedroom window. She rarely slept with her window open in February. "'A nine-year-old girl,' he says to me. Now that's funny."

With *Tigers in the Field* resting in her lap, Bell sat cross-legged on the floor beneath her bedroom window and seethed. She didn't know her dad's history with his boss. She just knew she didn't like him, but despite hearing him pee in her garden and laugh at her, she wasn't mad at Krull. He was entirely predictable. It was her father who was infuriating. She knew he couldn't discuss *all* the details of a case with her, but a few hints about where her tiger may have come from would have been nice. Apparently, there was some kind of amateur zoo in Alisaw Valley. No wonder he'd started to believe her.

For a few hours, she'd thought that he'd actually listened to her. That he had taken her seriously because of what she had to say and how she'd said it. Because she'd been out in the field doing his job for him. But no. He'd been led to the Target parking lot by other witnesses. The facts of the case had forced him to believe her, and that was not nearly the same thing.

21

FEBRUARY 4–7, 2005

THE EARTHY FUNK OF SAGEBRUSH WAFTED UP THE CANYON FROM the low place where streams collided and filtered into the cave. Bolt stirred. It was midafternoon, and for the first time in weeks, her sleep had been deep and unbroken. Because she'd found a safe haven. Shelter that was clean, dry, isolated, and blessed with an unparalleled vantage point. Most importantly, it was empty, and now, it belonged to her.

That comforting realization sent her spinning back into another satisfying slumber, which would have lasted all night if not for the return of the cave's rightful proprietor at sunset, who, after a long day of foraging and perturbed to find a trespasser snoring on her floor, did what any self-respecting crow would do. She fluttered down from her nest on a granite ledge near the roof, inserted her beak into the trespasser's radar ears, and let loose.

"Caaaaaaaw!" Her shriek ricocheted off the rock walls and echoed deep in the tiger's midbrain. Bolt's eyes snapped open and found a scrawny black bird with oversize wings, an outsize temper, and a spear-tipped beak hovering perilously close to her eyeball. The bird strained and screamed in panic and rage with every ounce of her being. "Caaaaaaw! Caaaaaaw! Caaaaaaw!"

Bolt did not walk out of the cave. She ran. She was gone so fast she didn't realize her whip of a tail had smacked the bird upside the head and knocked her over like a felled statue. Which was a bit of an issue in that this crow had just the one leg. She flapped her free wing with enough vigor to provide the lift needed to alight upright, but it took a while. Once the job was done, the One-Legged Crow fluffed her feathers with pride for having evicted her first squatter, and a rather intimidating one at that. Bolt spent most of that night lying awake in the grass above the cave, listening to rain patter the soft earth.

The One-Legged Crow didn't get much sleep either, terrorized as she was by the thought that the biggest cat she'd ever laid her bulging eyes on had chosen her perfect cave, where she'd lived alone and in peace for nearly two years, as its new home. But life was frequently unfair to the one-legged and feathery kind.

When she was a month old, her parents nudged her out of the nest for her first flying lesson. Her leg buckled when she hit the ground, and her head smacked the only rock in an otherwise open field. Knocked out cold, she was presumed dead by the Alisaw Valley Greater Crow Community, who, after hearing her parents' disconsolate caws, flew in from all ends of the valley. The communal wailing cycled from crescendo to piano before silence swallowed them up in a unified knot of grief. One by one, crows fluttered down beside her supposedly lifeless body. Some set sticks they'd used to roust termites and ants beside her or plucked feathers from her skin for a memento to decorate their nests. A few sprinkled her remains with colorful candy wrappers. Her mother spread a torn dryer sheet over her head. Such are the funeral rites of the American crow.

When she came to, tipped on her side and unable to rectify the situation, she was alone and in grave danger. Only her outrage at being orphaned so suddenly wouldn't let her die, and her ear-splitting calls lured two well-meaning humans. They took her to a local way station, where she was nurtured and taught how to pick herself up from the turf, hunt, and fly in an aviary by a third human, who combed the unlucky bird's velvety feathers each evening. Eventually, her benefactors released her into the wild, where she perfected the scavenging techniques she'd learned at the aviary and took care to avoid other animals. Particularly the crows who had abandoned her.

It wasn't difficult. When the 387 members of the Alisaw Valley GCC were confronted with the young One-Legged Crow's survival, they shunned her. Whenever she discovered a delicious piece of steaming carrion before they did, she typically could only manage a few bites before they descended en masse and bullied her away like an uninvited guest. In other words, the One-Legged Crow was no longer considered by the Alisaw Valley GCC to even be a crow. She would never mate. She would live and die alone.

So she leaned into solitude. That required her to become a skilled pilot capable of narrow escapes. Being underweight with oversize wings, she was light and fast, which made her acrobatic and daring. She did not favor trees. She preferred nesting in the rocky nooks and caves that peppered the Santa Susanas. If the dreaded feline only knew how many filthy holes and snake-ridden rock piles she'd explored before finding the cave of caves, completely vacant and awaiting her, as if from a fantasy, it might have understood why she was not about to surrender it, no matter who ambled in.

For three days, they traded places. In the morning, Bolt would watch the crow fly off before slinking into the cave. At sunset, like any smart squatter, Bolt would clear out before the proprietor returned. The tiger nestled in the grassy plateau above the cave each evening to await nightfall and watch the crow soar over Happy Camp Canyon. Bolt had seen these birds before but never a solitary one. Usually, they descended in twos or threes, and occasionally in mobs, to swipe the meat treats the Glenns tossed into her cage. She'd watched them move in a halting two-step. Sometimes, they galloped or skipped before taking flight. This one looked clumsy on land. It could only hop left to right and up and back. But in the sky, its skill showed.

On the third evening, when the rain had paused for a few minutes, Bolt watched the bird perform a series of gliding figure eights on its way home. That was Bolt's cue to depart, but she didn't want to. She preferred to stay dry and out of sight and sleep all night long. She took her time leaving but soon reached the meadow above the cave. She stared up at the bitter bird, who, fueled by her preferred cocktail of fear and rage, tucked her wings in and spiraled into a steep dive. She sounded her battle cry as she closed in on the cat's wide eyes like a missile, "Caw! Caw!"

Bolt barrel rolled left. The bird spread its wings to avoid slamming into the earth, and the wind filled them like sails. With a rightward arc and a few muscular strokes, the crow gathered enough altitude and momentum to make another pass. Bolt took off down the rock fall and bounded into the narrow canyon and shallow creek, where there were too many trees and boulders for the bird to attack from above. But that burst of exertion gave way to exhaustion and a hunger that was ferocious and painful.

She followed Camp Creek around three bends until it ran parallel to a fenced pasture. A gust of cold wind carried the pungent notes of horse manure, and she latched on to them. As a waxing moon sunk in the midnight sky, she crept from the stream, silent as a phantom.

Strauss Horse Ranch didn't have much stock on its forty-five acres beyond a trio of handsome geldings that were as tame as pet hamsters and nearly as round. Droplets of inky black were splattered like paint along the taut white hide of the closest horse. The other two were solid brown, one more chestnut and the other chocolate.

Bolt slunk along the Strauss property line, parsing the distinct aromas of horse patties and hay, wild grass and well water, which fed a manmade pond in the center of the ranch. The rambling ranch house's dim porch light barely dented the darkness. Bolt inched within a hundred yards of the horses. Only the Paint was clearly visible beneath the low crescent moon. The other two looked like three-dimensional silhouettes. The entire property was ringed with corral fencing, and not the cheap plastic stuff. This was a splintering redwood fence built back when Alisaw was primarily a fertile patchwork of ranches and farms. When there were more horses in the valley than cars. More avocado trees than single-family homes.

Bolt hurdled the fence and flared her nostrils. She tasted the horses' sweat on her exposed tongue, which hung limp and heavy. For the first time in her life, she was hypnotized by the hunt. Her fear of exposure evaporated. She had no thought of what would happen if some human caught sight of her. All that mattered was her untamed hunger.

She crept through the grass until she was fifty yards out, laid her belly flat to the earth, and raised her nose to the sky. The breeze blew directly at her, which meant she was undetectable to the horses. She crept forward another ten yards and lay down again. Then another five. She monitored the horses as they mingled beneath the walnut trees and listened to their hooves smack the wet soil around the drip line. Slowly and carefully, she moved to within twenty yards of her prey. She had hoped to get even closer, but the night exploded with howls and barks. Two hounds materialized from the shadows around the distant ranch house and raced toward Bolt. The horses registered the ruckus, but they didn't spook. Rather, they turned toward the disruption, nonchalant, and found a tiger's glowing eyes.

Bolt charged, but the horses, despite their condition and disposition, were faster than they looked, and the tiger had never been in a life-or-death footrace before. She stumbled in a divot and fell behind, then righted herself and found a rhythm.

Bolt's long, elegant strides carried her across the pasture as the horses sprinted toward the far fence that ran parallel to Suarez Road. They'd left the dogs far behind. It was only predator and prey now. Bolt drew up alongside the Paint, the slowest and thickest of the three horses. She gathered herself in two bounding strides and leaped into the air, landing on its back. The terrified horse bucked, and one rear hoof slammed into Bolt's exposed breast. Bolt tumbled sideways and rolled three times. The half-blind horses galloped on toward a fence they could not see until it was much too late. They smashed through the old wood and barreled onto the road, where they were illuminated by a pair of oncoming headlights. Lying on her side, panting, Bolt heard scampering hooves on asphalt, the screech of melting rubber, and the crunch of metal and shattering glass.

Bolt pushed up to standing and limped to the wreckage. Two of the horses were still running through the pasture across the road, but the Paint was sprawled on its side, half merged with a gurgling ten-year-old Honda Civic. The crushed car's last working headlight grew faint. The driver gasped, whimpered, and choked, bleeding from windshield wounds and blunt-force trauma to his head, neck, and chest. The hounds barked from a safe distance, but no other living thing seemed to have heard the accident.

Bolt stepped carefully through the shrapnel toward the horse's exposed rump. Ravenous, she unfurled her sandpaper tongue studded with papillae—dozens of small spikes that enable tigers to lick flesh clean from the bone. She licked blood from the horse's hide, flaying open a surface wound, then sunk her three-inch canines into the exposed thigh muscle. The horse didn't even twitch as Bolt tore away a bite, and then another, savoring hot blood on her thorny tongue.

The driver, who reporters would describe as a twenty-eight-year-old American male, lived for only ninety more seconds, and his reward was a vision as if from a dream. The spectacle of a tiger feasting on the horse that did him in. Bolt watched him carefully as she stole another taste from the dead horse's thigh. Then, she opened her jaws to the maximum, deployed her razor-sharp incisors, and tore away a long, thick steak.

The driver had already passed when Bolt felt a rumble beneath her feet and saw a distant glow growing in intensity. She leaped onto the shoulder and hid in the grass with her prized twenty-pound steak still dangling from her jaws as an SUV bore down on the tragic scene in the middle of Suarez Road. At the last second, the driver veered hard to the right and smashed the brakes at the same time, which sent her spinning. Her rear wheels rode up on the dead horse's hind legs and smashed the front end of the Civic, which caused the SUV to flip and slide on its roof for nearly thirty yards.

Bolt heard screams erupt from the second car before it stopped sliding. She turned to see two people hustling toward the road from the ranch house, which now had every light burning. Bolt's right paw had been lacerated by broken glass, and her sternum was badly bruised, but she streaked across the pasture and leaped into the creek. In the shadows, among lupine and poison oak, manzanita and sycamore, she laid her steak on a dry boulder and guzzled running water, rinsing blood from her nose and mouth. She hadn't made the kill herself, but her hunt had triggered it, and she felt a surge of satisfaction. Her genetic code was flickering back to life.

Bolt folded her strip steak over with her rough tongue, carried it between her teeth, and backtracked upstream into the now-familiar Happy Camp Canyon. She hopped from rock to rock until she could see the cave. She knew the crow was still home, but there was nowhere else to go. She limped inside and set her steak down on the cold stone floor. Placing one paw in the center, she tore away a healthy scrap with her teeth and left it as an offering. She scooped up the rest, hobbled toward the rear of the cave, and began to feast.

It took a few minutes for the suspicious bird to flutter over and investigate the bloody scrap. She pecked at it twice. It was still warm. She glanced over at the tiger, who was watching the landlord gobble her room service through half-mast eyelids. "Caw," the One-Legged Crow called out between gulps. "Caw." This time, it didn't come off as an insult or accusation. It was softer, more melodic. It almost sounded like a thank you.

22

FEBRUARY 8, 2005

MIRIAM'S CALL WOKE JAY BEFORE FIVE IN THE MORNING. HE DIDN'T like leaving Bell home alone at that hour, but it was either drag her to the aftermath of a bloody fatality or leave her a note and let her sleep. By the time he approached the scene, it was doused in flashing red lights and a sheer curtain of rain. Jay counted four sheriff's cruisers, one ambulance, a fire engine, and two flatbeds blocking both lanes of Suarez Road. All but the glow of the emergency lights was concealed from view when the rolling blacktop dipped, and it was easy to see how a driver could be blindsided.

Jay pulled up beside Miriam's van and clocked the zipped body bag in the back of the ambulance, the totaled Civic—with its crumpled front end, chopped back right corner, and shattered windshield—and the Chevy Tahoe standing on its head further down the road. Miriam met him at his window. Jay saw the mangled carcass pinned beneath the late-model Honda. "Sad way to start the day," he said, "but that doesn't look like deer to me."

"The deputy who called swore it was wildlife," Miriam said. "Sorry to pull you out of bed. Go be a dad. Animal control will handle."

Jay considered the scene. There was open space on either side of the asphalt strip. The Strauss pasture to the north, delineated by a now-ruptured fence line, and an unfenced pasture surrounded by rolling savanna and chaparral to the south. That was where a thin, silver-haired cowboy attempted to soothe two spooked horses who must have run from something. Jay climbed out of his truck and arched his stiff back.

"I say go home, he gets out of his truck."

"Bell knows her way around breakfast detail." Jay gazed at the toppled Tahoe and recreated the incident in his head starring a certain fugitive Miriam didn't know about. He'd wanted to share his report on the Glenns with her, but Krull had forbidden it. "How's the other driver?"

"Not a scratch. Doesn't remember much but confirmed the main event had already happened by the time she came along. They took her to the hospital as a precaution." Miriam sipped from her steaming travel mug.

Jay watched PJ Strauss, the sixty-three-year-old rancher, loop bridles over the heads of his two jittery survivors. An oversize sleep shirt hung loose on his wiry frame. He wore boots with no socks, a cowboy hat, and soft leather gloves. He whispered to his trembling geldings as he led them slowly back to pasture.

Miriam pointed to the diagonal laceration across the chestnut's sternum. "That must be where he made contact with the fence. Poor thing busted right through it."

"Makes sense. Have you had a chance to examine our dearly departed?"

"Not yet, seeing as it's laying beneath a chassis." The Tahoe had knocked the Civic onto the unlucky horse's ravaged rump, concealing it.

Jay caught up to Strauss when he was halfway to his barn. "It's the damnedest thing," Strauss said. "Coyotes prowl the property, and the horses never take so much as a step to avoid them. Ain't scared of black bear neither. Shotgun blasts, backfiring engines. Don't matter. These horses don't spook. Gotta be mountain lion."

"This is their habitat," Jay said. "Did your dogs bark last night?"

"We heard them carrying on for a few minutes, which happens. Considered getting up, but they settled right down."

Why was that? Jay wondered as he watched Strauss lead his horses away. *Had the wind changed? Did his dogs scare the tiger off without the horses realizing it? Had the poor things run through the fence for nothing? Was there ever a tiger here at all?*

For the next hour, Jay inspected the broken fence and the churned-up ground all around it while Miriam handled the removal of the dead horse. Jay collected blood samples and horsehair, but there was no apparent physical evidence of a predator. His mind kept veering toward the same conspicuous conclusion as he combed the pasture for paw prints, fur samples, scat, and urine. If the tiger did have something to do with this, Jay's worst fear had already materialized. An innocent young man had been killed. A rather polite and beautiful horse, too, from the sounds of it. It was a tragic accident, but it would not spark a valley-wide search for a cat he couldn't prove caused it.

As much as Krull grated on him, the Lieutenant was right that hard evidence was the only thing that should mobilize the machine. A suspicious and tragic traffic accident was as circumstantial as the testimony of an anonymous, overimaginative kid. But with rain sweeping steadily across the valley, physical traces were scarce. The iron tang of blood had already been washed away. There was no odor in the pasture but wet grass. Something strange had happened, that much was clear, but when the news trucks turned up at first light, neither Jay nor Miriam, Strauss nor the deputies on the scene had anything worth sharing beyond the obvious.

Miriam found Jay kneeling among the fence shrapnel on the roadside. "Think Strauss is right?"

"Mountain lion," he said, trying it on. "Sure. What else could it be?"

23

FEBRUARY 9, 2005

AUBREY SLID ONE OF TWO PLATES OF OVER-EASY EGGS BENEATH Eden's nose, which was currently parked inside the morning edition of the *Ventura County Star*. Alongside the eggs were three crispy strips of bacon and a mound of wilted spinach. He sat down opposite her with the other plate and sipped his coffee, which she'd prepared the way he liked it: milky and sweet.

"You know I hate sad stories," Eden said. She shook the paper out, folded it twice, and picked up her fork. "Especially this early."

"They said it was a tame horse, dear." Aubrey pierced his runny eggs with the side of his fork. "What was the term they used? Broke?"

"Dead broke." She picked up a strip of bacon, closed her eyes, and crunched. Bacon was a meditation, her nitrate-packed portal to inner peace, a respite from the latest sign they'd received from the universe that the walls were closing in. Aubrey sipped his coffee and opened the paper. Eden kept her eyes closed and took another bite.

"You say it, Eden, or I will."

She opened her eyes and attempted to exhale all the stress away before turning her attention back to her plate. It was that ability to take in chaos and process it with confidence that first drew Aubrey to her. Nothing flustered her. Not his lawsuits or his debt. She was the one who'd suggested a new identity, and it had worked. All her schemes worked, which was why he had believed her when she said Alisaw Valley would be another new beginning. That it would bring him and Bolt back together and save them from financial ruin.

"We should have gotten ahead of this."

"Well, Aubrey, sweetie, we obviously can't say anything now."

He watched as she arranged artfully layered forkfuls of bacon, egg, and spinach with precision and chewed each bite fifty times.

"Plus, you're reacting, not thinking. Read the story again. They're searching for a mountain lion with no evidence to go on. No tracks at all." She set her utensils down and sipped her coffee. She took her coffee black. "And what if we had volunteered something, and they'd found Bolt? How far back would that investigation go? To the forgery of federal documents? All the way back to that mall? Like I said from the beginning, let this rain do its work. They won't find any tracks, no scent or scat, as long as the rain keeps falling. And that will give us time to take care of this situation ourselves." As if on cue, the sound of crunching gravel beneath heavy tires came through their security monitor. "Speak of the devil."

She looked almost cheery as she padded to the front door, coffee in hand, but when she opened it, Jay wasn't waiting at their gate. It was a tall, older Black man dressed in blue jeans and a white cowboy hat standing next to an idling Dodge pickup. He tipped his hat.

"Morning. Name's Ben. I own a small ranch not far from here. We have a mutual friend in the animal-transport business. He told me you folks know a thing or two about big cats."

"How can we help you, Ben?" Eden asked.

Aubrey and Eden followed Ben to Dry Creek Ranch and parked behind him in the circular drive. "A historic horse ranch," Aubrey said. "That's what I call ideal retirement."

"It's supposed to be a business," Ben said. "Turned out to be a glorified hobby." Ben led them past three old valley oaks, around the back of his restored barn, and onto a rise that overlooked Camp Creek. The grass had receded into patches of clay soil, and Ben knelt in the mud beside a single, large cat track: four circular toes set above a thick, broad pad. "Tell me what you folks make of this."

Aubrey made a show of inspecting it. He leaned forward, changed angles, and measured it with his fingers, framing it just so. "Mountain lion," Aubrey said. "A hungry one, too, I'd bet."

"Would have to be a mighty big mountain lion, don't you think?" Ben said.

"Not necessarily," Aubrey said. "These are roughly six inches in diameter. We used to own a cougar with bigger paws than that."

"I'll bet you did," Ben said. "No offense, but that sure sounds like a strange and hazardous line of work." Their tense silence was mocked by the babbling creek. The stream itself was the property line and had been ever since the Suarez heirs subdivided it. "Just to be sure, come have a look at these."

Ben led Aubrey to the periphery of his property, where he pointed out four tracks on a muddy slope with unfenced access to the creek. Eden had lagged behind at first but joined them as Aubrey knelt for a closer look.

"Like I said—"

"Mountain lion." Ben finished his thought. The rain picked up.

"If you're concerned for your animals, we'd be happy to help search the area for your cougar," said Aubrey.

"My cougar. Funny." A gust rattled the wind chimes dangling from the eaves of the ranch house. "So you haven't lost any big cats."

"Now, Ben," Eden said. "You must have heard, considering the way word seems to travel around here. We lost them all."

WITHIN THE HOUR, BEN WAS SHOWING THE EVIDENCE TO JAY. OR he'd planned to, but instead of cat tracks all they could find on the muddy slope between the pasture and Camp Creek was a parade of partial boot prints. The track behind the barn was gone too. "I haven't felt this stupid in a long time," Ben said. "There were five tracks here a little over an hour ago."

Jay believed him. Not only because he and Ben were friendly but because Dry Creek Ranch bordered the Strauss property and this patch of mud—a classic track trap—did look to be intentionally erased.

Undeterred, Jay walked Ben's property line, which ran along Camp Creek for some one hundred feet. He moved slowly and mindfully, upstream then back downstream. The water was running higher than usual, but it was still only shin deep. On his return trip, he spotted a depression in a muddy bar that rose from the center of the creek. It was sheltered by a large sycamore, its white bark mottled and peeling. From his vantage point, it didn't look to be much more than the shape of water running through the soil. He sloshed across the creek to get a closer look, and he was glad he did. That depression was a cat track, and it was large. Jay placed his wet boot beside it for scale and snapped a photo.

"What do you think?" Ben was leaning against the tree trunk. "Aubrey swore up and down that it's a mountain lion."

"Could be," Jay said. He didn't buy it, but he had to fight to remain skeptical of the notion that a tiger was on the loose. Because he wanted it to be true, and there was no space for personal preference in any investigation. "Better call the expert."

Miriam arrived twenty minutes later, calipers in hand. Jay had already cordoned off the area with yellow tape, taken three dozen photographs, and covered the track with a bucket. She lifted the bucket and took her measurements, recording the track's length and inner and outer diameters on her forearm with a sharpie.

"All cats have similar prints," she said. "House cats, bobcats, mountain lions, and the bigger exotics are all basically the same. Four toes arced around a central carpal pad." She used the tip of her pocketknife to point out each section. "They have a useless fifth toe on their front feet, but those don't show up in their tracks." She set her knife down and opened her calipers. "It's the size that tells them apart. This one is six by six inches."

"That's what Aubrey said. That's big, right?" Ben asked.

"Aubrey Glenn? What was he..." Miriam rose and thrust her calipers at Jay. "I knew you were acting funny yesterday. You've been holding out on me, Tern!"

"Just following orders, ma'am," Jay said.

"You think this...and that they..."

"It doesn't make one bit of difference what I think." He knelt and gestured toward the print. "I need to know what I can prove." Miriam sighed, knelt beside him, and double-checked her work.

"I'd estimate a cat with a paw this size might weigh somewhere around four hundred pounds."

Jay had looked up the statistics. The largest mountain lion documented in North America had weighed less than three hundred pounds. If Miriam was right, this track was the closest thing he had to confirmation that a tiger was loose in the valley. So far, the body count was one horse and one late-night commuter, but it could have been much worse. There was the other driver. Plus, Bell had hiked the Camp Creek corridor. She would have been easy prey. Unless the tiger was found soon, there would be more blood. The situation was as absurd as it was outrageous, and yet the news pleased him. Because it meant that Bell's tiger was no delusion. If Miriam was right.

"You said, 'might.'"

Miriam spread her fingers and pressed her palm into the mud next to the track. The ground was sloppy, and the print she made was much larger than her hand.

"I'm afraid the substrate here is too loose to get an accurate reading. Some cats spread their toes when walking in soft mud to get better traction. That would make the paw look bigger than it actually is. Plus, look at the top right edge." Miriam pointed out where the edges of the toes blurred. It was as if Jay were seeing the track in double vision. "Cats have a natural inclination to overstep."

"Meaning this could be two prints in one," Jay said.

"Precisely. The carpal pad is deep, which might mean the cat weighs a quarter ton, unless it placed both its front and hind paws in the same exact place, one after another. The best I can do is give you a range. Let's call it between two hundred fifty and four hundred pounds."

Jay stared at the inconclusive pugmark. He felt a growing certainty that somewhere out there was a dangerous cat that did not belong in Alisaw Valley, but he still couldn't prove it.

24

WHEN HER DAD WORKED A CASE AT HIS DESK, BELL WAS NOT PERmitted to ask questions or peep at his computer screen, notes, photos, or loose files. These were crimes akin to snooping through his drawers and closet and led to solitary confinement in quarters. Which was unfortunate since it had become abundantly clear there would be no briefing forthcoming from the most annoying game warden in the known universe.

Bell read *Tigers in the Field* while pretending not to spy on him. The author, Ulias Murthy, was the foremost tiger biologist in India, and he'd just finished explaining that twenty-five thousand years ago, tigers migrated to India from China and flourished. There were forty thousand Bengal Tigers in India alone at the population's peak, not to mention the related subspecies in Java, Thailand, Sumatra, and Siberia. Then, humans began clearing land for crops. They built towns and cities, and wherever humans and tigers met, tigers lost. By 2005, there were less than four thousand Bengal tigers left.

Now, she was deep into Chapter Seven, "Effective Communication Strategies of Wild Tigers," which was her favorite so far. According to Murthy, tigers had the loudest and most spectacular roar in the animal kingdom. In fact, the MGM lion's roar—the one seen and heard before big blockbusters—was a tiger dubbed in. Yet their roar was seldom heard in the wild. They chuffed much more frequently, which Murthy described as part burp, part grunt, and part purr. It was their way of greeting loved ones, like their cubs or parents, siblings or friends. Bell considered this an important piece of intelligence and practiced chuffing as she read on, when she took a break to feed the fire, and when simply staring at her father in a vain attempt to use her psychic powers to get him to tell her everything.

Jay was too busy compiling his report to notice. In it, he referenced the car crash and included photographs of the dead and the new print he'd found that implied a big cat was near the scene that night. He reported Miriam's analysis and his interview with Ben. He also included the Glenns' multiple denials, the suspicion that Eden had destroyed evidence, and his deployment of two camera traps in the sycamore grove on the Dry Creek Ranch property line. Once he'd emailed it all to Krull, he shut his computer down and locked his paperwork in the filing cabinet. Then, he returned to his map and surveyed the whole of Alisaw Valley. When he heard Bell grunt again, and louder this time, Jay looked over.

"Why are you grunting?"

"It's not a grunt. It's a chuff. It means 'love' in tiger. Also 'hello' or 'goodbye,'" Bell said. "I guess a better translation would be 'aloha.' Or 'shalom.'"

She still took Jay by surprise. When he watched her hike and run trails with him, climb trees like a monkey, or reveal some new ability or chunk of knowledge harnessed while he wasn't looking, he felt it like the splash of a winter wave on an early morning. It snapped him wide awake, and despite all the variables spinning in his head—chiefly her vice-grip headaches, what they might mean, and the possibility of a starving tiger roaming the neighborhood—when those moments arrived, there was nothing else. The fire crackled, throwing light on the dated cabin walls, overhead beams, scrap-wood bookcases, and quirky collectibles. Everything they had—and it wasn't a whole lot—looked golden, and Bell's eyes sparkled.

"Can I at least look at the map?" she asked.

He met her on the floor and raised his map to the firelight. He'd marked four new locations—places where a tiger might have been—with an X, which gave him five total. There was the Glenn property, Chelsea Road, Target, the accident site on Suarez Road, and Dry Creek Ranch. He watched her trace a path between them with her fingertip.

"What happened here?" She stopped at the site of the fatal accident.

"Car wreck," he said. "I'm only telling you that because it's public information."

"Somebody get hurt?"

"Two somebodies." Jay folded his map and crossed to his desk. "A young man drove his car into a gentle old horse that was running from something. They both died."

"Was it running from her?"

"That's one theory."

"You mean your theory."

"Maybe."

Bell shot to her feet.

"Then why aren't you looking for her? Why aren't there, like, twenty wardens out there looking for her?"

"Because I can't prove it. We still don't have hard evidence. I've set up two camera traps. Hopefully, she comes back down the creek looking for another meal."

"Two dead bodies and you put up camera traps? There's a tiger loose in Alisaw Valley, and that's what you're doing? Camera traps?"

"Bell, it's not that simple. Based on the track we f—" He stopped himself. When it came to sensitive information, Jay found it was generally better to share nothing at all. Which was why he'd created the house rules in the first place. It made things easier on everyone.

"A track? You said there wasn't any hard evidence. Wait, was it on Ben's ranch. Was it one of *his* horses?"

"I've said too much already," Jay said, "but since you are my only eyewitness, you get one more question."

"Those people who lost Sierra had other cats, didn't they?"

"Yes, they did." He filed the map away and locked the drawer with his tiny black key.

"Great. I've been right this whole time, and you and your *boss* won't take me seriously. I heard him laughing that night, you know. He was laughing at both of us!"

"Enough of that talk," Jay said. "You are smart enough to know that the fact that you're my daughter and the lone eyewitness only hurts us."

"Then we'll look for the cat ourselves."

"No. We won't."

"Fine. Then we'll do nothing because it's easier and more acceptable!"

"I said enough!" He slapped his metal desk with both hands. "One man and one brave little girl out there all alone will not find this cat."

"See, that's your problem," she said. "You still think of me as a little kid." Her freckled cheeks roasted with anger. Her lower lip quivered. Her temple throbbed in two-four time. "And I'm not. I'm not your little girl anymore!"

"Well, you are to me." He grabbed a bath towel from his closet, threw it over his shoulder, and shut the door.

By the time he'd returned from his overdue shower and shave, dressed in a white t-shirt and gray sweats, Bell was asleep in front of the fire. He scooped her up in one arm and grabbed her drawing pad and colored pencils with the other, stuffing the pencils in his pants pocket. Her warm breath seeped from pursed lips onto his neck as he stepped softly down the hall. She was right. She wasn't little anymore, and there weren't many more of these moments left.

He tapped her bedroom door open with his toe and dropped her pad face down on her drafting table. He held her for a minute longer than necessary, then tucked her in. On his way out, he pulled her colored pencils from his pocket and set them alongside her pad, which he turned over, revealing a work in progress. The title read, *Family Tree: Due February 28*. Below that were the bare bones of what looked like an artful valley oak, its branches twisted and thick. Bell's name was perched like an owl at the top of the canopy.

Isabella "Bell" Tern (that's me!)

His name was slotted in below hers and beside her mother's on the next level of branches.

Jay Tern (Dearest Daddy) + Ling Tern (Poor Dead Momma Bear)

The lower branches were empty, and the tree itself was rootless, floating above a golden savanna. Its disconnected roots, a mirror image of the canopy, wriggled from the earth, groping for connection. Jay stared at Ling's name until he wobbled to the floor with a soft thud. Bell stirred but didn't wake, and he remained there, listening to the rain fall and counting her riffling breaths, for the better part of an hour, in clear violation of his house rules.

25

FEBRUARY 10, 2005

THE RAIN LET UP ON THE WAY TO SCHOOL, AND THE BUS WAS drenched in sunlight when it parked in front of the flagpole. Bell stepped off and looked up at the surrounding hills. After nearly two solid weeks of rain, she was pleased to see as much green as gold. When she reached her classroom, her enthusiasm fizzled. A handful of students had turned up with highly produced renditions of family trees, which Ms. Levine fawned over. Never mind that the project wasn't due for eighteen days.

Ashley strode in with a handmade scroll. Bell sat at her desk and watched Ms. Levine unfurl it, revealing an artful giant sequoia pinned with photos and handwritten captions. The teacher was obviously impressed. She was still admiring it when Ashley slid into her seat, kitty-corner to Bell.

"I didn't know you could draw," Bell said. She doubted it was Ashley's work alone but didn't mind using it to defuse any tension that may have resulted from Bell having seen Ashley's mother drag her away by her hair.

"Don't worry," Ashley said. "I'm sure your mom will help with your project too."

So that's it, Bell thought. *Psycho soccer mom has skills.*

"After she gets back from Milan," said Charlotte. "When's that again?"

"Good morning, everyone." Ms. Levine stood at the blackboard waiting for the morning chatter to simmer down. "Settle...settle. We have lots to cover today."

"I'm pretty sure she said next week," said Ashley.

"That's what she said."

"Yeah, right," Bell said. She knew better than to respond, but she couldn't help herself. "I never gave you a specific day."

"Isabella Tern! Mouth shut! Eyes up front, please! Thank you!"

Bell looked up to find Ms. Levine peering down at her from the front of the room. The entire class laughed. Ashley's and Charlotte's laughter was especially loud, which inspired Bell to spend the rest of the morning brainstorming all the many ways she might destroy Ashley's fraud of a family tree. She could simply march over to the wall and tear it to shreds. Or wrap it around Ashley's long neck and use it to drag her across the classroom floor. Better yet, she could stuff it into her pack, take it home, and use it as kindling. Yes, she needed to see it burn.

When the morning recess bell rang, the class was set loose to play in the sun. Bell took her time gathering her things and paused along the wall where Ms. Levine displayed the trees. The canopies overflowed, and Bell lingered over photographs of parents and grandparents, brothers, sisters, aunts, uncles, and cousins. There were time-worn black-and-whites, high-end color prints, and faded Polaroids. These trees—these families—looked to be ideal specimens, as her father called them. In comparison, the Tern tree was spindly and malnourished, starved for light in a crowded grove. The kind destined to sag to the forest floor. Unless they were all frauds like Ashley's. Maybe they all deserved to burn.

Bell's vision went fuzzy at the edges as she pictured herself at the front of the room preparing to unveil her own canvas, which was on an easel behind a tiger-print curtain. Her impressed classmates leaned forward in anticipation. With a snap of Bell's fingers, the curtain dropped, and she presented one of her tiger drawings. She snapped her fingers again, and all the family trees Ms. Levine had mounted on the walls burst into flames while her tiger blinked and came to life.

It leaped from the canvas into the classroom, saliva dripping from its black tongue. Students scattered as it closed in on the perfectly coiffed teacher, who trembled in her shiny heels, with Ashley and Charlotte cowering behind her.

"Getting some good ideas, I hope." Ms. Levine snapped the spell by draping her arm over Bell's shoulders and leading her to the door. "With your skills, I know whatever you create will be very special too."

On the playground, Bell retreated to the far corner of the field, pulled out her field glasses, and scanned the ridge closest to the school. She saw segments of the trail system winding through the chaparral and a string of homes clinging to the cliffs, but no tiger. She panned the playground and focused on Miles playing hopscotch with two friends his own age. Being associated with Bell hadn't done him many favors with the school bullies. Speaking of, she found Ashley and Charlotte playing four square with a larger group.

Ashley caught the ball in one hop. She raised it overhead, prepared to pass, and spotted Bell spying on her. She called out to Charlotte, who looked over and laughed hysterically. Soon, the entire group was laughing and pointing. Bell dropped her binoculars, stuffed them into her backpack, and attempted to recede deeper into the shadows. But her back foot slipped, and she landed face down in a puddle of mud.

She raised up slowly. Mud caked her lips, nose, eyebrows, cheeks, and chin. It was inside her mouth. She choked and coughed. Laughter billowed across the blacktop. Her eyes stung with tears. The dam was about to break, and she could not let that happen. She slammed both fists into the muddy field, pounded the grass like it was a heavy bag, and howled like a wild animal.

She raged at the ridicule—all those daily blank expressions and the constant laughter at her expense—and at her father's failure to listen and share even the most basic family history. She raged at her own lies and runaway fantasies and at her mother for leaving her alone. She raged at the unfairness and unkindness of everything. And in her outrage, she failed to register that the click-clack of high heels on asphalt was headed straight for her.

"Isabella Tern." Bell gazed up at Principal Ono's polished boots, designer skirt, and blazer, then compared them to her own soiled clothes. She was one gigantic mud stain. Principal Ono crouched down and extended her hand. "Come on up now. Don't make me beg."

The principal helped Bell to her feet and led her inside to the faculty restroom, where Bell rinsed her mouth clean and washed the mud off her face and palms. The principal did her best to clean the soil from Bell's overalls, then attempted to peel the mud-crusted beanie off her head, but Bell held it in place with both hands.

"It's okay, Isabella."

She normally cringed when anyone called her that, but this time, it soothed her. Her hands fell to her sides, and she stood facing the mirror with Principal Ono behind her. She watched the principal remove her hat and set it on the edge of the sink.

"Is that door locked?"

"You're embarrassed."

"Duh," Bell said. "Doesn't help that I'm standing next to perfect you."

"Now, if I were perfect, would I spend so much money on hair, nails, and clothes?" Principal Ono threaded her manicured fingers into Bell's hive, picking through snags, dreads, and clumps of mud, and found one blue pencil reduced to a nub.

"We look like a couple of baboons," Bell said.

"Is this what they do?" Principal Ono continued to untangle knots and remove foreign solids from the environment. It took some force and caused Bell considerable pain, and when she was done, Bell's hair was still a complete mess. "You know, I paid my way through college by doing hair. I still keep a pair of shears in my desk drawer."

"How come?"

"Memories, I suppose. The nurse has some shampoo. It's lice shampoo, but that might not be the worst idea."

"No," Bell said. "I mean, hello…you've barely ever said a word to me, and now you want to wash and cut my hair?"

"Yes, I do."

"Why?"

"Because it is the only thing I know I can do right this second to help you, and that's what I'm here for: to help kids whenever and however I can."

Bell tensed when Principal Ono washed and combed her neglected hair and when the principal gathered a tangled handful and sheared an inch and a half off the bottom where the ends had split and fused. But as she thinned out the rest, Bell relaxed and became absorbed in watching Principal Ono work until her damp dark-brown hair grazed her shoulders in tidy waves. It was the first time she could remember feeling a woman's touch so intently.

Afterward, they sat across from one another in Principal Ono's office, sipping mugs of hot chocolate the principal had made with steamed milk courtesy of that espresso machine. "This is yummy," Bell said, blowing steam from the surface of her mug.

"It's my guilty pleasure," Principal Ono said. "Sometimes, we need something sweet to make us feel better."

Bell giggled.

"What's funny?"

"All the kids are afraid of you. Everyone talks about how mean you are. You have a reputation."

"Oh, that's happened at every school I've worked in. I'm Japanese American, and I don't go around smiling all the time, so students assume I'm strict. Teachers and parents too. Is it a little racist? Sure, but I don't really mind because it keeps everyone in line." The principal sharpened her expression and glared at Bell from across her desk. "So don't you blow my cover."

Bell laughed, took another sip, and inspected the office walls, which were decorated with framed abstract photographs taken in the exotic markets, plazas, narrow laneways, and broad boulevards of Hanoi, Vienna, Seoul, Nairobi, Jakarta, Cartagena, and New York. Not that you could tell from the photographs themselves. "Did you take all those pictures?"

"It's a hobby," the principal said, blushing. "My husband finds them too angular or arty, so here they hang." Only one of the images looked vaguely familiar. It was a blurry snap of an older man on a grassy hillside wearing a broad hat and an orange poncho. It could have been any old man on any old hillside, but Bell felt she'd seen him before.

"That's Alisaw." Bell pointed at the image.

"Good eye. He was the first person we met here. Lives down the street from us." Principal Ono picked up her mug and took a slow sip. Chocolate clung to her upper lip. She erased it with a strategic swipe of her tongue. "He's an inventor."

"I've seen him working on the ridge. He's building something."

"Mm-hmm, his latest creation. He calls it the Windphone."

Bell stared at the man in the photograph, the steel frame glinting in the background.

"He sees it as a way to contact people we can't call with normal phones. People we've lost touch with, maybe, or...loved ones who've..."

Bell turned to her, and the principal stopped short.

Bell knew it was possible to use the wind to communicate. Once, she and Jay had hiked to opposite sides of Suarez Canyon. They were 150 feet apart, separated by the ravine, and when he whispered into the breeze, she heard every word as if he were whispering into her ear. The Inventor was hinting at a different sort of chasm.

"Dead people," Bell said.

"Well, he is an eccentric." Principal Ono reached for Bell's empty mug. "I'd take it with a grain of salt."

Bell thought of the trees tacked to her classroom wall. If it was somehow possible to speak with her mother directly, she wouldn't need her father's help. She could ask all the forbidden questions, catalog the details of her past, draw the most lifelike tree, and put Ashley in her place. Maybe then she wouldn't have to lie so much. Maybe then her life would make a little more sense. Five minutes earlier, she hadn't heard of anything like a Windphone. Now, it felt like the key to everything.

26

FEBRUARY 13, 2005

LEFT TO LOOK AFTER HERSELF ON A SUNDAY MORNING, BELL SET out on a reconnaissance hike while Jay was at work. About a mile and a half beyond the Hawk's Nest Overlook, she had a better view across the northwest corner of the valley. She wasn't looking for the tiger this time when she raised her field glasses toward the far ridge. She wanted to see the Inventor.

And there he was, dressed in his sleeveless orange poncho and wide-brimmed hat, unbothered by the steady showers. His forearms and hands were hairless and muscular, as if they belonged to a much younger man. He was moving brass fixtures and angular panes of blue glass into a tarpaulin tent he'd put up around the structure. When he was done, he rolled a cigarette, slid it between his lips, and gazed back across the gap, as if he sensed he was being watched. Then, he looked up into a split seam in the sky. Golden light flooded through it, attempting to pry the heavy clouds apart. He snapped open an old Zippo lighter, lit his cigarette, and peeled the tent back far enough for Bell to see the six-sided stainless steel frame glint in the sunshine spotlight.

Around that same time, Bolt woke up in the cave above Happy Camp Canyon to find the One-Legged Crow perched on her ivory belly, inspecting her fur for fleas and ticks. The crow found a fat tick on the inside of Bolt's back leg. Bolt watched her yank it out, then swallow it whole. The tiger chuffed in appreciation. One scrap of meat was all it took. They'd partnered up.

Bolt rolled over and watched sunlight seep toward her front paws. She yawned, reached forward, and sunk deep into her back hips. Then, she arched her back, yawned again, and sat upright. The clouds were scattering, and bright sun burned and beckoned.

She descended the rocky slope, where the air was thick with birdsong and rustling trees, bees, and the gurgling creek. The meal she'd eaten had energized her, and that deep mini hibernation had left her feeling refreshed. Her bruised sternum ached, and the cut above her ear had begun to fester, but the pain was tolerable.

Dragonflies skimmed the glassy surface of Camp Creek as Bolt followed it downstream through the canyon. She stopped to drink her fill, then peered up at the One-Legged Crow, who had landed at the top of a nearby sycamore. She climbed out of the cut and rubbed her haunches against thick stands of ceanothus, its buds balled up like tiny fists.

The tiger followed the water toward the subdivisions, parks, and shopping malls, and the crow followed. Suburban life played its symphony of honking horns and screeching tires. Doorbells chimed, and parks and playgrounds filled with chatter. Each sound was a reminder for Bolt to remain cautious and out of sight. She sloshed through two culverts and crept into the open space that unfurled between the Cummins Aerospace campus and the Alisaw Valley Country Club. An overpowering scent stretched toward her. A herd of Holstein dairy cows had been set loose to graze.

Bolt couldn't survive off roadkill alone. She needed to take advantage of every opportunity, and her awakened instinct demanded she track the herd. She took care to remain downwind and edge closer. She got within twenty yards of a grazing Holstein, a silky web of drool unspooling from its bottom lip, and lowered her belly to the earth. She'd thought she was well camouflaged, but Bolt was still a novice hunter. The sun was shining, and after such a long drought, the savanna wasn't very thick. The cow caught a glimpse of her through one clouded eye. Half-chewed grass tumbled from its gaping maw and clung to its foaming lips as it wheeled around, brayed with terror, and triggered a stampede.

The young cows weren't nearly as fast as the old horses, but they were bigger, younger, and stronger. Bolt remembered what it was like to be kicked by an old horse, but she bounded after the cows anyway. Top gear wasn't necessary to pick up yardage as the entire procession bore down on Tierra Rejada Road. This time, there was no fence to impede Bolt's prey and no vehicles to transform fleeing cows into big cat food. Every burly Holstein maintained its footing as they all ran for their lives toward the rear of the Reagan Presidential Library.

The terrified herd clamored up the limestone steps of the massive Spanish-style compound that loomed over the valley and gathered on its rear terrace. They turned to face their stalker as one immovable force. Bolt remained halfway down the hill, tucked into the tender grass. Good thing because a member of the museum's security staff soon appeared, alarmed at the intrusion. He searched the slope for the source of cattle anxiety, but from his vantage point, all he could see was a solitary crow arcing in tight circles.

Bolt turned tail and crept away. For hours, she moved through the recovering savanna in slow motion. She avoided all structures and roads and reached an old-growth oak grove rooted into a crease in the Alisaw Hills that felt like a safe place to take cover until nightfall.

She attempted to remain alert and watchful, but she was exhausted, and the warm afternoon won out. Her eyes closed of their own accord. She was roused an hour later by the shrieking crow and growling chainsaws. Six men dressed in faded jeans and long-sleeve work shirts were cutting down two oak trees less than fifty feet away. Bolt darted behind the largest tree in the woodland

and peeked around the trunk to see one of the men point toward a string of her fresh tracks meandering through the trees.

"¡Cuidado! Hay un puma por aca," he said. The sawyers killed their chainsaws and huddled around the tiger's tracks. Bolt assessed her position. There was less than thirty feet of open ground between her and the chaparral. She covered the distance in a few strides and bashed through the sagebrush. The men sprinted downhill to their trucks, leaving Bolt to the bushes, where she couldn't stop shaking. The tiger was no longer a shadow. She'd been spotted, and now she would be hunted.

27

VALENTINE'S DAY, 2005

FINGERS OF FOG THREADED THROUGH THE ALISAW HILLS AS JAY waited on the shoulder of Tierra Rejada Road. He pounded his boots on the asphalt. His breath merged with a mist that was sticky and cold. A single afternoon of sunshine had managed to convert the El Niño storm clouds into sponges that felt like they had been dunked into a cooler of ice water and filled to dripping.

The dim yellow headlights of a beat-up late-model Datsun pickup cut through the gloom as it rolled toward him and screeched to a stop. A short, thin fellow wearing Dickies jeans, a creased blue button-down, a secondhand Nike running hat, and well-worn pale-leather work boots hopped out. He was alone.

"Warden Tern, Fish and Wildlife." Jay extended his hand. The man checked both sides of the road.

"Luis Vallejo," he said with a thick Central American accent, shaking Jay's hand. Most Central American immigrants in Ventura County were undocumented, and weren't in the practice of calling law enforcement with tips. The fact that Luis had done so and was willing to return to an area where he'd seen a big cat demanded Jay's respect and discretion.

Luis led the way up the steep grade into the hills. Jay followed armed with his Olympus and a pack stuffed with evidence bags, tarps, and stakes. He was also strapped with his dart rifle and his Remington shotgun. Jay smelled wet sawdust and regarded one of the oaks in mid-destruction. It had been topped and chopped but was still alive.

"You were hired to clear all these trees?" Jay asked.

Luis nodded.

It was illegal to chop down native oaks in the state of California, but some developers ignored the law, and they tended to hire undocumented workers to do it. If anyone called them out, they blamed labor. Typically, the destruction of native plants was something Jay would investigate. Oak trees were vital habitat for mammals and birds who ate their acorns or lived in the canopy of healthy specimens and the trunks of decaying trees. Jay had handled a half dozen cases like this one. Krull had too. His boss was always happy to pin it on labor. Jay did his best to make it stick to the landowners. Today, he'd have to ignore it.

Luis was several paces ahead, pointing to the ground behind the largest tree. Most of the tracks had eroded, but three were still there in the clay soil. The sizes weren't consistent, but that wasn't necessarily a bad thing. Big cats tended to have larger front paws, which meant two of the three tracks were likely from the same stride. And that stride looked massive.

"That's a big puma you saw, amigo."

After speaking to Luis's teenage son over the phone, Jay had felt deflated. Finally, a reliable witness had seen what had to be the same huge cat, and it turned out to be a mountain lion after all. Or so he was led to believe.

"No era un puma," Luis confessed. "Is orange. Orange with…black stripe."

This was it. The break Jay had been waiting for. He chuckled and peered into the trampled sagebrush. "That is not what your son told me."

Luis laughed too. The notion of a tiger running loose in Alisaw was a laughable offense. That was why Jay had refused to believe it for so long, but he could no longer deny that Bell had been telling the truth. And that felt good.

Jay captured images, tented the prints with tarps and stakes, and cordoned off the entire area with caution tape. He sent two incoming calls to voicemail as he got down on his hands and knees to sift through the underbrush and search tree trunks for snags of fur. Empty-handed, Jay put Luis on tape. The new tracks coupled with another eyewitness account would have to be enough.

"I'll keep your name out of my report," Jay said after they'd returned to their trucks, "but it would help if you'd keep all this to yourself for another forty-eight hours. We don't want to cause a panic."

"Por supuesto," Luis said.

After Luis drove off, Jay smoothed his map on the hood of his F250 and added another X. The oak woodland would remain off-limits to its owners now that it was part of his investigation, and given how word traveled on the street, he doubted the developers would be able to find another crew willing to clear it anytime soon. Which meant the tiger had inadvertently saved it. Jay measured the distance between the marks on his map. Compared to the pens he'd seen on the Glenn property, the tiger's new territory probably felt infinite.

He was tempted to believe his fortunes had turned, but on his drive home, he checked his voicemail. There was a new message waiting for him. The number had a Hollywood area code.

"Mr. Tern, it's Dr. Ambrose. I'm afraid Bell's scan was inconclusive, and we'll need to have her back in for another one. Nothing to be overly alarmed about at this stage. We're still ruling things out. See you both soon."

28

FEBRUARY 15, 2005

"THERE IS A SIBERIAN TIGER LOOSE IN ALISAW VALLEY, AND THIS IS the team that is going to find it." Lieutenant Krull paced the stage, hair slicked back, uniform crisp. Four dozen game wardens from nine counties looked on from the auditorium seats. Jay watched them exchange glances and murmur to one another. Some looked anxious, others curious. "Now, if you repeat that to anyone outside this building, you will be written up," Krull said. "We're describing it to the press as a feline situation. Use that. It goes down nice and smooth."

The new evidence had turned out to be more than enough for the honchos in Sacramento to authorize a robust search of the area mapped out in Jay's report. Incident command was set up at Mission Butte Middle School, which was about three and a half miles from Strauss Horse Ranch, four miles from Dry Creek Ranch, six miles from the oak woodland, and across the street from Bell's school. Jay wasn't surprised when Lieutenant Krull was named warden in charge.

On their way into the auditorium a few minutes earlier, Krull had stopped in front of a small scrum of reporters and television cameras. When asked if he was referring to a mountain lion, the lieutenant had not said no, which led to welcome morning news reports of a lingering cougar.

"So far, so good," he'd told Jay when they were out of earshot of the reporters. "We do not need escaped tiger stories terrorizing our valley. Sacramento frowns on that kind of thing."

Jay couldn't quibble with that, but the more compelling reason to be vague had to do with the Glenns. They hadn't reported a tiger missing, and it was smart not to alienate them any further. They may still turn out to be useful.

Krull ceded the floor to Jay. He stood in front of an enlarged set of his maps tacked to three rolling whiteboards and offered a virtual tour of the tiger's known range. The nine-mile-long, six-mile-wide corridor ran from the Glenns' property in the east to Target in the west and from Dry Creek Ranch in the north to the Reagan Presidential Library and the old-growth oak woodland in the Alisaw Hills in the south. Jay described the contours of the land and the flow of water in Alisaw Valley. His audience was rapt.

Krull was more decorated and enjoyed the higher rank, but word of Jay's unrecognized heroics, fitness, and field work had circulated for years and inspired a sterling reputation among his colleagues. Jay knew how much that gnawed at Krull. The younger wardens had even studied some of his casework at the academy—primarily, his weekslong investigation of the lucrative local squid industry that began when he discovered a spent shell casing during a routine inspection of a squid trawler. He'd uncovered numerous by-catch violations. Dolphins caught in nets had suffocated. Sea lions dumped out of the nets and onto the deck alive had been shot in the head and tossed overboard with the dolphin corpses. Jay took his time and built a landmark case.

"We've identified three hundred ninety-seven landowners in the search area—that includes seven ranches, an orchard, a country club, and a cemetery. We'll need team leaders to secure access to each property," Jay said. "The success of this search will come down to the tenacity and intelligence of the people in this room. We can't use hounds because one swipe from the tiger would kill them. And this rain has been so relentless, we can't necessarily rely on infrared air support."

"Correction." Krull stepped forward and snatched the mic from Jay. "I've got the latest ten-day forecast here. The weather is supposed to clear up. We will have air support soon. Remember, if we all maintain a positive, can-do attitude, we'll have this wrapped up quickly. Now let's move out!"

Krull clapped his hands and hooted, and most of the rank and file joined in the hooyah. Jay waded quietly into the orchestra pit to direct team leaders toward a stash of gear that included GPS units, walkie-talkies, ammunition, rain ponchos, field glasses, and canteens. Meanwhile, a tall, slender woman who had been lurking in the shadows peeled herself off the back wall and made her way down the aisle.

"Before we all shuffle off, I, too, have a correction." Her voice floated on the wings of an accent that sounded South Asian poured through a London filter, and it froze all activity in the orchestra pit. She wore black equestrian breeches, a cashmere turtleneck, and a charcoal overcoat. She held a black duffel with her right hand and gripped the handle of a long burgundy case with her left. She had the attractive, corporate look of a news anchor or a catalog model, but the gear didn't fit. "Your tiger is not a Siberian."

"And who the hell are you?" Krull asked as he sucked in his belly enough that his overstarched uniform crinkled audibly.

"Sorry. I meant 'feline situation.' Your feline situation is not a Siberian." She stepped on stage, slipped out of her overcoat, and extended her hand. "Geeta Murthy, Wildlife Services. Is this the 'command' 'post'? I was told to meet a Lieutenant Krull at the 'command' 'post.'" She used air quotes around "command" and "post."

"I'm Krull." He shook her hand, albeit reluctantly. "Typical feds. Wildlife Services promises me two of their best guys and sends me a lady from Rodeo Drive. We have a good idea who the owners are and what breed the feline is. Tern, show her the permit."

Jay had copies of all his relevant reports stapled into packets for visiting wardens to read through. There were two left. He bounded up the steps and handed one to her.

Geeta accepted it as she surveyed the uniforms in the room. It was bloody 2005, and she was the only woman on the hunt, as usual. Krull stepped closer than necessary, snatched the packet out of her hands, and fumbled with it until he found the permit.

"See, right there: Siberian." She glared at him for a few seconds before allowing a patient smile to spread across her face. He wasn't the first bloated misogynist, stinking of hair gel and cologne, she'd met on the job. When she wasn't working for the USDA, she led big-game hunting trips in Africa, India, and Central Asia, and they turned up there, too, among her fellow guides, safari support staff, and elite clientele. Age, income, rank, nationality…none of it made any difference. They were everywhere, these simple men. She'd won an Olympic medal in skeet shooting and hunted her first big cat as a teenager, and she was aware of no one who had put down more large felines in the last ten years anywhere on earth than Geeta Murthy, yet men like Krull assumed she was the one out of her league.

"Oh, I've seen the permit," she said. "Washington sent me the case file yesterday. I read it on the plane." Geeta moved as she spoke, and the wardens watched her every step. She was used to that kind of thing too. She cut an imposing figure at nearly six feet tall with sharp features, high cheekbones, a slender build, and a tight black braid running down her back. "By now, you may have guessed that I come from India, where nearly four thousand wild tigers still live. Those are Bengal tigers, of course, which is one of nine subspecies. Think of the subs as purebreds, unlike the tigers here in America, who were not captured from wild stock but bred in captivity. Therefore, the tiger you are after is definitely not Siberian, Bengal, Amur, or Sumatran. It is an American tiger, one of twelve thousand born right here in the glorious melting pot that we all call home."

"So you're some kind of tiger expert," Krull said.

"I knew you'd catch up, Lieutenant."

"You're saying it's a mutt," Jay said.

She nodded.

"Okay, fine, so it's not a purebred. Does that make it easier to kill?" Krull asked.

"Normally, yes," she said. "American tigers are genetically programmed for speed, stealth, and lethal power, but they aren't as accustomed to using their equipment. However, yours has been on the loose for at least four weeks, if memory serves, which means its instincts and natural abilities are emerging from dormancy." Geeta paused in front of the maps and studied the annotations, which detailed the dates, times, and activity recorded at each relevant pinpoint. "We're not the only ones with this map. Our cat has been building a working map in its head too. Do we know if it has eaten?"

"We believe so," Jay said. "After animal control removed the horse from Suarez Road, it looked like a chunk of flesh was missing."

"Oh, yes, fresh roadkill. Nevertheless, it has got to be hungry, desperate, frustrated, perhaps even angry—at its owners, at humanity. In my experience, all of that would make it lethal. It has already killed once."

"It didn't kill anybody," Jay said.

"It caused a fatal collision, Warden Tern," Geeta said, reading his name tag. "According to your report. My point is that it might be extremely difficult to find our target, and the more pressure we put on it, the deadlier it will become. The good news, gentlemen, is that I've worked sixty-seven cases for Wildlife Services, and all targets were eliminated within seventy-two hours." She'd decided it was better not to mention that when the job was done, Wildlife Services would award her a $175,000 bonus on top of her regular rate of $5,000 per day.

"That's the second time we've talked about killing an animal we haven't even begun to search for," Jay said.

"Damn right," Krull said. "No more human blood."

"You've never seen what a desperate tiger can do to somebody, Warden Tern. I have." Geeta addressed the group. "Their jaws are twice as powerful as an African lion's. A simple swat from their paws can break a human neck. Their claws are so sharp they can disembowel their prey with only the slightest effort."

"Let that sink in, people," Krull said. "Stay vigilant! We have a deadly animal out there."

While Jay continued to equip warden teams with gear, Krull offered Geeta the choice of a pickup truck or an all-terrain vehicle to use on the hunt. She had other ideas. "I hunt on horseback, Lieutenant. I'm surprised no one mentioned it."

"We don't have horses readily available, Murthy," Krull said. "We aren't a stable."

"It's nonnegotiable," she said.

Krull sucked his teeth.

"Tern!" Jay glanced up at them from the orchestra pit. "Find the lady a horse."

29

GEETA HUNG BACK AT THE TRUCK AND WATCHED JAY GREET BEN, who looked tense and had a Remington rifle slung over his shoulder. Three other ranch hands patrolled the property with shotguns. Smart. Someone had to protect the horses with a tiger on the loose.

She spotted what looked to be a thoroughbred and some quarter horses resting beneath a large valley oak in the pasture, guarded by one of the ranch hands. Three of the horses were male—two geldings and a stallion. The stallion was the thoroughbred, which meant he had both speed and endurance. Geeta headed in their direction.

It had taken her years to accept that her ears were useless on a hunt. Unlike those of other predators, human ears told nothing but lies. In the forest, savanna, desert, or out on the ice, sound came at you from all angles, riding wind currents or bouncing off tree trunks, rock walls, and glaciers. She'd chased too many stale echoes and false footsteps to count. Cats, on the other hand, could process each distinct sound no matter how layered and were able to discern exactly where they were all coming from. Tracking a tiger, or any big cat, from the seat of a loud quad or behind the wheel of a clunky pickup was as silly as wearing a bright-orange vest in the evergreens and expecting to sneak up on a herd of elk. Plus, Geeta grew up on horseback.

She smooched her lips and clicked her tongue. The stallion lifted his head and trotted toward her with his ears pinned back. An anxious ranch hand ran after him. Geeta raised her palm in reassurance, locked eyes with the edgy stallion, swayed her hips in two-four time, and broke into song.

Her song of choice was "Heroes" by David Bowie, albeit a modified version. The stallion stopped cold and watched her with big brown eyes, his head swaying back and forth. Still singing softly, Geeta extended the back of her hand. She didn't favor thoroughbreds in rugged country, but he was clearly the alpha, and she needed to kiss his ring before she could inspect the others in peace.

Before long, all three males were gathered around Geeta, eating grass out of her hands. When the stallion jostled to keep the others in line, she whispered in his ear, and he promptly lowered his head onto her shoulder with something approaching an apology. The other two males were quarter horses. Geeta had always been partial to the American quarter horse. They were fast, hearty, and versatile. They excelled on the racetrack, were used by pioneers during the Gold Rush, and didn't spook easily. But lying beneath a tree in the distance was a fourth horse with a glossy chocolate coat and a back end that looked like it had been splashed in white paint by Jackson Pollock, then peppered with black ink. She was a young filly, and a beauty.

Geeta left the boys behind and sashayed toward her new target. She swam through the air as she sang her take on a Bowie classic, a song she considered solely responsible for keeping her sane and alive between her seventeenth and twenty-fourth birthdays. She'd belted it out in a smattering of depressing rented rooms, dorms, Olympiad housing units, closet-sized studios, and studio-size walk-in closets. Not to mention all those airplane, train, and bus lavatories and rifle-range latrines. She'd performed it in a handful of karaoke bars and once on stage in Kolkata with a trending Bowie tribute band called Stardust. At some point, she'd noticed her horses liked it too. She'd sung it to the spooked mixed-breeds she and her Fortune 500 clients rode on hunts in the Maasai Mara. She'd used it to encourage a confused Arabian in the Sahara and soothe a gorgeous, if exhausted, Bhutia in Kashmir. And now, she was serenading what looked to be the product of a tryst between a quarter horse and an Appaloosa in a suburban Southern California paddock.

The filly gathered herself and stood. To Geeta's surprise, she was nearly as tall as the thoroughbred. She stretched her neck forward and nuzzled Geeta's fist with her moist, stubbly nose. Geeta stroked the filly's platinum-blond mane, then crouched and ran her hands up the horse's lower legs and rippling thighs. The Appaloosa was at one time the choice breed of the indigenous Nez Perce nation, who used their hearty horses to trade with tribes from the Oregon coast all the way to Montana. They weren't especially fast, but their endurance was mind-boggling. She'd read accounts of them covering seventy miles a day for weeks at a time.

Geeta peeled back the animal's lips and examined her teeth. She drummed her fingers along the filly's flanks and inspected all four hooves before leading the horse around the paddock to study her gait. Geeta coaxed her forward by placing the tip of her finger on the filly's chin. The horse moved with a light and fluid grace.

"That one is called Billie!" Ben called out through cupped hands. Geeta turned and waved in acknowledgment, then whispered in Billie's one speckled ear. The men watched from a distance as the horse raised her front right hoof, and Geeta used it to mount her, bareback.

Geeta led Billie to the barn where she slipped into a fresh black turtleneck, zipped her camo jacket, and laced up her riding boots. She found a clean brush to work with and hummed as she brushed Billie down. She needed her mount to feel cared for. She selected a chocolate-brown wool saddle pad from a clean pile on a shelf and draped it over Billie's back. Geeta grew up riding English, but Ben only kept western saddles, and she knew how to ride like a cowboy too. She found a well-oiled, black leather saddle and adjusted the girth so it wasn't loose but didn't chafe or constrict Billie's stride. Then, she dropped her stirrups, looped a bridle around Billie's neck, and slid the bit into her mouth.

With Billie's head leaning on her shoulder, Geeta opened her compact, added a touch of gloss to her lips, puckered to smooth out the coat, and snapped the compact shut again. Then, she knelt in the hay with her back to the barn door and thumbed the proper numbers—090988—into the digital combination lock on that long burgundy case. Inside was her beloved matte-black M-14 .308-caliber sniper rifle with a night vision scope, ideal for taking down big game from hundreds of yards away. The trick would be finding the cat, which was her secondary reason for renting Billie. The tiger already had a taste for horse meat.

"Why not carry a dart gun?" Jay was silhouetted in the open barn door. Geeta rose to her feet holding her rifle.

"It wasn't in the specs I received from the agency, for one. What did your friend say about the horse?"

"Ben? He said that you certainly know how to handle them. That his stallion is rough on everybody, and that Billie here cannot be bothered to do a damn thing she doesn't want to. And he said that you can ride her, so long as I vouch for you."

"And did you?"

"I told him that I don't know you at all."

"Very well," said Geeta. She slung her rifle over her shoulder and closed her left hand around Billie's reins. "I'll organize things with him myself."

"That's probably best," Jay said. He pulled a walkie-talkie from his holster and handed it to her. "You know, if you do manage to find the tiger, the safest play might be to pin it down and call for backup. I'll come in behind you with darts."

She smiled coolly. "Thank you, Warden Tern, but I won't be requiring any further assistance from you."

"I didn't mean to insinuate that you needed help..."

"None of you ever *mean* to, but you do say it, don't you?" She led Billie out into the muted gray light and glanced back over her shoulder. "Don't worry. This will all be over quite soon."

"DON'T WORRY," JAY MUTTERED TO HIMSELF AS HE PUT HIS TRUCK in gear and rolled down Ben's driveway. "Quite soon!" Horns blared as he bulled his way into traffic and headed east. He wasn't being presumptuous. She was. This *feline situation* had been going on for nearly a month. The tiger may not be wild yet, but it was getting there. Geeta had said so herself while revealing that Jay was the only one in the entire search party concerned for the tiger's well-being.

He couldn't imagine breaking the news to Bell that her tiger had been shot dead. Especially considering her inconclusive scan and its horrifying implications. He'd ignored her pleas for weeks and wasted precious time. Now, there were fifty-some rifles and one expert big cat hunter on the ground amped to eliminate it. There was only one solution: Jay had to find Bell's tiger first.

The back tires sprayed gravel as Jay veered up the Glenns' driveway, where he was forced to stop short. Aubrey's truck was parked diagonally, blocking access. Jay hopped out with the engine still running and darted around the truck and up the gravel drive. Eden stepped out of the slanted shadows of the wild walnut trees that grew on either side of the driveway, rifle in hand. Jay froze. Though the barrel of her gun was angled down, she was in a shooter's stance. Her feet were set apart. Her weight was balanced, and her small, hard eyes looked mean. He felt danger buzzing close.

"The hunt continues, I see." Jay didn't bother blunting the edge to his voice. Ben had mentioned that he'd watched two people search the Camp Creek corridor most of the night and that they'd been armed for a hunt. Then, this morning, Jay's camera traps were nowhere to be found. The only people who could have known about the tracks on Dry Creek Ranch last night were Miriam, Jay, Krull, and the Glenns. If he sounded like a man down to his last nerve, that was because he was, and for some reason, it made Eden smile.

"I don't know what you mean by that, game warden. Carrying a permitted rifle on your own property is legal." She was dressed in jeans and a purple cotton blouse, which the steady rain had pasted to her pink arms and neck. She looked sleep deprived and stressed.

"You and Aubrey were walking Camp Creek last night."

"Warden, we are awfully tired of this...harassment."

"You've got it wrong, Mrs. Glenn. I'm not here to harass you," Jay said. "You made a mistake. You're scared. Talk to me. I can help you fix this."

"Help us? So far you've invaded our privacy and ordered us to foster our innocent animals—including the lynx you *shot*—on short notice and at our own expense, and all we have done is comply, comply, comply." Eden stepped toward him and began walking him back down the driveway toward his truck. "Now, I am sorry that you have a rogue mountain lion on the loose and that someone has died. I really am. But our animals are our entire lives, and if one of them was missing, we would tell you. If you are not willing to believe that—to believe us—then you cannot help us. Which is why I'm asking you to leave." Jay was practically pinned to the driver's side door of Aubrey's truck when Eden turned on her heel and headed toward their double-wide.

"Anything you say that leads to the safe recovery of your cat would be a very good thing for you and Aubrey. Bolt's gotta be hungry by now. Maybe even starving to death. Tell me what to feed him. I want to catch him alive before somebody kills him!"

Eden stopped and looked back. A dazed smile flickered on her lips, like the nanosecond between frames of a black-and-white film. "Oh, Warden Tern. Bolt died two years ago."

Jay felt his world tilt as he watched Eden Glenn recede into the trees. This case had been murky from the beginning, complicated by fuzzy permits, anonymous witnesses, wrecked cars, dead broke horses, pounding headaches, CT scans, a Siberian lynx, Bell's unhinged imagination, and too much rain. Was Eden finally telling the truth? Had Bolt died? When? Two years ago? Last night? Where did certainty end and wishful thinking begin?

It had been a long while since Jay had been certain of anything. Ever since he and Bell had been left alone, he'd done his best to cope. He'd turned their cabin into a lifeboat, a small ship they could navigate together to seek out and collect moments of beauty, exhilaration, and joy. They kept to, and relied on, themselves. They stayed close to trails and trees. Nature and their own independence were the only moorings they had, and he'd always told himself that was enough. But he knew that even the soundest lifeboats could break apart in the fiercest storms and that there was no such thing as a thriving independent organism in the wild world. That truth had haunted Jay in his darkest hours countless times over the past six years. Two was not a big enough number for a family of modern primates to thrive. Because where there were only two, eventually there would be just one. He'd considered what would happen to Bell if he got sick or dropped dead, but he had never dared contemplate what would happen if he were the one left alone.

Bolt died two years ago. Truth or lie, he scribbled Eden's statement in his notebook and tagged it with a date and time. He knew it would be impossible to verify because there was also no such thing as a death certificate for an American tiger.

30

BY MIDDAY, THE VALLEY CRAWLED WITH GAME WARDENS. JAY combed the Camp Creek corridor. Geeta scanned the rain-soaked savanna from Billie's saddle. And from the relative comfort of Incident Command, Lieutenant Krull barked into his radio and demanded everyone's location at the top and bottom of the hour.

Bolt, meanwhile, was miles from the active search zone, completely dry, out of sight. On her trek home from the oak grove, she had been extremely cautious. No human or animal had tracked her. The search party could look where they liked, but as long as Bolt stayed put, she would remain free from human interference, control, and violence. If only her belly would quit rumbling.

When Bell stepped off the bus in front of the Mystic Heights gateway later that afternoon, Jay was waiting in his mud-stained uniform. Soaked to the bone, he leaned against the hood of his idling work truck, cell phone glued to his ear, a staticky walkie-talkie in his off hand. Bell noticed the other parents staring. The entire valley was on edge. At school, she'd overheard teachers debating whether it was safe to take the trash out at night. Jay nodded at Bell and buckled into the cab of his patrol truck. He wrapped the call as she climbed into the passenger seat. A second later, his radio chirped.

While driving them home, Jay helped a pair of visiting game wardens lost in the bush find their bearings. Miriam called for an update on the search as he was reheating a batch of frozen veggie chili on the stove. Bell slipped the wooden spoon from his fingers, climbed the step ladder, and watched the rain as she stirred. The muted light gave the showers a depth of field.

"I know I put you in a tough spot with your homework assignment," Jay said. He had turned off his cell phone and was busy prepping garnish. Bell tasted the chili for warmth, turned off the burner, and scooped it into two bowls. Jay sprinkled chopped red onions and tender sprigs of cilantro on top.

"I don't even care about that dumb assignment," Bell said.

"Oh good...because...I mean...I don't really..." Jay reminded her of a novice swimmer, flailing and struggling to stay afloat. "Not right now anyway...you know?"

Bell was his lifeguard. "Dad, seriously. You have much more important things to do."

"That's not it."

"Yes," she said, "it is." She slid one of the bowls in front of him. "Eat. Anyway, I can make this stuff up. Ms. Levine will never know or care." Jay nodded and managed a half dozen bites before his radio crackled again.

"Tern. Come in. Over."

Jay arched an astonished eyebrow but ignored his lieutenant and kept eating. Bell pretended to laugh while irritating questions populated her brain. She'd overheard Jay mention a professional tracker to Miriam, and she wanted to know who he was and if he planned to kill her tiger. Then there was the family tree situation. Had Ms. Levine called him? No, it had to have been Principal Ono. The hot chocolate and haircut were a ploy to get closer to her and meddle. She should have seen that coming.

"Tern!" Krull barked. "What's your twenty?"

"That sounds urgent," Bell said.

"I'll be back late." Jay swallowed one last spoonful and grabbed his coat and radio. "Lights out at nine."

An hour later, Bell was lying on the living room floor, staring up at the beamed ceiling. The tin roof rumbled like a rhythm section as she pictured teams of wardens and one expert tracker wandering the drenched savanna. She wished she could join them. She flipped onto her belly and opened her drawing pad to the unfinished family tree, which she'd dog-eared at the lower right-hand corner.

Of course, Bell thought. *He was so obvious! The most private person in Alisaw Valley had broken his own sacred code and snooped my pages without permission!*

She stood in a huff and scanned the room. She had plenty of time. Who knew what she'd find with a thorough search. She crossed to his closet door, grabbed the knob, and turned. It opened right up.

The walk-in was just large enough for a small dresser, two overhead wraparound shelves, and two hanging rods, one on either side. Standing on the stepladder, Bell took down his hanging clothes and emptied the pockets. She found a blue whale lapel pin without the backing in the inside pocket of the charcoal blazer he wore once a year, along with a receipt from a late-night run to Lily's taqueria. She traced that to the annual CDFW dinner he was obligated to attend. In his favorite black denim jacket, she found a pharmacy receipt for cough syrup from when she had strep throat and another for pain medication to help with her headaches. She discovered an unpaid parking ticket from Westward Beach in a pair of chinos. She smiled at that one.

His dresser was next. It had three drawers: one for underwear and socks, another for shirts and sweatshirts, and the bottom one for long pants. Predictably, most of the clothes were rumpled and tangled, and she set about smoothing and folding crewnecks, flannel button-downs, and hoodies, which she stacked in tidy piles. Once a given drawer was empty, she tapped the sides and base, but she found no false bottoms or secret compartments. Not that she expected to find anything so significant. Maybe she'd get lucky and find an envelope with a few pictures, a letter, an heirloom. Something to hold in her hands.

Her hope was fading by the time she reached Jay's jeans in the bottom drawer. She folded and set them aside and palpated the wood. Again, nothing. To be sure, she tried to yank the drawers out completely. She wanted to inspect the backs and bottoms, but they were anchored to the rails. Luckily, her arms were just long enough to reach into the guts of the dresser and feel around behind the drawers. She moved from the top down and made four passes on each drawer. During her final pass on the bottom drawer, her left pinky caught a metallic edge. She extended her arm as far as it would go and grazed a thin piece of metal with her middle finger. Something was taped to the back. She batted at the object the way a cat might. The tape loosened. Then it tore, and a vintage copper key fell into the palm of her hand. She had no idea what it unlocked, but she was determined to find out.

Above the hangers, the wraparound shelves were piled with clear tubs of camping and sports gear. She wasn't strong enough to wriggle the tubs down without falling backward, so she took inventory from the top of the stepladder but didn't see anything that sparked interest. The gun safe was in the rear of the closet, but she'd seen it wide open too many times to believe there was anything inside but weapons and ammo. Abandoning the closet, she turned her attention to Jay's desk. She jimmied the locks on his side drawers and filing cabinets with her pocketknife and found almost nothing but casework. There was one file marked *Personal*. It held their birth certificates, income and property tax forms, mortgage details, a pink slip for the Chevy, and a faded blueprint folded into quarters. She opened the blueprint and found creased plans for an addition to the Tern cabin. It called for a second story, a full garage, a tiered back deck with a hot tub and outdoor kitchen, and an outdoor shower below that. The plans had been designed by an architect and approved by city hall in April 1995. Four months before she was born.

The kitchen was next. She tore through the knotty pinewood pantry and removed clasped metal containers filled with oats, flour, rice, dried lentils, and black beans, along with jars of house-canned tomatoes. She patted down the walls and shelves. She opened the kitchen cabinets, removed dishes and glassware, and climbed onto the tiled counter to peer into the high cabinet above the fridge, where Jay kept his Buffalo Trace bourbon, Michter's rye, and Fortaleza tequila but no family secrets.

In the bathroom, she knelt on worn 1980s linoleum, opened the chipped powder-blue cabinets, and dug through spare rolls of toilet paper and packs of cotton buds, Band-Aids and athletic tape. The drawers were sparse, containing only new toothbrushes, tweezers, Jay's safety razors, and a beard trimmer. The medicine cabinet was too shallow to hide much, but she looked anyway and inventoried the pill bottles, ointments, and herbal tinctures she'd seen hundreds of times before: her headache meds, his unused Prozac, echinacea, and yin chiao. Medicines old and new, over-the-counter and prescription, reliable and iffy that had been deployed to this troubled pair over the years, with mixed results.

The only room left to toss was her own, but she already knew every inch of that one. Unless he was hiding his secrets right under her nose. She dove into her closet without the care she'd taken with her father's things. She dumped drawers of underwear and socks on the floor and piled secondhand, ill-fitting shorts, jeans, overalls, hoodies, and cotton t-shirts onto her bed. She swept books and field guides from the shelves and threw sneakers, roller skates, hiking boots, cleats, and her black baseball mitt against the wall. The only items left standing were a jar filled with shells and stones, her mirror, and a fanned-out stack of recent illustrations on her drafting table.

"One picture," she screamed. "One! Is that too much to ask?"

For years, Bell had fantasized about stumbling upon a forgotten family photograph with a clear image of her mother. She knew exactly what she would do with it. She'd begin by sketching an outline on vellum, then rub it with a soft black pencil to transfer it onto good stock before inking the lines of her mother's face and neck until she was no longer a mystery.

Her mother was the one subject Bell could never draw. She made up stories, conjured occupations, adventures, and hobbies, but she couldn't illustrate the evidence because she had no frame of reference. Jay made sure of that. Her whole life, she'd considered her dad to be strong in every way. Now, she felt his sharpest, most glaring weakness. It had cut her deeply and left her with a pooling wound.

Drained, she turned toward her nightstand and read the digital clock. It was after ten, and the cabin was in total chaos. There was more searching to do. She hadn't been in the toolshed yet and still had the carport to deal with. This was not over, but Jay would be home around midnight, which gave her less than two hours to make everything right.

She shoveled her own mess into the closet, hit the bathroom and kitchen with a rag and sponge, and restocked his dresser drawers with his folded and fluffed clothes. Bell wasn't trying to cover her tracks. She wanted Jay to notice the surface and miss the deeper meaning. She was still dusting his boots and dress shoes when she heard his engine rumbling up the driveway. The glow of his headlights arced through the living room windows as he crested the final incline. Anxious, she set the last boot down on the shoe rack in his closet, turned to sprint back to her room, and caught her foot on the dresser's front leg. She fell forward. Her knees and elbows smacked the wood floor hard and jarred a wobbly panel slightly askew. The plank extended below the dresser to the wall. Bell felt an urge to slide it out. She didn't want to wait to peer down into the joists to see what may or may not be there. But she was out of time.

Jay pulled into the carport. Bell jiggled the plank until it fell flush. His engine died, and his car door slammed. She swiped the cut on her knee with two fingers, blotted the floorboard with her blood, and dashed to her room. Her heart thumped as she heard the front door open and close. She wriggled out of her jeans under the covers. She heard footsteps and shut her eyes. She'd left her bedroom door cracked on purpose, knowing that gave him permission to check in on her. The hinges creaked as he pushed the door open a bit further. Bell yawned as if waking from a peaceful dream.

"Did you find her?"

Jay shook his head.

Bell shut her eyes gently and rolled away from him. When she heard the shower running, she kicked off her sheets and crossed to her bedroom window. Rain was still falling, and somewhere out there, a tiger was still free.

31

FEBRUARY 16, 2005

STORM CLOUDS SMOTHERED THE MOONLIGHT, AND THE SKY WAS dark as coal as Lieutenant Krull piloted his ATV along the western edge of Highway 23 at half past one in the morning. Needles of rain stung his face and neck, and they felt damn good. So far, his small army of game wardens and one uppity tracker had delivered exactly zilch. Let them all sleep like little children. Lieutenant Corey Krull was on the hunt.

The warden teams had filed into Incident Command before midnight, soiled and soaked. Any enthusiasm they'd begun the day with had faded into a realization they were searching for a ghost. They had worked the neighborhoods, shopping centers, and ranches east of Highway 23 all day and night. They'd canvassed door to door, checked out all the quirky tips that flooded the phone banks, and never come close to a promising lead.

Geeta was already on stage, her coat dripping onto the boards, hands on hips, one muddy riding boot tapping the ground, when Krull ducked away from the news cameras in the parking lot and stepped inside. Geeta didn't mask her contempt as she regarded

Krull's still-crisp and mostly dry uniform, stained only with chocolate frosting.

"Hard day on the job?" she asked before placing her rifle back into its case and snapping it shut. Krull tracked the laughter rippling through the ranks as he joined her on stage.

"And is our community better off now than when you showed up this morning?" He stepped close enough to hover over her. "You know, I put in three seasons with Wildlife Services as a tracker in Idaho in the nineties. Easiest job I've ever had."

"Idaho." Geeta hooked one arm through the shoulder straps of her duffel and stood. "You killed wolves."

"We tracked wolves, yes." Krull sucked his teeth. "If they messed with livestock."

"Right. You 'tracked' them," she said, redeploying her strategic air quotes.

"Technically, I'm still on the Wildlife Services roster. Which means that if I get the tiger, I collect the bonus. Not you. Which would be unfortunate, given that nasty divorce of yours. Too bad about the pesky prenup." Krull had done some googling and called Jason Caudle, an old buddy who worked with Wildlife Services in DC. Murthy needed that bonus given her current credit card imbalances and lack of cash flow from her CEO husband with a knocked-up mistress.

"Lieutenant," Geeta said, "tracking down a tiger in the rain is quite a different thing from taking target practice from a helicopter." She placed her hands on his shoulders and backed him up two steps. "So be a good lad, and stay out of my way."

Krull ran that conversation on a loop in his head as the vibration from his quad bike hummed up his spine. He wore backcountry boots, a rain poncho, and two assault rifles strapped across his back in an X. Accessible by his left hand was his vintage M-1, originally developed for combat in the Vietnam War but modified, modernized, and outfitted with a night vision-enabled scope and a longer barrel to target game from distances of over four hundred yards.

Within reach of his right hand was his Pneu-Dart tranquilizer rifle, a weapon with a range of ten to forty yards, but one that could be unreliable in heavy brush and strong wind. He also wore a Glock 10mm as a sidearm for firing at close range and a six-inch hunting knife on his opposite hip.

Despite Geeta's assumptions, Krull's relationship with wolves hadn't always been adversarial. He'd studied wildlife biology on the GI Bill after being discharged from the Marines, where he'd trained as a sniper. The summer after graduation, he'd heard the National Park Service needed riflemen to tranquilize wolves so they could be collared, moved, and released into an ecosystem where they had gone extinct. He was hired two weeks later.

Wolves once roamed across the United States but were hunted to near extinction as ranchers spread out West. Cattle was good eating to a wolf, and ranchers couldn't stomach losing stock. Wolves were trapped, skinned, hunted to the nub, and eventually eradicated from most of the Rocky Mountains, including Wyoming, where Krull was hired to be part of Yellowstone's wolf program, one of the most ambitious rewilding initiatives in history. It was pitched by environmentalists as a remedy to heal the land, though not everybody was thrilled. Local ranchers still didn't want wolves around.

The individuals Krull darted in Alberta were released in Yellowstone National Park. If they migrated outside park boundaries, Krull and his coworkers tranquilized and moved them again because neighboring ranchers could legally shoot prowling wolves on their property. That first wolfpack flourished, mated, and had pups that also thrived. Their presence helped control elk populations in the park, which allowed marsh habitat and wild grasslands to regenerate, to the great benefit of the buffalo herds. Eventually, the wolf population expanded well beyond park boundaries, and some did feed on livestock. Problem wolves were identified, and after he moved to Idaho, it became Krull's job to destroy them.

The first time he took a kill shot from a hovering chopper, he was paid three times what he'd been paid to tranquilize wolves. That night, he drank himself sick and didn't leave his house for six days. He hated killing such an intelligent animal for doing what it was born to do. It was pure cruelty. He promised himself he'd quit, but the calls kept coming, and the money was too good and too easy. Yet each time he pulled the trigger, he fell into the bottle to numb it all out.

One night, after destroying three wolves in ninety minutes, he stumbled into an Idaho Falls bar, where he met a wealthy ranch owner. She raised sheep on a big, showy spread outside Elk Bend and once witnessed her lambs and best ewe get ravaged by wolves. She'd tried to defend them and been mauled. She showed Krull her scars. Her lower left leg had been used as a chew toy. Just fifty-three years old, and she walked with a cane. She convinced him what he was doing was righteous. This was our world to manage, she explained, and any beast that harmed a human being or threatened their livelihood had to be dealt with. From that point on, whenever he had a kill shot, he pictured her, bloody and sobbing and clutching a dead lamb, and he squeezed his trigger guilt-free. The lesson stayed with him. He dealt with dangerous nuisance animals as a game warden from time to time, and though he carried his dart gun for show, he still believed the bullet served the greater good.

Wind rippled his poncho, and rain funneled down the bridge of his nose. Fields of cattails flew by in a blur as Krull splashed down the dark frontage road. It had been nearly ten years since his last hunt for hire, but he was still a crack shot, took his limit of two mule deer and one elk each hunting season, and could not wait to meet this tiger.

"Laugh all you want, little peons," he said to no one in particular. "This time, I'll pin the medal on my chest myself." He skidded into a turnout near the overpass and killed the engine. "No. I'll make Tern do it."

Tern had been vague about where he was searching most of the day, but Krull had leaned on him when they ran into each other at the auditorium that night. He'd confessed he planned to begin day two by searching around the Highway 23 culvert, an aluminum drainage pipe where seasonal streams converged on the east side of the highway and became the Alisaw River as it flowed out the other end. The lieutenant aimed to beat him to it.

Krull slid down the muddy embankment toward the western mouth of the culvert. With his assault rifle in his hands, he stepped into the Alisaw River, which, despite all the rain, was still only knee-deep. He heard the echo of heavy footsteps coming from the far end of the culvert. Thirty yards away sat an immense, four-legged silhouette. The beast was bent over with its rump to Krull, lapping up running water by the gallon.

Krull hadn't expected it to be this easy. He edged into the head-high pipe, certain he was about to become a two-time hero, but by the time his eyes had adjusted to the disorienting darkness, the silhouette was gone. A big rig roared across the overpass above. Krull watched river water swirl between his legs. He heard three loud bangs and felt the flow shift when the beastly shadow waded back into the river at other end of the culvert. It was sniffing a disturbance in the air.

Steeped in cold water on a frigid night, Krull broke into a hot sweat. He could smell and feel the presence of a predator and switched on his night vision scope. When he peered into it, his flickering scope winked out, and the culvert erupted in a rumble as loud as thunder.

Krull flicked on his headlamp to see what was charging him. Not a tiger, but a five-hundred-pound black bear that filled the entire tunnel with its girth. Krull attempted to pull the trigger of his M-1, but he hadn't disabled the safety. Now it was too late. He braced for unhealthy contact, but the bear slid to a stop two feet in front of him and emitted a low growl.

The black bear wore one of those bulky radio collars, the type used to track wildlife, and despite his current position, Krull was thankful he hadn't shot it. This was a known animal, and it was no longer bear season. If he'd killed it, the press would have run a humiliating story. Sacramento would have been furious, and he'd have been the big joke among wardens on search detail. His rifle trembled in his unsteady hands, but Krull held his ground, stood tall, and raised his voice. He knew how to move a bear along.

"Hey! This is my river! Move out!"

Somewhere close, a pack of rambunctious coyotes erupted in hysterical yips. The bear tilted its head, growled, and took another step toward the lieutenant. Krull stumbled backward and landed on his behind in the muddy water. The coyotes kept shrieking and howling, and the bear advanced, baring its teeth. Krull scrambled to get to his feet, slipped, and fell again. The light from his headlamp glinted off the animal's vampire-like incisors. When bears fight, they battle mouth to mouth, and this bear was close enough for Krull to smell its putrid breath.

The beast lunged for Krull's face. Krull kicked and landed a vicious shot to its nose. The bear retaliated by sinking its yellow teeth into Krull's calf and dragging him against the flow. Muddy water filled Krull's ears, eyes, and nose. He couldn't breathe or see, and the back of his head kept thumping the ridged bottom of the culvert as the bear pulled him deeper beneath the highway.

Krull felt his skin tear. Blood gushed from his lower leg. It took all the strength he had left to lift his head up out of the water and draw his handgun. He pulled the trigger twice. Bullets pinged the metallic walls. The bear released him and bounded away.

Gasping, Krull sat up to wipe the grit and mud from his stinging eyes. He pulled his gashed left calf above the surface, rolled up his pants, and lit the wound with his headlamp, which, by some miracle, he hadn't lost. His calf looked like it had been kissed by a chainsaw. A running thread of his blood meandered on the surface of the brown water. He could only hope he'd left the bear with its own wound to ponder.

Krull stood and limped downstream toward the west end of the culvert. He climbed the short slope on all fours, then continued crawling to his quad. Kneeling, he popped the seat, grabbed his first aid kit, and retreated to the shelter of the culvert's concrete ledge. His eyes watered from the pain. His brow was slick with hot sweat and cold mud. He extended his palms and washed them in the downpour, then compressed his wounds with gauze pads. He squeezed a shot of disinfecting bonding agent directly into his punctures, which burned like grain alcohol. He rocked on his backside and rifled through his first aid kit in search of relief. He found a faded prescription bottle: tramadol, his favorite. He popped the cap with his teeth, tipped three pills onto his tongue, and washed them down with a slug from his hip flask. He dressed his wound and waited for the medicine to do its work. Once the pain had mellowed enough to test his leg, he limped in wobbly circles on the shoulder of the highway while debating whether to stop by the ER on his way home.

His radio chirped. "Lieutenant Krull, Tern here." Krull checked his watch. It was after two in the morning. "I noticed your GPS shows you're by the highway culvert. So is BB-One-Twelve. Keep your eyes open. He's a troublemaker."

32

JAY OPENED THE DOOR TO THE AUDITORIUM AT SIX IN THE MORNING to find Geeta already inside, studying his maps. She was dressed in tailored navy-blue breeches and knee-high leather riding boots. She sipped from a steaming travel mug, her rifle case at her feet.

"Is Lieutenant Krull here?" Jay trudged toward the stage.

"These maps are hand-rendered," Geeta said without turning around. "I'd assumed you'd be using GIS topo maps. You know, like every other agency I've ever worked with."

"We recommend folks in the field go back and forth between the two," Jay said as he joined her on stage. "Whatever is most comfortable."

"Right. I did that yesterday, but the detail here is superb. It is worthwhile to know the proper bend of a wash and where exactly the grasslands are and where the chaparral takes over. In comparison, the GIS maps are quite useless. Especially to someone on horseback."

"I'm glad they're helpful," Jay said. "How'd you get in here? The lieutenant and I are supposed to be the only ones with keys."

Geeta turned and trained her studious gaze on Jay before responding. "I picked the lock," she said. "Most useful thing I learned in uni."

"Breaking and entering does sound useful."

"Can be," she said. "Fun, too, under the right circumstances."

Jay's uniform was fresh, but his eyes felt heavy. He'd been too bothered by his confrontation with Eden to lie down when he got home. Instead, he'd spent the night at his desk going over the Glenns' permits, beginning with Bolt's. Later, after he'd noticed Krull's beacon pinging close to BB-112 and alerted him, he'd opened Bell's original evidence file to examine her illustrations again. He'd zeroed in on the distinguishing mark on the tiger's face until his vision blurred. Then, he'd laid his own cheek down flat on his desk, closed his eyes, and slipped into a dream.

Ling was lounging under the needle in a Ventura tattoo parlor. He sat beside her with nineteen-month-old Bell on his lap, close enough for Ling to grip his hand. She looked scrawny and fragile, with dark circles under her penetrating eyes. When the needle pierced her skin, her brow twitched, and a tear slipped free. She stared at the new art coming together on her forearm, which Jay couldn't see from his vantage point. Anyway, it was meant to be a surprise. The needle cut deeper, and Ling squeezed his hand, hard.

Jay bolted upright at his desk, wide awake. Spooked and disoriented, he stared at his hand as if he could still feel her touch. He hadn't dreamed of her in years. Had barely thought about her. In defiance of his grief counselors, he'd consciously reeled those impulses in and stashed his memories away. It had taken some doing, but it had worked. He and Bell had moved on. *Must be the stress*, he thought as he shook out his hand. He'd need to be more mentally disciplined, and the only reliable way to tame an anxious mind was to occupy it.

Which was why he'd found a folding chair on stage and was rereading his team leaders' nightly reports, which only confirmed what he already knew. No prints, snags, scat, or scent had been found. Geeta's bootheels echoed through the empty auditorium as she crossed the stage and sat beside him.

"Riveting, those reports," Geeta said.

"Due diligence, Ms. Murthy," Jay said. "Maybe there's something in the notes a visiting warden wouldn't find significant, but I might."

The old furnace woke up slowly, and the room was still cold enough to see their breath. She gestured to his thermos, and he refilled her empty mug with steaming black coffee. She took a sip and nodded, impressed.

"Thank you, Warden Tern."

He nodded back. Although he still considered her an adversary, technically, they were on the same team. He knew the local terrain better than anyone, and she was the tiger expert, a world-class hunter. Which meant the best way to save the tiger might be to convince her it didn't have to die.

"What if we set traps?"

Geeta smirked.

"Miriam at Animal Control and I have some experience—"

"This is not a job for Miriam at Animal Control," Geeta said. Jay sensed he'd offended her again but pressed his case.

"She has a PhD in wildlife biology. We've had success trapping mountain lions."

"Traps make sense for mountain lion, jaguar, or Florida panther in its natural habitat. But what would Dr. Miriam at Animal Control do if a starving four-hundred-pound tiger saw her first? How would she defend herself whilst she built her trap from sticks and leaves?"

"Funny," Jay said. "I would be there to watch her back."

"Well, lucky her then." Geeta stood and returned to his maps, and they fell into an uncomfortable silence that lasted until the other wardens trickled in, dressed in their baggy forest greens and khakis. Their boots were still muddy, their jackets and hats already damp. Jay continued to flip through their flimsy reports until Krull limped in from backstage, sixteen minutes late.

He was no longer clean and pressed. His hair was wild, his eyes bloodshot. His uniform was streaked and pitted with sweat, mud, and blood. Everyone watched, stunned, as he sank into the seat next to Jay, guzzled his canteen dry, and wiped his wet mouth with his stained shirtsleeve.

"Quick show of hands," Krull said. "Who got some rest last night?"

Some wardens raised their hands more tepidly than others. "Good, good. Now, who stayed out all night and found five tiger tracks." The rank and file dropped their paws in unison. Krull smiled wide.

The lieutenant had always loved the feeling of a room tilted in his direction, and he seemed to savor it before explaining that after an unlucky fall on a broken wine bottle in the culvert, he'd used his rifle as a crutch to scale the muddy slope back to his ATV and found a large, conspicuous track sheltered from the rain by the culvert's concrete embankment.

"It's a front left paw, twice as big as any mountain lion I've ever seen," he said. "I spent the rest of the night in and around the culvert and found four more." He hobbled to the map board and pointed out the exact locations.

"It has a bigger range than we thought," Geeta said. "What made you search the culvert?"

Krull's eyes darted toward Tern before drifting out to the other wardens seated in the auditorium. "Instinct and experience," he said.

Geeta rode with Jay as they followed Krull to the new evidence. Jay called Miriam on the way, but the Animal Control truck was already there waiting when the CDFW caravan arrived. Krull had staked the area down with a tarp to preserve the prints, which had been made in stiff clay soil. Miriam measured them with her calipers.

"Yup. Front left," she said. "Probably a match."

"Definitely," Geeta said. "Look at how the wonky third toe leans toward the second. I noticed the same thing when I inspected the tracks by the oaks yesterday. Unfortunately, there's no texture to them. No color difference between the track and the ground around them. They are at least twelve hours old. Given this substrate, perhaps days old."

"Where would the useless fifth toe be?" Jay asked.

Miriam motioned toward the bottom left of the carpal pad.

"Who told you it was useless?" Geeta snapped. "The fifth toe gives cats more stability and grip up front. That's precisely what makes them such good climbers and superb hunters."

Geeta examined the tracks from multiple angles. The lieutenant's discovery was significant, but good trackers hope to find a story in the sign—something to propel the search forward—and it looked to her as if this cat had been pivoting, stuck in neutral, unsure where to go next. The feeling was contagious.

For the next hour, Geeta slalomed wardens in the overrun riverbed, searching for a lead, until a Toyota Tacoma pulled onto the shoulder of the frontage road. She watched a young man get out of the cab and approach Jay with a handshake and a point-and-shoot camera. Krull peered over Jay's shoulder. Geeta arrived at the scrum in time to hear a tale about a midnight visitor to nearby Treeland Farms twelve nights ago. Marco toggled to an image of one of the tracks next to his size-ten-and-a-half boot. Jay handed Geeta the camera. Her eyes went right to the third toe.

"That's our cat," she said.

Jay smoothed a map of the search area across the hood of his truck and called the others over. "Treeland Farms is right about here," he said. "So, really, the tiger's range is upward of one hundred ten square miles."

Krull sucked his teeth, impressed.

Geeta watched Jay amend and annotate the map and realized it was his hand that was more reliable than the GIS.

Jay traced the Alisaw River back to the headwaters on his map. "Yesterday, we focused our attention east of here, in this twenty-four-square-mile box." Jay pointed out a cross-section of the valley known as Tierra Rejada, home to Alisaw's last remaining working ranches. "Clearly, the search has been too concentrated. We've been fixated on livestock, but west of here, there is access to higher ground and plenty of deer to hunt."

Krull shouldered in to get a better look. His complexion was beet red, and his forehead pearled with rain and sweat. He leaned on Jay's shoulder and winced.

"You alright, Lieutenant? You haven't slept. Maybe you should get that leg looked at."

"Pain is transitory, Tern," Krull said. "I learned that in the Marines." He patted Jay's shoulder, slipped on his pack, and cinched it tight. "Glad we're back in sync. Fan the teams out as far west as you see fit. Team leaders report to you. You report to me."

"Roger that, Lieutenant," Jay said. "Where you headed?"

Krull limped downstream, heading west. "I'm going to get me a tiger-skin rug!"

33

BELL HAD EVEN MORE DIFFICULTY THAN USUAL CONCENTRATING in class, consumed as she was with the wonky floorboard and the possibilities of what might lie beneath. Hope made her pulse quicken, but she knew better than to give in to it. The cabin was old and showed signs of decline. A chipped doorframe here, a missing crown molding there. Her closet doors constantly derailed. A wobbly floor plank fit right in and was probably the reason her father had placed his dresser there. Ignoring or covering up problems was a daily routine at the cabin. Yet she'd found a key.

Jay picked her up from the bus but didn't have time to come inside when he dropped her off. "I've gotta get back to it," he said. "We found new evidence."

"That's good, right?"

He seemed optimistic.

"Yes, but it means we have a lot more ground to cover."

Bell badly wanted the specifics she knew he wouldn't divulge but hopped out of the truck without pressing him. She had a hunt of her own to get back to.

The cabin was see-your-own-breath cold. Goose bumps rippled her arms and the back of her neck as she kicked off her shoes and knelt at the hearth. She built a tent of ash and pine kindling above a bed of crumpled newspaper and wood shavings. With a spark from the flint, the paper curled in a rush of flames that caught the wood. She fed the fire and crossed to Jay's closet, where she dropped to her hands and knees and found her smear of blood. She rubbed the yellowing scab on her shin and pressed into the floor plank. It didn't budge, so she pressed harder and felt it give. She would need to move the dresser to pry it up. She rose to her feet, put both hands on one side of the dresser, and leaned in with all her might. The dresser stayed put, but Bell slid backward until she fell to her hands and knees and bashed her scabby shin.

She limped around the living room until the pain faded, then stared the dresser down. She wouldn't be able to move it fully stocked. Once again, she stacked her father's clothes in neat piles until it was empty then put her shoulder to it. She pushed until her feet slipped out from under her again, and she fell, hard. She peeled herself off the floor and tried a third time, only to taste dust a third time.

Bell rose again, panting and sweating. She glared at the unmovable object of her discontent and backed up four paces. She howled as she crashed into the dresser with a running start. Two of the dresser's legs popped off the ground for a split second before she smacked her bleeding shin on the bottom edge, tumbled onto her backside, and yelped in pain. But when she examined the fresh blood oozing from her aggravated wound, she noticed something else too. There were clean circles on the dusty floor where the back legs used to be. She'd moved the dresser.

She glanced around Jay's closet and located his leather jump rope dangling from a nearby hook. She looped it around one of the front legs, tied the rope in a hitch around her waist, and laced up her hiking boots for better traction. She stepped forward, remaining low to the ground. The taut rope dug into her hip bones, burning the skin, but she took another step, and then another, dragging the dresser behind her. She'd cleared less than two feet of space, but it was enough to squeeze in among the dust bunnies and feel around for the wobbly plank. The board didn't jostle. She hammered away haphazardly, drummed all the floorboards within reach, until she struck the sweet spot at the top right edge of the correct plank, and it popped up at an angle.

Breathless, she peered into the sliver of shadow beneath the elevated plank. She tried to raise it up a bit more, but it wouldn't give, so she tugged, and the floorboard slid free from a slotted metal hinge. This plank hadn't come loose with age. This was a stash.

She grabbed her headlamp from her go bag, but when she knelt in front of the hole, her sphere of light revealed only sawdust. She dug into it with her fingers and found no ants, termites, worms, roaches, or ticks. Nothing was alive down there. It was sterile. Bell retrieved her trowel and probed the sawdust repeatedly, deeper each time. She heard a satisfying clunk. Excited, she dug out the sawdust into sloppy piles on the floor until she could make out the side of an engraved wooden box.

She wriggled it free with her fingertips and used a moist cloth to rub clinging sawdust away. The box was painted indigo blue, with brass hinges, and it was clasped with a miniature padlock. Bell searched her pockets and found the key. It was a perfect fit.

She opened and set the padlock aside, then unlatched the box. The interior was lined with velvet and contained a silk Chanel scarf decorated with a turquoise paisley pattern. She unfolded the scarf and found a photograph of a young Asian woman with long, unruly black hair corralled by the same scarf now spread across Bell's lap. The woman wore beads and silver bracelets. A constellation of freckles twinkled across her flat nose and spread along her full cheeks. Her lips were the color of red wine. She sat on a pillow in a tiled room bright with sunlight in front of a dark-red wall. Bell had never seen the woman before, but she knew exactly who she was. Because in that photograph, Bell saw herself.

There were other pictures. One with Jay when he was younger and without a hint of gray. They were emerging from the ocean. Ling was in a bikini, her smile brilliant. Jay was laughing, dressed in a Speedo with a mask on his head, fins in one hand, and a lobster in the other. In the next, Ling was writing by candlelight in what looked like the cabin's living room. Her hair had fallen in front of her face, but she held it back far enough to reveal one eye, attempting at the same time to raise her exposed eyebrow with her fingertips. Bell could only imagine what Jay's acrobatic eyebrow had been doing at the time. Next was a single wedding-day snapshot. They stood arm in arm and barefoot on the beach beneath the bluffs, flanked by Miriam and Ben. It seemed even then the Terns didn't have many friends.

Another picture was taken on a mountain trail. It was a close-up, and the contrast of the photo made Ling's freckles stand out. Bell brought it to the bathroom mirror. Bell had lighter hair, and her freckles were more golden brown, but the spray pattern was almost identical.

In the next photo, Ling was naked and pregnant, soaking in the cabin's bathtub. She had a washcloth plastered to her forehead. Bell knew the posture well and figured her mother was dealing with a migraine, but she still managed a faint smile for Jay's camera. The final image was captured when Bell was a toddler. Ling was cradling her on the back porch, wearing the same scarf, but her thick hair was gone, and she looked frail. Her sunglasses didn't completely cloak the sagging bags under her eyes as she stared down at her two-year-old daughter, smitten. Little Bell was beaming.

Bell could feel her pulse in every inch of her body. Her heart was thumping so hard it blended with the unmistakable pounding of rotors overhead. She rushed to the window. For the first time, a chopper, and its heat-seeking infrared radar, was scanning the valley. The search had intensified outside and inside the cabin's paneled walls, where Jay's clothes teetered in loose piles. Sawdust was scattered about, and a panel of flooring was leaning against the wall of his closet, but Bell didn't feel an ounce of guilt.

This was his doing. He'd deceived and betrayed her, forced her to imagine what her mother might look like. What her tastes might have been, how she dressed and spent her time. For years, Bell had constructed possibilities. Her mother was a pilot, then a sculptor, a mountain climber, then a radio disc jockey, but leafing through the photographs, she could see just how much the imaginary paled in comparison to pure reality. The revelation was almost too much to bear.

With the sound of the helicopter receding, Bell folded the silk scarf over the small pile of photographs and set them aside. There was something else in the box: a faded and tattered leather-bound journal.

34

GEETA RODE BILLIE TO THE TOP OF A RISE, RAISED HER RIFLE, AND stared through her scope. Below her was an anxious alpaca herd milling about a misty pasture. Normally, such a gathering might interest a hungry tiger, but there were boots on the ground among the herd, and they weren't the best and brightest. These game wardens were prone to banging through barns and shouting across pastures—not the shrewdest way to find a fugitive. Although most of the warden teams were working west of Highway 23, Tern had assigned a few to Tierra Rejada. And as she'd suspected, he soon appeared in the field below wearing a loaded pack and carrying a heavy sack over one shoulder. He patted the side of one alpaca, tickled the chin of another, and shook hands with the team leader. Geeta lowered her rifle. The purist was much sneakier than he let on.

She'd had her suspicions that Tern was playing Krull when they'd huddled at the culvert. Tern was too smart and too logical to conclude that tracks so old would demand such a radical redistribution of manpower. Which was why, in the absence of viable tiger sign, she'd spent the day tracking Warden Tern instead. The story she told herself was that Tern had a notion where the tiger might be hiding and had used Krull's tracks as a smoke screen to divert most of the guns out of the heart of its range. That was one way to save the cat.

Few would suspect such a thing from a goody-good like Tern, but he did seem to be guided by his own holier-than-thou moral compass.

At first, she'd worried her hunch was misguided. She watched from afar as he spent the morning in and around Treeland Farms with the bulk of the search party. He slipped away in early afternoon, but all wardens were carrying GPS units with transponders to make it easier to send backup should anyone happen upon the beast. Geeta nicked a CDFW pickup, drove herself to Dry Creek Ranch to collect Billie, and felt a surge of satisfaction when Jay's icon swerved east, into the Santa Susana foothills.

She rode Billie hard through the suburban streets to Mystic Heights. She dismounted behind a particularly garish new build in time to watch Jay greet his freckle-faced daughter at the school bus. The child's clothes were ill-fitting thrift-store finds. Her backpack was stuffed to the seams, and strands of chestnut hair poked out from her grotty beanie. *Where is the mother?* Geeta wondered as she watched Jay's transponder wink off. Instead of following him, Geeta directed Billie toward higher ground above Mystic Heights and waited. Within a half hour, she watched Jay's truck roll toward the alpaca pasture. Her scope was on him when he stepped out of the cab, slipped into the straps of his heavy backpack, and hefted that strange sack from the bed of his pickup. He wished his colleagues well on his way through the herd to a wooded stretch of Camp Creek.

Geeta led Billie to a valley oak grove one hundred yards from the creek and set her loose. She found a blind to tuck into along the water and smelled Jay coming long before he paused ten feet away, oblivious to her presence. His pack was strapped with a rifle case, and the funk of raw meat wafted toward her from the sack on his left shoulder. He dropped it at his feet and aimed his field glasses at a rocky outcrop where tendrils of fog drifted through gaps in the burnt-orange sandstone. Geeta followed him as he picked his way along the stream banks until he reached the first bottleneck, where the flow gathered with a swirling force.

Eleven and half months a year, Camp Creek was dry. This year, it was knee-deep and the color of mocha, and now there was no avoiding it. Jay would have to get wet if he hoped to reach his target: the cave at the top of Happy Camp Canyon. Thanks in part to a complete lack of trails, he hadn't explored Happy Camp Canyon in years, which was why he hadn't even considered the cave until Marco showed up with his point-and-shoot. After he'd amended his map, Jay had mulled the options open to a frightened beast on the run. Sure, it may have headed west, out of the valley, but what if the tiger had found a safe place? Somewhere dry and out of sight.

Judging by the depth of the stream and knowing what was to come, Jay suspected he was overloaded. He dropped his sack, wriggled out of his pack, and was contemplating where to streamline when Geeta stepped close enough to read the branding on his rifle case.

"Aren't you supposed to be ransacking innocent barns or interrogating dizzy alpacas?" she said. He'd managed to shake every gun in the search party but the deadliest. He turned to her. She nudged the stinky sack at his feet with the toe of her boot. "What is this?"

"Bait," he said. "Miriam found me a mountain lion trap to deploy. Showed me how to put the sticks and leaves together and everything." Although, given the flow of the creek, it was obvious bringing it all along was a better idea in theory.

"Brilliant." Geeta smiled wide. "Where are we off to then?"

"You're not invited." Jay grabbed his gear and stepped around her into the brush. He needed to find a suitable tree. He stopped at the base of a sycamore, opened his pack, and jettisoned extra layers, protein bars, and a thermos of green tea as well as the animal trap Miriam had loaned him. He bundled the excess in a tarp, which he cinched to the sack of thawing beef.

"Because you don't approve of my approach?" she asked.

"No," he said. "You're the expert. I suppose you have your reasons." He tossed a weighted line tied to a coil of rope over a high branch and used it to hoist his gear into the canopy. "Some of them might not even be any of my damn business."

"Perhaps not," she said.

"But you are out for blood." He tied his rope off at the trunk. "And there are better solutions." He knelt and opened his gun case. Inside was his jet-black rifle, four darts, and two vials of ketamine. When Geeta saw it, she looked amused. Jay kitted up, made his way back to the creek, and sloshed upstream with pace. Geeta cinched her pack and followed.

"I'm not really asking. It's quite easy to track you. I've been doing it all day."

"That's not creepy." He turned and caught a glimpse of her profile. Fine raindrops gathered on her eyelashes and glinted in the soft light. One dripped from her tapered eyebrow directly onto her left pupil. She blinked it away. It wouldn't be easy to shake her. She was fit and tenacious; she'd changed from her riding boots into hiking boots, and even if he picked up a mile on her, she'd track him right down. Nonetheless, Jay pushed to widen his gap as the shape-shifting creek snaked through the hills.

Geeta took her time to examine the corridor as she followed him. She clocked a pair of large, overturned boulders and a trampled manzanita half submerged in the creek. They might have been byproducts of the storm cycle, but she didn't see any evidence of a rock or mudslide. More likely, something heavy and alive had impacted them on its way up or downstream. She smiled to herself. The biggest limitation for any great tracker was their familiarity, or lack thereof, with the terrain they were operating in, and it was abundantly clear that Jay Tern was the authority on the flow of life across this valley. But she'd need to set his mind at ease to fully leverage his knowledge and finish the job.

It took effort to navigate a hairpin bend with water up to their thighs. A bit further on, Camp Creek narrowed into an even deeper channel that ran fast and foaming around three slick boulders. Jay scrambled onto the last stack of dry rocks on his side of the corridor. On the other side, a grassy slope paralleled the creek and could take them further up the canyon, but the stream was too wide to jump from a standstill. Jay's hesitation allowed Geeta to catch up.

"We're heading to the top of this canyon," Geeta said. "You noted on your magnificent map that the rock is compacted sandstone. Meaning there is a cave up there, which you like because it could make for a sensational tiger's nest. Of course, if you'd bothered to ask your tiger expert what she thought, she would have told you that in the wild, tigers don't den up unless they are having cubs."

"Yet here you are."

"Well, without any fresh cat sign to track, I figured this could be good fun. And I suppose it does make some sense that our besieged beast might hunker down, but I can see that you're concerned, and you really shouldn't be. Because you're probably wrong." Geeta yanked the load lifters on her pack until it was tight to her slender frame, then leapfrogged from slick stone to slick stone and onto the opposite bank with the grace of a dancer.

Jay teetered on the first slick boulder but managed to find good footing on a gritty edge at the last second as foaming mud-water tore around him. He leaped toward the next boulder, but his back foot snagged. He would have belly flopped into fast water and pinballed the jagged rocks if not for Geeta's long limbs and world-class reflexes. She caught his one extended forearm with both hands and tugged him hard enough that he fell face down into the muck at her feet.

When he raised his head, mud dripped from his cheeks and chin. Geeta pulled a bandana from a side pocket of her pack and dangled it above him. Jay grudgingly accepted, sat up, and wiped his eyes and mouth. He took a swig from his water bottle, swished, and spit. Then, he wiped his mouth with the bandana again.

"You can keep that," she said.

Sheepish, Jay rose to his feet and pointed the way forward. They picked their way up the slope until it became a wooded creek-side bluff. Sycamores leaned over the water at odd angles. Once the stream broadened out, Jay found a deer trail that led them back down to the channel, where he stayed out front and calculated how to play it—if he wasn't wrong. If they did find the tiger.

"Tell me more about your lieutenant," Geeta said, breaking their silence. "How does a man like that become a commander?"

"He was a big hero," Jay said. "Took down a cop killer."

"That doesn't sound like our dear leader."

"It's well documented. They pinned a medal to his chest and everything. I was there."

"And why were you there? Did they pin a medal to your chest too?"

Jay didn't answer. Not because she was being her typical pushy self but because the roar of falling water had grown impossible to ignore. The principal reason Jay had streamlined his gear was around the next bend, and he hoped it might dissuade Geeta from going any further. But when the seventy-foot-high tumble of boulders loomed into view, she didn't seem so spooked. Or maybe she'd seen something in the creek he'd missed and was eager to get a clean look at that cave.

"We don't have a lot of light left," Jay said. The crag wasn't completely vertical. There were slopes, ledges, angles, and handholds, but it was saturated with stormwater that rolled over the top and gushed through the cracks. Jay noticed that the middle route, where the bouldering was typically easiest, was completely underwater. He had never seen that.

"Then let's not waste it." Geeta shed her pack into his arms. "Don't slip this time. That would be bad."

Yeah, she was eager all right. Within seconds, she'd scrambled up onto the first ledge. So much for outclimbing her. He handed her up her gear and then his own. With two quick moves, he joined her. From there, three boulders leaned into one another and led to the next tier. Bolts of water gushed between them. The pitch was more diagonal than vertical, and though the rocks were damp, they weren't slick. The two scrambled up onto a ledge no more than two feet wide at the base of a twenty-foot vertical ascent. Jay didn't see any decent handholds. Geeta pointed to a twisted sycamore overhead. Its root system snaked between the wet boulders above them and extended down like a fire escape they could scale to the top of the column. If they could reach it.

"Give me a boost, and I'll pull myself up," Geeta said. She swiveled to point out the best handhold, but her front foot slipped, and she lost her balance. Jay grabbed her left wrist with both his hands, and she dangled above the exposed and shallow rock fifty feet below. Her heels thumped stone like a metronome.

Jay saw fear in Geeta's eyes. Then, he felt his own boot begin to slide. If he lost his footing, they were through. He reached for the lowest-hanging sycamore root, gripped it with one hand, and pulled Geeta toward him with the other. He let loose a guttural growl as she kicked her legs and swung back onto the ledge.

His lungs heaving, Jay peered into the darkening sky and didn't like what the swirling clouds had to say. They had to get off the rock. Fast. He was still gripping that sycamore root with one hand and her wrist with the other, so he let her go, dried his free hand on his undershirt, and grabbed another more significant root. He pulled himself up slowly and with complete control, high enough to insert his right toe into the knotted root system, which gave him the leverage he needed to lean down and offer Geeta his hand. She accepted it, and once again, he pulled her toward him until she could grab hold of the roots herself. Then, they kept climbing up onto the angled tree trunk and into the canopy. They paused to rest on the thickest branch, and within seconds, the misty rain gave way to a deluge. They watched in awe as water and mud peeled down the slopes and formed a roaring waterfall that spread across the entire wall. They'd barely made it.

"I honestly don't know what I was thinking," she said, still breathless. "You saved my life."

"I was returning a favor," Jay said.

The downpour had eased by the time they dropped from the tree onto a plateau that sloped away from the creek and toward yet another fifty-foot-high sandstone bluff crowned with the cave. Jay gazed up at it and tried to work out the best way to get there. Geeta swung her rifle into her hands and dropped to her belly. She scanned the opening, her cheek pressed to the smooth mahogany handle, her view stabilized by a built-in tripod on the muzzle. Jay needed to get closer; Geeta was already well within range.

"There is definitely something up there," she sang with delight. Still standing, Jay peered through his field glasses and detected no movement at all.

"An hour ago, you said I was wrong."

"I said you were probably wrong, but it turns out you're a devious genius, game warden."

"I'm too simple to be devious."

"*You* are not so simple," she said. "Unique. Capable. But not simple."

"Uh-huh. Well, we'll need to get closer to dart it. You can use my rifle. I checked it out. You don't need to kill the cat to collect your bonus. Capturing him alive pays too."

She lifted her gaze from her scope and peered up at him. Her eyes were ice cold.

"Warden Tern, I am sorry, but this isn't your call."

She was right. Geeta was with the feds, which meant she had the authority, and it didn't matter that she'd tailed him here or that he'd saved her life. Even if he spilled it all about Bell, her health and bond with the tiger, his failures as a warden and father, she still wouldn't do the right thing. Because Geeta was a predator, and predators were not wired to show mercy.

She closed her right eye and placed her left back on the scope.

"Not to worry," she said. "Any minute now, our cat will step out of that cave, and tomorrow, you'll be happily rid of me."

Bolt had smelled and then heard them coming. First, it was a delicious whiff of rank meat. Notes of marbled fat and coagulated blood rode the breeze and filtered into the dank lair, setting her nose to twitch and appetite ablaze. She'd padded to the shadow line, where the last of the daylight leaked in. She'd been hiding out in that cave ever since she'd slunk back after being spotted, and her hunger had grown deep and painful, but crossing the threshold was no small thing.

The crow fluttered over from her nest and landed beside her.

They glanced at one another and then back out into the world, when they heard a garbled shriek and a tumble of splashing rocks. Terrified, Bolt withdrew to the recesses. The crow, however, did not retreat from the fading shadow line as darkness set in. Blessed with telescopic eyes of her own, honed by evolution to see sharp images from great distance even in low light, she watched Jay and Geeta swing down from the tree onto the plateau. They did look to be trouble. Of course, when you were a One-Legged Crow, every animal was a threat. On the other hand, nothing was ever afraid of her.

Smaller birds didn't fuss much when Old One Leg swooped over their nests. Even baby squirrels shrugged her off. People felt so sorry for her, they were moved to share snacks, tossing her seeds, popcorn, peanuts, stale breadcrumbs, or beef jerky as if she were incapable of spotting carrion from hundreds of feet up. As if she were half a wild thing. All the many scenes of disrespect she'd experienced fluttered to the front of her perpetually underestimated crow mind as she fluffed herself up and hopped back and forth across the threshold, knowing full well that her movements were being tracked from below. After all, being a crow, she was as keen as some primates and as self-aware as most dolphins. She was a natural problem-solver, and when it came to flight, she had few peers.

Geeta watched the flickering shadow and felt a familiar rush of pleasure that came on when her mind, body, and rifle were aligned and aimed directly at her target. Her brow and underarms bloomed with perspiration. Her senses sharpened to maximum, and her heartbeat slowed. She only felt this engaged when a kill was moments away, and this wasn't just another kill. Jay had been right about that too. There were reasons this tiger had to die that had nothing to do with keeping the people of Alisaw Valley safe, pleasing her bosses at Wildlife Services, or fixing her messy, post-divorce finances. And they weren't anybody's business but her own.

"Please do not take what is about to happen as a referendum on my respect or appreciation for your strength, skill, and desire to do what's right, game warden," she said, her long, slender body a humming wire of tension and focus. "There is more to this particular feline situation is all, and…it's best to think of what you are about to witness as nature taking its bloody course."

That was when the One-Legged Crow breached the cave and caught an updraft. She glided through the growing darkness—silent as an owl—sliced through the rain, arced back toward the cave to gain another spike of altitude, then tucked in her oversize wings and dove straight for the barrel of Geeta's gun.

Startled by the strange sight of a black bird materializing from the shadows and bearing down upon her, Geeta pulled the trigger. The crow banked left. A white-hot shell zoomed over her right wing, singed the barbs of her feathers, and smashed into the cliff above the cave. The crow closed the remaining distance in a series of corkscrews. Jay hit the dirt, and Geeta buried her nose in the rocky soil as the One-Legged Crow swooped close enough to grab a lock of Geeta's hair with her talons and yank it out by the root. Geeta yelped, reached for the silver-dollar-sized bald patch on her crown, and found a blossom of blood. The bird pulled up, settled in the sycamore, and scattered Geeta's silky strands in the grass. Then, she puffed out her chest and dialed up her loudest and most furious, "Caaaw!" She kept them coming too. One after another after another.

"Oh, caw, caw, caw!" Geeta howled back, her hand on her bloody scalp.

And Jay laughed. Harder than he had in almost seven years. So hard he could barely breathe. Until he noticed something curious about that enraged bird in the sycamore tree. "How 'bout that," he said, catching his breath. "A one-legged crow."

35

AS NIGHT SPREAD ITS SOGGY QUILT OVER ALISAW VALLEY, BELL LAID her favorite Pendleton blanket down in front of the fire, sat cross-legged on the floor, and cracked her mother's journal. There was an inscription on the inside front cover that snapped her solemn mood.

Random Mutterings, Lists, and Brainfarts
If found, burn for warmth.
—Ling Wong Tern

"Brainfarts," Bell said, giggling. She passed her fingers over her mother's name. For as long she could remember, she'd been weighed down with unresolved foundational questions. All she'd ever wanted was a clue, some knotted line leading to a fuller notion of who she was. Now, she was holding it in her hands, and it wasn't one of those hyper-organized time-stamped diaries with places and dates. Ling's journal was a dump site, a painter's palette, a laboratory. And it started with a list:

Nomi di bambina
Raven
Hooper

<u>Plum</u>

<u>Isabella/Bell</u>

Charley

Lotus

Bell tried them all on. She ordered herself to clean her room, do the dishes, build a fire. She liked Lotus and Charley and thought she would have made a decent Hooper. "Get dressed, Hoop," she said standing behind her dad's desk and holding an empty coffee cup as a prop. "Time for school, Hooper. Hooper, what did I tell you about leaving your art supplies spread all over the floor?" The one name she sneered at was Plum, but it was underlined along with Bell, which convinced her it must have been a close second. The list held a strange power. It reduced Bell to a shadow, a phantom, an idea in her mother's mind. Which was exactly what Ling had always been for her. When she turned the page, Bell found a blurry twenty-week ultrasound photograph with the caption: "Isabella Ái Wong Tern."

Ling was a funny writer and a splendid artist. She sketched in pencil, chalk, and charcoal and always in black and white. Sprinkled throughout her journal were mountains and river valleys, herds of elk. A spotted fawn. A family of foxes. A mother bobcat and her cub. She scribbled recipes (*apple cider donuts, lentil soup, chili crab curry, tofu rice noodle bowls with baby bok choy*) and jotted down old movies to watch (*New York, New York*; *Trading Places*; *Seven Samurai*; *8 ½*) and places to visit (*Kyoto, Porto, Seville, Tierra Del Fuego, the Komodo Islands, Alaska: all of it, and sure, everywhere else too*). There were pages of long-hand prose, and about halfway through, Ling began writing about the intense migraines that surfaced during pregnancy.

> *I feel them everywhere. Even in the tips of my toes and fingernails. I become the rawest nerve. Immobilized, terrified, enraged. I refuse to go numb with medication. I'd rather take the pain and combat the storm with visualization, which drives Jay crazy. He means so well but cannot understand. You know what helps? Repeating certain words or song lyrics. Mostly Bob. "Stir It Up"*

helps every time. I play it on repeat and picture my soul lifting up and out of my body until I am uncontained. Content to watch all the drama happen way down there in "real life."

Jay had taught Bell some of these same strategies when her headaches started, but the word *soul* was what grabbed her. She'd obviously heard it before, but the meaning her mother infused it with felt different. More potent.

Some pages held only a few random thoughts. Others were jammed to the margins. One had the word love spelled out in different languages.

Love, amou [french], amor [spanish], amore [italian], hubun [arabic], lyubov [bulgarian], aahkyit [burmese], ái [mandarin], milovat [czech], kærlighed [danish], liefde [dutch], pag-ibig [filipino], rakkus [finnish], liebe [german], agápi [greek], prēma [gujurati], aroma [maori], maya [nepali], sailing [korean], aloha [hawaiian], mapenzi [swahili], cinta [bahasa]

She found a full-page sketch of a black lightning bolt frayed at the edges on the very next page. The one after that was pasted with two photographs. The first was a picture of Ling, her head shaved, reclining at a tattoo parlor as an artist worked on her forearm. The second was of Ling and Jay lying in bed with two-year-old Bell pinned in a cloth diaper. Jay wore boxers. Ling was naked. She looked too skinny. Her ribs were exposed, and her head was still shaved. Defiant, she held up her forearm to show off her lightning bolt.

With rain pounding the tin roof and the hum of blood in her ears, Bell flashed on Bolt's face. Jay had made it perfectly clear that he didn't believe in life after death or messages from the beyond. Naturalists, he liked to say, believed only in what could be objectively observed. Chaos and coincidence, luck, choices, conflict, habits, pain, and tragedy were all real. Life and death were real. The moon and stars were as real as the mountains and the sea. Magic, in his estimation, was a made-up bedtime story. But what about *soul*? She grabbed the Oxford English Dictionary from the bookshelf and found it halfway down page 797. Definition 3b felt like what her mother was hinting at.

> *Soul /sōl/ the spiritual or immaterial part of a human being or animal, regarded as immortal.*

Bell had seen the world through her father's viewfinder for her entire life, and she had embraced it, but now, she found herself wondering if there wasn't some connection between her dead mother and an escaped tiger. Her father would dismiss it as random, if not ridiculous. "How many people with lightning-bolt tattoos are there on planet Earth? Thousands? Millions? Not everything should be considered some sacred sign from the universe," she could hear him say. Yet she couldn't help but wonder how Ling might interpret it.

By then, the fire had smoldered to embers. Bell yawned and checked the kitchen clock. It was 10:23 p.m. Her father would be home around midnight, and she still wasn't ready to discuss any of this. Not yet. She swept up his closet and slotted the plank back into place. She managed to bully the dresser back up against the wall and put his clothes away. Then, she scooped up the box, scarf, and her mother's journal and shuffled to her bedroom. She made a tent with her bedsheets and used her headlamp to keep reading.

Ling's penmanship became shaky in the final pages. The subject matter was a lot to take in and mostly beyond her years. There were entries referencing her mother's many doctors and procedures and what would happen after she was gone.

> *Today he told me that he doesn't know if he can do it. That he's not strong enough. What does that even mean? I snapped at him. I told him he had to stop. That nobody knows how strong they can be until it is absolutely necessary, and I begged him NOT to project worst-case scenarioisms into this sad, beautiful world. Because they DO NOT HELP!*

The final page was transcribed. Bell knew that because she'd heard the passage before.

Do you imagine the universe is agitated?
Go into the desert at night and look out at the stars.
This practice should answer the question.
The superior person settles her mind as the universe settles the stars in the sky.
By connecting her mind with the subtle origin, she calms it.
Once calmed, it naturally expands, and ultimately her mind becomes as vast and immeasurable as the night sky.

The passage Jay had read to her in the desert last Thanksgiving was linked to her mother, and he'd never told her. Of all the insults she'd dug up from his stash, this one stung the most. Until she found two envelopes taped to the inside back cover that had faded and softened with time. One had her father's name on it. His was creased and torn open, illustrated with islands and cacti, mountains and stars, the letter still tucked inside. The other was addressed to Bell. It was decorated with sailing canoes, whales, waves, a scoop of pelicans soaring in a v-formation through the sky. There were rain clouds on the back with a bolt of black lightning, and it was still sealed. Her mother had written her a letter, and her father had kept it from her.

Outside, the sky cracked with two flashes of lightning and an explosion of rolling thunder. Clouds burst above the cabin, and rain bucketed down. Bell's eyes burned. She held the sealed letter to her chest and trembled with confusion, sadness, and fury. Two giant teardrops swelled and spilled over the dam, triggering a flood. The tears came fast and free as her cries merged with the raging storm. There was no stifling it this time. She flicked off her headlamp, lay down, and let it all flow until she faded into a dreamless sleep.

36

"YOU ALMOST SHOT AN INNOCENT CROW," JAY SAID. "THAT'S GOTTA be against tracker code."

Geeta fingered the empty patch on her scalp. "Crows should be culled. They're invasive. They crowd out more pleasant songbirds. Every game warden worth their badge knows that." She turned to the scrawny crow as its caw rang through the night. "Besides, are we supposed to believe that this...*thing*...is the king of that glorious cave?"

"You're suggesting our tiger and the bird are in cahoots?"

"It's not impossible. I grew up on a tiger reserve in India where my father became science-famous for a book he wrote about a Bengal tiger who spent the better part of two years shacked up with a crane."

Jay watched rain dribble down the ski slope of Geeta's slender yet substantial nose. She had a bloody scalp and a cut on her cheek where she'd bashed her face on the handle of her rifle, and her ego had been bruised purple. Self-assured Geeta Murthy actually looked vulnerable.

"Granted, the crane was blessed with a regal elegance that *some* birds lack, and it certainly didn't have that hideous cackle."

On cue, the crow let loose its parting shot and flew home.

"A one-legged crow, roommates with a starving tiger," Jay said. "That's your theory?"

"Eating that wouldn't do much for anyone, especially a big cat." Geeta dusted herself off and strapped her rifle to her pack. "Are you coming or not?"

Jay considered his options. He had read enough to know that odd couples occasionally coexisted in nature, but that didn't mean it was a good idea to scramble up the bluffs in the rain on a dark night to confront a hungry tiger. If it was there, she'd kill it. The sane thing would be to figure a route out of their current predicament that did not involve descending through the canyon or climbing any more near-vertical walls. He opened his map and found something that could work. There was a touch of moderate bouldering before they could move cross-country through the savanna to an old Jeep trail favored by mountain bikers that snaked down to the alpaca ranch off Suarez Road. On the other hand, they were so close, and it did make sense to be 100 percent certain.

"I liked it for a lair," he said, folding his map. "I really did." His knee and tailbone throbbed. The cliff in front of them was no El Capitan, but it was a fifty-foot stack of boulders with crumbly sections and narrow ledges, and they'd already had one near-miss. Plus, Geeta was agitated and angry—humiliated, even—and humiliated people made questionable decisions. Which was why he couldn't let her go it alone.

They foundered in the darkness, bickering in hushed tones. They argued about who should go first and which were the optimal hand and footholds. Three times, they reached the top of a rock column only to find themselves cut off, forcing them to backtrack to an alternative route. During one turnaround, the rain eased to a drizzle, and they paused to rest, sitting side by side.

"I just put it together," Jay said. He watched a crack in the clouds widen enough to reveal starlight. "Your dad is Ulias Murthy. My daughter is reading one of his books, but I don't think there's a crane in it."

"Poor dear," she said. "*Tigers in the Field* is quite dry. It did not exactly fly off the shelves."

"She's enjoying the heck out of it."

"I'd say he'd be touched to hear it, but I haven't spoken to him in a decade."

"Your doing or his?"

Geeta picked up her rifle and wiped it down with another dry bandana. She seemed to have an endless supply. "Warden Tern, what is the point of this dreary line of questioning?"

"I suppose I'd like to know why Ulias Murthy's daughter feels the need to kill a lost and innocent tiger."

"It instigated a fatality," Geeta said, "according to your own report."

"Fair, but I'd stipulate it has not deliberately hurt any human being that we know of."

"So stipulated." She laid her weapon across her lap. "Go on then. You must have a theory."

"Okay. It's revenge. Your father spent all his time with tigers and ignored his little girl, who happened to be bright and precocious and certainly worthy of fatherly attention. Nevertheless, his love was lacking. Because he preferred the company of big cats. Or, more precisely, tigers. Although he enjoyed leopards too."

Geeta cocked her head, slightly impressed. "You've been reading some Dr. Murthy yourself by the sounds of it."

"Ah, but tigers were his true love. Even his daughter couldn't compete, and that shamed him. Only his shame pushed him even further away until he found it easy to prioritize tigers and sacrifice the needs of his family for his own ambition. Resentful and rebellious, his baby girl grew into the thing he hated most: a predator's predator, with a penchant for killing the cats he loved. All to get back at dear old dad."

"That's quite a story." Geeta shook her hair out before taking a moment to peer into her compact and touch up the gloss on her lips. "You have a daughter and, from what I can tell, prefer animals to humans. Do you worry she will become everything you despise?"

"No," he said. "That is not what I worry about with her."

He watched Geeta attempt to read him like he was a collection of fresh tiger tracks while he loaded his dart gun.

"His work isn't the reason I don't speak to my father, and it's not why I neutralize big cats for a living."

"You mean kill."

"Oh, right. I'm the evil tracker lady, and you're the angel who wants to see the tiger spend the rest of its life in a cage."

"Don't give me that garbage," he said.

"Well, you can't release it into the wild. Best case, it lives out its days in a 'sanctuary,'" she said, flexing those air quotes of hers, "where it has a slightly bigger, greener cell but not much of a life. Not for a cat that has tasted freedom."

"It's the humane thing to do—that's your motivation? I don't buy it. Doesn't track with your big speech about the trail of devastation you've seen. No, this is personal for you."

"Maybe so, but it's a long story, Warden Tern."

"Jay. Please."

Geeta rose to her feet, rifle in hand. "Let's go, Jay. We're so close to the top."

They climbed the last section in silence and pinned themselves to the right of the cave's entrance. Geeta stood closest to the opening. Jay was behind her, armed with his tranquilizer rifle.

"Give me one chance to dart it," he whispered. "I did lead you up here. Not to mention save your life."

She turned and glared.

"Your words, not mine."

"I won't be hearing the end of *that* anytime soon." She switched her headlamp to red, dipped into a shoulder roll, and came up ready to fire, but the only thing she'd illuminated was the raggedy crow half asleep in its nest on the ledge. It barely squawked at the intrusion.

Jay had only set foot in the cave once before, a long time ago. It was larger than he remembered and so dark it was difficult to perform a thorough search, even with headlamps. The floor was all rock, so there were no tracks, and they found no fur, scat, teeth, or spoiled meat. It smelled faintly of rot, but Jay attributed that to moisture and the funky bird. After the clouds opened up again, all they could smell was rain.

"I'm calling it," Jay said. He bagged a single black feather he'd found on the floor and stepped to the mouth of the cave. Geeta joined him there. On a clear day, you could see for miles from that cave. It overlooked the entire valley all the way to Highway 23, but the wet night smothered the lights, and everything remained murky. "This was a monumental waste of time."

"Agreed," Geeta said. "I suspect we're both better off working alone."

They scrambled up two more boulders, reached a meadow above the cave, and cut cross-country through thigh-high grass. With the trail in sight, Jay heard something rustle nearby. Geeta placed a hand on his elbow to stop him.

"What was that?" she whispered.

"Cattle, probably," Jay said. "There are grazing rights up here."

"Better to be sure." They remained still for a moment, and then another, until lightning flashed, thunder cracked, and Geeta agreed to walk on in the bucketing rain.

Bolt remained in the grass, flat on her belly, until their footsteps were no longer audible, their bouncing lights were swallowed by the darkness, and the lingering trace of their scent had faded. Then, she waited another full hour before heading back down, but she didn't reenter the cave. Not right away. Something pungent was still blowing up from the roaring creek.

She plunged down the bluffs and used the sycamore to work her way into the canyon. She navigated the edges of the churning falls with skill and ease, then rock-hopped to avoid the fastest flow in the channel. Near the bottom, she followed her nose to a sack tied high up a tree. She leaped, snatched it with her jaws, ripped it down, shredded the sack, and found a fatty shank of beef that was starting to turn. Bolt took two bites to soothe the gnaw in her gut, then carried it back up the canyon.

Soaked yet satisfied, she entered the dry cave, dropped the meat on the floor, and shook out her soggy mane. The crow hopped down from her nest. Bolt tore off two sizable chunks with her teeth and pushed them toward her friend with her exceptionally large front left paw.

37

BELL WOKE IN THE MIDDLE OF THE NIGHT STILL CLUTCHING THE letter. Fully clothed with her headlamp askew, she sat up in bed and smoothed out the crinkled envelope on her lap. When she was ready, she straightened and switched on her headlamp, and, with a care bordering on reverence, peeled the envelope open.

My Darling Bell,

I'm writing this by the light of a fire in our living room. You're fast asleep on your knees, with your head resting in my lap. I can feel your warm breath tickle my shins. You are three years old, talk all day, and climb everything in sight, especially trees with your daddy. You love animals and strawberries and hiking on our trails. And I love you more deeply than I have ever loved anyone or anything.

When we first brought you home from the hospital, I'll admit to being shell-shocked, but Daddy was ready. He swaddled, rocked, held, and changed you while I rested between feedings. Something special happened between the two of us on your third day on planet Earth. We locked eyes; our hearts merged, and you and I became one.

You are so strong and so smart. You walked before you turned one. You jumped for the first time at thirteen months. You said your first words around then too. Always advanced. I don't want to miss a moment with you because I know I will miss so many, and it's not fair. To you or me.

I wish more than anything that I could have held your hand on your first day of school or brushed your thick hair every day of elementary school—thirty times on the left side and thirty times on the right—or found you the perfect outfit for picture day. I wonder what you will look like when you finally read this. I wonder so much about you, but I suppose I would wonder even if I weren't so sick.

I suspect you will be an adventurer like Daddy and a daydreamer like me. I hope you will share our love of nature and books and jazz. But maybe it will be different books and music we don't know much about and adventures and dreams we couldn't have seen coming. And that's okay too. More than okay. That's how it should be.

You have learned early that sometimes we do not get the time we need or deserve and that there is nothing we can do about it. We must accept life as it comes and try to find the beauty, energy, love, and possibility in every situation. Even the sad ones. That takes a quality of spirit that I know you possess because I can feel it.

Bell Tern, whatever happens in your life, whenever you feel sad, lost, left out, or unappreciated, know that there is LIGHT and MAGIC inside you and enough STRENGTH to overcome anything. Because your life will not be limited by what you've lost. The only thing that will ever limit you is the extent of your wild imagination.

Did you know that when a valley oak falls, from the axe or disease or fire, her daughters rise through the soil all around her? They absorb the sun she can no longer feel and suckle the moisture and nutrients they need from their dead mother's roots, even after her leaves are long gone, her branches and bark have turned brittle, and she begins to fade away. Remember the lesson of the oak trees, baby Bell. Just like them, we are connected! Believe that! Not because I say so but because Mother Nature proves it every day.

Okay, you're stirring now, and I get to go play outside with you. Stay magical, my darling girl. It is your magic that will make you indestructible despite all the unfairness in this world. And remember, I am sending you kisses, nourishing hugs, and my bottomless love from across the big sky and great sea, always and forever.

XX—Momma

Bell read the letter twice. First, she felt soothed. Then came the frustration. She'd found the treasure she'd been aching for. All of it was beautiful and affirming—especially Ling's letter—and just as her father had predicted, it wasn't nearly enough. Exhausted but wired, Bell knew she wouldn't be able to sleep. Not anytime soon. There was only one thing to do. She opened Ling's journal to her favorite photograph and reached for her sketch pad.

38

FEBRUARY 17, 2005

JAY KNOCKED ON THE DOOR OF MIRIAM'S TWO-BEDROOM BUNGAlow around one in the morning. She was still dressed in her Animal Control uniform when she answered. "Surprised you're up," he said.

"I just got home from the hospital. Obviously you haven't heard. I was there with your boss."

Miriam invited Jay in and poured him a cup of tea. He gripped it with both hands as he dripped on her kitchen floor. She filled him in.

"I drove to Santa Paula for animal feed this afternoon and saw a CDFW ATV parked at the Santa Paula Ridge trailhead. Which was strange because I'd been on comms all day and hadn't heard about our cat or any warden teams heading that far west. I decided to check it out and found your lieutenant lying face down in a patch of white sage about thirty feet off the trail. He looked a mess. Clammy and pale, and he kept mumbling about how close he was. 'Help me up, Long,' he said. 'I'm gonna finish this thing myself.' I tried to get you, but you were busy or out of range."

She shot Jay a skeptical look. He sipped his tea.

"I managed to get him up onto his feet and back to my van. He was still mumbling when we arrived at the emergency room. And that's when it got interesting because once the doctors unwrapped the filthy gauze around his calf and wiped away the mud and coagulated blood, it was obvious that he didn't slip on any broken wine bottle." Miriam blew the steam from the surface of her teacup and took a healthy sip. "He was *bitten* by something in that culvert, Jay. Something with long canines."

"Did he explain himself?"

"Not at first. The docs pressed him. I pressed him, but he was vague. Which made sense. He hadn't slept in two days. The details didn't much matter to the doctor, who gave him a rabies shot, scrubbed that nasty wound, and stitched him up. But word must have gotten out because the press trickled in. That perked Corey right up, and he spun them a story about how he'd been mauled by a big cat in the culvert and tracked it all the way to Santa Paula. You can read about it in tomorrow's paper."

"Doesn't follow. At all."

"I know it. But two warden teams went out searching for the cat near Santa Paula Ridge and found eroding mountain lion tracks not far from the trailhead."

"Wonderful. So now residents and ranchers in Alisaw and Santa Paula are going to be nervous."

"Ding. Ding," she said.

"Did you get a good look at his wound?"

"Looked like bear to me."

Jay's anger warmed him. BB-112 spent a lot of time around Santa Paula Ridge. Jay made a mental note to check the bear's movements as soon as he got home.

"Where's Krull now?"

"Sleeping it off. You might have to lead the team tomorrow."

"Negative. He's going to lean into this publicity." Jay drained the last of the tea from his mug, set it down on the counter, and placed an evidence bag next to it. Inside was a tail feather from an American crow.

Jay was aware of Miriam's habit of cataloging the DNA of her hardest rehab cases, which invariably were her favorite rehab cases, and that the One-Legged Crow remained at the top of her all-time list. When Bell and Jay had brought her over, the poor thing was concussed and underweight with wings that were out of proportion to her small body, but the bird had spirit. She would dance back and forth, left and right on Miriam's examination table, her chest all puffed out and cocky as hell, until she fell on her face or rump. Then, she'd pump her one good leg in a vain attempt to right herself until Miriam cupped her in gentle, gloved hands and set her upright, at which point, the wonky bird would go right back to bobbing, weaving, and pecking like a plucky young boxer who had more heart than talent. As was often the case when she had orphaned animals, Miriam spent the first three nights in a cot beside the crow's cage at the way station, waking to syringe feed her every two hours. Jay and Bell visited them on the third night. The bird was already sitting on Miriam's shoulder and eating out of the palm of her hand.

"You think you saw her?" Miriam asked and picked up the evidence bag for a closer look.

Jay nodded.

"At close range?"

"Dangerously close," Jay said.

"And you're sure there was just the one—"

"Maybe it's a coincidence, but I figured you'd be able to tell." Miriam's hugs could be so sudden and strong they were almost confrontational. Jay wheezed as she wrapped him in her arms. She was old enough to be his aunt, and that was exactly how he felt about her. "I filed my report before coming over and emailed you a copy so you can see where I found that. Now, I'd better get home to Bell." Miriam pushed him away and slapped him on the chest.

"Do not tell me you left her alone all night!"

"Okay, I won't."

"Jay Tern! I do not approve!"

"I don't make a habit of it."

"Yes, you do," Miriam said, "and you know it."

That night, Jay fell asleep on the floor in front of a dying fire and slipped into another strange dream. A freezing fog had rolled in and swallowed the cabin. Barefoot, Jay stepped out into the garden with his tranquilizer rifle and stared at the frost on the ground. It was pocked with fresh tiger tracks. The frost crackled as he followed the tracks into the avocado grove. Visibility was poor. He couldn't see further than the barrel of his gun, but he heard a menacing growl and smelled a predator lurking perilously close. He pivoted, frightened and unsure. A blade of moonlight pierced the fog and revealed the tiger's enormous shadow dancing against the tree trunks. But it wasn't a cat that stepped out of those trees. It was Ling.

She was completely naked save for a beaded bracelet. She took his hand and led him back inside, where they sat on the floor in front of a roaring fire. He traced her tattoo with his fingertips. The beads she wore on that same wrist were made from a variety of reddish-brown quartz she'd always favored. Tiger's eye.

"I've missed this place," she said. Jay quivered as she ran her icy palm down his cheek and pulled his shirt over his head. When she moved to unbuckle his belt, he stopped her.

"No," he said. "I can't. I mean...I haven't...not for a long time."

"You shouldn't do that to yourself." She laughed and kissed him softly. "Anyway, it's only me." She kissed him again and undressed him, and they lay down together. Her touch wasn't cold anymore. It radiated through him like light and heat. Skin to skin, their kisses increased in depth and passion. Ling brushed Jay's hair from his forehead with her left hand. He gazed at her lightning bolt in the moonlight and saw it reflected in her transparent cheek.

Part III

39

FEBRUARY 17, 2005

CLEANED UP, SLICKED BACK, AND LEANING ON A TREKKING POLE, Lieutenant Krull was holding court on stage when Jay rushed into the auditorium, twenty minutes late. Geeta was up there too, glued to the back wall, looking freshly swabbed with a thin coat of her burgundy lip gloss, a black beret tilted over her scalp wound.

Jay's head was fuzzy, his hands jittery, and his patience thin. For the second straight night, he woke up rattled and drenched in sweat. He hadn't dreamed about her in five years and hadn't had a romantic dream of any kind in longer than that. He'd assumed that side of him was still dormant. Now, Ling was alive in his head again, and he was becoming unspooled. It didn't help that at breakfast, Bell complained about another migraine that kept her up half the night too. She said she felt weak and didn't have the energy for school. Jay remembered what Miriam had said the night before and that he still hadn't called Dr. Ambrose back. The right thing to do was to blow off the search and take Bell directly to Children's Hospital. Instead, he left her alone again.

Jay found a seat in the orchestra pit among the rank and file and berated himself. *What am I doing? What the hell is wrong with me?*

On stage, Krull held up the front page of *The Ventura County Star*. They had published their largest feature on the search yet. A copy of the paper was draped over the back of the seat in front of Jay's, and he grabbed it. The headline had punch. "Trail Goes Cold After Game Warden Mauled by Killer Cat." The lede was high on drama too. Both were low on facts.

> *Acting on instinct and his background as a federal tracker, Lieutenant Corey Krull with the California Department of Fish and Wildlife, who was previously honored for taking down a cop killer on the run, was the first to discover that the big cat had headed into the mountains around Santa Paula. Sometimes, one hero is all a community needs. Usually, however, it's not quite enough.*

The story explained that Krull was attacked by a big cat in the culvert and that without pausing for medical attention or sleep, he remained in the field and tracked the same animal all the way to Santa Paula before his body gave out. The Glenns made the paper too. The reporter acknowledged there had been rumors of a tiger on the loose, but the lieutenant's words paired with the tracks the wardens found supposedly confirmed it was a native mountain lion that had caused all the havoc. The editors printed an image of what wardens believed to be its front left pawprint. It was half gone already, and the rain was busy wiping it away for good, but one thing was clear: that cat's third toe was perfectly straight.

From Jay's point of view, the only revealing information in the entire piece was the amount of rain that had fallen in the past two-plus weeks: eleven inches. More than enough to wash away scent or scat and ensure that any tracks that might have recorded the tiger's movements had melted into the mud like an Etch A Sketch.

"One hero is not enough," Krull said. "Let that sink in, people. Who here is ready to join me and give it all they've got? Who here has the makings of a hero inside them?" Wardens exchanged awkward glances. Geeta smirked at Jay, who raised one eyebrow. "Tern, I read your report, and I'm not at all impressed."

"Yes, sir," Jay said, sitting up straight. He'd considered keeping the details of last night's mission to himself but opted for at least some transparency. In a brief report written in the cab of his truck, he described exploring Happy Camp Canyon and making it all the way to the cave. He didn't mention Geeta's presence or her entanglement with a certain crow. "You'd agreed the cat had headed west. You redeployed 80 percent of the team west of the culvert. Then you went offline in the opposite direction without telling a soul."

"Yes, sir. I did."

"Why?"

"I played a hunch."

"A hunch. That's always been your major malfunction, Tern. You think you're smarter than everybody else. So enlighten us. Tell us what you found last night by playing your hunch."

Jay leveled his gaze at his boss. He didn't think he was smarter than *everybody*, but his hunches had solved poaching cases across Ventura County, and he felt he'd earned some leeway. However, with Krull's lies in the media and the tiger still a ghost, his brilliant strategy had made him a convenient scapegoat. "Nothing, sir," he said finally.

"'Nothing, sir.'" Krull imitated him. "I've heard that from you before." Uncomfortable laughter rippled through the ranks. When Krull rattled off the morning patrols, Jay's name came up last of all. "Tern, I'll need you at the Glenns' all day. With your transponder on."

"If it's a mountain lion," Jay said, "why pester poor Mr. and Mrs. Glenn any further?"

Geeta laughed out loud. Krull wheeled around to look at her.

"Murthy. So far, you've given us squat-diddly while I'm out there leaving my blood on the trail!"

"Indeed," Geeta said. "I read all about it, Commander."

Krull crumpled the paper and hurled it into a trash can.

"We're expanding the search area again today. We'll be fanning out from here all the way to Santa Paula Ridge. I know that's a lot of ground to cover. Sacramento will be sending in reinforcements. I expect everyone in this room to keep their GPS unit engaged at all times. If you find something, anything of interest, radio me directly. I'll be in the field again today, too, despite the twenty stitches in my calf. No more freelancing or wild hunches. From now on, the only thing any of you need to follow is my orders."

By the time Jay had climbed into the driver's seat of his truck, Geeta was already sitting shotgun, her rifle case slotted between her legs. Around them, wardens loaded up in teams of threes and fours. Truck engines sparked; tires squealed on wet asphalt. Krull limped through the doors last and crossed to his truck, which he'd conveniently parked in the lot's only disabled space. He glared at Jay and Geeta as he sped away.

"Geeta Murthy. Are you trying to get me fired?"

"I am trying to find a tiger before it kills again."

Jay watched her lay her case on her lap and manipulate the combination lock until it read 090988, which didn't strike him as the most secure secret code. She opened it and gazed lovingly at her oiled and polished weapon of choice.

"You're trying to kill a tiger who hasn't killed at all so you can win best tracker and a hundred billion dollars."

"Semantics." Geeta set the case down in the rear of the cab, exposing the back of her long neck. That dormant side of him was most definitely stirring now. "The thing is, you *are* smarter than the rest of them. That's why they are using your maps, and you know as well as I do that our tiger has been in that cave. I felt it!"

"I only know what I can prove," Jay said as he watched Miriam's Animal Control van roll into the parking lot right on schedule. He flashed his lights. She pulled up beside him wearing the crow's feather in her hair. Jay hopped out of the cab and scooted around to Miriam's window so Geeta couldn't eavesdrop from the passenger seat.

"The DNA is a match," Miriam said.

"I'm very happy to hear that," Jay said. It was the only good thing that had come out of this mess so far.

"I cannot believe you found her. I'd been so worried that I made a huge mistake."

Jay knew the science. Rehabilitated crows must be released in pairs or groups to ensure their survival. He'd watched Miriam work the phones, but she couldn't find another crow in any rehab center in Southern California, and she couldn't keep a healthy bird penned up when it was ready to fly.

"I've checked every major crow roost in Ventura and Santa Barbara Counties looking for that dang bird. And you found her in a cave above Happy Camp Canyon."

"I never knew you were looking for her."

"They say a crow never forgets a face." Miriam blinked through tears. "I wanted to see if it was true."

"I'd bet it is in your case."

"Well, your instincts have always been pretty good." Miriam sniffed and glanced over at Geeta. "Not perfect, but pretty darn good." She took both his hands in hers and slipped him a small vial.

"Don't look at it with her around. What's happening there, by the way?"

"Nothing. She needs a ride."

"Mm-hmm."

"What's in the vial, Miriam?"

"Oh, just a strand of fur I found in the quills of a certain feather."

Jay arched his inquisitive eyebrow.

"Ding. Ding," Miriam said. Jay leaned in for a hug and hung on a bit longer than necessary. "Now, go save that tiger, game warden. I'm already looking for the right sanctuary. We're gonna find someplace special. Guaranteed."

Miriam frowned at Geeta as she pulled away. Geeta sneered back. Jay did his best not to look too pleased with himself as he buckled up. "What was she on about?" Geeta asked.

"That crow you like so much. Those two are old friends."

"Ha ha."

"Why are you still in my truck? 'We work better alone.' Those were your words."

"I was embarrassed, but I woke up thinking clearly, and the fact is you know this land, and I know tigers."

"Maybe so, but I am not going back to that cave with you. I'll drop you as close as I can to where you left Billie and wish you good luck."

"So it's like that," Geeta said.

"The tiger isn't there. We checked that box last night. And even if it were, I still wouldn't take you because I'm not the cat killer's caddy. You heard Krull. I have a job to do. If I get fired, who's going to pay my salary? My daughter's health insurance?"

"Please. They aren't going to fire one of the heroes who saved the valley."

"See, that's the thing about me," Jay said, firing the ignition. "I've never needed to be the hero."

40

BELL COMPARED HER SKETCH TO THE PHOTOGRAPH AS SHE REREAD Ling's journal over breakfast. She could finally see her mother and hear her voice, but basic facts and the tiny, mundane details that would tell the true story of Ling's life remained fuzzy, which made her more mirage than solid presence, a collection of dreams too fluid to hold. Bell ripped a page from her drawing pad, pulled a black pencil from her Pringles can, and jotted down some questions.

When she was done, she unfolded the topographic map she'd pinched from Jay's desk and laid it out on the floor. He'd drawn it in 1:50,000 scale, which meant that every centimeter of map space represented half a kilometer, or just over a quarter mile. She used a ruler to measure the approximate distance and saw that though the Windphone was roughly five miles away as the crow flies, it was seven miles away by road and even farther on trails. Wardens were everywhere, so she couldn't use roads. Lying on her belly propped up on her elbows, she planned a route that would take her up the Jagged Spur Trail from their garden to the Alisaw Rim Trail, which traced the entirety of the Santa Susana ridgeline and would lead her to the Inventor's neighborhood. It was a nine-mile hike each way. That was a long day—too long. She went over the route again and found a shortcut. She could leave the trail, descend into Sheep's

Canyon, and after a relatively simple traverse, carve a path through the savanna directly to the Windphone. That would save at least three miles.

Bell stepped outside and stared into the sky. It looked soupy, but the rain had slowed to a gentle shower. She packed some granola, three carrots and an apple, and filled her canteen with water. She pocketed her compass and house keys and sealed the map in a Ziploc bag that she slid into the front pocket of her pack. Kitted up, she stared into her bedroom mirror until her eyes turned glassy. She was only nine and had already lived two lives but could only remember one of them. She turned to her bed, where Ling's journal lay open to that snapshot of all three Terns. Her mother was naked, her hair buzzed and her tattooed forearm raised in defiance.

Bell plucked a pair of scissors from her drafting table and gathered her hair into her fist, slicing it off in chunks. She slipped the pack from her back, stripped down to her socks and underwear, and stomped into the bathroom. She found her father's beard trimmer in the cabinet, switched it on, and buzzed away all the remaining knots and tangles until she'd reached the base layer. When she was finished, she ran her palm over her fuzzy scalp, pleased to find she looked an awful lot like Ling. Then, she ran out into the avocado grove and let the rain wash clinging strands down her neck, shoulders, arms, and legs and into the dark soil.

She dried off in front of the fire, stepped into her overalls, wiggled into a t-shirt and fleece, double-knotted her boot laces, zipped up her rain shell, and put on her Dodgers cap. Then, she slipped her arms back through the straps of her pack and locked the front door behind her.

The rain stopped, and a gust of wind stirred the clouds like tea leaves. The emboldened sun split the tapestry apart at the seams. Patches of blue sky expanded, and a rainbow arced over the Santa Susanas. It had turned into a glorious day, but those first two miles took much longer than expected because the Jagged Spur was being swallowed up by the bush. Bell ducked heavy branches and pushed through thickets of funky white sage. She had never seen chaparral grow in so thick or so fast, but then, she'd never seen this much rain.

Sagebrush narrowed the Alisaw Rim Trail too. Steam rose from the burly shrubs. A pair of willow flycatchers darted overhead. Western fence lizards did their push-ups in the sun, and painted ladies, Bell's favorite butterflies, seemed to be everywhere, fluttering here and there, waiting for all the plump buds to unfold into flowers. Some of them already had. Bell noted scattered early bursts of California sunflower, delicate lavender blossoms of black sage, and pockets of sweet-smelling powder-blue ceanothus blooms.

Despite the encroaching vegetation, she kept a decent pace. When she reached the viewpoint overlooking the northwest corner of the valley, she sat on a flat rock the size of a milk crate, ate an apple, and took a swig of water, then peeled off her long sleeves and stuffed them into her pack. Then, she pulled out her field glasses and focused on her destination.

The Windphone's steel frame had been wrapped in a mosaic of clear blue glass. There were triangles, ovals, parabolas, and trapezoids. The Inventor stood at the top of a tall ladder and set what looked like an antenna from a different age onto the sparkling copper roof. He climbed onto the roof itself to bolt it down and paused to admire his work afterward. It looked to Bell like he'd finally finished.

She tipped her head back and let the sun warm her freckles as it rose to its apex and attempted to dissolve the lingering clouds. This was the second sunny day in weeks. Everything felt clean and new, but there was work to do. She still had to ascend another mile or so and gain over five hundred feet in elevation before she'd reach the top of Sheep's Canyon and the first of three cross-country sections. It was past noon already, and light was a finite resource in February. She'd better hustle.

41

JAY STASHED HIS GPS DEVICE IN THE BRUSH AT THE BOTTOM OF THE Glenns' driveway and drove to the old Jeep trail. He unlocked the vehicle gate and accelerated up the rutted fire road toward the ridge above Happy Camp Canyon. That strand of fur Miriam found suggested the tiger had been in that cave at some point, perhaps last night, and may even be there right now. Geeta would be on her way to take another look, too, but she'd have to find her horse first, which meant he had at least an hour on her. That was plenty of time when the road looked passable, but brush had quickly taken over. He managed to steer around it and bash through it for close to two miles. When he could drive no further, Jay killed the engine. He kicked off his boots and laced up a pair of trail runners. With his tranquilizer rifle in his hands, he charged up the slope for three hard, fast miles, desperate to get there first.

The final approach required him to climb down from the top of the cliff above the cave. He strapped his rifle to his back, locked his legs, and lowered himself from handhold to handhold before dropping onto the sandstone ledge with a soft kiss. He approached the entrance to the cave with his back to the rock, his heart thrumming. This time, there was an unmistakable animal scent. He cocked his dart gun and turned, ready to fire, but the cave was empty.

Geeta wondered if Billie might have made her way home to Dry Creek Ranch after being set loose, but their bond was strong, and she took a chance. She asked Jay to drop her on the road closest to the bottom of Happy Camp Canyon. Unfortunately, the filly was nowhere to be found. Geeta whistled as she hiked through the woods toward the rushing creek that sounded as loud as a river. She followed it up through the trees and heard the thrashing of a large animal in the nearby chapparal. She slipped her weapon from her shoulder. The animal thrashed again, and Geeta stepped slowly toward the rustling shrubs. Then, she heard a familiar whinny, and a broad smile swept across the tracker's face as she began to sing softly.

Billie pushed through the sagebrush and reared up on her hind legs. Her coat was gleaming, her big brown eyes shining. Geeta plucked an apple from her pack. Billie devoured it in three bites. "Thank you for waiting for me, my darling." Geeta hummed as she unsaddled her mount, brushed her down, and straddled each leg to clean the grass caught in Billie's shoes with a hoof pick. Judging by the chewed ends of the tall grasses, Billie had eaten well. *Good girl*, Geeta thought. *You'll have energy to burn.*

Great trackers built working maps in their heads whenever they were on the job, and Geeta didn't have to consult Jay's map to know the fastest route to the meadow above the cave. She asked Billie for speed, and she got it. On the way, Geeta surrendered to the darkness she'd been working hard to suppress since she'd first arrived in Alisaw Valley. Grainy images flashed in her mind's eye. Bloody bodies ravaged and torn. Her own mother left stranded and trembling in a swamp of hip-high water a quarter mile from their front door. Her father, for so long a towering presence, caught between love and duty. It was the same newsreel that had haunted her whole adult life and that she'd never defused.

Within forty minutes, they'd reached the meadow. Geeta dismounted and redid her long ponytail. Not because it needed it but as a hack to help her channel her demons and focus on the task ahead. She ditched her heavy boots for simpler shoes, slung her rifle over her right shoulder, and kissed the bridge of Billie's nose. "This time, I really will be right back."

Geeta dropped down from the roof of the cave and landed in silence. The floor inside was almost all solid stone, but she'd noticed small piles of decomposed rock in the corners. Not enough to trap a track, but enough for Geeta to detect movement as she crept toward the entrance. She cocked her weapon, placed her slender finger next to the trigger, and took two deep breaths to reduce her heart rate to kill speed.

It seemed to happen in slow motion. She heard shuffling coming from the cave and wheeled around to face it, but instead of a tiger, she found Jay kneeling in the rear of the cave, aiming his weapon at her.

"Wow," Jay said. "You made good time, and you're in luck." He thumbed in the direction of the crow's nest. "The proprietor is out."

Geeta seethed. She could have killed him, and it would have been his own bloody fault.

"'The tiger is not there,' he said! 'We checked that box last night,' he said! I offer to work together, and you sabotage me."

"It's not personal, Geeta," Jay said, standing. "You want the tiger dead for some secret reason, and I don't."

Geeta leaned her weapon against the outer wall of the cave and sat on the ledge. Her legs dangling, she watched the frothing creek tumble toward the valley floor. "He did love tigers more than people in the end," she said. "You had that part right." Jay joined her on the ledge. It had been years since she told anybody what had happened. Her soon-to-be-ex-husband didn't even know her long story, but given the situation, it felt natural to reveal it to Jay.

"I grew up in a village adjacent to a national park that had once been a raj hunting reserve. That's a place where English colonists and the upper caste met up to shoot tigers for sport. Even after independence, hunting on these reserves was very popular until Indira Gandhi formed her Tiger Task Force. She had read one of my father's early papers and appointed him to run one of her new national parks.

"His mission was to restore tiger habitat and protect them from poaching. He spent most of his time speaking to villagers and village leaders and asking them to leave the forest and the cats alone. The theory was that tiger tourism would bring them prosperity. And it did, here and there, especially for those he hired as guides and rangers, but watching from a safe distance was not the only way people interacted with tigers.

"When I was fifteen, a disfigured tiger who had been shot in the face by a poacher turned up mad with hunger. It couldn't catch its usual prey—you know, sambar or chital deer or gaur—so it focused on a much easier species to kill."

"It became a maneater," Jay said.

Geeta turned to him.

"It left a trail of bodies. Mangled faces, crushed rib cages, skulls cracked with a single swat. Spinal cords torn out and left on the side of the jungle path. Many times, all anyone could find were bone fragments and shredded clothes. It wasn't just our village. For sixteen months, it cycled through every village in its two hundred fifty-square-mile range. As you might imagine, my father felt a lot of pressure to put an end to it.

"I was with him one day early on. We were on horseback doing his usual rounds when the news came in that a young girl had been attacked while collecting bananas miles away. It was just the second death. Every ranger in the park left to track it, so nobody was with us when the cat with the mangled jaw stepped out of the jungle dragging the girl's lifeless body in its teeth. It dropped her, turned, and roared. Our horses were spooked but held their ground. My father was armed, of course, and he raised his weapon but purposely shot over the cat's head. Frightened, the tiger picked up its meal and ran off. That night, he barricaded himself in his office and sobbed.

"Neither of us told anybody what had happened, but as months passed and the bodies piled up, he felt more and more paralyzed with guilt. The villagers wanted to kill every tiger in the park, and he was powerless to stop them. Several were culled—none were the maneater. One night, my father mustered the nerve to protest to village elders. The blame they heaved in his direction sent him back into hiding.

"Any of us could have been next. It could have been my father—I'm sure he wishes it was—or me. But it was my mother who left the house first on the morning of September 9, 1988. When we heard its unmistakable roar, a group of armed villagers gathered and took off in pursuit. I panicked when I couldn't locate my mother, but my father insisted that she was fine and refused to leave the house. She'd gone off to the market, he said, but our Land Rover was still parked in the drive, and her keys were on the hook in the kitchen. I loaded his rifle and caught up to the hunting party. We found her sandals thirty-five yards apart among fresh pugmarks.

"We'd all told ourselves the same story during those months. That the attacks had been lightning strikes. It was over before the victim knew it or felt any pain, but this wasn't like that at all. Judging by the tracks, the tiger allowed my mother to run, cornered her in a swamp, and dove in after her. Then, they both disappeared. I was still with the hunters when they found her bloody sari hours later and used it to wrap up her meager remains."

"Alright," Jay said. "I get it now." He offered her his canteen. She waved it away.

"Many of our neighbors considered it karma."

"They were wrong. They were and are wrong. You know that."

"It destroyed her, Jay. As if it were making a very specific point."

"Did you ever find the cat?"

She nodded and sighed. "He was holed up in a ravine. It felt like something out of the early twentieth century. A dense mist had rolled in, and three dozen men beat the bushes. They strung white linen in the trees to create corridors that would funnel the cat toward the riflemen. There were six of them. They rode in on elephants and horses. But when the tiger was flushed out, everyone missed except… well, I'm not sure anybody realized that I had tucked into the perfect blind. Unfortunately, the tiger was too quick for me. I managed to squeeze off two shots, but neither was a kill shot. I grazed its shoulder and hip, and the beast vanished again like a demon in the fog.

"I never went home after that. I took a bus to my auntie's house. She lived in the countryside near the Nepali border, and I spent the next few months shooting in ranges. I got good. Really bloody good. I wanted to go back and kill the maneater myself. I was obsessed. It was all I could think about, but the day before I was scheduled to leave, we heard that someone else had shot and killed it. I had no money. Few prospects. So I stayed with my aunt and kept shooting. I even started competing. I became the most accurate young gun in South Asia. Then one of the best in the world. Made it to the Olympics. Came in sixth place."

"I heard," Jay said. "A few of the wardens googled you."

Geeta rolled her eyes, but she was flattered. "After that, I tried uni. Dropped out in my second year to chase a boy to Kenya and ditched him when I was offered a gig as a hunting guide in the Maasai Mara. Right away, I knew tracking big animals was my true calling. Not for the bush meat or the thrill of the hunt. I considered it training. I'd made a promise to my mother on the day she died, and I swore to myself that the next time I was presented with an opportunity to avenge her, I would not miss."

Jay offered his canteen a second time, and water trickled from her lower lip as she drank deeply, her fingertips tracing the scabbing bald patch on her crown. It didn't matter that this wasn't the same tiger that had killed her mother. She was hunting something else entirely. Jay knew what it was like to have a void open beneath you—to live with a darkness that wanted to swallow you.

"My wife died when Bell was three," he said.

"Your daughter's name is Bell?" Geeta turned and smiled through a single tear. "That's lovely. How old is she now?"

"She's nine."

"Nine. A tender and vicious age." Geeta wiped the stray tear away with the heel of her palm. "Nobody wants to join our miserable little club, do they?" She retied her hair and banished her beret to her rucksack "Now, why don't you tell me why you're here. It's not a hunch this time. I can see that."

"You called it," Jay said. "The crow and the tiger." Jay explained Miriam's find and how he'd scoured the cave looking for more evidence. "I haven't found any fur, urine, blood, or scat. Maybe it used this cave at one point and left."

"No." Geeta pulled her pocketknife and a flashlight from her pack. "It can't be that simple." She crossed to the crow's nest and peered into it. She worked the tip of her blade from the edge of the nest to the cradle. She set aside two splintered chopsticks and a single forked stick: keepsakes from foraging runs that had become tools. "What do we know about this crow, Warden Tern?"

"Well," Jay said, "crows are like us. Or like most primates anyway. They're social creatures by nature, which means they need to bond to survive. This bird had been orphaned, so she bonded with Miriam during rehabilitation, meaning she was already geared toward interspecies connection. Also, she's tough. The world kicked her in the face, and she survived to give some back, if you don't mind my saying."

"Yes, wounded souls tend to have an edge."

"And obviously, the darn thing can fly its butt off."

Geeta huffed in agreement as she probed the cradle. It was layered with pine needles, tender sycamore leaves, and something else. Woven through the leaf litter was an insulating bed of fur. "And it used that skill to risk its life for its only friend," she said.

"Two lonely beasts surviving in a hostile world together," Jay said. "Who would ever believe a story like that?" He pulled the tweezers from his Leatherman and three plastic evidence bags from his pack. He tucked two into his waistband and shook the third one open.

"You cannot call this in," Geeta said. "You'll lose your job, and we still haven't a clue—" She stopped herself and returned to the ledge. She raised her rifle and peered through the scope.

"Let me worry about Krull," Jay said as he plucked knotted clumps of fur from the nest. He would send them off to three different labs to be certain. "Anyway, you should be pleased with yourself. You were right. Doesn't that usually light you up, being right?" Jay braced for a zinging retort, but Geeta was already gone.

42

AVOIDABLE TRAGEDY, JAY ONCE TOLD BELL, WAS THE RESULT OF several dominoes falling in sequence. Looking back, an experienced forensic investigator could pinpoint where and how the chain reaction began. The first, second, or third domino doesn't feel like much of a risk, but that's where you need to stop the tragic sequence: when the daring is still innocent enough to feel doable. That theory occupied Bell's mind as she detoured from the trail down a faint, overgrown deer path into the wooded crease known as Sheep's Canyon.

She'd been here once before and remembered it as one of the gentler folds of the Santa Susanas. On the way down, she could see that the typically dry Shepherd's Creek was running too high to ford. She considered backtracking to the trail immediately but opted to follow the water upstream to look for a broader section to rock hop. She was rewarded with a recently uprooted sycamore tree that had fallen onto its side, spanning the creek like a floating bridge of convenience. It was plenty wide enough for Bell's small feet, and she made quick work of the crossing.

Difficult tasks often look more doable from a distance, and the grade on the far slope was steeper than anticipated. The ground still saturated and slick, Bell skittered like a crab from one tree to the next. She clutched branches and roots for stability and scolded herself for her choice in shortcuts. Eventually, she topped out into the savanna, where the slope was gentler.

The grass grew out of the soil in bunches and swayed above Bell's shoulders, higher and denser than ever. Stalks rattled in the wind. It sounded as if she were marching through a garden of rattlesnakes, and she couldn't see much. Her pulse quickened. She repeated her mantra. "A cauldron of bats, a dance of cranes, an orchestra of crickets."

She'd felt thrilled for the adventure when she set off without so much as a note, but there was a dark side to every thrill ride. Nobody knew where she was or where she was headed, and as she marched blindly forward, the grasses became a tripping hazard. Her foot caught, and she fell forward into blades, slicing her bare forearms, cheeks, and chin. The savanna, which looked so soft and lush from afar, was more of an obstacle than she'd anticipated.

Bell hiked blind, using her compass to chart a northwest course she believed would take her through roughly two miles of savanna and deliver her to the Windphone, but the slope intensified unexpectedly. A little at first. Then a lot. She kept climbing until she felt a trickle of mud thread into the eyelets of her boots. She looked down. The ground seemed to be eroding from beneath her feet, and her traction became tenuous. She tried to keep going, but it felt like she was on ice. She grabbed fistfuls of sharp grass to steady herself, but the flow increased. She lost her footing, fell hard on her side, and was swept away in a mudslide. She could see she was careening down a melting slope toward a sheer drop-off, where mud and water drained over the frayed lip into empty space.

She hurtled toward the drop, too scared to scream. *I misread the map*, she thought. *I should never have gone off trail.* The cliff was less than fifty feet away. She flipped onto her belly and clawed at the slick earth, which slowed but did not arrest her slide. A few body lengths from certain doom, she spotted a stubborn ceanothus shrub clinging to the cliff's edge like it had refused to give in to gravity. She rolled up onto her seat, splayed her legs out like a starfish, and aimed for the thickest root, which had been shaped by wind, water, and time into a smooth handle. Bell grabbed it with both hands, swung her body parallel to the lip of the mountain, and stopped just short of free fall. Her compass tipped end over end into oblivion, and her Dodgers cap spun down after it like a parachute in the wind.

Clutching a shrub that was thick and hearty but stunted by the wind, Bell was still overcome with the sensation of falling. Her heart pounded as she scooted up closer to the roots. She held on even tighter and built up the courage to look out over the edge.

Topographic maps were laced with elevation lines, arcs that signified gain or loss in altitude and offered a cross-country hiker an idea of the best places to move across the landscape. When Bell had planned her route, she'd misread the map. She'd seen a plateau that linked two slopes and missed the slot canyon below her. *That was the first domino*, she thought. Unless it was her discovery of her father's secret stash beneath his dresser. Or Principal Ono's explanation of the Windphone or the family tree assignment itself.

No. It was Ling's death. By the time she was three years old, Bell was already working with one domino down.

Clinging to the shrub that saved her life, she looked across the gap and found the gleaming Windphone taunting her from the next ridge. It was roughly one mile away, she thought, as she watched a crow bank overhead and corkscrew into the canyon. "As the crow flies," Bell said out loud. "One mile as the crow flies."

She was so close, but lacking wings, she had far more than a mile of ground to cover, and without a compass, she had no clue how to get there. The first step was obvious. She had to climb up and out of harm's way. Water and mud were still sheeting down from above her, but she'd slid at an angle. She was already out of the main flow. There looked to be better footing to her right, but there was only one way to know for sure.

She pushed up into a squat, still clutching the shrub. Her clothes heavy with mud and her legs jelly, she let go and began crab walking up and to the right. Each step was deliberate. She planted the sole of her boot as deep as possible into the soggy slope for stability and continued to stomp that way even after she was well beyond the reach of the mudslide and the sheet of water that had caused it. She wouldn't stand upright until the lush savanna took her in again and closed its curtains behind her.

Orienteering is problem-solving. Bell heard her dad's voice in her head as she fought through head-high blades of grass that scraped most of the mud away. *Roadblocks and hazards are par for the course.* She checked her progress against the map in her head and the fading daylight. If she was right, this slope would level into a wooded meadow, and beyond it, she would find the Alisaw Rim Trail at its highest point. From there, it was all downhill.

Her traction improved as she climbed higher. Adrenaline and energy thrummed through her. "I should be dead," Bell said out loud. "The last domino fell, and I'm still alive." She laughed at her own audacity and dumb luck, which had made her somehow immune to the cosmic forces of tragedy.

If only she had lingered in the arms of that ceanothus shrub on the precipice a few moments longer or observed the ravine a bit more thoroughly, she might have seen that beneath the circling crow lurked a familiar figure slipping through the shadows in search of higher ground and burning with hunger.

43

JAY PARKED OUTSIDE THE GLENNS' GATE AND KILLED THE ENGINE. He retrieved his stashed GPS from a rangy patch of artemisia and checked his watch. It was 1:47 p.m. As far as Krull knew, Jay had been monitoring the Glenn property since eight that morning, but now his stakeout had truly begun, and he planned to be thorough. He wore his side arm and carried his dart gun over his shoulder, slotted his notebook into his back pocket, and holstered his field glasses. Then, he walked the perimeter of the property, which he would do every half hour. He'd called ahead and received access from the absentee owners of the neighboring plots to loop around the north side of the Glenns' spread, where he'd discovered the snow leopard, and the west, where the big cat barn was visible.

On his second patrol, he noted Aubrey shuffling in circles in the horse corral. Jay could see a dozen things that needed to be done. If it were him, he'd begin with breaking down and removing the horse trailer. Then he'd replace the corral fencing, repair the barn, and clean the enclosures. The stench was strong, even from fifty yards away. Maybe the Glenns had been paralyzed by losing their animals, or maybe they didn't work that hard period, and their animals had been forced to live in filth.

Between patrols, Jay sat in the cab of his truck and listened to the stagnant updates of the search on his scratchy radio feed. He had planned to send out an alert about the cave but reconsidered. Geeta was right; the tiger could be anywhere, and he was not operating from a position of strength. Their breakthrough had to come from her, with his name kept out of it. He checked her transponder. Geeta's deliberate yet consistent advance coupled with her radio silence was concerning. It meant, at the very least, she'd seen something that interested her. She might even have a bead on the cat. Moored at the Glenns, Jay could do nothing to stop her.

His cell phone rang while he was walking the western perimeter for the fourth time. He answered without checking the incoming number, hoping it was Geeta.

"Tern."

"Mr. Tern, I'm so glad I caught you. Dr. Ambrose, Children's Hospital."

Jay froze. "Hello, Doc."

"We still don't have Isabella on the schedule, and we do need to see her as soon as possible." Her tone was as warm and calm as he remembered. "We have an opening tomorrow."

"Right. Well, uh, work has gotten...honestly, you wouldn't believe me if I told you...and with me being a single parent—"

Jay cut himself off. He never could stomach the excuse-makers—people who failed to take personal responsibility for falling short. Now he was one of them, and even he didn't want to hear it.

"Mr. Tern, pardon me for being blunt, but it is *vital* we clear up this inconsistency. We both want Bell to feel better, and if any treatment is required, we must—"

"No, you're right," he said. "You're absolutely right."

"Obviously, it's best to begin as soon—"

"You're right! Okay? You're right!" Jay clenched his jaw, attempting to stem the tide of nausea rising from his gut. The sun felt blistering. He unbuttoned his shirt and pulled the excess from his waistband.

For years, he'd thought of bad luck like a freak storm cycle. It materialized in the atmosphere with little to no warning, then proceeded to drench, spin, and shatter you. Almost everyone and every place would get a taste of it at some point or another, but even a casual survey of human history proved that some places and people got served much more than their fair share.

He visualized Bell at home alone, drawing the afternoon away, the side of her right hand smeared with graphite. For the second time that day, he felt an urge to abandon his post, go home, and hug his daughter. Load her up in the truck and drive to Dr. Ambrose's office. And he would have done just that if he hadn't seen Eden Glenn kneeling in the grass at the edge of the woods. With the phone pinned to his ear, he watched her stand in shock, then move slowly into the trees.

"I'm sorry, Mr. Tern," Dr. Ambrose said. "I know it's challenging to confront these possibilities, especially given what you've already experienced. That is not lost on me."

"Challenging," Jay said. That was not how he'd describe losing a wife and now possibly a daughter in less than a decade. It wasn't how he'd describe the very worst luck of all. "That's one word for it."

"Aubrey!" Eden shouted over her shoulder. "Aubrey! Come quick!" Jay raised his field glasses and focused on Eden. She was staring at the ground as if she'd found a track.

"Look," Dr. Ambrose said. "I am on your side here. Yours and Bell's."

"Warden Tern..." His radio chirped. It was Geeta. "Warden Tern. Paging Warden Tern."

"Aubrey!" Eden yelled again. "We've got something!"

"I'm putting you down for tomorrow at eleven," Dr. Ambrose said. "That way, you don't have to deal with traffic coming into the city."

The more earnest and confident Dr. Ambrose sounded, the more rage Jay felt until it was the only thing keeping him upright, but it needed a target, and the doc wouldn't do. With a stab of guilt, he hung up on her and locked in on Eden. His cell phone rang again. He glanced at the number and answered.

"Geeta? Where the hell are you?"

"Oh, you know," she whispered, "face down in the shrubs in ticky-tacky suburbia measuring a fresh pugmark against my palm."

"Do you see him?"

"No, but I'm getting very close. This track was made within the last two hours."

"Where, exactly?" Jay unfolded the map in his mind. The thing about tinkering with maps was that it allowed you to commit a place to memory. Whenever he woke in the middle of the night and stared up from his lumpy futon, his maps of Alisaw Valley and Ventura County unfurled across the ceiling. The exposed beams were mountain ranges; depressions and cracks in the paint were canyons and creeks. Knowing a place so well could be read one of two ways. It either meant that was where he and Bell belonged, or it was a sure sign that they had nothing left to learn from it and should leave it behind. If bad luck was like weather, maybe they could outrun it. The debate was a familiar one, but he always came to the same conclusion. He couldn't leave Alisaw without confronting everything that had happened there, and he wasn't ready.

Geeta gave him the waypoints, and he drew a line from the Glenns' place to Sierra's red dot on the map in his head. It couldn't be a coincidence. Had Bolt been nearby on the day he found Sierra? How close had he come to ending all this before it began?

"Why are you calling me?" Jay snapped. "Just finish it already."

"Oh, I plan to," she said, "but don't you want to see it walking around free at least once?" Jay didn't feel guilty when he hung up this time.

The woman is twisted, he thought. *She's damaged goods on a misguided vengeance trip.* And he could not let her win. He raced back to his truck, fired the engine, and watched the Glenns jog downhill after him. Whatever they had to tell him was stale news by now. Jay punched it.

His uniform still unbuttoned and untucked, Jay leaped from the cab and knelt in the bushes beside Geeta. She was a sight. The small scab below her left eye had punctured, and her face was streaked with dried blood. Her shirt was torn at the elbow where the skin had been gouged, and she was bleeding there too. Then there was the exposed patch of scalp where her hair used to be. Not that any of it seemed to trouble her. She was too busy admiring her discovery. There were three tracks and among them, a full stride of nearly six feet. It was magnificent.

"You think it's in this subdivision?" Jay asked.

"No. It skirted the perimeter. I think it's heading west, but Camp Creek is running too high to use the corridor. It had to find another way." She had her map open on the ground in front of her. "It left the creek bed at the bottom of the canyon. I know because I found a toppled boulder with soil still clinging to the side right about here." She tapped the location with her fingertip. "It ate your bait, by the way."

"Huh. So you saw my stuff and that rock, and it led you here?"

"Not exactly. First it led me to a fresh, green sycamore leaf, which I found in an open meadow with no sycamores anywhere close. It had to have hitched a ride, perhaps on the bottom of a tiger's paw or in the fluff of its mane. I didn't really *know* I was on to it until I found a tiger-sized mat of trampled grasses that looked like a bed, with the front and back legs stretched out in opposite directions. Just back there."

Jay was looking in the other direction, at a familiar pepper tree in the distance.

"Okay, this is disappointing. I've found our tiger's trail with very little to go on, and you aren't making any of your brilliant annotations. What do you see?"

"It's where the lynx was first spotted," Jay said. "Maybe the tiger is looking for its friend."

"I thought we agreed that its friend is an ill-tempered crow," she said. "Let's not add a bandmate because you're, I dunno...sad? Furious? Which is it?"

"Both," he said. "I'm almost positive it came by the Glenn property at some point too. Could it be retracing its steps?"

"We did flush it out of its haven," Geeta said. "Perhaps it's expanding its range. Do you know how wild tigers do that?"

"You're the expert," Jay said.

"By cycling through their turf."

They scanned her map. Jay leaned in and pressed his thumb onto a red X that was less than two miles away.

"Dry Creek Ranch," they said it in unison.

"Told you it was headed west," Geeta said. She stood and clicked her tongue. Billie ambled over.

"It's leaving the valley," Jay said.

"It's certainly worth looking into." Geeta saddled up. "Once I have it in my sights, I'll pin it down and call you to meet me."

Jay nodded and shook his head at the same time. "There won't be time for all that," he said and slotted his tranquilizer rifle between her saddlebags. She tried to shake him off. "Take it. You don't have to kill this cat, Geeta. It won't help."

"And how would you know?" Geeta said, her eyes glistening.

"Because there's a kind of pain that never goes away," he said. "We just have to figure out a way to live with it. And when that stops working, find another."

44

IT WAS THE ROAR OF A CHOPPER OVERHEAD THAT DROVE BOLT INTO the slot canyon. She'd spent much of the afternoon slinking between parking lots and loading docks, a condo complex and a medical office building, a soccer field and a multiplex. She'd skirted several subdivisions too. Now, once again, she was in a wilder place, where there was no evidence of human activity, aside from that monstrous mechanical bird swooping this way and that.

She found no cave or shelter as she approached the canyon's back wall, but there was a flowing waterfall and enough chunky sandstone stacked up on the edges for Bolt to ascend the deconstructed staircase. Loose boulders slipped from beneath her back legs, tumbled, and crashed into the pooling water below as she climbed. She topped out in the savanna and pinned her belly to the wet earth, scanning the airwaves with her hypersonic ears. She brushed her whiskers against the ground and detected soft footsteps and the parting of the grassy sea. There was life nearby.

Bell was still mired in the tall grass when she heard the helicopter, but she caught a brief glimpse as it completed its circuit of the valley. When the rumble of falling rocks echoed toward her, it sounded curious but not dangerous. She'd seen water move the land right out from beneath her feet. That was what record storm cycles did;

they transformed the landscape. Anyway, she was on flat ground now and what she believed to be a northern tack toward the Alisaw Rim Trail. The sky was mostly clear, and she was alone. Unless you counted the crow spiraling above her. When the chopper roared by a second time, Bell hit the dirt. She could not allow herself to be *rescued*. That would be humiliating.

The sun angled low in the western sky and infused Alisaw Valley with golden light. Bell glanced at her watch. It was nearly five o'clock. Darkness would descend soon. The bunch grasses had become sparse, which enabled her to jog up a short rise to a group of boulders blotched with lime-green lichen. She could see a dense huddle of live oaks up ahead and a lush meadow beyond it that stretched out toward a saddle where she hoped to find her trail.

Bell entered the oak woodland and was stunned at the sight of thousands of painted ladies swarming the canopy. They clung to the crackling bark, crawled on the forest floor, and floated through the dusky light. They were orange with black-and-white stripes and polka dots, and like a tiger's stripes, each one offered its own intricate pattern, its own expression of what it meant to be a painted lady. Knowing that made Bell feel even more connected to them.

"A kaleidoscope of butterflies," she said. They were spinning, falling, and rising all around her. Bell weaved between the trees. Butterflies alighted gently upon her head and shoulders. Some looked pristine and vibrant. Others had faded, their wings ravaged by wind and rain. She held out her left palm, and a pair perched there together.

Mesmerized by the kaleidoscope, Bell didn't sense she was being stalked until the wind shifted and carried with it the sour heat of her predator's breath. A shiver traveled the length of Bell's spine. She knew exactly who was behind her. The tiger stepped closer, and her growl rippled through Bell like a wave. Bell turned slowly to find a thick thread of saliva dripping from the tiger's open mouth less than ten feet away.

Time stopped as Bell mapped the face she'd committed to

memory. She checked off the tiger's two-tone nose, her yellowed canines, her swiveling ears, and the pools of molten amber that were her eyes. Then, she lingered on the lightning bolt. At close range, it looked eerily similar to her mother's tattoo.

The big cat's whiskers rippled. Her short mane flared with static electricity, and her powerful jaws opened and closed as she stepped within arm's length of Bell. All around them, painted ladies danced. Bell could feel the small hairs on the tiger's wet nose as she sniffed her from the top of her boots to her hips to her navel all the way to her shoulders. Bell whimpered and emptied her bladder. She saw the tiger note the dark spread in the crotch of her overalls, but she was too terrified for embarrassment, too frozen to run, too overwhelmed to speak. Her only choice was surrender. The tiger's tongue hung heavy from her open mouth, and Bell could see the papillae she'd read about. She felt their roughness when the tiger ran her tongue across the length of Bell's right cheek from her jawline to her hairline. A bloody rash bloomed and burned.

Bell knew she wasn't much of a meal, but she was there, and this cat was obviously starving. Separated by inches, immersed in a sublime swarm, the sound of a soft rain filtered through the canopy. Bell sensed the tiger's hesitation and wondered if she'd been recognized as the girl from the bus, which sprang a radical thought loose. Bell chuffed. It wasn't a tiger-quality chuff. It lacked the classic guttural, bass-note rumble, but it was a statement that said, "I am here, and I am your friend."

One of the tiger's ears folded over in surprise, and Bell chuffed again. This one was better. The tiger cocked her head and chuffed back. They stared into one another's eyes for nearly a minute. The tiger chuffed again and placed her front paw onto the toe of Bell's boot before moving it onto her shoulder. Bell raised her hand slowly and grazed the tiger's lower leg with her fingertips. She petted her matted fur all the way down to the topside of her paw. She traced her underside by the pads and realized this supposedly vicious animal had no claws.

The tiger retracted her paw and took a step back. Running on a blend of fascination and instinct, Bell stepped forward and reached out her left hand. The tiger leaned into it, arched her back, and dropped her tail. The sky above was a shattered patchwork of orange, pink, and gray. Storm clouds had steamed in again from the northeast, and light was draining fast. Tears streamed down Bell's cheeks. Nobody would ever believe her. If she weren't right here experiencing it, she wouldn't believe it herself. That hardly mattered. Her mouth was dry. Every inch of her skin was drenched in sweat. Her legs were sticky with urine, and she'd never in her life felt so perfect.

"Caw!" The crow darted through the grove and swirled the butterflies into a frenzy. The tiger jerked her head up, and her ears swiveled as she registered a distant pounding, then the thundering of hooves. The crow flew directly toward the ruckus. "Caw! Caw!" The tiger turned hard, knocked Bell down, and sprinted in the opposite direction, back toward the canyon. From her hands and knees, Bell watched the cat pivot, searching for the best possible escape route. The thundering of hooves grew louder, closer. Bell heard a gunshot, immediately followed by another. She stayed low and crawled behind one of the trees as a hunter galloped through the grove on horseback, stopping at the edge of the woodland to raise their rifle once more.

Geeta scanned the savanna through her scope and detected a glint of orange in the green. The tiger wasn't running; it was hiding. She took a deep breath, steadied herself, and settled her finger on the trigger. She'd admired Jay's insistence that she carry his dart gun and his confidence that she would come to see things from his gentler point of view, but she needed this kill to set things right, to recalibrate the rotation of her inner world, to finally spark the funeral pyre and torch her darkest memories to ash. And she could not remember the last time she'd missed her target three times in a row.

Geeta exhaled. Billie whinnied, and the tiger took off, bounding in and out of her crosshairs. Geeta gauged the cat's tempo and stride. She had the timing locked. Redemption was imminent.

"Billie?" A child's voice rang out from behind. The startled horse made a sharp about-face. Geeta had been leaning so far forward that she slid off her saddle and now dangled by one stirrup. Inverted, she had a perfect view of the One-Legged Crow, who soared after the fleeing tiger, shrieking in mockery.

"Caw! Caw! Caw!"

"Damn you, Geeta!" She wriggled her boot free, fell flat on her back, and seethed. "When you have the bloody shot, *take it!*"

Bell stepped through the trees, stunned. Dead butterflies littered the forest floor where Billie had trampled them thanks to the wretched hunter—or, more precisely, the tracker. "You're a girl," Bell said.

"Don't sound so surprised." Geeta used her rifle to push herself to her feet. "What's your name?"

Bell hesitated. The walkie-talkie on Geeta's hip squawked with game warden chatter. Bell had said too much already. She'd jeopardized her mission.

"You know you're not supposed to be out after dark. Or alone."

"I was fine until you almost shot me."

Geeta stepped forward, took Bell's chin between her thumb and forefinger, and turned her head to examine the rash on her cheek. "That tiger would have eaten you alive if it weren't for me."

"Yeah, right. You didn't even see me, and you missed. Twice."

"And you are an impolite little twerp. You pissed your pants, and you're breaking the law." Geeta pulled Billie close and slapped her saddle. "Up you get. You're riding with us."

"No."

"Don't make me hog-tie you to the back of my bloody horse."

"It's not your horse!"

Bell turned and sprinted away into the gathering darkness in what she hoped was the direction of her trail. A cloud burst above her, and rain sheeted down. It would wash away her urine, sweat, and blood, along with the last traces of the mudslide and the tiger's saliva, but the feel of fur was still alive in Bell's fingertips, as was the shape of a spiked tongue against her cheek.

Geeta watched the child go, then glanced in the direction of her target. The choice was clear: take off in pursuit of a beast that was almost certainly looking for an angle back into the box canyon, or catch the little snot who had no business being outside in the rain with a starving tiger on the loose. She grabbed her walkie-talkie and sighed. The girl's parents were obviously criminally incompetent. "Evening, everyone. I've just had a visual," Geeta said as she guided Billie down the tiger's trail of trampled grass. "I chased him into Colibri Canyon. Set a perimeter in the valley, and you'll funnel him right back to me."

"Sounds like you missed." Krull's voice crackled through the radio. There was a fuzzy pause. "Sending three teams now. Bird's gonna fly too."

"Splendid," Geeta snapped. Then she considered the other fugitive still running through the mountains. Someone had to corral her before she became cat food. "Also, there's—"

In a flash of recognition, Geeta lowered her walkie-talkie. Shaved head or no, it shouldn't have taken her this long to realize that she'd seen the girl before. Over the past few days, word had circulated among the search party that the first person in Alisaw Valley to have seen the escaped tiger was a schoolgirl and that Jay had kept this detail out of his original report. No wonder he was so interested in capturing the cat alive. He wasn't some angel who couldn't bear the thought of spilled blood. This was personal for him too.

"You cut out, Murthy," Krull said. "What else you got?"

45

JAY WAS IN HIS TRUCK PARKED OUTSIDE THE GLENNS' GATE WHEN Geeta's APB came over the radio. He opened his map and marked where Geeta was and where the tiger was likely headed: back into Colibri Canyon. On the map, it looked like there were two ways in and out of Colibri Canyon—one in the valley and another at the top of the rock fall—but Jay knew that in the upper elevations, there were multiple exits. The cat would have figured that out. He radioed the lieutenant to share his knowledge. Krull interrupted him, overconfident as always.

"We got this," Krull said. "Stay on the Glenns. Over."

Stuck on the sidelines, Jay tuned in to the local news on AM radio, where the latest big cat sighting was being reported. He counted the guns on their way to take Bolt down and felt a compulsion to join the search with his tranquilizer rifle, but he'd already surrendered it to Geeta. He felt useless. He was failing when it mattered most, both as a father and a game warden.

He pictured Bell at home in front of the fire, keeping tabs on the search. She had probably heard the same report, and he knew how painful it would be for her to imagine the tiger running for its life while the whole world closed in, armed to the teeth. For most of Bell's life, Jay had advised her that when the tide of emotions swelled like that, it was best not to believe everything she felt. He called it "staying neutral," but the lesson never took. Not really. Even when she tried to hide her feelings from him, it was obvious she felt so much. Which was for the best. He knew firsthand that the cell wall between neutrality and numbness was permeable, and once you crossed over, it was near impossible to get back. Not that he'd ever wanted to. If he didn't feel anything, he couldn't feel sorry for himself, and he considered self-pity to be among the lowest forms of human misery. But in that moment outside the Glenns' gate, he was confronted with how much his numbness had distracted him from his most important mission: keeping Bell healthy and safe. Krull was right after all. It was long past time to follow orders. Dr. Ambrose's orders. It was time to go home.

He reached for the key in the ignition but was stopped by the crack of gunfire ringing through the woods. He was out of the cab and up the long driveway in a blink. He gripped his sidearm with his left hand, pressed into the top of the gate with his right, and swung over in one clean motion. The rain blurred his vision, but he could see Eden and Aubrey arguing through their living room window, illuminated by the television. Eden was barefoot in a pink tank top and white cotton boy shorts, waving a pistol over her head and screaming. Aubrey was pleading with her. He held a Maglite and was dressed head to toe in dripping rain gear. Jay saw the muzzle flash again and heard glass shatter as the light went out in the living room.

"Shots fired! I repeat, shots fired!" Jay yelled into his radio as he reached the front porch. He banged on the door. "Drop the weapon, Mrs. Glenn! There is no reason for anybody to get hurt tonight!" He banged on the door again. Aubrey opened it, and he looked shaken.

"This is a private discussion, Tern." Jay clocked the smoldering television behind Aubrey and the steady drip in the center of the room where a bullet had pierced their roof. "She don't mean nothing by it."

Both hands on his pistol, Jay watched Eden set hers on an end table, retreat to the sofa, and weep. "Shots were fired, Mr. Glenn,"

Jay said, holstering his weapon. "Sheriff's deputies are on their way. What were you two arguing about?"

Aubrey pulled off his poncho, flung it to the floor, and sunk into the couch beside Eden, wrapping his arms around her. Quaking with sobs, she leaned into his bulk and muttered her breathless apologies. "It'll be okay, darling. It was an accident," he said. "It was all an accident."

46

THE CHOPPER ROARED OVERHEAD, ILLUMINATING THE DOWNPOUR in yellows, blues, and reds. Bell dropped to her belly on a muddy deer path and watched the chopper bank toward the drop-off, which she took to mean the tiger was still very much alive. She pushed herself back up to her feet and kept running until the deer trail curled into a much larger cut that had to be the Alisaw Rim Trail. If she was right, the Windphone was just over a mile away.

Her feet were raw, soaked, and blistering. She barely felt them as she charged downhill. Lights burned in the hills below, and when the trail veered left, she could see that the Inventor had tented the Windphone in his blue tarp. Although she was armed with her interview questions, she still hadn't decided how to begin. What do you say by way of greeting to your dead mom? She would have stopped and run through a few takes if not for the sound of hooves bearing down upon her. Bell ran even harder. She was too close and had endured too much to let anyone stop her now.

She reached a Y-junction, left the trail, and sprinted onto a gravel spit that became asphalt, with large houses sprouting up on both sides. Lightning flashed and thunder exploded as Billie closed the distance. Bell shot through a narrow gap between homes and pushed up onto a tiered flagstone wall that divided the backyards of two properties. She leaped to the ground and rolled, then sprinted across a sprawling lawn, clambered onto a trampoline, and used it to spring onto another flagstone wall. From it, she could see a strand of similar homes strung out along a wide, grassy ledge that overlooked Alisaw Valley. Streetlights glimmered below like tethered stars. And directly in front of her was the Windphone, its blue tarp rippling in the breeze.

"Bell Tern!" Bell looked over her shoulder and there was Geeta standing with her rifle strapped to her back atop the far wall. "How far are we running tonight? Because I must tell you, the indignities of this evening are beginning to pile up."

The sound of churning rotors reverberated off the mountainside as they lifted the chopper above the ledge and bathed Bell in the helicopter's hot light. Bell dropped to the ground, stuck the landing, and kept running. Steam poured off her as she shed her pack, unzipped her shell, and ripped off her soggy fleece. The chopper pulled away, and her world was dark again by the time she could feel the blue tarp between her fingers. Geeta ran up beside her and doubled over.

"You're bloody fast," she said, gasping for breath.

Bell glanced at her, peeled back the tarp, and stepped into the tent. The structure was even more magnificent up close. It was almost twelve feet tall and looked less like an analog phone booth than an interstellar portal. She ran her fingers along the brass seams between panes of beveled blue glass sealed with an aquamarine glaze. She took hold of the ornate brass door handle and paused to gather herself, but when she opened the door, she didn't find a telephone, only loose wires dangling from the antenna menagerie on the roof. The Windphone was as empty as a spent abalone shell.

Bell heard a door open and shut and soft footsteps on wet grass. The tarp peeled back. The Inventor stood, bowlegged, with a lit, hand-rolled cigarette between his lips. He was a small, older man with outsize hands that were rough and muscular. His wispy white hair was wavy and unkempt. His sparse silver whiskers were days old. There was a scar on his cheek that reminded Bell of the red splotch on the belly of Jupiter and a mole peeking out from one of his hedgerow eyebrows. Her tiger's attempted murderer stood behind him.

"There's no phone," Bell said.

The Inventor seemed oddly unruffled by her appearance on his back lawn. She watched him evaluate his creation as if compiling a checklist of edits and updates. He took a drag from his soggy cigarette, folded his arms, and sighed.

"Not yet, no. I am terribly sorry about that," he said. "Behind schedule as usual."

47

BRUISED AND BLOODY, FILTHY AND SOAKED, BELL SAT SILENTLY, wrapped in one of the Inventor's handmade quilts. A frenzy of faces appeared, etched with a blend of concern, anguish, and fascination. Most of them were strange. A few were familiar, and all were curious as to the condition of the lone hiker they'd heard about on the scanner. The child brave and foolish enough to trek into nocturnal tiger country.

Bell caught snippets as Geeta explained to the gathering wardens how, though she'd missed killing the beast, at least she'd saved the girl from certain death at the claws of a starving cat. Bell heard the word "claws" clearly, but her head was throbbing, and she didn't have the energy to protest. More sirens swam toward her. She retreated within to distance herself from the scene, from the ridiculous notion that it was possible to speak to the dead, from her entire messed-up life. The Inventor shuffled over and sat on the wet grass beside her.

"Why did you build it?" Bell asked. He contemplated the freshly rolled cigarette between his fingers and flared his Zippo.

"I want to use it," he said. "Same as you."

Krull was among the wardens who arrived in the second wave. His hair was slick, his uniform crisp and camera-ready, and he was so keyed up and focused on the cameras gathering around him, he limped past Bell without recognizing her.

"Evening, everyone," he said. "I'd like to begin by saying that my team has performed admirably tonight. While zeroing in on the cat, we saved the life of a child lost in the mountains, and that makes me incredibly proud."

"Is that the girl?" a reporter asked. A bright light pierced Bell's tunnel vision. Krull squinted in her direction, trying to place how he knew her.

"Back off!" Principal Ono shoved the camera's all-seeing eye away. Her arms flexed, shoulders square, she unleashed her signature searing glare that had convinced thousands of children over two decades to *behave*. "This child is nine years old, and you do *not* have permission to air that footage."

She'd rushed into the yard flanked by two paramedics, who knelt before Bell to examine her. Principal Ono draped another blanket over her shoulders and sat beside her. Bell wanted to tell her that the Windphone was a fraud, that all this chaos was for nothing, but silence felt safer.

"Her temperature is low. I don't like her color," one of the paramedics said. "Are you her mother?"

"No," Principal Ono said. "I assumed her father would be here by now. He's a game warden."

Bell had assumed the same thing. Not that she wanted to see him. This was all his fault. Because of him, she'd almost slipped to her death. Because of him, she'd pissed herself and had to hit the dirt to avoid getting shot by that psycho over there. Because of him, she knew how to get herself into some perilous situations but also how to survive them. Because of him, she was resourceful, athletic, and mentally strong enough to overcome the dangers and the setbacks and reach the Windphone. She was banged up, shivering, dehydrated, and hungry, but she'd made it. Not because she'd wanted to. He'd forced her into this by sharing nothing. He'd made her defy his rules and break curfew all in a vain effort to decode her insignificant life. Because of him, she had met the tiger she'd been dreaming about for weeks. All of it was him—the sad, the dysfunctional, and the heartbreakingly beautiful.

She heard an engine strain with a familiar rattle in the cul-de-sac out front. A door slammed, and Jay burst through the side gate, the last to arrive. As soon as she saw him, Bell stood, shedding the Inventor's quilt and her principal's blanket. Jay ran to her. The paramedics backed away, and he knelt in front of her, searching her eyes for answers. He brushed her unevenly shaved scalp with his palm and placed the back of his hand against her cheek and forehead. He massaged her ghost-like fingers, wrinkled into prunes by the rain. She collapsed into him. Wild sobs rattled her ribs. Hot tears and snot soaked his shoulders. Her release was contagious.

Jay lifted her into his arms. Geeta handed him Bell's backpack as he breezed past Krull and his bright-light news cameras and stomped through the gate and out into the street, where his truck idled. With great care, he placed Bell in the passenger seat and buckled her in, then turned the heat up to blasting.

He slung her pack into the back of the cab, shut the door, and ran around to the driver's side. With his hands on the wheel, he turned to her. Then came a knock at his window. It was Lieutenant Krull waving him out of the truck. His eyes were narrow, his expression severe. Jay ignored him and hit the gas.

48

FEBRUARY 17–18, 2005

THE BATHROOM FLOOR WAS STILL LITTERED WITH BELL'S HAIR when Jay ran her warm bath. He left her to soak while he heated up a batch of her favorite vegetable barley soup on the stove and built a fire. He emptied her pack, found the map, and checked her route. He saw her mistake immediately and guessed where she must have backtracked based on where Geeta reported finding her. And he found the Windphone, whatever that was.

When she reappeared wrapped in towels twenty minutes later, he waved her over to the fire. He'd set up a first aid station prepared to do what he'd been doing her entire life: catalog, clean, and disinfect her many surface wounds. He washed the scrapes on her knees, shins, wrist, and elbow with a soft sponge while she sipped her soup. He blotted the deeper cuts dry and hit them with a swab of bonding disinfectant before wrapping them in cream-colored gauze and moving on to her chin. Dressing her flesh wounds was easy. It was her headaches and heartache he wasn't equipped to handle.

"That was one heck of a hike, sweetheart," he said. He dabbed the gash on her chin. She shut her eyes and winced. "Some impressive orienteering and problem-solving. Not flawless, but you made it." He examined the rash on her cheek. "What happened here?"

"I don't know," she said. "Did I get you fired?"

"TBD. I imagine I'll be off the search, so no solo cross-country missions for you anytime soon."

He kept his eyes down, focused on the physical work of first aid, and as Bell warmed up, her anger came rushing back. He was taking this much too well. He had to know that she'd picked his locks and raided his maps, that she had been in his dresser and closet. Even he wasn't this clueless.

"Honestly, what is wrong with you?"

He gazed up at her.

"I could have died out there, and you're acting like none of this is a big deal. Like everything is okay. Like *we* are okay. And we're not! Not even close!" She ran to her room and slammed the door.

It was after midnight by the time Jay mustered the strength to check on her. Bell was already asleep. He knelt by her bedside to pull up the blankets and found himself staring at Ling's journal lying face down on the bed. He couldn't compute how she'd managed to find it. He turned it over and saw his late wife's face for the first time in more than five years.

Jay hadn't been with many women before Ling, and he hadn't been with anyone since. She'd once told him that she'd fallen in love with him because he knew what the plants were called. Because he was good-looking in that shy, unkempt way of his. Because he liked to drone on about the benefits of basking in the buoyant energy of Mother Nature. By then, it was established fact that she could convince him of anything. After she'd been diagnosed during her second trimester, he believed her when she said that whatever happened to her, he was strong enough to take it, that he and Bell would be just fine. It was her most beautiful lie.

He woke up on the living room floor at eight the next morning, fully clothed, next to Ling's open journal and a half-spent bottle of Michter's. Bell was standing over him. She sat beside him, picked up the journal, and flipped through it. He inhaled sharply and sat up into the gathering storm of a hangover.

"What does this mean?" Bell pointed to a page in the middle of the book. It was a chart with three columns of numbers labeled *frequency, duration, time stamp*. The page had been creased and smoothed out. There were ink splotches and water stains.

"That's you," Jay said, leaning over his daughter. "Those were your mother's contractions when she was in labor. That's why there are so many hearts and butterflies in the margins."

"Painted ladies," she said. "I saw thousands of them yesterday."

Jay stared at her. There were so many things he needed to know about her trek, and there was a lifetime of details he still hadn't shared. The journal sketched a fuzzy outline, but looking at Bell, he could finally see how badly she needed to know more. He began with their origin story.

He'd met Ling on Santa Cruz Island. He was freediving the rock reef offshore, came up for air, and saw her on the beach picnicking with a group of friends. He could have sworn she smiled at him. He found her on the ferry back to Ventura Harbor and clumsily asked her to join him for coffee the next day.

"Our second date started immediately after that coffee date," he said. "We drove up to Big Sur on a whim, hiked through the redwoods, and camped in a river valley. We soaked in hot springs on and off for three days and told each other everything."

"Mr. Privacy told a stranger everything?"

"I know. It's one of those impossible-to-believe love stories. I mean, look at her. Totally out of my league."

Ling's parents were Malaysian immigrants who overstayed on a tourist visa and settled in Oxnard, where she was born. Her dad started a house-painting business, but his real passion was tennis, and he trained her to be great. She rose through the junior national circuit, and when she was invited to play a tournament in Singapore, she applied for a passport. A few weeks later, their home was raided by immigration enforcement agents, who hauled her father away.

He was deported, and her mother couldn't cope without him. Ling quit tennis and dropped out of school. When she turned seventeen, she moved in with her high school boyfriend's family and drifted away from her own.

"You're an only child too," Bell said. Jay nodded. His parents were older when they had him. His father died when he was twenty. His mother died eight years later, and they didn't leave him much.

"So were your grandparents, on both sides," he said. "I'm afraid you come from a long line of loners."

They moved into the cabin a little over a year after that Big Sur trip. She planted a modest garden. He pruned the old avocado trees. Around the time of their first harvest, they started to wonder aloud what it would be like for two wounded animals to raise a child.

"She had big plans for this place," he said.

"I know," Bell said. "I found the blueprints." Jay shook his head and laughed. He knew something was up when his dresser drawers were suddenly organized but never guessed anything like this.

"I suppose I left you no choice."

"I don't get it. We're always broke and buying secondhand, but you guys were going to redo the cabin? How? Did Mom work?"

"She freelanced as a photographer, and she was great at budgeting. The secondhand shopping came from her. We never spent much. She always seemed to find whatever we needed at estate or garage sales, flea markets, and on the street," he said. "She'd call me while I was on patrol and ask me to pick up someone else's curbside discards on the way home. She found some gems. Like that mirror of yours. Anyway, we saved enough to hire an architect, who drew up the addition.

"We were planning to do most of the work ourselves and have a baby after the renovation, but she got pregnant, so we put the remodel on hold. When her headaches came on, we thought she had a wicked case of morning sickness, but twenty-three weeks in, she had a scan. They found a brain tumor. Cancer. Then, in front of the fire a few days later, on a morning like this one, she told me how things would have to be."

Jay held his breath as the emotion had its way with him. To stave off the flood, he clenched his eyes shut and jaw tight. His rib cage and arms quaked, but he did not shed a single tear, and within a few minutes, he'd gathered himself enough to continue.

"She insisted that nothing could be done until after you'd nursed for six months. Once treatment started, she did really well. Yeah, she lost her hair, lost weight, but she responded to the chemotherapy, went into remission, and was strong enough to care for you while I was at work. It came back after you turned two.

"The end was torture. Ling was in the hospital for weeks on a morphine drip. Her scapula showed. Her skin was loose, almost translucent. She was evaporating.

"You and me, we spent most nights on the floor or in the cramped hospital bed beside her. The nurses kept threatening to kick us out, but I guess they took pity on us. We read to her. I helped you spill water between her chapped lips. We marveled at her eyes, which were electric right up until she faded away."

"I must have been a mess." Bell wiped tears away with her shirt sleeve.

"No," he said. "You accepted it. There I was trying to pretend I was strong enough for you, but you were the strong one. I didn't get you through it; you got me through it. You never once cried for her or said you missed her. You knew the score immediately. And I guess I thought the best thing for both of us would be to keep facing forward…to try not to remember. That must sound so silly, so selfish to you now." Ashamed, he stared at his trembling hands. "I'm sorry for keeping your mother from you, Isabella. I should have been stronger."

"And the letter she wrote me," Bell said. "You kept that from me too."

Jay chose not to protest. Ling had asked him to wait until she was thirteen to give it to her. She'd wanted Bell to be old enough to understand it, but tragedy makes kids grow up fast, and Jay could now see how deeply Bell understood. He wished he'd seen it a lot sooner.

Jay didn't share everything with Bell. He opted not to reveal their financial devastation in the wake of Ling's death. He and Ling weren't legally married. They'd had a ceremony and exchanged rings but never followed through on the license. When she got sick, his health insurance didn't cover her. Their savings weren't enough to pay for her care, and they took on tens of thousands of dollars in credit card debt, which he carried for years. He was too proud to declare bankruptcy and had only recently paid it off. One day, he'd explain that part, too, but when it was happening, he'd considered it almost irrelevant—the most miniscule part of the unraveling. He still felt that way.

Their silence stretched on as they watched the fire feast on crackling wood. "Do I have the same kind of headaches?" Bell asked finally.

"I hope not, kid, but we're going to find out."

Bell stood, kissed him on the forehead, and padded into the kitchen, where she filled their scorched pot with two cups of rice milk. She sprinkled in a pinch of salt and lit a burner. Then, she filled the bell bottom of his stovetop espresso bubbler with water, packed the metal filter with fresh grounds, and lit another burner.

"Which one of you named me?" The question snapped Jay out of his haze, and he moved to the bar while she peeled and chopped an apple for oatmeal.

"That was me," he said.

"You get an A-plus for that, Dad," Bell said. "I am not a Plum."

"No, you are not."

Jay answered every question Bell still had about her mother on the drive into the city after breakfast. As he steered the old Chevy onto Hollywood Boulevard, she told him what she knew about the Windphone. They were in the elevator, heading up to the seventh floor—and an appointment that would shape the rest of their lives—when he finally mentioned the tiger.

"We're lucky Geeta was there to scare it away before it could get to you," Jay said.

Bell laughed out loud.

"That tiger is starving, Bell. It was stalking you. It would have killed you."

"That's definitely what she's telling everybody."

"She called and asked about you this morning. You know who her father is?" The elevator doors slid open, but the hospital's cheery wallpaper didn't do much to ease his anxiety. When the doors tried to close, Jay stopped them with his hand. "Your favorite tiger biologist."

He stepped into the hallway. "No way," she said, scurrying after him. "Then why does she want to kill it?"

"That's a long, sad story."

"Well, I'm ninety-nine percent sure she didn't see me until after she pulled the trigger. She's the one who could have killed me. Not the cat."

"How close to it were you anyway?" Jay stopped in front of Dr. Ambrose's office and opened the door for her. Bell took his off hand and placed it on her irritated cheek.

"This close," she said. He pulled his hand away, shocked. Bell giggled and entered the waiting room.

"Are you..." He lowered his voice. "Are you *kidding me*?" She found an empty seat. He signed her in, then rubbed his face with both hands and slumped into the one beside her. "Have you told anyone else about this?" Bell shook her head. "Good. I wish you hadn't told me."

"She's definitely female," Bell said, "and she's not dangerous."

Jay offered a skeptical arch of the eyebrow.

She gave him one right back. "I'm serious."

"Isabella Tern?" At the other end of the waiting room, a nurse waved from an open door. Bell stood and offered her father a hand to hold.

"She doesn't even have claws."

49

JAY WAITED IN THE DOCTOR'S OFFICE, CHOOSING TO WATCH RAIN drench Los Angeles rather than bear the sight of Bell swirling in the medical mind for a second time. While he waited, he fielded a call from Child Protective Services. He wasn't surprised. *That's what happens to clueless parents when their kid breaks the law and almost gets herself killed.*

"A house visit and at least one round of interviews will be required," the emotionless social worker said, "to ensure there aren't any issues with neglect or delinquency."

Is that what Bell has become on my watch? Jay thought as he looked out over a thousand puddles collecting on Hollywood rooftops. *A neglected juvenile delinquent?*

He agreed to terms, politely ended the call, and crossed to a bank of floor-to-ceiling windows. He leaned forward until his overheated forehead met cool, double-paned glass and found an angle that allowed him to stare straight down onto a land where a once-teeming savanna basin had been hunted, plowed, tamed, mowed, and paved into a reflection of the human condition.

Civilization, they called it, but nothing was ever completely civilized. There were always cracks in the concrete shell where grass and trees sprouted. Squirrels, possums, rats, coyotes, cottontails, and birds—

some native, others exotic—made the city their own too. Because wild things, like viruses and rogue cells, would always prowl, evolve, attempt to take root, and multiply. Wildness could be caged, beaten, declawed, paved over, and ignored for a while, but none of that would extinguish the unifying force within all matter. Wildness was the will to live and thrive. And when wild bumped up against wild, there entered random chance. The potential for love and conflict, illness and healing, birth and death. Loss. Every wild thing eventually lost something.

Nature being nature, it was often the case that good and bad things came in multiples, one after another, like waves. Like attracted like, they said, and when things were good, it was tempting to believe that the fortunate deserved their bounty, or worse, cultivated it on their own. Industriousness, sound choices, and good deeds led to stable, abundant outcomes, or so the thinking went. And when bad piled on top of bad, it was just as tempting for the afflicted to believe that the world was against them, that they were the playthings of brutal gods, or that they created the conditions that allowed their terrible luck to blossom, that they deserved it.

But whether you were a fugitive tiger attempting to fend for itself, a presumed-dead and abandoned One-Legged Crow, a widower in over his head, or a motherless nine-year-old girl, the fact was that almost everything wonderful and horrible that had ever happened was mostly beyond your control. It was nature at play. It was random, but nature didn't get the whole say. Often, it was how a particular beast reacted to the randomness of their life that determined how their story ended. The key, Jay knew in his heart, was not in the anticipation of good or bad news. It was in the acceptance that either could come at any time and the willingness to stay ready on all fronts. He'd forgotten that—or, more precisely, chosen to ignore it.

"The tiger has no claws," Jay said to himself. Bell knew this because evidently the animal had touched her. She had provided the most relevant eyewitness description so far, and it was exactly the type of disclosure that could lead to the loss of jobs and child custody, broken hearts, and the collapse of everything that mattered.

AFTER BELL'S APPOINTMENT, THEY DID SOME SHOPPING ON MELrose, then settled into a molded, candy-colored booth at Astro Burger for veggie burgers with grilled mushrooms and onions, french fries, and chocolate shakes. Between bites, Bell described nearly sliding off the cliff in detail. Jay had to push his fast-food feast aside.

"Okay, that is a perfect example of what not to tell a social worker," he said. "Nothing eventful happened on this hike until…well, they know the tiger was close, but you never saw it. Agreed?"

Bell spared him further details of her close encounter, what the tiger smelled like, the roughness of her tongue. How when the tiger chuffed, Bell felt it from the tips of her toes through the top of her skull. The man could only take so much.

"I wish you were still on the case, Dad," Bell said on the drive home, somewhere around Calabasas. It was still coming down hard. The raindrops were the size of quarters. "Someone has to stop that lady from killing the tiger."

"You mean, someone has to stop that nice lady from killing…Bolt."

"Bolt. That's her name?"

Jay nodded.

"It's perfect." Bell reached into the open pack of gummy worms sitting between them on the bench seat. She popped two into her mouth. "She's not that nice, by the way," Bell said. "Ms. Murthy, I mean."

"True, but it's impolite to hold that against her."

"Oh my god. You like her."

Jay kept his eyes on the road. "Not really. She's the know-it-all type. Full of herself. But I do…I mean, I respect her."

"Gross! I'm gonna throw up."

"Because you ate too much junk food."

"No, because my dad's girlfriend is out there trying to kill Bolt."

"Girlfriend is a reach. And nobody is finding Bolt in this rain."

That night, Jay opened Ling's journal and followed her recipe for her favorite Panang-style vegetable curry. He and Bell listened to the local news as they ate it over rice in front of a blazing fire.

Bolt remained at large. The chopper had been grounded, and the trail was cold thanks to El Niño's magic eraser. After dinner, Bell leaned over a fresh sheet of vellum and sketched a tiger wandering through a woodland filled with painted ladies. Jay cleaned the kitchen, thumbed through the case file on his desk, and checked his voicemail. Miriam had called, and she was not happy.

"I'm glad you didn't pick up," she began, "because I don't want to hear your lame excuses, but I just got a call from someone who volunteered with the Glenns at Cat Heaven, and since you haven't been suspended...*yet*...I figured I'd try you. But I swear, if you ever leave Bell alone like that again, we are going to have some real problems, buddy."

The number she left had a Riverside County area code.

50

FEBRUARY 21, 2005

THEY MET AT THE ENTRANCE TO THE OLD CAT HEAVEN IN THE GEN-trifying cowboy town of Temecula. Cliff Yarborough was taller than Jay had expected—at least six feet, five inches—neatly dressed, and suntanned, with a thick mop of wavy hair silvering at the temples. Lois Yarborough had a salt-and-pepper bob and was dressed in a hoop skirt and black boots. Cliff confirmed over the phone that the couple had volunteered with the Glenns for a decade, but their appearance, and their pleasant dispositions, didn't match Jay's low expectations.

On their way out of Alisaw Valley early that morning, Jay had passed the middle school parking lot where Krull was hosting his daily press conference to quell the public's growing anxiety. It was the fourth consecutive day of heavy rain since that single day of sunshine, and the increasingly lush landscape provided plenty of cover for a tiger on the move. The press throng had grown since Bell's adventure. All the Los Angeles papers, television stations, and news radio stations were in attendance, and CNN sent a remote unit too. Each of them had run a similar version of the story. There was the unnamed lost minor, the ravenous tiger who'd stalked her, and

Geeta, her brave savior. Bell had wanted to correct the record, but Jay barked off any media that called up at the cabin.

"I don't suppose you have identification?" Cliff asked.

Jay wasn't in uniform—he wore blue jeans, a Dodgers cap, and a Patagonia shell—and he wasn't armed. Officially, he was off the case, but he extended his badge and ID. Bell was with him. She wore brand-new black denim overalls that fit her perfectly; her shaved head was covered by an oversized Carhartt beanie, also brand new. Both of them wore fresh boots, all purchased during that shopping spree after leaving Children's Hospital.

Cliff glanced at Bell. "You his deputy?"

"Supervisor," she said, easing the early awkwardness.

Jay could see the ranch was vacant. There was nothing but muddy corrals and an empty ranch house, which he considered a level up from where the Glenns currently resided, until he peered through the window. Inside, the carpeting was stained and shredded, the wood floors buckled, and the walls clawed and dented. One day soon, the bank would foreclose.

As they strolled the grounds, Jay sensed the Yarboroughs' wistfulness. Where there was ruin, they saw the so-called refuge at its apex. Cliff and Lois were drifting with the purposelessness of early retirement when they stumbled upon the Glenns. Working at Cat Heaven in its glory days brightened their lives immediately, and they volunteered five days a week for over three years.

"Aubrey and Eden had a variety of cats here, but tigers were their obsession," Lois said. "Eden had a tiger bathrobe, tiger coffee cups, tiger stuffed animals, tiger bedsheets, tiger towels."

"She was damn good with them too," Cliff added. "They both were. It wasn't long before we bought a house down the block. It's addictive, being around big cats. They are so powerful and loving. It's a rush. The only thing we've found that comes close is riding motorcycles."

"Even that doesn't compare," Lois said. "When these animals imprint on you—when they recognize you as someone they can trust—that is something you never forget."

"It's impossible to fully explain," Cliff said, "but it's a deep, deep connection."

"You have to feel it," Bell said. Jay shot her a look that suggested she was one step closer to waiting out this officially unofficial interview in the truck. He worried that a slip from her could spark the rumor mill in the big cat chatrooms the Yarboroughs still visited and add fuel to the hiker-girl stories, but he also suspected Cliff and Lois wouldn't want their cat friends to know they were speaking with law enforcement.

Standing in one of the sad corrals, the dashing older couple looked fragile. Jay could see the cats on them. His scarred knuckles. The faint echo of an old gash on the back of her neck.

"We've both been down since the Glenns left," Cliff said, "but we would have stopped working with them even if they'd stayed."

"Why?"

Cliff looked at Bell and hesitated.

"She's not fragile," Jay said.

"I can see that," Cliff said. "Their money dried up. This place was falling apart. Some days, there wasn't enough food. Cats got sick, and the vet stopped coming. We buried two of them."

"Any runaways?"

"No," Lois said, "but there was an incident on moving day. One of the tigers lunged at Aubrey. Eden had to step in with a loaded shotgun to stop it."

"Was that Bolt?" Jay hadn't asked about Bolt over the phone. He had wanted to save it for when they were face to face so he didn't miss things like the way Cliff worked his jaw as he searched for the right words.

"Yes, it was," Lois said. "We were all shocked. She'd been docile for years, but she had snapped once before, when she was a cub."

"Is that right?" Jay said.

"There was an incident in the Midwest somewhere," Cliff said. "A beauty queen mauled by a tiger cub. She was declawed after that."

Jay glanced at Bell.

"So terribly sad," Lois said.

"For the tiger," Jay asked, "or its victim?"

"Declawing a cat is an amputation, Warden Tern," Lois said. "People think of it like toenail removal. It's not. They saw off the tips of their toes at the joint."

"Aubrey didn't want to do it," Cliff said. "He had to. It was the only way to save Bolt's life."

They were a curious couple. Regular people drawn into the Glenns' bizarre orbit who fell hard for the animals they tended. Jay empathized with them...to a point. They were participants in all this.

"Do you still talk to the Glenns?"

"Just once since they left," Lois said. "After years of daily contact."

"I would have thought you'd want to know how the animals were settling in."

"It wasn't for lack of trying. We called them both several times. They never called back. Then last week, Eden did call, and she sounded strange. She said Bolt took sick and went downhill quickly. Said she died two days after the move."

"You didn't believe her." Jay said.

"Why would she bother to call weeks later to tell me that? Why not immediately after Bolt died?"

"Bolt was fond of that lynx you found," said Cliff. "They rode in the same trailer when they moved. If one got loose, maybe..."

Bell gripped Jay's hand. He tapped the back of hers twice.

On the three-hour drive home, Bell napped while Jay's mind churned. He'd defied a direct order to stay off the case but felt a familiar buzz that came from getting closer to the truth. He had eyewitnesses who saw Bolt get loaded up with Sierra, alive. Hounds could be deployed with the confirmation the tiger had no claws. Of course, Krull, Geeta, or some other warden might still kill Bolt, and this wouldn't necessarily save Jay's job, but lives were at stake. Sharing this intel was the only honorable move. He called Geeta first. She didn't answer. Neither did Miriam or Krull. Maybe he'd been fired already, and no one had bothered to tell him.

As Jay rolled into Alisaw Valley, fat raindrops peppered his windshield, and he stole glances into the green hills. According to the news, the chopper had been grounded indefinitely due to what a reporter called "inclement weather," which was a funny way of describing an unprecedented atmospheric river that had delivered rain of contrasting quality for three weeks straight. It had come down in teardrops and pearls, in slanted downpours and feathery showers. It pierced like needles and billowed like curtains dancing in the wind. The scrubby mountains looked almost tropical. Chaparral grew in tall and thick. Oak trees became cloaked in soft green lichen seemingly overnight. The hills were shedding water. Canyons were choked with frothing run-off. It spilled out from small washes, saturated the side roads, and poured over ledges and ridges in once-in-a-generation ephemeral waterfalls. The valley had become a jungle oasis fit for a tiger, and Bolt was on the move.

From the moment she'd dodged Geeta's bullets, Bolt had blazed a disappearing trail. She'd ranged from horse ranch to golf course to an abandoned construction site to the back forty of the community college. She seldom stayed in one place for more than an hour. Whenever the search party crept within a hundred yards of her, she heard them coming and slipped away through the grass. Her hunger was severe, yet prey was scarce. Horses and cattle were locked away in barns guarded by men with guns, and most other critters were hunkered down, waiting for the sun. Even the One-Legged Crow was nowhere to be found.

Loneliness tracked Bolt like a shadow, and the wound above her ear throbbed with infection. She was sleep deprived, shivering from the cold, and starving, but her senses had never been so sharp or her instincts so keen. She was truly wild now, and Alisaw Valley was her territory. Which was why, even in failing strength, she could easily outmaneuver the small army desperate to track her down.

51

FEBRUARY 24–25, 2005

GEETA LOOPED THE VALLEY ON HORSEBACK WHILE GAME WARDENS continued to canvass door to door. The same properties were searched, the same homeowners and ranchers questioned. Krull marauded from one end of the search area to the other on his ATV, and when he wasn't in the field, he drove reporters and their photographers around so they could watch the search unfold. He posed on his quad surrounded by the wardens he'd assigned to stand sentry at every mark on Jay's map. One unit monitored the Highway 23 culvert. Others were posted at Treeland Farms, Ben's ranch, and the oak woodland. He even posted a unit at the cave. But what the cameramen and reporters and their editors and producers really wanted was a shot of the tiger itself. Preferably in full flight and then splayed out on the ground, lifeless.

Jay spent the days after the meeting in Temecula at his desk investigating the Glenns. He was convinced they had already cost one young man his life, and Jay had almost lost his daughter. His anger sharpened his focus as he burrowed into the fledgling internet and criminal databases. He found a single five-hundred-word story buried in the archives of the *Cincinnati Enquirer* that documented an incident involving a female tiger cub and a mauled college student at the Kenwood Town Centre. A subsequent call to the Kenwood Police Department yielded a scanned copy of a police report that documented the questioning of a man named Cooper Stills, the owner of the tiger-petting concession, who "reluctantly and tearfully surrendered his animal." According to the report, once traces of the girl's dried blood were found on the cub's claws, it was euthanized. Had Stills switched the tigers on Kenwood PD and sold Bolt to Aubrey to save her life? That didn't mesh with what he'd heard from the Yarboroughs. Of course, their story could easily be a mishmash of rumor, presumption, faulty memory, and fact.

He kept digging and got the feeling that Cooper Stills was an empty shell. He had no bank accounts or credit cards, no driver's license, and no prior arrest record. Jay couldn't even find a photograph of him on the internet. The victim filed a lawsuit that was never served because Stills either vanished or never existed in the first place. On a hunch, Jay ran a search for Aubrey Stills, and his screen lit up. There were thirty-six of them scattered around the country. None in Ohio, but one used to live in Indiana. Jay traced that address to a filing with the Riverside County Recorder, where Aubrey Stills officially became Aubrey Glenn.

Jay figured he had the Glenns for violation of their permits and possibly animal cruelty. Those were misdemeanors. There was also a strong case to be made for felony perjury for lying about Bolt's sex on their permit application, presumably to protect her. And if Aubrey had switched out the tiger cubs back in Ohio, that could lead to state felony charges for intentionally misleading law enforcement and tampering with evidence.

Bell was home too. Jay kept her out of school because he knew how pushy journalists could be and didn't trust the faculty to protect her. Ms. Levine wasn't his daughter's biggest fan, and Principal Ono was the one who'd told Bell about that so-called Windphone in the first place. While he hunted and pecked his keyboard, Bell transferred sections of her cathedral valley oak to a piece of poster board they'd picked up at an art supply store in West Hollywood. The tree trunk was thick and majestic. The drip line sprouted with poppies, and the canopy was a chaotic spread of intersecting limbs that mirrored the root system, which extended deep beneath the savanna. She took most of the day to sketch it out and transfer it. Then, she deployed her pencil palette and infused the scene with color. In the early evening, the pounding rain finally took a commercial break. Soon after, a chopper roared overhead.

"The forecast looks great for the rest of the week," Jay said as he spooned black beans and cilantro rice onto her plate alongside half of one of their homegrown avocados and two warm flour tortillas. Bell knelt on her bar stool and stuffed a steaming tortilla.

"Better weather means it will be easier to find her," she said.

"It's not safe for anybody until we find her." Jay folded one of his own tortillas over a hunk of avocado and a spoonful of black beans. "Especially her."

"Either way, she's not safe."

"Because she doesn't belong in this ecosystem."

"But I was thinking…" Bell set her tortilla down and licked her fingers clean. "What's one more big cat left alone in the hills? She's been a prisoner for her entire life. You heard what the Yarboroughs said. She has no claws and can't have babies. What's the harm?"

"One man is dead already."

"I don't blame her for that."

"Some people do, and she's only going to get hungrier and more desperate until she either hurts someone intentionally or starves to death. I know it's unfair, but this is one of those situations when nobody wins."

Bell slid off her bar stool and stepped to the kitchen window, where a passing shaft of dusky light illuminated the natural highlights in her buzz cut. "The valley is so lush. When was the last time you saw it like this?"

"I've never seen the valley like this."

"Maybe it's her. Maybe she's…"

"Maybe she's what?"

"Magic."

"My bet is that it's El Niño's doing," he said, taking another bite. "Not the cat's."

"I know it looks that way, but there's something I still haven't told you. That lightning stripe on her cheek? It's almost identical to mom's tattoo." Jay put his utensils down, wiped his face, and stepped to the window beside her. "I swear."

"You think there's some connection between them."

"It must mean something. All this…it can't just be random."

Every instinct Jay had told him to dismiss Bell's claim as coincidence. Because he was an earthbound realist. He didn't have fantastical visions or create evocative art. He drew maps, not connections that weren't there. He worked the soil, groomed trails, harvested fruit and vegetables. He ran hills, roamed deserts, and swam in the sea. He believed only in the tangible. Except Ling had reappeared in his dreams after the tiger turned up. And what were dreams if not a swirl of memory, desire, fear, and anxiety? Weren't those things real, if not completely tangible?

"We should be looking for her," Bell said. "These are our mountains. We can find her, and we can save her."

Jay scanned the jade hills. There were good reasons to at least attempt to do the brave and virtuous thing, but the stakes had become too high now that CPS had them in their crosshairs. Plus, no matter what Bell thought she knew about the tiger, Bolt *was* dangerous.

The clouds parted late that night, and the full moon glowed like a galactic floodlight, which led to the fiddling of crickets, the scratching of mice and possums, the calling of the barn owl. The land could finally breathe now that the spigot had shut off, and wildlife were busy investigating, instigating, hunting, gathering, and rebuilding.

Lying in bed, Bell could not stop thinking about Bolt. The tiger was stuck dealing with the chaotic randomness like everybody else and trying her best to cope. So what if she didn't belong in their ecosystem? Bolt never asked to live in Alisaw Valley. She didn't set out to make a mockery of her owners or the CDFW or the tracker brought in to find her. She was born with several dominoes down, and all she wanted was freedom. Her own piece of this wild world.

Restless, Bell padded out of bed and slid her window open. There was a chill in the air, and the sky was a deep navy blue, but the first members of the songbird brigade were already tuning their instruments. She yawned as she got dressed, pinched her earlobes to eradicate lingering drowsiness, zipped her parka, laced up her boots, and slipped out the back door and into the avocado trees. One had a limb low enough to grab hold of. She hooked her arms and legs around it and pulled herself up to sitting. She walked up its slant on hands and feet until she could access a thicker horizontal branch further up, where she laid down flat. She hugged herself warm, stared through the patchwork of foliage, and waited for the sky to brighten. Her eyelids shut on their own accord, and within a few minutes, she'd fallen sleep.

She woke with a start nearly an hour later, teetered but steadied herself, and sat up in time to see two deer streaking downhill past the cabin. A few seconds later, she smelled a familiar musk. She swung to the lower branch, then clambered down the slant until she was low enough to jump to the ground. She landed on all fours a few feet from Bolt. The tiger raised her nose, shook out her mane, and chuffed. Even in her emaciated state, she looked regal.

A light flickered to life in the kitchen, and Bell heard Jay cough. She wanted to call out to him. They could do it after all. They could capture and protect Bolt. Find a place somewhere way out in the wilderness to set her free again, as if she were just another nuisance animal, a baby rattler, an orphaned fox, a snooping possum, a confused cougar. But Bell knew that was not what would happen to her tiger if Jay darted her. There was no place safe to put her besides another cage, which would only diminish her. That was, if her dad's bosses didn't come up with some excuse to put her to sleep forever.

Yeah, that's what would happen. She'd already escaped once, they'd say, and caused a fatal car crash. Then they'd ask their loaded question. *Is keeping her alive worth another human life?*

Jay coughed again. Bolt cocked her head toward the house. In the distance, a truck fired its engine. The drumbeat of a chopper pounded into a sky that was burning hot pink. The sun was rising, and Bell knew that Bolt's only chance was escape.

"You have to get out of here," she said. Confused, Bolt chuffed again and moved a step closer. "No!" Bell stomped her foot. "Run! Go! Now!"

Jay shut off the bathroom faucet and heard his daughter's distressed voice outside. The toothbrush fell from his mouth in the hallway a second before he burst through the back door, where he could see Bell standing alone in the avocado grove, stiff and agitated. "Are you okay?" he asked. Bell turned to him with a smile that looked forced.

The radio broke the news while Jay washed the breakfast dishes. He stopped to listen and called out to Bell, who came running from her bedroom. Bolt had been spotted pacing outside a woman's yard in Mystic Heights while staring through a wrought-iron fence at a cowering labradoodle. The yelping dog barreled around the side of the house and through the kitchen door to safety. The panicked homeowner dialed 911. Within minutes, a procession of CDFW trucks, sheriff patrol cars, and news vans arrived at the caller's house. Game wardens fanned out on foot while deputies managed the traffic, and Lieutenant Krull announced that they'd found a string of fresh tracks.

Jay steered his Chevy past all the action and through the Mystic Heights gates on their way to school. He pulled into the drop-off zone and watched the chopper make another low pass.

"I cannot believe you're making me go to school," Bell said. "What are you gonna to do?"

Jay was unarmed and in street clothes, but he felt very much on duty. "They have enough boots on the ground as it is," he said with a shrug. "The best I can do is make my case against the Glenns after everything is done."

Bell didn't look convinced. Neither was he.

Warden teams had established perimeters north and west, east and south of Mystic Heights. Additional teams searched around the flooded culverts, corridors, and bike paths, and several turned up on the highway near the school. Bell hopped out of the truck and noticed the gathering of patrol cars and emergency vehicles, their lights flashing. Up above, a chopper hovered, and Bell's calm veneer unraveled.

"Let me come with you!"

"Back home?"

"We both know what kind of doctor I went to. We know what happened to mom, and we know *you* aren't going home. What is the point of school?"

"Did you see something in the avocado grove this morning or not?" When her eyebrows pinched together, he knew the tiger had been in his garden. He reached across the bench seat, yanked her door shut, and pulled away.

Furious, Bell found herself ditched beneath the flagpole, where the giant banner hung limp. She was surrounded by anxious children, hysterical parents, and flustered teachers. A scatter of deputies attempted to herd them all into the safety of the building. Bell submitted to the flow but paused at the doorway long enough to watch her father park down the road in front of the middle school auditorium. He got out of the truck and aimed his binoculars at the treetops across the highway. Then, he dashed inside.

"I guess they think the tiger's close by."

Bell turned to find Miles swaying like a metronome.

"Wanna see her?" Bell asked. After a few more beats of the metronome, he nodded. She took his hand, and together they dashed into the chaotic hallway. Foot traffic was thick, but that made it easier to weave through the madness undetected and reach the reliable side door that was perpetually unlocked. Miles stood watch while Bell opened it just wide enough for them to slip through and race out onto the empty playground.

52

WITH ALL HANDS IN THE FIELD, THE AUDITORIUM WAS DESERTED. Jay found his tranquilizer rifle leaning against the wall beneath the map, not far from where Geeta liked to stand during morning briefings. He checked to make sure it was still loaded and used the map to get his bearings. He zeroed in on a shallow gully across the highway from the school. Bolt favored canyons and depressions. This one was sealed off by the Alisaw River's manmade embankment. It was a dead end, and it was dry.

He grabbed a stray walkie-talkie, charged up the aisle and out the door, and hopped into his Chevy. He cranked the key. It turned over slowly but didn't catch. He took a breath and tried again. No joy. He grabbed his rifle and bailed out.

He hurdled a pipe fence, sprinted across the frontage road and onto the highway, crossed the overgrown median, and reached the far shoulder where he'd seen a solitary crow disappear into the dense brush. The way it dove for cover struck a nerve. He pushed through the vegetation and started down the slope, taking care to move as quietly as possible, but his boot slipped in the mud, and he slid on his backside all the way down the slick hill. He held his rifle in front of his face as he bashed through thorny foliage. Then, he caught air and fell the final five feet to the bottom of the gulch, where he landed with a loud and painful thud. So much for the element of surprise.

Rotors beat furiously overhead. The morning sun was warm, and vapor rose from the wet earth. He scanned the brush for a flash of orange and white, the mossy canopy above for a flush of black feathers. Bolt had to be close. Jay crawled behind a tangle of ceanothus and checked to make sure the safety was off. Then came a rustle followed by an unmistakable animal scent. He swiveled right and saw a banded tail slither past. Jay crawled out of his blind and followed Bolt as she moved deeper into the gulch toward a smooth, near vertical wall reenforced with concrete.

Jay's direction was her only escape, and thanks to a favorable wind, he hadn't been detected by the tiger or the crow who hopped from rock ledge to tree branch and back again in its usual stop-motion cadence. Jay tucked into a snag of sage and raised his rifle. The longer the tiger stalled, the more his pulse would settle.

The sound of pounding hooves rose behind him. Geeta was riding hands free, her weapon cocked and ready. She never felt so free as when she'd bonded with a horse enough that the animal knew what she needed without so much as a soft tug of the reins or a gentle nudge with her bootheel, when she could focus on hunting and trust the horse to do the driving. The one good thing about the prolonged hunt was that it had allowed Geeta and Billie the time to get there, and now it was all about to end as she'd envisioned, with a big check, a tiger pelt, and a cleansed conscience. The specifics of her tragedy would recede into the depths of Geeta's swampy memory, and the great tracker would be free to recall her mother's easy grace and all the wonderful moments that came before. In fact, she already had the kill shot.

After forty-five days of running and hiding, Bolt looked resigned to her fate. She turned toward Geeta and dropped her head as Billie closed the distance. Yet with success virtually guaranteed, Geeta felt an unfamiliar pang, a desire to let the tiger live. Had she been hypnotized by the cat's liquid movement, its athleticism and beauty, like so many tiger hunters before her? Or was she starting to believe Jay's argument that killing this tiger wouldn't bury her demons? Because Bolt wasn't her maneater or even much of a predator; she was just another victim.

Sensing a shift in the game, Bolt shed her malaise and sprinted toward the horse. Billie spooked and veered. Geeta grabbed the reins in time to save herself from being tossed and righted the horse as Bolt kept running for the slope that dropped from the highway. Shaken from the tiger's spell, Geeta felt a renewed zeal to finish the bloody job. Once again, she raised her rifle and steadied her aim.

Jay rolled free from the brush directly into her line of fire. He pulled his trigger, but the dart whizzed over Bolt's backside as she bounded up the slope and disappeared into the woods along Highway 23. Geeta came riding up alongside him.

"Well, that won't get you back on the job, will it?" She looked angry, and even more so when he regarded her with sympathy. Twice she'd had the shot, and twice she'd failed to act.

"I can see you don't want to pull the trigger, Geeta."

"Watch me," she said, tears in her eyes. "Yah!" Billie responded and galloped up the steep slope, leaving Jay in the mist.

Highway 23 had been sealed off by law enforcement. Three news choppers had joined the CDFW helicopter in the sky, and they all marked Bolt as she burst from the wooded margins of the highway and dashed across the northbound lanes. From the playground, Bell and Miles gripped the fence and watched a panicked Bolt spin in confused circles on a grassy median that had gone feral.

Dozens of wardens marched toward the cat from the north and south. Krull parked his quad on the shoulder, not forty feet from where the kids were white knuckling the chain-link fence. He stood on the seat and aimed his rifle at the jittery tiger. Geeta did the same from her saddle on the opposite shoulder.

"No!" Bell screamed at the top of her lungs. Krull, Geeta, and Bolt all turned and stared at her as an alarmed sheriff's deputy sprinted onto the playground, followed by Principal Ono. The deputy grabbed both kids and attempted to drag them from the fence. Miles surrendered. Bell held on and unleashed a deep and wild howl. The stunned cop released her.

Principal Ono hugged Bell, attempting to calm her, while the deputy carried Miles to the safety of the school building, where students, parents, and teachers, in classrooms and in offices, were pressed noses to glass watching it all play out. In Ms. Levine's classroom, Ashley and Charlotte gawked in stunned silence as Bell refused to yield. The principal simply held her where she stood, and the deputy returned to watch over them both with his gun drawn.

Out on the highway, wardens communicated with hand gestures, adjusted their positions, and edged closer to a tiger caught between panic and surrender. Bolt feinted left, then right, up, then back, staying as low to the ground as possible. She was starving and spent. Where there once had been thick bands of muscle and a plumpness that came from eating regularly and doing a whole lot of nothing, skin hung loose from her bones. Her coat was backbitten and frayed, and it was abundantly clear that her time had come.

Bell let go of the fence and stepped back into the principal's arms. "I can't," she said. "I can't watch them kill her."

"Then let's go inside," Principal Ono said.

Bell nodded, turned her back to the tiger, and allowed herself to be led away.

Krull directed game warden traffic over the radio. He forbade anyone—including Geeta—to shoot the animal without his approval. He blamed it on the proximity of the schools and the potential for crossfire, but really, he wanted the first clean shot. Jay was done following Krull's orders and emerged onto the southbound shoulder of the highway without anybody realizing.

Bolt sensed her end and stood tall. Her amber eyes pulsed as a final burst of fight-or-flight adrenaline detonated in her bloodstream, and she unleashed a roar that shook Alisaw Valley. Wardens flinched. Geeta lowered her weapon out of respect. Even Krull shook his head in wonder. Principal Ono and Bell froze halfway across the blacktop. Standing in a hopscotch court, they turned toward one of planet Earth's finest and most ferocious beasts making its last stand. When it roared a second time, Bell shook loose.

"Bell!" Principal Ono yelled and lunged for her, but there was no stopping Bell Tern. The tiger crouched low and shifted her weight to her back legs as Bell made for the fence.

"Everybody relax now," Krull said. "I have the shot." Krull was in perfect position and about to pull his trigger when a news van cut in front of him. They wanted a clean shot too. "Dang it!" He gunned his quad and swerved toward higher ground. "Who gave media the authority to be out here?"

"You did, sir," someone answered.

Jay edged across the southbound lanes toward the cat's right flank. He would need two direct hits to put the tiger to bed. Krull spotted him from his new vantage point and barked into his radio. "Stand down, Tern! If you attempt to dart that animal, you're finished with the department! It's my shot!"

So be it, Jay thought. *It would be the perfect way to go out.* Then he saw Bell leap from the top of the nine-foot-tall chain-link fence, roll onto the frontage road, and run toward the ravenous tiger. He didn't have time to hit Bolt twice. Not with his daughter in harm's way.

"Do it now then," Jay snapped, "and don't miss!"

Krull exhaled as his crosshairs settled on Bolt's jugular, certain that his fantasy was about to become reality. His public life would begin with an onslaught of positive local press followed by a handful of national television interviews, the governor's commendation, and—who could forget?—a fat check from Wildlife Services. But locked on his target, there was so much about that cat, about the valley, and about his own predicament that Krull could not see. Like a nervy, stealthy One-Legged Crow headed for the back of his neck.

When it dug its sharp talons into the soft spot to the left of the lieutenant's spine, Krull sputtered and squealed. When it burrowed its bill into his ear, he yelped like a wounded puppy and toppled off the ATV in a fit of pain and profanity.

AMERICAN TIGER · 319

"Vile creature. Impeccable timing," Geeta said into her radio. "My shot, then." She raised her weapon as Bell reached the highway, where a sheriff's cruiser cut her off. Two deputies attempted to corral her. Bell juked them easily and stepped into Geeta's line of fire.

"The girl..." Geeta said and lowered her weapon.

Krull picked himself up off the turf and barked into his radio, "Tern, is that your kid again?"

But all Jay could hear was the blood in his ears as he sprinted for his daughter. Bolt pivoted toward him and sized up the threat. Her mouth hung open. Her canines glinted in the sun. Jay froze. The tiger crouched deeper, prepared to pounce, but Bell got to her first. She smashed into Bolt at full speed, hugged her around the neck, and buried her nose in the tiger's mane. Surprised, Bolt turned to Bell and snuffled her cheek.

Jay edged close enough to place his hand on Bell's shoulder. Bolt retracted her upper lip and growled. "Shhh," Bell said. "He's not going to hurt you."

"Come with me, sweetheart," Jay said. Still clutching the tiger, Bell turned and gazed at him with the same calm confidence he'd once seen in Ling's eyes.

"Not until everyone puts their guns away," she said. She ran her finger down Bolt's lightning stripe. "See what I mean, Daddy? It's the same."

Stunned, Jay knelt beside her, leaned closer, and saw it too. It was impossible to believe yet so obviously true he couldn't help but surrender to the evidence and to his daughter's point of view. His mind felt loose and elastic. Time slowed way down, and a wave of calm washed over him. He didn't even know that he was smiling when he panned the tense scene and clocked all the twitchy riflemen gawking at them in utter disbelief. *Bell was right*, he thought. *This whole time, she'd been absolutely right. And it must mean something.*

"Don't worry, Bolt," Bell said. "We're here now, and we're not going anywhere."

Everyone watching assumed the hungry beast would tear them

both to pieces. It was what they had all come to expect from the fugitive cat based on the wildlife footage and frantic news reports they'd consumed. Eventually, the tiger that did not belong would exert its physical dominance, leverage its primordial need for red meat and blood, and claim human life. Except Bolt never was a maneater. And in those slow motion seconds, an unexpected gale came out of the north.

Winds billowed and snapped the giant flag at Big Springs back to attention and funneled one last swirl of swollen storm clouds into Alisaw Valley. Lightning slashed. The purple sky melted into a downpour, and a tiger calculated her odds. With the Terns in the way, the riflemen were forced to reposition, and they'd left the western flank wide open.

Bolt leaped out of Bell's grasp, knocking her flat, and took off in a dead run. Jay helped Bell to her feet, and they squinted through the squall to watch Krull, the last line of defense, kneel and take aim, but he was much too slow. Bolt bulled him aside and kept running, faster than any American tiger had ever moved across open space. She accelerated past twenty, beyond thirty, and then over forty miles per hour, her stride as elegant and athletic as any cat's in history.

Krull picked himself up off the turf one last time, climbed into the bed of a nearby CDFW pickup parked on the shoulder, and smacked the side with an open palm. The driver took off hot, and Krull was back to tracking Bolt through his scope. They gained on her, but visibility was poor, and Krull chose a dangerous angle. Geeta was the first to notice.

"Hold your fire, Lieutenant!" Geeta shouted over the radio. Krull squeezed off three rounds. Two bullets ricocheted off the roof of the middle school. The last one lodged into the concrete wall inches above a classroom window where two dozen students were watching it all happen. "Hold your bloody fire!"

The helicopter pilots and aerial cameramen stayed with Bolt, through slanting rain and unstable air, as she charged downhill toward the Highway 23 culvert and the frothing Alisaw River. Krull and his driver accelerated after her. They were followed by two sheriff's cruisers. Bolt had a lead, but the machines growled, strained, and gained. Krull took aim from the truck's bed. Behind him, two deputies hung out their car windows, armed with shotguns. Then, the culvert burst at the seams in a yawning crunch of twisted metal, and a great tide crested the highway.

What was once the mostly dry headwaters of a meager river had become an otherworldly sea. Bolt felt and heard nothing but the touch of her paw pads to the earth as she sprinted headlong toward the safety of the flood. In the churning, muddy water, she would leave no tracks, no scent, no trace at all. In the water, she would stay free.

Behind her, the cruisers hydroplaned and swerved as panicked drivers abandoned the hunt, aimed their hoods in the opposite direction, and smashed the gas to save themselves. Krull's driver couldn't shed speed so easily and skidded onto a lumpy median already filled to the wheel wells with floodwater. Krull's ribs smashed the top of the tailgate, and he fumbled his weapon into the flood. The truck choked and gasped, its tires groping hopelessly for traction as water continued to rise.

Bolt remained on high ground for as long as she could, then launched into the foaming brown rapids. She paddled hard to remain at the surface and craned her neck toward clearing skies, where her friend glided in the thermals. The One-Legged Crow spotted her, tucked her oversize wings in, and dove close enough to issue a final farewell. It was the usual verse. Bolt chuffed back, then filled her lungs with fresh air, sensing that soon the untamed river would swallow her whole.

53

APRIL 7, 2005

ONCE THE RAINS BROKE, IT DIDN'T TAKE LONG FOR THE WATERS TO recede. Seasonal streams continued to run, but not like raging rivers. Waterfalls dried up, but the mountains remained green, and Alisaw Valley burst with a super bloom of wildflowers. The hills were abuzz with wild bees. Troops of hummingbirds zipped this way and that. After a winter of water, spring was a celebration.

Bell stood at her father's desk and opened the map she'd used on her solo trek. Jay showed her two fixes that shaved a nine-mile hike, one way, into a twelve-mile round trip. There were things about reading maps Bell still needed to learn, and she had a willing teacher.

"Don't forget your migraine meds," Jay said. He folded the map and handed it to her. She zipped it into the front pocket of her pack. Outside, the wind was already howling. It was expected to gust over twenty knots by midafternoon, which would make the hike less pleasant, but that was part of the plan. According to the Inventor, windy days were ideal for placing calls.

"I have them," Bell said, "but I won't need them."

The Windphone had been operational for five weeks by then, and

Bell had been the first to use it. The Inventor had made sure of that. Her invitation came in early March while she was having dinner with Principal Ono and her family, part of her new routine implemented by a Ventura County social worker, who insisted Bell needed more structure. Jay was now required by law to ask for help.

When her dad worked nights, Bell helped Miriam with the kennels and the way station or had dinner with her principal. There was more routine in her life than she'd ever had before, and she was surprised by how much she liked it.

On that first Windphone call, Bell felt jittery as she turned the crank of a vintage phone in an ironwood cabinet. A waxing half-moon hung in the sky. The breeze spun the brass weathervane on the roof, and the array of steampunk satellite dishes swiveled with each turn of the crank. Bell glanced up through the ceiling, dazzled, and repeated her mother's name as instructed until a pink light beamed from a crystal mounted on the phone's cabinet. She picked up the receiver.

If her mother was on the line, Bell didn't hear her. The only voice in the booth that night was her own. She started with whispers, her mind a mush of questions, but after a minute or two, she slid to the floor and rattled them off one at a time. The answers didn't come as she'd hoped. But when she stepped out of the booth, she wasn't disappointed.

"She didn't talk," Bell said.

The Inventor nodded. "The dead can't always respond," he said, "but they do listen."

She tried again the next time she went to Principal Ono's house. Instead of asking questions, she told her mother everything she knew about Bolt.

"Nobody has seen her since that morning," Bell said. "The search went on for another week before it was called off. Most people assume she drowned and was carried out to sea, but I don't. I think she found another cave, somewhere in the high country where no one will ever bother her again."

Bell went on to explain how her father managed to keep his job. With the floodwaters still rising, he placed Bell on Billie's saddle with Geeta and ran to his Chevy. This time, it fired right up. Everyone else was clearing off the highway in search of higher ground, but the old truck was heavier and rode higher than those CDFW pickups, and Jay accelerated downhill toward danger. He waded into the churning, hip-deep water, threw Krull over his shoulders, and grabbed the driver by the forearm, saving them both.

Over the following days, Jay built a compelling felony case against the Glenns for animal cruelty and perjury that reached back to that fateful day in Ohio. But since Bolt was never recovered—and Ohio was well outside even the most motivated California game warden's jurisdiction—prosecutors wouldn't file charges. Thanks to Jay's diligence, however, the Glenns were forever banned from owning exotic animals anywhere in the United States.

In the end, it was Lieutenant Krull who lost his job. After Bolt's escape, the higher-ups in Sacramento found flaws in the way he managed the search. His lies to the local media were an embarrassment, but it was his irresponsible gun play that did him in. He became a lieutenant on the assumption he'd shot down an armed killer, and he lost his post after nearly firing into a classroom full of children. Ventura County required a new lieutenant. Jay applied, and though he wondered how Sacramento would evaluate his own motivations and actions during the failed tiger search and was concerned they might dig into the circumstances surrounding a certain scrapped development in Alisaw Valley, it was all a formality. He got the job.

"I know what you're thinking," Bell said near the end of the second call. "Before he applied, Dr. Ambrose told us my brain was fine. I still get migraines, but it's not what you had. She thinks by the time I'm in college, they won't happen so often."

Bell stayed in the booth for nearly two hours that evening but left out the part about Jay's semi-frequent phone calls and occasional dinners with the now-out-of-work tracker lady who'd moved to Santa Barbara and turned out to be vaguely entertaining in small doses.

Once again, the Inventor was waiting when she hung up. Her eyes were puffy, cheeks streaked with dried tears. He smiled gently and lit one of his cigarettes.

"Next time, bring your dad," he said. "Tell him I said it will help him."

On what would have been Ling Wong Tern's thirty-seventh birthday, gravel turned to tarmac, and Bell took Jay's hand. Front-yard wind chimes sang from the branches of swaying trees in the cul-de-sac, and parked cars were sprinkled with tumbling flower petals. The Inventor met them in front of his house and escorted them to the Sapphire, as it had come to be known around the valley. Dozens of locals had made calls already, and he was beginning to get inquiries from grieving people all over the world thanks to a news feature in which he confessed he built it to speak to his son, who'd drowned when he was twelve. Jay ran a finger down a pane of blue glass coated in pollen. Like it did everything else, nature was in the process of marking the cosmic phone booth.

"It's better this way," the Inventor said. "It was too pristine before. Too pretty."

Bell reminded Jay how it worked as they stepped inside. With her hand over his, they turned the crank, visualized Ling, and repeated her name. Once that pink crystal was shining, Bell picked up.

"Happy birthday, Momma." She gazed up at her bewildered father. "I have a surprise for you. I brought someone with me today."

Bell handed the receiver to Jay, stepped outside, and shut the door behind her. She nodded encouragement through dusty blue glass. He stared at the phone in his hand, nodded back, and turned to face the valley.

The Windphone had been built on a ledge overlooking the place Jay Tern had lived and worked nearly all his adult life. It was a view that encompassed habitats and hideaways, oak woodlands, savanna, seasonal streambeds, working ranches, and way too many subdivisions and shopping centers. More were always on the way, but it gave him comfort to know that within and surrounding all that, were animals: furry, feathered, and finned; two-, four-, one- and no-legged. They lived in caves, creeks, crevasses, and canopies; houses, condos, and a cabin. They traveled by hoof, paw, sole, wing, and wheel. All of them strands in the same wildly interconnected and interdependent web of life.

With a sigh, Jay tipped his forehead to the glass to get a better angle on it all, to see the familiar from a fresh perspective, and to let his tears flow like rain. Until finally, he managed to catch his breath, clear his throat, and speak.

ACKNOWLEDGEMENTS

IN 2005, A TIGER AND A LYNX ESCAPED FROM A RANCH NEAR SIMI Valley, California. Whether or not they were in cahoots is impossible to say. The lynx was recovered quickly, but several more days passed before a ranch hand happened to see a tiger slinking through the tall grass. By then El Niño was soaking the city and surrounding hills, intent on washing away all scent, scat, and tracks.

In 2010, Itaru Sasaki, a grief-stricken landscape designer from Otsuchi, Japan, installed a disused and disconnected phone booth in his garden so he could speak to his dead cousin. The following year, a 9.1-magnitude earthquake triggered a devastating tsunami that killed more than 16,000 people on the northeast coast of Japan. In the aftermath, Sasaki opened his Windphone to the public. It has since been used by tens of thousands, including many who never had the chance to say a proper goodbye to their loved ones.

I was a young(ish) reporter in 2005, and I spent a day with the game wardens in charge of the fraught search for the tiger. I filed my piece with the *LA Weekly* and figured this quirky wildlife story had run its course, as far as I was concerned. But it wouldn't let me go, and in 2013, I started dreaming up a fictionalized version with an alternate ending. In 2016, I tuned into episode 597 of *This American*

Life and learned about Sasaki's Windphone. It's a wonderful piece, reported by Miki Meek, and it inspired me.

I'd like to thank the California Department of Fish and Wildlife for their help during my research, especially Lieutenant Chris Long and Warden Jorge Gross. Thanks also to Ben Pryor for his research assistance, and to expert tracker Preston Taylor, who took me out trailing deer and mountain lion in Ventura County. We were unarmed.

Hope Edelman's seminal book, *Motherless Daughters*, provided valuable insight into what it's like for girls to grow up without a mom. Dr. Sarah Menacho and Dr. Rene McNall helped me better understand how cases like Bell's and Ling's would be handled.

My deepest gratitude to early readers Lia Barrett, Dan Cohn, Paul Feinstein, Ann Napolitano, Carrie Garber, and Chris Douglas, and to my editor, Will Bennett, whose insights have made me a better writer and elevated this manuscript. Thanks also to my agents at UTA, Byrd Leavell and Ariele Fredman; to the team at Scribe, especially Ellie Cole and Eric Jorgenson; and to the talented Aidan Yetman-Michaelson for the cover art and hand-drawn topographic map.

I'd also like to thank David Goggins, Jennifer Kish, and all of David's readers and listeners. If not for the success of *Can't Hurt Me*, it is unlikely that I would have been able to take the time to write this book, let alone publish it. Thanks also to Rich Roll, Greg Anzalone, and *The Rich Roll Podcast* community for their continued support.

Of course, none of this happens without my number one collaborator, April Wong. Nobody has read more of my stuff, or read more versions of this book, than April, and nobody believed in it more. Ling's backstory is based on April's childhood trauma, when her father was apprehended in the middle of the night and deported from Australia. Wounded souls do tend to find one another, and I am eternally grateful that I found her.

Speaking of the wounded, thanks to the One-Legged Crow, who I first conjured on the page, then spotted in the wild—on our block, and eventually in our garden. You were the sign from the universe I needed, more than once.

ABOUT THE AUTHOR

ADAM SKOLNICK is an author and journalist who covers travel, adventure and endurance sports, and the environment. His work has appeared in *The New York Times*, *Outside*, *Wired*, *Lonely Planet*, and *Men's Health*. He's the author of *One Breath: Freediving, Death and the Quest to Shatter Human Limits*, and the ghostwriter and audiobook narrator of the bestselling David Goggins memoirs, *Can't Hurt Me* and *Never Finished*. A frequent contributor on *The Rich Roll Podcast*, he lives in Southern California where he was born and raised. This is his first novel.

www.ingramcontent.com/pod-product-compliance
Lightning Source LLC
LaVergne TN
LVHW041620060526
838200LV00040B/1359